Praise for
All the Happiness You Deserve

"Beautifully written and deeply rewarding. Piafsky is heading toward becoming a major writer."
— *Booklist*

"Moves seamlessly from the poetic to the humorous to the vernacular...a brilliant book that serves as a cautionary tale for anyone over thirty who feels certain about his or her future."
— *ForeWord Reviews*

"Michael Piafsky finds the remarkable in seemingly unremarkable things. He is a poet of everyday details, and *All the Happiness You Deserve* is a beautiful, confident novel, full of unique and unexpected energy."
— Scott O'Connor, author of *Half World* and *Untouchable*

"A distinctive, insightful portrait of the everyday rhythms of life and the fragile, complicated threads that connect us, *All the Happiness You Deserve* is a wildly original, mesmerizing debut."
— Amy Hatvany, author of *The Language of Sisters*, *Heart Like Mine*, and *Outside the Lines*

"What I love about *All the Happiness You Deserve* is its gentle irony and humor. This book captures both a family's caring and the way it can descend into absolute chaos. Michael Piafsky is one of America's most promising young writers."
— Speer Morgan, author of *The Freshour Cylinders*

"*All the Happiness You Deserve* delivers much more than that to readers, actually. It's a long, lovely poem of a book, a kind of literary kaleidoscope that reveals beautiful, intricate patterns with each turn of the page."
— Liam Callanan, author of *The Cloud Atlas* and *All Saints*

"In Michael Piafsky's superb Everyman novel, all the big questions—fate, fortune, free will, happiness, pain—spin round and round like a carnival Ferris wheel ride you hope will never end."
— Michael Kardos, author of *The Three-Day Affair*

"Through beautifully written episodes, *All the Happiness You Deserve* takes us right into the unavoidable melancholy of life."
— Sahar Delijani, author of *Children of the Jacaranda Tree*

"*All the Happiness You Deserve* is a terrific novel, one that succeeds in the rarest of ways: through a combination of experimentation and accessibility. It tells the story of a man's entire life, and in so doing reveals a great deal about the way we tell stories, to others and—most dangerously—to ourselves."
— Christopher Coake, author of *You Came Back* and *We're in Trouble*

"Michael Piafsky is quite a good writer: smart, playful, energetic, and a skillful hand with words, besides being very funny when it's the appropriate time to be funny, and touching when the situation calls for it. I hope he gets the readership he deserves."
— Stephen Dixon, National Book Award–nominated author of *Frog* and *Interstate*

"Michael Piafsky takes a deep and unflinching look into the soul of the average American male. In *All the Happiness You Deserve*, the narrative arc of an 'ordinary' life is writ both large and small in the finely wrought and telling details laid by the hands of a master craftsman. Precise, amusing, and tragic—this is a remarkable debut."
— Brian Payton, author of *The Wind Is Not a River*

"With a pointillist painter's skill and vision, Michael Piafsky uses brief scenes to create a full canvas. *All the Happiness You Deserve* succeeds brilliantly on both a microscopic and telescopic level, with the sum of its parts being greater than the whole—and yet somehow each part stands on its own as a perfect jewel, a flash of light."
— Marly Swick, author of *The Summer Before the Summer of Love* and *Evening News*

ALL THE HAPPINESS
YOU DESERVE

Michael Piafsky

PROSPECT
· PARK ·
BOOKS

Published by Prospect Park Books
969 S. Raymond Avenue
Pasadena, California 91105
prospectparkbooks.com

PROSPECT
·PARK·
BOOKS

Distributed by Consortium Book Sales & Distribution
cbsd.com

Library of Congress Cataloging in Publication Information

Piafsky, Michael.
 All the happiness you deserve / Michael Piafsky.
   pages cm

 ISBN 978-1-938849-15-2 (pbk.) -- ISBN 978-1-938849-16-9 (e-book)
 1. Men--Fiction. 2. Life change events--Fiction. 3. Life cycle, Human--
Fiction. 4. Psychological fiction. I. Title.
PS3616.I212A55 2014
 813'.6--dc23
                            2013019553

First edition, first printing

Cover design by Brad Norr. Interior design by Kate Hillseth.
Printed in the United States of America.

For Julie

TAROT SPREADS

The Three Gates

Two of Wands
The Fool
The Chariot

The Dagger of Truth

The Hanged Man
Seven of Swords
Nine of Swords
The Magician
Seven of Cups
Page of Wands

Mind, Body, and Spirit

Strength
Nine of Wands
Knight of Swords

The Sacred Quest

Knight of Cups
Six of Swords
Eight of Swords
Five of Wands
The World
Justice
Three of Swords

Consequences

Four of Swords
Four of Wands
King of Cups
Wheel of Fortune
Queen of Cups
Ten of Cups
Eight of Wands

Teacher and Helper

Ace of Cups
Two of Cups
Two of Swords

The Cusp of Aries

High Priestess
Three of Cups
Three of Wands

The Golden Dawn

Four of Cups
Six of Wands
Ace of Pentacles
The Hermit
Two of Pentacles
Queen of Swords

Temperance
The Devil
Ten of Pentacles
Four of Pentacles
Three of Pentacles
Knight of Pentacles
The Lovers
The Sun
Seven of Pentacles

Celtic Cross

Page of Cups
Five of Swords
King of Swords
Knight of Wands
Queen of Pentacles
Page of Swords
The Star
Eight of Pentacles
Page of Pentacles
Nine of Cups

The Tree of Life

Ace of Wands
Ace of Swords
Six of Pentacles

The Hierophant
Nine of Pentacles
The Emperor
Six of Cups
Seven of Wands
King of Wands
Judgment

The Horseshoe

Five of Cups
The Empress
Five of Pentacles
Ten of Wands
Ten of Swords
King of Pentacles
The Tower

The Arrow of Time

Death
Queen of Wands
The Moon

Every New Day

Eight of Cups

The Three Gates

Setting Forth

Charlotte wakes you by jumping on your bed. "Look what happened," she whispers, opening your curtains to reveal a foot of snow on the ground. She laughs in delight as you struggle out of your sheets, your eyes clumsy in this new light. She helps you into your snow pants and raises the zipper, careful not to catch its teeth in your shirt, then drags you to her door. You pause at the threshold—surely she remembers how she has decreed this room "boy free" and yes, that means especially you too—until she laughs, "come on," and takes your hand to pull you across.

Her room, opposite your own, stays dark in the mornings so that invariably you wake up first and have to coerce her (always from the doorway, never farther in) downstairs to help you with breakfast. Some mornings she is good about helping, dutiful in preparing your cereal and readying whatever you will need for second grade. But most mornings she refuses your pleas, covering her ears with her pillow, hurling stuffed bears at you until you retreat, taunting you that your breakfast can "wait until Mom gets up," a solution certain to result in starvation, as she well knows. Never is Charlotte as giddy as she seems this morning, as optimistic, and as willing to share her world with you. You sit on her bed while she gets ready.

"Turn around," she admonishes, removing her pajama bottoms, "in the presence of a lady," and you face toward the wall, to a postcard she has tacked up from a friend's trip to a desert country, a shard of sea glass dangling from a string and a small picture of Sal Mineo dotted liberally with sticky pink hearts, symbols of her ten-year-old body. When she is done with her own layers you are invited to turn back around, and, while she brushes her hair, she describes the snow fort to which you will devote your day.

Charlotte has drawn up a plan. While she brushes, you examine it. It depicts the snow fort from any number of angles, all superimposed on one another, so that the drawing resembles the spider webs that accumulate under the eaves of the carport in the springtime, and its intricacy confirms even to your eight-year-old mind that you and Charlotte could never hope to build such a palace, not in one winter morning nor in a thousand of them. But of course you would never think of telling Charlotte this—Charlotte, who gushes about the moats and walls and drawbridges ("We can use the old rusted grill top from Dad's barbecue"), who uses the word "us" to describe the day's participants, whose reflection smiles at you from the silvered mirror, whose hair crackles with electricity in the dry air, and whose crayoned blueprint suggests in its fanciful geometry that anything is possible.

You are out of the house and into the yard before your parents wake, admittedly not a Herculean task considering it is Sunday and you could hear their laughter and the clink of glassware last evening as you slipped between the cracks of dreams. This morning, this winter Sunday, is for you and Charlotte alone.

As everyone knows, a good fort begins with high walls. Unfortunately the snow, tantalizing as fallen clouds from your window, is not the right kind for fort making. It takes only a few gathered handfuls disintegrating as soon as you release them, floating gently back to the earth instead of clumping together, for the two of you to realize that this is not going to work. "You're not doing it right," Charlotte snipes, her goodwill ebbing away in disappointment, even while the remains of her own attempts lie at her feet, no more substantial than yours. Finally she gets up. "Wait here," she warns.

Beyond the wreckage of your fort, the snow is as flat as an untended field, with only the paired sets of footsteps to disturb it. When you lie down, it makes a wonderful bed. The snow, poor for fort building, is perfect for lying on: so dry it does not melt into slush, so cold it resists your heat. The sky above is an uninterrupted blue, the clouds having spent themselves into nothing with the snowfall. Lying there you can feel the earth spinning underneath you (in all the years you will tell this story, almost nobody will understand the phenomenon, but every once in a while you will catch a certain look that encourages you to keep trying), the entire world rotating counterclockwise, a funnel with you at its stem, and you watch the naked branches skate their circle above you, no sound, no interruptions, until Charlotte's face appears, upside down, so that the look of consternation she wears presents itself to you as a smile.

"What are you doing?"

"Making snow angels," you reply.

In her arms she carries your mother's mop bucket, filled to the top with water, and the rinsing cup from your bath. "Watch," she tells you, and ladles the water from the bucket.

Where the water touches it, the snow becomes malleable and firm. Used judiciously, and you both learn quickly all manner of tricks, the first bucket is enough to forge the walls into a rough omega, with a narrow passage for you to leave and return by. Working together, you fall into a rhythm, until your building process becomes automated, your breathing in syncopation, your hands as courteous to one another's as valued guests, your fingers arriving just as hers pull away. You work together through two buckets until the walls are smooth, reaching as high as your waist, until the sun is nearly overhead, until there is only an inch or so of water at the base of the bucket. These dregs Charlotte dumps near your leg as she rises to trudge the bucket back to the house. "When I get back we'll start on the tower," she promises.

Perish the elf that plots in your mind and compels your actions. You tend to the watered snow, assured in your timing, deliberate in your preparations, so that when Charlotte reemerges a few minutes later, a full bucket in hand, your mother's wavering voice promising lunch in a half an hour, it will be to this image: you, buttressed inside the fort, protected by its heavy walls, a single immaculate snow globe poised in your hand. You will recognize the disappointment in her eyes, but also some measure of gratification. She devoted her morning to building the fort, after all. What hollow veneer of honor could be claimed by depriving the fort of its battle?

"Picture it," your father says, glass in hand. The family lore. "Christmas party, revelry, eggnog, you know the rest."

You're seven years old. And you do know the rest, having heard it all many times. The family lore.

And then your mother: "I'm sitting with Sharon Bingham, discussing her cheating boyfriend and along comes this, this *creature*. Ten miles tall and wearing a lampshade on his head." She shifts back on the sofa. "Can you imagine such a thing?" You—fidgety, weak of bladder, increasingly myopic, a nascent male—cannot possibly be the audience she has in mind. Even your sister, newly nine, her birthday dolly always close at hand, is far from ideal. "Honestly, who can imagine such a thing?"

"So I wander up, cool as a cuke, and extend an arm. 'I'm Garland,' I say, and shake hands with the both of them."

"I had this terror, as this apparition reached for my wrist, that he was going to do something awful," your mother confides. "I thought he was going to try to kiss the back of my hand."

Next to you, giggling, Charlotte takes this liberty with her dolly.

"Wouldn't have done that, Lu," your father says, shaking his head. "Wouldn't have done that."

"I thought he was going to do something awful."

"Wouldn't have done that," your father repeats. "Couldn't get my lips under the lampshade."

"Anyway," continues your mother, "this giant creature, reed-thin back then if you can imagine it, introduces himself and asks what we're talking about. Sharon turns beet red, looking for that lout of a boyfriend—bad as he is, he trumps a space alien, she'd tell me later—and I say to him 'We're discussing the issues in Berlin, if you must know.'"

"All I had was this opening," your father says. "Good opening, but still. I'm there with two guys from work, mostly for the free hooch…" He trails off, finally remembering his audience. "I'm slated to meet this woman Eileen. A matchmaking thing. Everyone swears we're perfect for each other. Destined to be together, the whole sales pitch. Never got to lay eyes on her, turns out she missed her bus. So my friends, we're bored stiff five minutes in, and then one of my buddies takes a lamp from the corner, drops the shade over my head. 'Well, Garland, you're the life of the party,' he tells me. Hal Scott, moved down to Dallas. Anyway, I'm looking out through the muslin of the shade and all I see is this shadow…" He glances at your mother and winks, "a nice shadow, if I may add." Your mother, smiling, brushes him away with her arm as he continues: "I'm so scared that I just stand there and a little voice inside my head speaks to me. Hell, I'd been living in my parents' basement, back from overseas nearly a year. Something told me to be open to it all. Just let it all happen." Your mother looks over to him expectantly, but your father misses this cue. He looks confused, disoriented. Then his lacquered eyes refocus on yours. "And that's when I knew." He reaches for his highball glass. "The trick to comedy comes to me like my gift from the heavens. For the rest of the night I stood there, Cary fucking Grant, excuse me the language, kids. Discussed world events with a lampshade on my head. Refilled her drinks. Talked about housing shortages and the new GM line. And I never needed to look at her face."

Your mother raises her eyes reproachfully to the ceiling, "How was I to know that fool didn't mean it ironically? Like expecting irony from a houseplant. Underneath the lampshade Cary Grant, and underneath Cary Grant? Another lampshade. Story of my life."

"You loved it," your father says. "And you love me." And the way she looks at him, almost shyly, over her own glass, and the way he grins back, the frequency with which they tell the story, their legs on the couch kissing at the knee, all tell you that she did and that she does.

His breath is a cloud hovering above your pillow.

"Get up," he says, and you look around blearily.

He's wearing his heavy coat, lambskin and wool. You try to reason through the hands of the clock to conclude that it is four a.m. Even at twelve years old, you know that nothing good has ever come at four a.m. Even Christmas needs to wait till daybreak. But your father is standing over your bed, holding out your winter jacket and a pair of shoes. The keys to the Buick twirl in his fingers.

"Get up," he says.

Outside, the air is so cold you can feel it hammering into your sinuses. The liquid in your eyes crinkles. Giant snowflakes are falling, soft as the pillow on your bed. There's baby-blue light coming from the streetlamps and you don't know if it's from the cold or the time of day. "Are we going to wait for Charlotte?" you ask, looking out the window at the house. No lights on. Your sister allowed to sleep. The Buick coughs to a start and your father pulls away from the curb.

"We'll keep this between us men." Your dad taps your shoulder, which, even at this hour, makes you feel good.

He drives a few miles out of town, until the snow on the road gets thicker and there aren't any more streetlamps. The Buick shoulders through the snow, headlights like a submarine's. Your dad's hands shift gears, knuckles hunched up on the steering wheel. When he turns, you can spot something in his eye. Something like hunger or mirth. It's something close to joy, only not quite. This is what joy would look like if it drank too much coffee. You can smell the scotch on his breath, but it's nothing to worry about. It smells like last night, stale and benign. Whatever is pushing him forward, it isn't the booze. Finally he stops the car, his hand jerking the shift upward. The headlights are on high, reaching out to absolutely nothing.

He opens his door and gets out, bending onto the hood. You pull open your door, the steel cold and heavy under your fingers, the air dashing underneath your pant cuffs straight toward your privates. You walk up to the hood and examine your father, who's staring straight outward, eyes sheathed. He's got a ten-mile stare on.

"What do you see?" he asks.

Flat land for a hundred miles in every direction. The snow piled up in dunes that groan and sway like mammals do just before they go extinct. It's a test and you don't have any answers. "Nothing," you offer.

He grunts. Then grins at you, his eye teeth stained darker than the rest. "Ever drive through a snowdrift?" he asks.

You tell him you've never driven at all, although this isn't true. You've pulled the car in and out of the driveway for six months now, and two weeks ago your mother let you idle in front of the supermarket. He motions you into the driver's seat and waits while you calibrate the darkness in the mirrors. Once you're ready he starts talking, gesturing, his hands covering your hands.

"No surprises," he begins. "The trick is speed. Come at them quick but leave enough to accelerate through."

You nod.

"At least to start, you're going to want to try a lower gear. After that we can experiment."

Then he sits quiet for a while, so long that you think maybe he's gone to sleep. With the headlights straight ahead, the car is pitch black. His breathing is shallow and even. Then: "Don't touch the brakes. We've got a shovel in the trunk but I don't want to use it."

You adjust yourself in the seat. Your jacket is bunched underneath your armpits, constricting your arms. The cotton of your pajama pants is so thin that you can feel the cold vinyl. The pedal feels strange until you realize that your father has brought your baseball cleats, the metal elevating your foot so that you are meeting the clutch midway. With no socks, the hard leather and mud from last fall dig into your heel. Just as you reach out to put the car into first, your dad reaches over, draping you with his body. You can feel the stubble from his cheek and smell him, animal sour, the lambskin and scotch and gum decay. He exhales in your ear and then pulls back with your seat belt in his hand. He straps you in and checks the belt's excess.

You hit the first bank at fifteen miles an hour. The car rumbles through, not enough momentum, only the eight cylinders grinding through the dense snow. The car emerges like it's coming up for air. Your dad grunts, "Faster."

You pick out another one forty feet away, accelerate smoothly. This one you hit at twenty plus, and the car makes a satisfying noise as it connects. The headlights go dark and then light again. You pull around in a long loop and your father points over the wheel to a large target.

"Faster."

By now the car is swerving east-west from the ice, but it's a giant, hogging the road like gravity's litmus. You both seize when the car smashes through, the antenna pointed back at you like a broken arrow. You target another bank and shift into third gear, the wheels in cartoon acceleration until they find the ground and grab. This bank is higher than the rest, maybe wider too.

"Faster."

This time it's like going through sea foam, the car catching briefly before tearing through. You hear a sharp ping and, opening your eyes, you can see that the antenna is completely gone. If your dad notices, he says nothing. Only his breathing, ragged and wet. "Faster."

The car hits forty, everything accelerator and inertia. Your foot pushed so hard against the floor that your bottom thrusts high into the air for leverage. When you come at the dune, your fingers tense against the wheel.

"Faster."

Everything explodes hard and quick. The chunks of snow atomize against your windshield and you can feel the front wheels buck. For a second it feels like you're flying, and then the wheelbase jars back down. You are almost out of the snowbank but not quite, the headlights lighting nothing but themselves, snowbed elevating the front axle just off terra firma. It is ocean-floor dark and quiet. Next to you, your father retreats into the vinyl, his lungs slowing down, finally getting the oxygen they need. His fingers, clenched on your knee, finally relax and recede. Beneath you, the wheels are spinning helplessly, rubber in the air, whirring impotent, lovers mourning their distance from the Earth.

The Dagger of Truth

THE HANGED MAN.

It begins, not unusually, with the dishes. Your father pushes back from the table, starting off to the den and the early innings of the Cardinals game. Your mother reaches out a thin arm (thinner as your father grows thicker, as though there's a certain amount of matter in the house and someone's gain must come through someone else's loss) and taps your father's plate with her fork. "Sit down, Chump. Some of us haven't finished yet."

It had been a quiet evening.

So down he sits, like a marionette jerked back into place, eyes straight ahead. Your mother, herself three bites from finishing her shepherd's pie, begins to pile food onto her fork with exasperating slowness. You and Charlotte watch, rapt.

Meat, corn, potatoes.

When the tower topples, she builds it again. No one says anything. It never reaches her mouth.

At Charlotte's feet her dog whines. Lady, a diffident spaniel, is six months old, new to the family. It is her presence, strangely, to which you attribute these troubles. The four of you, it seems to your nine-year-old mind, had had the family dynamic pretty well worked out. But for her eleventh birthday, Charlotte had begged for, and received, this dog.

Even the delivery was rough. Your father stomping into the house with a cardboard box, your mother holding the door. You and Charlotte had been playing with matchsticks, building them up into stacks, but when she saw your father, smelled the cardboard and newspaper, her leg jerked the matchsticks into a pile. Your mother, face gleaming, handed the puppy to your sister. "Look at her," Charlotte whispered. "Just look at her."

Your mother came from behind and hugged your sister's shoulders. "Someone didn't want to do this, but I convinced him for you." The puppy, meanwhile, buried her nose under your sister's arm, to Charlotte's squealing delight.

"He's very pretty," you offered. You had, in the past, shared birds and fish and once, until the weather turned, a bunny hutch in the backyard.

"She's a girl, stupid," hissed your sister, turning her body away, shielding the puppy.

"She's a dog," corrected your father. "She needs to be fed, walked, played with. None of which, you better believe, will take care of itself. What she is is a pain in the ass and a giant mistake."

"Oh hush," waved your mother, swatting at your father in a way that in recent months suggested that she would have liked nothing more than for a giant wave to blow him back to sea. "Charlotte's a big girl now and she's ready for this."

Your offers to help were firmly and ungraciously rebuffed. "She's Charlotte's dog," your mother reminded you. "Let's all try to remember that."

And, to be fair, Charlotte is very good with the dog. She takes her out at the allotted times and doles out scoops of dog food supplemented by bites from her own plate. "Stop feeding the damned dog," your father mutters every night—the new family ritual. "That's why it begs all the time."

Your sister sticks out her tongue. "She isn't a dog, she is a little girl in furs. And she deserves the best."

Your father motions down to whatever dinner your mother has cooked. "Then why are you feeding her this gruel?" The punchline. Poorly received. Every time.

"You deserve the best," your sister coos, while the dog flicks her agile tongue at the hamburger, the spaghetti, the meatloaf. "You are my little lady."

And so Lady.

And so the fights.

Meanwhile, your mother is rebuilding her tower. Meat corn, potatoes. She tips the tines with her teeth, toppling the tower (there is plenty of time for poetry). "Oops," she smirks.

Your father folds his hands in front of him, as if saying grace for all the meals and hours to come, his smile tight on his lips.

Eventually the dog wanders into the living room, confused.

Whole minutes pass. You watch the hands on the clock, count down from one hundred and then repeat. The refrigerator compressor clicks on and then clicks off.

By now, the food left on your mother's plate has hardened. The potatoes have grown skin, the meat and corn congealed. The whole thing sticks to the fork with urgency, making your mother work all the harder to ensure none of it passes into her mouth. It would be, you think, poetry for her to actually have to eat it.

By the time the sun has gone down, you have worked out a new pattern. Every five minutes you lift yourself onto your knees and rock slowly back and forth on the chair. Every ten you slide back onto your bottom to rest.

Charlotte keeps her face down even though you wish she would look up at you. You sense that she is the only one who can stop all of this, the one who can turn your mother back.

Instead it is your father, finally, who breaks. "You might think," he says, very quietly, "that a man who works all day would deserve better than this in the evenings. You might think this, but of course you'd be wrong because the Fates are assholes." His eyes meet yours and he repeats this, his tone no longer quiet. "Assholes."

"Don't swear at the dinner table," your mother says mechanically.

"Swearing, my ass. I'm giving him pearls of wisdom here. Remember this, because it is important. Nobody gets what they deserve." And then he gets up and walks into the den. In a moment, you hear the radio. All this time it turns out it really was that easy, a cheat like the Wizard of Oz was a cheat.

Your mother, a strange smile on her face, clears the dishes. She pushes your help away. "This is my job," she says. "Go tend to your homework."

You are about to tell her that you don't have any, a falsehood, when you hear a shout and then a yelp from the other room. Charlotte is crying, scrambling atop your father's back. Your father holds the dog by the neck, pushing its face into the carpeting while it reaches behind, teeth bared, snarling.

"Garland," your mother screams from behind you, the dishtowel still in her hands. She flings it at your father's arm. "Let go, you're hurting her."

"Goddamned dog pissed on my rug." Your father doesn't look up, his eyes locked onto the dog's.

Charlotte and your mother pull at his arm but you just stand and watch the scene; your father like a giant hunched over this dog, his muscles straining. The dog, teeth bared, for once no longer diffident, for once no longer a lady. The lake of urine underneath her neck, the bitter fumes burning your nostrils. When your sister and mother finally succeed in slackening your father's grip, the dog uses this resultant leverage to twist around and clamp down on your father's thumb, top and bottom canines finding flesh. Your father's foot, reflexive, sends the dog hard against the side of the sofa.

"For God's sake," pleads your mother. "It's the children's dog."

"She pisses in the house again and I'll kill her," your father says and, for reasons you can never fathom, he points his finger at you.

Your sister is bent over Lady's body. "I couldn't take her out," she cries. "It wasn't her fault that nobody let her out." She rubs at the dog's haunches, and Lady shakes like she does during her bath and then licks at her front paws.

Charlotte races to find the leash while your mother and father stand there. Your father glares at the dog, who looks warily back at him. Your mother stares at your father. Charlotte returns and attaches the collar to Lady, who moves with her usual gait toward the doorway. Just as she passes your feet, your father lunges at the dog and raises his fist. "She pisses in the house again and I swear I'll take a shovel to her head." At the volume of his threat, the dog lowers herself in submission and pees on the rug.

Nobody moves. Your father stares at the dog and then at the puddle leaking under her flanks. Then, suddenly, he smiles. "That goddamned dog," he says, "is the only one here who understands what I am saying."

While Charlotte and the dog are outside, you get some rags and move them over the floor with your feet. Initially the smell pushes something up from your stomach, but after a while you hardly notice it. Your mother has disappeared. Your father, slumped in his chair, does not offer to help. When you are done with the doorway, you move the rags to the original stain, drying near his feet.

Afterward, you retreat to your room and rinse your hands. You pull off your soiled shirt and shorts, find new ones, and, without even realizing what you are doing, push your arms through the pant legs. After this, it is a simple measure to thread your legs through the T-shirt's armholes and tuck its hem into the elastic of your underwear. Your glossy dress shoes fit snugly over your hands. You walk back into the den, your arms pumping their own pantomime of walking, a giant smile on your face. You stand in front of your father and attempt a simple burlesque.

He adjusts himself in the seat, stare fixed on the radio. Your dance grows more animated until finally, with a sigh, he rises past you to turn off the radio. "Of course. Why should a man who works all day have a single moment to himself?"

Your mother, in the kitchen, examines her hand. You churn your shoed hands like pistons. "Ask me," you beg your mother.

She pushes her hand toward you. "Does this look like a liver spot?" she says, then tilts it back toward the light.

"That's not the right question," you whine. "Ask me the question."

She looks up and surveys you, top to bottom, bottom to top. "Are those your good shoes?" she asks. "Put them away before you scuff them." Her eyes move back to her hands, and then she straightens a leg and angles her neck to look at the purple veins on the back of her knee. She pokes a vein with her fingernail and it pulses slightly. She looks at you and grimaces. "Ugh." On your way out the door, she calls, "That man is a total zero."

Back in the front hall your sister has returned with her dog, who seems no worse for wear, trying to shake off her leash. Charlotte looks you up and down and shakes her head, the look you will come to recognize in a million spent waitresses in a million mediocre bars.

Your arms push up and down while your bare toes wave to her. "Ask me the question," you beg.

"What are you doing?" she says in a tired voice. Lady, anxious to get to her food dish, jumps up and nips at your heels.

"Ask me the right question," you beg again. "Ask me, ask me, ask me."

"The circus has left town, Freako."

"Ask me when I got so good at walking on my hands," you crow, and raise and lower your bare feet.

Your sister bends down to free the dog from her collar, and Lady sprints off into the kitchen to scavenge whatever might be left of dinner. Charlotte collects the dog's things in her hands and rises from her knees. She looks at you almost fondly, at your brand-new feet still swinging in space. "I'll tell you one thing," she sighs. "You certainly are your father's son."

The Lord of Unstable Effort

This time he comes with a pamphlet in his hand. "Your mother sent me."

You move over on your bed and clear the comic books into a tower. You hope he'll notice how much you like them, maybe bring a few home from work next week, but he's got his eyes straight ahead, his mouth working furiously at an olive. He pulls close, then skates away. "Your mother sent me," he repeats and then sits there, not touching anything, robotic, until you realize finally that it is your turn to say something.

"How was work today?" It is all you can think of, a parrot of your mother at the dinner table, which makes you wonder whether it is all she can think of too.

"I'm not good at this kind of crap," he says, with a vehemence you can't quite place until it comes to you that he sounds like he's listening to the Cardinals game on the radio. Like he did when you were younger. The sudden memory of it curls around your insides. He takes the olive pit out of his mouth and rolls it between two fingers, examines it for a moment then jabs it back into his mouth. "She knows I'm not good at this crap."

You nod, sympathetically.

He looks around the room at the comic books and your school bag over your chair. "Getting pretty tall. What are you, thirteen?" You smile at the compliment until you realize he isn't joking.

"I'm eleven," you say. "Charlotte is thirteen."

"Don't tell me about Charlotte," he says, his face reddening. "I don't have to deal with that one. That one's all hers, I can promise you that." Then his face resets:

"So what grade does that make you, eleven?"

"Fifth," you say.

"You like it?" he asks.

You tilt your hand this way and then that, all those years of the question at the kitchen table preparing you admirably. "Beats digging ditches." His line.

"Anyway, your mother sent me." He lays the pamphlet between you, perpendicular to the length of the mattress. "I'm supposed to talk to you about the man and woman things."

Your head jerks straight. Your entire body focuses on a point on the wall in front of you. There is no power on Earth great enough to compel your eyes to his.

"It's biology, a complicated thing. I mean, I can tell you some stories," he starts, then coughs. "Jesus Fucking Christ."

There is some part of you that wants him to continue. What the other kids have been saying seems implausible to you, and your father can undoubtedly set everything straight, but then he takes the pit out of his mouth again and squints through its eclipse to the light on your ceiling.

"It's all right, Dad. We learned all this in school," you lie.

"No kidding?" He smiles. It feels nice to have given this to him. "That's good, real good." Then he reaches down to his feet and pulls out a Blackhawk comic book you were just finishing when he came in. "This one good?" he asks.

"Blackhawk and the team are attacked by Killer Shark's new secret weapon, Killer Whale. Even their bullets and bombs can't faze it," you say. You point your finger at the cover, which summarizes this more neatly than you ever could. You let your finger linger over the shiny boots, the watermark. Your dad's hand is pressed so tight against the bottom of the comic that you can see the tension creasing its way through the tissue pages.

"They get out alive?" he asks, looking past your shoulder.

"We don't know yet," you reply. "Won't find out 'til next issue. It's a cliffhanger." You nod sagely.

His lip turns up at the ends. He leans close to your ear, almost touching but not quite. "I think they're going to be okay," he whispers. He takes the comic and drops it neatly over the pamphlet. "They really teach you that stuff at school?" he asks.

"You bet," you say. "Definitely."

You ask him whether he wants to read the comic with you, but he waves your hand away. "Good night, Little Man," he says. "Get some sleep."

"It's eight o'clock," you want to tell him, but something in his look warns you not to.

Despair

Like the Mighty Casey, Musial has struck out. Nobody on and one out. Ninth inning. Pretty much just as Sayers had divined. Everything repeats itself if you wait long enough. The hum of electrical lines, and your father emits a long, wheezing sigh, as if he had expected nothing less, as if the count, the absence of runners on base, the slider in the dirt and the half-hearted whisk of the wrists, the game, the season, and maybe even the sport itself were concocted by some trickster god for the purpose of tormenting your old man.

"What does it mean?" he asks you, plaintive as a parishioner, "that between them, Stan Musial and The Splinter can't buy a base hit?" To you, it suggests that baseball is a game best played by young men called home to dinner at dusk, farm boys strong enough to lift plows above their heads. There is no mystery to it. Musial and Williams are nearly forty years old, stooped at the plate and in the field, like the men you see at the grocery store holding onto shopping lists and looking vacantly down aisles, hoping that canned peas and spaghetti noodles (and do make sure it's the thin ones this time, Roger) will just appear, clutching their lists like justification, citizenship cards that they'd wear pinned to the sleeve if their wives thought they could get away with it. Gray men, graying, the globe spinning through the air, the body just a rotation too late. "What does it say about this country?" your father wants to know. Your father shares a birthdate with Musial and, since long before your own birth, this has been an unerring source of pride, each batting title some affirmation of astrological prowess. "The stars were aligned that day," he'd crow. "Three fifty-five. Jesus Christ. Not bad for an old man, huh?" Then a slug on your shoulder and off he'd go, unfolding from his chair like a magic trick, hat on and out the door, the whole house breathing a sigh of relief. Now the house sits empty each day, awaiting its bodies' return.

"Seriously, I'm asking you. What does it say about our country that great men like Musial and The Kid are hitting the way they are?"

Your father, the same age exactly as a man whose career is nearly over. There is no answer that can satisfy the hollowness in his bones. He sneers at you from across the seat bench. "What did I bring you here for anyway?"

To this too you have no reply.

Earlier, you had drifted to sleep. Doldrums of the middle innings, lulled by the announcer's voice and the autumn stillness. You'd been woken by knuckles on the car window, your father reaching over you to roll down the window and smile up at a policeman shining his flashlight into the car. "Lousy reception," your father had explained, and the policeman had nodded and asked the score, which your father promptly told him.

It was a nice night. Your father fought the Buick through the drive, downshifting up the hills, chasing the smell of drying leaves and backyard parties with the abused engine's belch. Finally, rising to Makeout Point and a wry smile. "Only goddamned place in this entire town worth a good goddamn," he had muttered, pushing through the resistant gearshift. An autumn night, the kind they write poems about, Midwestern town so deadened it's a fixed point on the cosmos. Entropy. He pulled onto the lookout, so fast and hard you worried the car might slide down the embankment to the nest of trees below. Such accidents were a semiannual occurrence in this town (your mother was always quick to dismiss) of horny teenagers.

You'd heard the stories at school, but at fourteen you'd never been to Makeout Point and hadn't expected your first time to be with your father, who was busy kicking through the parking brake with his foot. "Let's try this fucker again."

This drive came only after he'd spent twenty minutes fiddling with the radio at home. "KMOX, two hundred miles and you'd think we were on Neptune." Meanwhile, you sat in your room and massaged your hunger through your intestines. The Cardinals games are a ritual for your father and the fiddling with the radio the grail quest he must complete to get there. The transmission from St. Louis and then cities unimaginably north and east. Airwaves beholden to some higher power. Every night the struggle and then Harry Caray's voice pushing through with its first hawk for an ice cold beer. This time, though, a snarl, "Sound is supposed to carry better in the fucking cold," and then a tremendous crash, epic and thundering, and you emerged from the stairwell to see your father standing over the wooden shell, the radio's innards leaking out, a single vacuum tube in your father's meaty palm. "Grab your coat, we're going out."

It was an evening that had begun with such promise, your father busy in the kitchen, having returned from work with a bloody butcher's bag of meat and a sack of potatoes. "Man food," he'd grinned and then disappeared into the kitchen, where you'd heard him wrestling the stove. Finally, his voice to the top of the stairs: "Dinner is served."

After pan-fried steak and potatoes, your father pushed back from the table and collected his napkin onto the plate. "Time for the ballgame. Let's listen to the first few innings. Leave the dishes," he commanded. "Your mom will take care of those when she gets back." Four weeks since she'd been gone and you'd have run out of plates a long time ago, but mostly your father has been coming back from work (good thing my route is compact enough to bring me home each night, huh?) with fried-egg sandwiches wrapped in waxed paper, sandwiches he encourages you to eat jackknifed over the sink. After school you've been mousing through soda crackers and ketchup and that novelty has long run thin. You think eventually your father will have to do the dishes himself, or buy new ones, but you know that asking him about this will lead to the inevitable questions about your mother and Charlotte and their own midnight excursion nearly a month ago. He's letting the dishes accumulate, fetid, in the sink, the fly hatchery of an omelet made a week into this strange halving—on a morning you woke to the smell of food in the kitchen. For a moment, your eyes fluttering, you had thought that your mom and Charlotte had returned home, but then you heard a bang and cursing—fading back, back, at the wall, your dream of marines on a beachfront—and the only surprise awaiting you in the kitchen was your father in an apron upon which was printed, improbably, a portrait of a trapeze artist high atop his wire. "Hey, Sport," he grinned. He tried to flip the omelet in the skillet, but it caught on the way up and folded back over in a defeated shrug. "Thought I'd whip up a little bachelor omelet." He had used the last of the milk, the cheese, the eggs, the last of most anything perishable. When you mentioned this, he nodded: "Like the last day of a camping trip, packing up light, leaving the trash for the bears." Your father brought the pan over to the table and cut the omelet in two with a spatula, letting each side fall onto a plate. The omelet looked suspiciously small, and on a whim you opened the trash can, discovered other omelet incarnations in various states of production. "There were some false starts," your father snarled. "You want some of this shit or not?"

The remnants in the sink haven't yet joined those still in the kitchen trash, the smell enough to necessitate an open window. You will get around to taking the trash out yourself, you know, but some sort of perversion makes you wait on this, like a test of wills with your father, the same game the tall tower of dishes in the sink tells you he is playing with your absent mother. You think maybe she'd come home sooner if he'd go ahead and clean them himself, but you are only fourteen, after all, and as everyone in the world is quick to tell you, you aren't a man yet.

From your vista in the car you could see through the middle of town, your eyes obeying traffic laws down Main Street until the river and then taking flight to the fading horizon. It was a beautiful view, even if you were the only one who had ever bothered to look for it. Almost immediately you heard Caray's voice bray, "And there's another ball looped into center field by Burgess. Flood will get it back in quickly. Another run plated and the Redbirds now trail three to two. Gibson's leaving everything out over the plate." Your father's balled fist twitched toward the radio and then stopped short, his fingers running lovingly over the dashboard, following a vein in the wood down the panel. You reached over and touched his wrist and his hand flashed upward, smacking at the knobs. The station jolted, Caray's voice dancing with a slow waltz a station number up, the two signals cutting in and out. Butterflies knuckling in the high sky.

"You going to start with me now?" he asked, rubbing his fingers against his left wrist. "Are you next in line? Even my Cardinals are turning on me. I've got a fucking bull's-eye on my back."

And for once you knew just what to say. Your hand moved slowly to readjust the dial between your thumb and forefinger. Caray's voice reemerged clear as space travel. "Don't worry, Dad. They'll come back. They're going to come back."

Ever intrepid, your father presses his hands and face against the glass and looks into the restaurant. A man seated directly inside the window, shadowed by your father's bulk, startles. Hunched over his soup, the man takes the paper napkin from his lap and daubs at his face. He looks up to your father's hulking form, still peering inside, then out toward the remainder of your family, sequestered on the sidewalk. The man assesses your mother, with two small children hiding behind her bare legs, and smiles. He flutters the napkin with his fingers for a moment and then looks down at his soup. "Hot," he mouths, fanning himself extravagantly. Your father, having divined a kindred spirit nearly a thousand miles from home, taps on the glass, mimes a spoon entering and leaving his mouth, and then offers both choices: a thumbs-up and then a thumbs-down. Inside the glass the man's brow furrows in calculation. Finally he raises his hand, still holding the napkin. He stretches out his fingers, letting the napkin catch an air current and return gently to his lap. Then he tilts his empty hand like a boat on a wave. Everything here is okay, his gesture assures you, so long as you don't expect too much.

Perhaps inevitably, this lukewarm encouragement elicits a split decision in your makeshift huddle (your father warning "we could always do worse," your mother countering that "who ever heard of coming to Memphis to eat Chinese food?"). And perhaps inevitably your eight-year-old bladder makes the decision for everyone, the door to the restaurant welcoming you with the tinkling of a bell and then your father's too-loud announcement to his newfound soul mate that "we've decided to trust you." Once you are inside, you notice that the mime is eating alone, his umbrella upright in the seat opposite him, his fedora resting on the umbrella's handle. Also, he is very heavy. He accepts your father's confidence with the same ambivalence he offered the soup, shrugging his shoulders (the gesture riding the bottom of his suit jacket up toward his elbows) as your father bustles you to the bathroom but, when your mother passes, the man reaches across the table to the umbrella and deftly tilts the brow of his fedora, your mother returning the gesture with a curtsy.

Throughout the meal you feel a buzzing sensation at the back of your skull. An older you would recognize this as the effects of MSG on your body, but for now you attribute it to the exoticism of the food, the paper dragon lanterns hanging on the wall, the elegant waitress with her sculpted eyebrows. It all feels like a magical spell as your family empties plate after plate into stomachs plumbed by a long day of sightseeing, your parents' squabbles no more affecting than the low-grade hum that massages your ears. A very busy day and your head nods forward while your parents discuss tomorrow's drive east to Nashville. The vacation, a weeklong car trip before returning home, is nearly half over and, even though it was all at your father's instigation and bullying (your mother lobbying for a beach farther south: "honest to God, Garland, there's such a thing as too much family time. And why would a traveling salesman want to spend more time in the car?"), now it seems your mother is the one enjoying herself. She looks out the window during the long swaths of road, content to let you and Charlotte bicker in the backseat, your father forever tweaking the radio dial. While the rest of you unfurl from the car as wrinkled as the clothes pushed into the recesses of your suitcase, your mother emerges gracefully, as if the automobile is the instrument of convenience and grace its advertisements have always purported it to be.

Since it has been a very long day, your parents let you doze. You wake up to the waitress placing a basket of cookies on the table. You reach for one, but your father knocks your hand away. "They're fortune cookies," he explains. "Inside each cookie there is a tiny slip of paper that will tell your future."

The cookies in the basket are golden brown, folded like crustaceans, with a waxy gleam. When you reach again, your father takes the basket in his hand and raises it above his head. "You don't choose the fortune cookie," he says in a Charlie Chan accent that causes the waitress to scowl and retreat back into the kitchen. "The fortune cookie chooses you." Charlotte rolls her eyes. Your mother busies herself with the makeup in her compact. After holding his pose for a few seconds, your father lowers the basket to the middle of the table. Then he takes Charlotte's hand and moves it slowly above the cookies, finally settling on one. He then motions to your mother, who plucks her cookie indifferently, her eyes never wavering from the mirrored compact. Then, still grinning at you, your father deliberates between the remaining two, his finger twitching like an antenna. After his choice, there is only one cookie left in the basket, but when you reach for it, your father pulls the basket back. His mouth already full, he cracks your cookie and removes the slender piece of paper. "Open up," he commands, and you sit very still to let him reach forward to place the cookie on your tongue. Then he chews his own cookie for a moment, reading and burying his fortune in the jellied remains of a sweet-and-sour sauce. Finally, with the showmanship he applies any time he has managed to coerce an audience, he unfolds your piece of paper, your fortune, and reads it silently to himself. "What does it say?" you ask, and he shakes his head, his eyebrow raised, an enigmatic smile on his face. Inside your mouth, the cookie melts down to sugar. You stare at your father. "What does it say?" you beg. "Why won't you just tell me what it says?"

Potential

Her dangling girl legs muss your hair then disappear until your masculine pride urges you upward. You strain for clues (which branch she uses to pull herself up, which knob steadies her sandaled feet). Midway up the oak tree your pipecleaner legs give way and you scrape down the bark until finally you're able to steady yourself against a stronger limb. You can feel the bits of sap and splinters, the welt already rising, the sap gluey on your fingers.

Charlotte is a good ten feet above you, perhaps thirty feet off the ground, balancing a sandal on the end of her toe. Like a metronome keeping time for your weakness. "Do you need a hand?" she sneers.

"I'm wearing shorts," you complain. She runs a branch up her own bare thigh. "Ow," she mock grimaces, "mean leaves."

She has, in the past few months, suddenly become funnier than you. Stronger than you. She has always been smarter than you. Companions and well-matched through eight and ten, you could feel her pulling away when she turned eleven. Already your games are stupid, your stories childish, your contests uneven. "You never want to do anything anymore," you whine to her and she cocks her head to the side like her spaniel—that newest flag of independence.

She has less and less time for you, less and less time for your father, whose every sentence is now punctuated by Charlotte's eye-rollings and mocking songs. Like the adaptation of "Greensleeves" she invents for your behalf:

"Mean leaves a weakling boy, mean leaves a villain…"

Dinners have become a struggle. Your father, formerly a joker, an arm-puncher, a kidder. Your father, who would order away for gadgets from catalogues: Groucho glasses. A plastic squirting lapel flower. A tiny device that would cube a soft boiled egg in a matter of moments, if only anyone would ask it to. You know from the stories (if stories are to be trusted) that there was a time everyone thought he was a hoot, couldn't dream of a weekend without him. But this father is in hibernation, like the pair of wax lips growing hair in the back of the kitchen drawer. All that's left are the stories, the family lore, mined and repeated even as that man (if ever he existed) wanders further away, leaving the tired husk who blinks at you like he's trying to remember your name. Now your mother distances herself from your father's rare jokes. There was a time when the two of them finished each other's skits, the joker and the straight man. Once all they did was laugh. Burns and Allen. A vaudeville act your sister has recently shown a critic's inclination to cancel.

And so dinners are a struggle. Strangely, your mother sides universally with your sister, as though she has been biding her time for this ally to emerge. She too is pulling away from the act, her tone imploring in ways it had never been before. When now she forces her arms rigid and admonishes your father "seriously," it is *seriously* that she means, whereas once it wasn't. The landscape is changing, although of course it will be years before you can make sense of any of it. For now, you know only the sudden arguments and the lulls between. Once your spilled glass of milk, your belch, your glib retort were lauded and dissected as formative Buster Keaton; now they are reduced to acts of stupidity, each transgression further proof of your genetics, your gender, your shortcomings. Every wrong thing brands you more deeply in your mother's and sister's eyes.

This weekend then, an attempt. Your father's manager has a

summer place in the woods. Doles out two days as a reward for sales quotas. Cheaper than a Christmas bonus, maybe even cheaper than a ham. But an attempt nonetheless. Even your mother smiling on the way up, whistling a duet with your father, the two holding hands. Your sister's goodwill offering to take you for a walk behind the cabin, the lushness of the trees and undergrowth, the overwhelming greenness of it all. Even Charlotte's shorts are green. And then, in a clearing, an enormous oak tree and behind it a pond skimmed with moss. "Race you," Charlotte said, already running. She raced you to the giant oak tree and then raced you upward. And now here you are, an unexplored pond at your feet and Charlotte's song above.

"Mean leaves something to fear, For none but my baby brother."

You grab hold of the branch above but don't have enough leverage to push with your legs, nor enough strength to lift with your arms. You are trapped, swinging, terrified. Finally, in desperation you slide down to your initial perch, to the rough comfort of its bark against your cheek and belly. By now your sister has stopped singing, her disgust lower on the register. "Coming?" she asks, knowing the answer as well as you do.

"I can't," you admit.

"So jump into the pond," she urges.

But you are afraid. The algae on its top masks its depth. Your instincts, your bowels, tell you no.

"Then you might as well climb down," she sighs. Then, looking out from a vantage you can't fathom: "God, you are such a baby."

From the base of the tree, your sister seems unbelievably high. Even the low branch you'd gotten stuck on is a summit, fifteen feet off the ground. You can't imagine your sister's height, her bravery. You cannot yet imagine what it must be like to be so high off the ground, thirty feet, untethered. And never, not if you live to a million, will you be able to imagine perching on the branch, arms above your head, and diving arrow straight into the pond. Even after you've witnessed her doing it. Down like an angel, down like a woman, down into depths unknown, singing as she flew. Heroic.

A Child of Inspiration

The teacher welcomes your parents into the classroom and directs them to two chairs in front of her desk. You, she motions to stand next to her. "Young legs like his," she informs your father, "can hold themselves up for a few minutes."

"So let's hear it. How's he doing?" Your father dwarfs his chair. Even though there are parent-teacher conferences twice a year and have been for all recorded history, and therefore simple arithmetic dictates that the number of parents participating must stretch into the thousands, if not beyond, there are never enough chairs for the adults to use. And therefore your parents are now sitting in wooden chairs so tiny that even you, so skinny that strange old women tsk at your mother in public, would be hard-pressed to fit onto them. The wood groans under your parents' frames, the seats producing alarming noises that seem the harbinger of structural catastrophe until your mother glares hers into submission. This leaves only your father, whose girth, while by no means inconsequential, cannot possibly be as substantial as that of some of the other fathers who have spawned the doughy burlap sacks now idling between their schoolyard bullyhood of early elementary school and their future glory as offensive linemen, the pride of Harry S. Truman high schools across the Show-Me State. Ultimately, your father subdues his chair by balancing his entire weight on a single leg that he keeps rooted to the floor. Mrs. Watson waits with a barely tolerant smile until his dance concludes.

"Ah," she says, "I must admit that I've been waiting for this particular meeting." She looks up at you, your arms folded behind your back, and then to your parents.

"What'd he do wrong?" your father asks, anchoring his leg against Mrs. Watson's desk for balance.

This is an excellent question. You cannot think of a thing. You are not a resident troublemaker, nor even much of anything. In this, your fifth grade year, you are not yet tall enough to play basketball, although you burn for the chance (the desire for a growth spurt dominates your conscious prayers). You are neither popular nor unpopular, rarely picked on, cordially ignored by the upper caste. You are, in short, as successfully invisible as any twelve-year-old longs to be, and therefore surprised to hear that Mrs. Watson (herself a rather unmemorable presence, never Teacher of the Year, never the source of scandalous rumors or vitriol, the sort of teacher who will eventually rise to be vice-principal or else secretary of the union) has been looking forward to this meeting.

"What was I just saying?" Mrs. Watson turns on you, her tone sharp.

Very quickly, you replay the beginnings of her conversation in your mind. Unfortunately there's nothing there but scraps, not enough evidence to piece together, so you have to shrug and admit you don't know.

"You see?" Mrs. Watson asks your parents.

They nod and claim they do, although you would bet whatever meager birthday sums you have squirreled away that they are as confused as you are. Mrs. Watson seems suspicious as well and reprimands them with a look nearly as hard as the one allotted you. "He's a dreamer," she hisses, before tempering it with a laugh.

The looks on your parents' faces turn so quickly from confusion to understanding that you feel a bit betrayed. Your mother offers a commiserating smile. "Tell me about it," she jokes. "You should see him before he's had his morning coffee."

A few seconds pass before Mrs. Watson realizes that your mother is kidding, and when she does she seems slighted (although also gratified) by your mother's reaction. "Yes," she replies coldly. "Ha. The problem of course is that when he is not listening, he is not learning anything."

You wonder whether this is true. On the surface it seems irrefutable, yet you spend so little time consciously listening (and in this, you can't help but complain, you are hardly alone) that it seems impossible. After all, if it were as simple as that, you would still be a lump of newborn flesh, incapable of any but the simplest tasks. As it is, you have a thoroughly unremarkable report card, equally unlikely to provoke punishment or reward, the perfect representation of that neutrality you have worked so hard to achieve. Besides, if she really knew how the human brain worked, you doubt she would be teaching at an elementary school. Your mother, always the lioness in public, scoffs. "I don't think wandering off makes him unique." She picks up her purse from the floor and places it neatly on her lap. "So he's a spaceman. How many parents have you done this with today, anyway?"

There would be something laudable about this, your mother's retort, another tidy family story to tell, but the look on Mrs. Watson's face is completely wrong. For the scene to work, that face needs to be stuffy, affronted, grotesque, pursed. and ridiculous as your parents rise from their tiny chairs, growing taller with each proud stride, and you following triumphantly in their wake.

But instead it is a look of profound sadness. It is the look of a woman who cares deeply, who derives no pleasure at all from this encounter, who often has something important to say and whose curse it is to be relegated to a career where no one is willing to hear it. It is an entirely different look than the one your parents need to make her a punchline, and a tribute to her that after all her years she can still bear to offer it.

"I'm well aware that my students," Mrs. Watson replies gravely, "that *all* students, for that matter, are not always able to concentrate their full attention on their lessons. I don't mean that your son sometimes gets distracted."

"Then what do you mean?" your mother asks.

"I mean simply that he goes somewhere very far away, somewhere deep inside his mind."

"And you think it's a problem?" your mother concludes.

"I don't think it's something that is going to prevent him from memorizing state capitals or early algebra," Mrs. Watson replies. "His report cards, for whatever little that is worth, do not concern me. But it *is* something you need to be aware of and something about which you need not be dismissive."

Your mother, fully chastened, promises to keep a closer eye out. It's funny because everything had been going so perfectly according to script, everyone playing their stock roles so marvelously, the punchline teed up as big as a balloon, before Mrs. Watson had to ruin it. Your mother cannot adjust. Thrown suddenly into this different role, she promises changes at home, augers more discipline. She and Mrs. Watson orbit each other for a few moments, now comrades. Your mother, apologetic, the penitent, allows that she "never thought it was so severe," Charlotte having never posed this exact problem, Mrs. Watson now whispering her dispensations, assuring your mother with lazy prophesy that it is all undoubtedly a phase, that it will pass. They transition so neatly into these new roles that you almost think you missed something, staring over Mrs. Watson's head to the window behind, to the headlights blinking like stars in the darkened parking lot. It takes the sudden protest of your father's chair to bring you back. He alone is still angry, he alone out of character. "So the kid's a dreamer," he barks. "So the hell what?" Your mother and Mrs. Watson, now aligned, this time share a very different conspiratorial look. "I'm serious," he says. "So the kid goes off into his own world." Your father rises and his seat, finally released, comes crashing down onto the checkerboard floor. "Let me ask you a question," he says, looking in turn to Mrs. Watson and then to his wife. "Look around and tell me what you think he's missing."

That night, as he tucks you into bed, your mother having rushed from the car to her room, promising only that she was well-rid of the both of you, the slams and thunders continuing unmuffled from behind the locked door, you thank your father for earlier. "With Mrs. Watson," you explain. It's a long time before he speaks, his face flushed with anger, wincing at the detonations in his bedroom. And finally his look silences you as neatly as Mrs. Watson's had done your mother an hour ago, a look whose sadness and pain mirror her own, a wistful look as he cups your chin in his hand and asks you where you go.

Mind, Body, and Spirit

The real problem, as it turns out, is the dog. For weeks after your mother has left, taking the car, taking Charlotte in the middle of the night, taking few of their clothes, nothing in the way of keepsakes but, if you can trust your father's angry rants, taking all his hard-earned money from his wallet as well as those little piles he'd stashed round the house, for an emergency, for a rainy day. "I don't know about you," he said, his face as red as an overtaxed heart, "but I sure don't see any rain."

Eighth grade under way and it's amazing how this single fluke of the calendar (if indeed it was a fluke) tempers anything you might have felt about your mother's disappearance. At night, late at night, you wonder where they've gone and worry whether they are safe, a thousand unbirthed questions, but in the morning there is breakfast to be scavenged, classes, homework. Your mind clings to the civics test, the nape of Jenny Hempel's neck from your seat behind, Bob Pettit's firm solidity under the basket. And Lady, whose daily rituals have quickly shifted everything squarely at you.

Lady has been with your family for five years and Charlotte has done well by her—conscientious in her parenting, firm, even-handed. So in these five years she has been a very good dog. But the alteration in her routine, the reduction in the family's head count, and of course, your uneven schedule have all jolted something in her and she has reverted to the foibles of puppyhood. So evenings, between schoolwork and radio broadcasts of the Hawks' latest game (after winning the West last year, they're back in contention), are often spent wiping up messes and walking Lady through the neighborhood. "It isn't fair," you tell your father, motioning down to the darkened stain on the carpeting.

"I seem to remember you begging me for this dog," he replies. "I seem to remember you making me a promise that you'd look after it forever."

The cleanups cost less than the fights.

At nighttime, Lady sleeps in Charlotte's room, where she always has. A few weeks after they left, you stripped the bed but, having come in one night to find Lady nesting without purchase on a throw pillow, you are now careful to leave a blanket on the bed, swapping it out every few weeks with your laundry.

But even with your attentions, there are still problems. One night, your father comes into your room long after you've gone to sleep, dragging you by your shirt down into the living room where a turd festers. "Clean it," your father commands.

"Just so there's no confusion," you mumble. "We're both clear that I didn't do it, right?"

"I'm going to bed," he barks back.

Her begging escalates, as family mealtime becomes more fluid in execution. And you cringe every time she hops up onto your father's leg. He yells a lot now, and when he yells at the dog he looks at you (although often when he yells at you he looks at the dog). Regardless, Lady, now in her own middle age, now the sole generator of estrogen in the home, holds her own against him, wages her own guerilla battles in opposition to his regime.

All of which results in more work for you.

The second time he wakes you it's with a giant club raised above his arm. Even though by all rights you should be petrified, it is an indictment of the household dynamic that you take the image in stride. The second your mind processes it all—the clenched arm, the strain of his stomach against the bottom of his shirt—you realize that you've been waiting for this moment since they left.

The dog has chewed through a baseball bat your father keeps in his study. "It was a Solly Hemus," your father bellows. You tell him that it's hard to read with the bat directly above your head. Also, it's three thirty in the morning and pretty fucking dark in your room.

"Can you see it now?" he demands, swinging the bat forward until it stops just shy of your chin. The dog's teethmarks have chipped their Braille in the polish. He rotates the barrel until you can read the label beneath your eyes—Solly Hemus printed in neat letters, a generic signature burned into the lacquer. He was telling the truth.

"She really did a number on it," you whistle. "Who knew she was part beaver?"

"This was my bat," he says. Apparently your father had played baseball in high school, although this particular bat came far later (hardly a relic), for an aborted weekend beer league jaunt five or six years ago, one of the many Hail Marys of his depleted youth.

He takes a step backward and then a nice, even swing in the space above your head. He whistles through his teeth, his focus fixed on the dark wall. Then he whispers something inaudible and swings again. You remain motionless on the bed, watching the bat pass through the zone again and again. And then it stops.

"I was going to give you this bat one day."

"Thank you."

"Don't thank me now, you idiot. Now the garbage man can thank me for this, same way he thanked me for the rug and the lamp and my good stepladder."

"I'll buy another bat," you say. You don't play baseball. Too static. Too boring. You prefer basketball, the fluid motions, like water flowing downstream. You don't play baseball, as your father is fond of reminding you.

"Where is the little bitch, anyhow?" he snarls.

You sit up and shrug. "In her room, probably. Asleep, probably."

"In her room?" Your father rubs the barrel, confused.

"Charlotte's room," you explain. "Where she sleeps."

"Charlotte's room," he repeats to himself, running his hand up and down his chest, gathering the fabric of his shirt between his fingers. He leans the bat up against your wall. "Good night," he says. "That fucking dog," he says.

Down the street there is a little girl, perhaps seven years old. A freckled little girl whose mother you sometimes have occasion to think about at night. This little girl spends a lot of time sitting on the sidewalk, so you often pass her on your way to school. One morning, another morning of the same tired fights, dragging Lady behind you, her lead twisted around your legs, this little girl waves you over to tell you she likes your dog. "She's pretty," she says. "What's her name?"

By dinnertime you have carted all of Lady's stuff to the little girl's house: the food dish and bag, the collar, the leash, her chewtoys and throwtoys and even a homemade bumblebee costume crafted a lifetime of Halloweens ago. As you pass the mother in the opened doorway, your elbow caresses the full curve of her breast, a miraculous feeling. She smells beautiful. You return with the blanket Lady has been sleeping on for the last week, thinking perhaps the smell might help her transition, adding one of Charlotte's discarded shirts, wadding up the whole pile of fabric into a giant ball that you hoist onto your shoulders and muscle down the street. "My goodness," the woman says, her smile white against her tan face. "What's all of this?" You tell her about the blanket and the shirt, and she sits you down at the kitchen table and pours you a large glass of juice and asks you about your classes. When you tell her about your history teacher, she explodes into a laugh. "Mrs. Hermida! Is she still foaming at the mouth?" She reaches over and touches the bow of your lip. When you freeze she pulls her hand away. "I know," she says. "I'm a million years old." You tell her that wasn't what you were thinking at all. "Well, you're right," she laughs. "A million years old." She leans forward on the table, those breasts pressed up hard against the laminate. "Just think about how old Mrs. Hermida must be!" Then she gathers the laundry and starts climbing the stairs. "I'll get this ready for Lady's arrival," she calls over her shoulder, "so she'll feel comfortable immediately."

This leaves only Lady, who has watched all of this from her perch on the sofa, unmoving. Only when you reach for her missing leash at its post on the coat rack do you realize you've already given it away. You call for Lady but she declines, looking briefly at you before turning her attention back to the sofa. Raising your voice doesn't elicit a response, nor does slapping your thigh. The little girl's house isn't too far and you suppose you should go back to get the leash, laugh over your mistake, but for whatever reason you don't do that. Instead, your eye catches the newspaper still untouched on the kitchen table and the twine that secures it. You pry this open with your fingernails and Lady permits you to wrap the thin cord around her neck, leaning her weight comfortably on your forearm as you work. Once tied tight around her neck, the lead is only eight or ten inches long, but that ought to be enough for a half-block trudge, you reason.

"C'mon. To Grandmother's house we go," you say to Lady, and give the twine a brief tug. But she simply tucks her head underneath her leg and licks at herself. You wait a moment and then try again but the dog won't budge. Her obligation met by letting you tie the string, she declines any further commitment to this matter.

"Damn it," you mutter. "Come on already." You jerk at the string, hard, and this jolts Lady's head toward you but her claws dig deep into the fabric of the sofa, tenting it away from the frame until you worry that if you pull any more something is going to give. "Look, it's nearly dinnertime," you say, and Lady's ears perk up instantly. But the food and dishes are both in the kitchen down the street, waiting for the dog. "Yeah," you say. "And dinnertime Dad comes home. You want to try this shit with him instead?"

The firmness of her claws in the sofa fabric vouches for her willingness to take the risk.

"You want some food?" You let your voice go softer. "Treat?"

Lady's demeanor shifts but she's still unwilling to budge without seeing a leash that you, of course, can no longer show her.

"Tell you what. Come with me on a short walk, just a tiny one, and then you can have all the food you want," you beg. With food apparently not forthcoming, Lady turns her attention back to the bend of her leg.

You pull harder, hard enough for her nails to tear at the fabric, hard enough to strain the thin twine, hard enough to lift the dog into the air so that she is dangling above the sofa, her feet clawing madly for the world below, the string cutting deep into the muscles of her neck. You try to grab at her but the frantic gesture of her claws pushes you away and you can see the panic in her eyes and hear the labor of her breathing as the twine tightens itself around her.

When you think back on this moment, you wonder why you didn't simply drop the leash, let it and the dog fall to the ground. You think about this a lot.

But you don't do this. Instead you try instead to grab at the dog, her claws tearing into your arms, leaving jagged wounds along your chest and arms, leaving the twine to embed into her skin until finally something gives and the twine snaps, letting Lady drop to the ground.

You stroke her neck and she lets her head fall into your lap, letting her body deflate gently, licking at the salty blood on your arms. "Jesus," you say, your breath coming hard. "Jesus." You reach down and give her a hug and she remains perfectly still to accept it.

Without the lead, you hunch the entire way, your head never higher than the small of your back. Because of this you walk very slowly, station to station, taking tiny steps that make even the modest distance down the street seem far longer. Lady keeps your stride perfectly, never once distracted by smells or markers. The two of you walk like this, in awkward harmony, into the little girl's house where her mother's pretty face, her long yellow hair, and large bosom greet you warmly, assuring you how much they appreciate this gift, what good care her daughter is going to take with the dog and how much Lady is going to love her new home.

On Certain Displays of Determination

Now that you're aware of it, it's hard to concentrate on anything but Mrs. Hermida frothing at the mouth. Last class of the day and this is the most interesting thing anyone's seen yet. At the far end of the row, Jenny Hempel looks up briefly before returning to her doodling. You'd make a joke for her benefit but the last few haven't gone well. This has been an almost unbearable strain on you and, worse, a source of amusement to Jeff, whose solace comes in suggesting that maybe she likes older men. High schoolers, maybe. "I'm old enough," you retort. "If I were Jewish I'd be a man already."

Jeff, with predatory instincts, has been using this angle to try to convince you to throw a party. "I can't believe my misfortune," he complains to the fates, "to be best friends with the one guy in school blessed with an empty house and the only one who won't do anything with it. It's one in a million."

"Forget it," you advise him. "Besides, my dad's home at nights."

He isn't, sometimes, but you don't reveal this to Jeff.

"We're eighth graders. We should be running this place," he pleads, always pleading, whispering in your ear while Mrs. Hermida explains again about William Blake's versatile capabilities as an artist.

"Imagine," she sputters. You've been reading Blake's poetry in English class, his grand menagerie, and today as a special treat (the optimistic phrase itself enough to engender disdain) she's brought in copies of some of his artwork. She began, your notes tell you, with his *Pieta*, "a very common subject," she explained to no one in particular, "almost a rite of passage for artists coming into middle age. Blake was thirty-eight when he painted his so he was probably feeling the pinch of time." In an ill-considered moment, she had confided how she'd always wanted to be an artist herself, her entire life, something horribly transparent in her tone making everyone turn away, forcing her to retreat to the board: "Next we've got *The House of Death*."

"Speaking of which..." Jeff started in.

All of this because Jeff has just discovered that your mom and sister took off a few months ago. "I can't believe I just found out," he'd shrieked. "What an opportunity." Then he'd narrowed his gaze. "Why didn't anyone tell me?"

Jeff's family just moved to town. At first you'd assumed he'd befriended you (an unlikely choice, unremarkable, tangential to any large group) because of the oddity or opportunity of your living condition, but apparently not. It's strange. While everyone else has been walking on eggshells, refusing to discuss the situation directly, these people you've known since birth, Jeff won't shut up about it. "Why should I?" he says. "We've all got problems, right? Don't get me started on my parents." You don't. "What I can't understand," he admits finally, "is why your dad doesn't call the cops."

To be fair, you don't know either. Partly it was the timing of it. For the first couple of weeks you'd both just assumed they'd find their way back. And after that, after it had already been a month, well, it's hard to explain. Inertia? That was certainly part of it. "What if she'd taken me too?" you'd asked your father one morning, having slept through his late arrival the night before. "What would you have done then?" The man, hands vicelike around his coffee mug, took a long time in considering this. Finally he gave you a measured glance. "She wouldn't…" he began, but then he took a long sip of coffee and looked out the window and he never finished the sentence.

At the board, Mrs. Hermida produces a drawing of a floating head. "Where's the rest of it?" someone asks, a seventh grader of promise, accelerated into your class, accelerated and proving it, the only one paying attention. Mrs. Hermida, gratified, explains that this was Saint Christopher. "Extra credit," she offers hopefully, "if someone can remind the class what he was patron saint of." But no one, not even the seventh grade girl (who looks like she's considering it) cashes in. "Carousels?" someone guesses and everyone laughs. It's true, the way Blake had sketched it, Christopher looks like he's riding on a merry-go-round, rotating in circles, looking backward at what he has just missed (and will undoubtedly miss again), the half-considered cape stretching behind his body, making light of his fruitless motion.

Even Mrs. Hermida laughs, the act soaking those unfortunate souls sitting up front, and explains how she'd chosen this picture because it was drawn when Blake was a student himself, "not much older than you all," she points out. Then, when no one says anything, she winces. "Considerably younger than me."

Jeff called it crazy. "It's kidnapping," he whispered, but it wasn't that either. "Where do you think they went?" he asked minutes later, apropos of nothing.

It isn't the least bit clear why Jeff wants to have a party. As a new student in a school with few transfers, he isn't wildly popular and it's unlikely that hosting what could only be a modest gathering would increase his chances. If anything, it would only highlight the discrepancy between where he (and you) are socially and where he (and you) might hope to be. It is for this reason, among too many others to list, that you refuse. It's difficult to describe the dynamic you and your father have settled into since August, your uneasy companionship, what Lady's new owner referred to that afternoon as the company of men. But it is a fragile situation, unstable, and even though it is unlikely that your father would mind this party (even if it somehow lived up to its name), it might upset this new equilibrium. "And," you'd told Jeff, "things have been upset enough."

If Jeff felt any remorse, he never showed it. "We're nearly at the finish line," he said. "Once we get to high school, we've got to start all over."

"From what?" you snapped. At the sound, Jenny looked up again before burying her head to complete a garland around Blake's capital B on the page of her notebook. You'd motioned to Jeff: *see?*

"Now's the time," Jeff repeated. "I'm sick of starting over. Besides, your mother might come home any time and then it would be too late."

At the front of the classroom, time standing still, Mrs. Hermida comes to her special favorite, a picture called *Age Teaches Youth*. Despite her enthusiasm, which is considerable, no one listens to her. Even the seventh grader has drifted away. Mrs. Hermida must notice this (she has never struck you as particularly oblivious) yet while your doodled stickman shoots jumpers, she drones on about songs of innocence and experience. You can't help but feel badly for her, just not badly enough to listen.

"What are you afraid of?" Jeff pulls you away from your thoughts. "What's your old man going to do to you, anyway, ground you? How can he make that stick?"

It's true that your father would have a hard time punishing you. You doubt he'd even try. More and more he's been less and less like a father, turning into something else instead, something you can't name. All of a sudden, Jeff raises his hand, the act generating widespread unease among the class. "Mrs. Hermida," he interrupts. "Would you say that Blake was advocating experience over innocence?"

Mrs. Hermida takes a moment to recover from her surprise. "That's an interesting question," she begins, and then follows it up until whatever interest there might have been has been leached out. But the gist of it seems to be that experience is unavoidable, whatever our mortal desires. Buoyed by this sign of life, Mrs. Hermida transitions to one final picture, one of Blake's lesser-known works, an etching entitled *The Industrious Cottager*. Seeking relief from Jeff's nagging and Mrs. Hermida's humid drone, you get lost in the enlarged pastoral, let yourself go blank around it, let the colors blur into one another, let them shimmer and twitch for you until the bell rings and you can all head to your homes.

"Last chance," Jeff offers, and to his surprise (and to yours), through a jaw clenching in determination and then a grimace for the remorse inevitably in your future, you agree: "What the hell. Let's do it."

Toward a New Perspective

Five men sitting in the drinking car, near the fireplace, desperate for the heat coming off the crackling logs. Your father and his fellow travelers, commission driven, crowd together, their bones hollowed by the years. "Might as well spend a week with me," he had offered. "Might as well see what the old man has been doing all these years." It was an important trip for him, one that coincided with your spring break, and your father decided that fourteen was too young to spend a weekend home alone. For some reason (involving caps on his reimbursement miles and the idiocy of the highway system and how his boss has got him dangling by his short hairs), you are traveling by train rather than car. He tells you it's just as well, that you're in for quite an experience. Thus far, he has been proven right. The fireplace, initially an oddity (you are delighted to be allowed into the drinking car, the men quipping that they'll keep an eye out for the bull), becomes vitally important by nightfall as the ground loses its heat. You look at the fire and then across to the window and the landscape rushing by. You grunt and the other men grunt back. It is, in its own way, a conversation. Your grunt, "A fireplace inside a moving train car, imagine." Theirs, "Yes. We have long considered."

The train passes smoothly over the plains. This terrain was

hammered out over the eons, or perhaps just hasn't erupted yet. You have been allowed first one drink and then more, and your thoughts have slipped their reins, musing unmolested about glaciers and geological time and a hundred other whims that taunt you with their speed, your senses sluggish and deliberate, unable to keep up. It all feels very appropriate as you approach nightfall with dusk shading everything. You ruminate (audibly? The men next to you offer no clue) about the clickity-clack of the train being a lullaby for dead men. An entire world without women. It is possible you are drunk.

Across from you, a man pulls things from his bag. When the canvas opens, it releases an odor, sharp and meaty. It is a smell you recognize. It smells of your father. All of these men carry it with them. It is the smell of travel, or at least it was fifty years ago. Now it is the smell of railway coal, cigars and velvet, damp wool. It's the smell of history stripped of nostalgia.

Inside the car, the smoke from the fire and the cigarettes (your father looks away as you accept one from another man) tars the walls behind the peeling wallpaper. By your feet the spittoon is a guard dog, perched there since the James Gang at least, and your eyes amuse themselves with the pattern of the wear on the carpeting: threads pulled apart, every man walking the same path, dropping onto the velour seats until the whistled announcement of a destination finally reached, his arms pushing him away, tilting his hat in farewell to the strangers who tilt theirs back, a salesman's valise, a salesman's lower back pain. The windows: soot from the Wild West, cinders, and behind it all the tracks that rush and race with you, the towns like toys—wood framed. No one's built anything near the railyards for decades. So the towns are museum pieces too, fatigued, fatigued. Bone tired. Time for another drink, the shudder of the engine enough to soak your wrist with the bottle's foam, the men hooting at your expense, glad, so glad to have you aboard.

Nine of Clubs. Six of Hearts. The man's fingers shuffle at a deck of playing cards and drop them down onto the table. He hasn't shaved in weeks, his stubble grayed. His tweed coat falls, like his skin, down to his knees. His scarf tatters at its ends. His trousers were stitched for a fuller man. Queen of Diamonds. Ace of Spades. They tumble faster until half the deck piles up. Finally the suicide king (finally) so the remaining cards can go back into the pocket to rest. Then a photograph, then a tarnished silver cigarette case, then a pocket knife. He scrapes absently at some dead skin on his elbow, hacks off a scaly corner like shoe leather, flakes it onto the carpeting. Coughs yellow into a yellowed handkerchief.

The abstract painting outside slows into specifics. There's a clump of trees green with moss. A station outhouse with an indecipherable message scrawled along its siding. You can feel the train grumble to a stop, feel luggage piled upon itself, feel rather than hear the passengers embark and disembark. Inside the drinking car there is nothing to hear, insulated as it is, dark wood, five men standing watch for one another. On lookout for your bull to emerge. Waiting.

Finally the train pulls away and you lean back against the chair, feel the clickity-clack rearrange your insides. Here comes the motion. There's nothing to do but wait. The train will take you where it wants you to go. Time to rest. To weave the threads of your thoughts back into your head. Time enough, at least, for another drink. The voice escorting you into dreams, "Take a look at your boy, Garland. He's a natural."

The Sacred Quest

The Warrior of Sentimental Love

Coming into the house, well past midnight, to The Four Aces playing upstairs in your father's room. There was a time this wouldn't have been that unusual. Once, he loved to sing—crooning down the staircase, dancing the chairs across the kitchen. But of course long before your mother and sister left home, those days had passed. For nearly a decade (for most of your accessible memory), his only music has been the braying for quiet, the rhythmic pounding of his fist, the broom, an umbrella against the downstairs ceiling if Charlotte played her radio too loud or Lady's nails scrambled against the floorboards. In the months since they've been gone, it has grown much quieter in the house, but it is only at moments like this, welcomed by the dulcet murmurings of hearts in love, that you even pay it any mind. You've grown accustomed to the solitude and the quiet, like anything else. Yours is the house friends can come to after school. No need to notify your father should you find yourself out late. You have developed a certain amount of facility around the kitchen. This is far from the worst of all possible worlds.

Occasionally, though, you might wish for more. It's your fifteenth birthday, and while you hadn't expected much in the way of ceremony, you had at least hoped for some acknowledgment. To be honest, the results of your emotional audit have surprised you (as it turns out, you do care) in pangs that chime at odd moments throughout the school day and your shared, distracted supper. In a week or two you will let mention of it slip in some innocuous way, and while he will not apologize, your father will fatten your wallet. Since the women have left, it is only fair to point out, money has become far less of an issue around the house.

So it is a quiet house, a messy but relatively sterile one (twice a week an elderly Czech woman comes and does battle with whatever mess needs to be confronted), a place where things stay as you left them. But now a voice upstairs sings in the neglected registers of love anew on a high and windy hill. Also, staring at the early morning hours on the clock while you fill a glass with water from the kitchen sink, it is, technically, no longer your birthday.

The music is a mystery, absolutely, but it's very late, and just as your father is inclined to let your teenage transgressions pass unmolested, so too are you inclined to let this slide. Indeed, you are past your father's door at the head of the stairs and nearly to your own room before you catch a whiff of perfume. In coldly logical terms you enumerate possible explanations. It isn't the cleaning lady's day, and anyway she carries with her a distinct odor of bleach and skin cream. Neither is it any lingering scent from Charlotte's room, which remains closed and to whose odor you have long since been inured. Following similar logic, it is unlikely to be your mother's perfume for, while you cannot summon its smell at this time, its constant if ambient presence would surely register.

Followed to its logical conclusion, this line of reasoning dictates that a woman, a perfumed woman, has been in your house, in the upstairs of your house, in your father's room. Off the top of your head, you can produce no viable suspects. Your father, tall and thin in your early childhood, has grown wider in the last few years. Your metabolism, sports, and a healthy preoccupation with members of the opposite sex have saved your own waistline during these seasons of premade dinners, but the constant parade of canned foods and fried red meat (your father, cognizant of his inconsistencies with the stove, still shies away from chicken and pork for fear of contaminating you both) have wrecked your father, pushing him from paunchy into bloated, nearly unrecognizable. Still, you are not too young to know, biology conquers all. He is, after all, relatively young (you would have to do the math in your head), still retains most of his hair, his shoulders remain broad and unbowed, he holds a paying job and a mostly paid-for house. In addition to these most pedestrian of qualities, he is also not a particularly social man, and therefore more inclined to discretion. And, finally and least palatably, he's most likely hard-up and therefore less likely to maintain high standards. The perfume, after all, is overpowering and cloying. All of this, checks and balances considered and weighed, forces the logical portion of your brain to judge your father not unsaleable in all markets.

It is very late and most parts of you vote to go to bed, to leave this as one of life's unsolved mysteries, to let some you of the future study its forensics and implications. But unfortunately these parts lack voting rights, so you find yourself lying awake in your bed thinking more about the situation. While it is true that you have noted little interest from your father (the occasional oblique invitation from a waitress goes unanswered or misconstrued), it is also true that you are rarely home, and not exactly the man's confidante—if indeed he has one. It is also true he spends most of his time on the road. A chance encounter, a moment of weakness or even a newly constructed identity (he has exhibited this skill), none of these can be dismissed out of hand. After all, you smile, when one eliminates the impossible, what is left, no matter how improbable, must be the truth. The evidence— the perfume, the music that continues to preach love's divinity at you from underneath the door—is incontrovertible. Maybe he has been swept off his feet. Your imagination now runs unabated through scenarios of the waitresses you've grown to recognize in the greasy spoons you've come to frequent, the widows who prowl the grocery store and dispense unsought advice on the relative merits of baked beans. Even (this last thought banished instantly and permanently to the far reaches of your mind—even unabated imagination not without its pity) your old teachers, the ones who insisted on being called Miss rather than Missus.

This is what your mother's abandonment has reduced you to.

Your father's door remains closed. You put your fingers to it, worrying circles in the wood. The radio has switched to a more upbeat song, Frankie Laine, something with pep, as once your mother might have classified it. Nothing else. By now it is nearly two in the morning, and while your father's parenting could generously be described as laissez-faire, you have never before tested him to this extent. A vision pops into your mind, unbidden, of your father looking anxiously at the clock, the telephone, as desperate as Aegeus for news of you, and while nothing in your shared history validates this, you know as soon as it appears that the prophecy will haunt your dreams for this night and future ones unless you purge it now by wishing him goodnight.

You don't want to go inside, but the vision propels you to knock twice. Quietly the first time, and then louder. No rustling, no shushed giggles or frantic scrambles, nothing except for the bleating of the radio, which promises eternal love by the spoonful and big church weddings.

Your father is alone, of course. On the dresser sit four bottles of perfume, each one nearly full, each one dousing your mother's discarded scarves. None in the lineup, despite his guesses, your mother's brand. The mixture, without the prophylactic barrier of the door, makes you gag. It takes a moment for you to regain your poise (God, the smell, like a fist in your sternum), and in that moment your father rises from his dune at the far end of the bed. In the lamplight you can see his hair wisping up from his forehead, his face lopsided from his pillow's assault, his eyes wide at your sudden arrival, the bulk of the telephone on his chest, clasped securely in his cradled hands.

"I'm home," you tell him, this man, this stranger, still disoriented, still bested by sleep. "I just wanted to let you know that I'm home."

The Ferry of Souls

This one takes place on your way back from getting ice cream. Since your mother and sister have returned, the family has taken to evening outings. After dinner, the dishes safely corralled in the sink, your father asks in that blustery tone whether the kids might want to try their luck at bowling or pinball. One night, perhaps two weeks ago, he pushed back from the table and pondered aloud whether anyone might fancy a jog around the park. Tonight it is ice cream. "That's the third time this month," your mother grouses good-naturedly. "Keep this up and I'm going to have some trouble fitting into my pants."

"I can think of a solution to that." Your father reaches out a hand and tries to pull her toward him.

"None of that now," she giggles.

Everyone is trying very hard. Even Charlotte, who comes into your room with a book she has just finished reading. "It's great," she gushes. The cover doesn't look promising and neither does the plot— something about a guy in Connecticut who won't stop whining. "You'll like it," she augurs.

You promise to start it that night. "Did you read this in school?" you ask, but she declines the bait with a taunting finger. Frankly, you aren't even sure she's been in school for these last two years. If she was, she'll graduate in the spring, but if she wasn't, then surely she's going to need to drop down, putting her in tenth grade with you or even below, and you don't know how to feel about this. They returned in July, which suggests maybe they were waiting for the school year to end, but who knows? The women—and your sister has become a woman in her time away—share suntans that will fade gradually through the fall so that by December they are pale again, so that you can't even be sure if they are falling back to meet your memory of what they were or whether it is your memory that rises to meet what they have become.

Like many other things, ice cream is less enjoyable the more you have of it, and after six weeks of nightly outings, even Rocky Road is wearing thin. But still, all of you try, your father spooning your mother samples of his newest combination (pistachio/butter brittle, who would have guessed?), you and Charlotte admiring the pastel colors of the ice cream and painted shop fixtures. You want to explain to Charlotte how soothing they are, how much they're what you all are trying to be, but you can't think of how to say any of this, especially with everything between you so fragile. More and more, you are having these thoughts but are afraid to say or do anything with them, so instead you just point to the pink fluff of a sherbet and mouth—"neato."

"Angling for another one?" your father asks, his lips a greasepaint smear.

"Nah," Charlotte says. "We're just looking at all the different colors." Then, miraculously, she winks at you. "They make us think of childhood, right?"

It feels like something opening inside of you. You start to nod, are nodding, when your mother comes up from behind Charlotte and clucks, "a bit young for nostalgia, aren't we, kiddos?"

With another family outing nearing completion, your father steers you all back into the car, his spirits (all of your spirits) as high as you can remember, the radio playing, your mother's arm draped across your father's shoulder in the frontseat and all of you singing along. At a red light a new song begins, and because it is Del Shannon's new single, and because the car is stopped at the red light, and because of what Charlotte said earlier, you look over just in time to see her throw a glance diagonally across the front of the car to your mother, who casually drops her arm from your father's shoulder to your sister's knee, where she offers two quick squeezes before letting her arm recede back to her own lap. When you look back to Charlotte, her face is directed out the window, her eyes raised, her mouth silent.

"Why is no one singing?" your father asks and rouses you all with his ridiculous vaudeville baritone, in imperfect harmony with the song's meticulous vocals. "Come on," he implores. "You all know the words, right?" Your mother turns her head back to you and joins in, scowling for you to follow suit. From the reflection in the window you can see Charlotte's lips begin to mouth the lyrics, as contrived as a silent-film star, her gaze high on the horizon, the car pulling away, your father's voice running roughshod over everything else as the light changes from red back to green.

Interference

Your father would like you to know that your state university has an excellent wrestling team. "Not just excellent, one of the best. Hell, it may be *the* best, for all I know, although a lot of that depends on recruiting classes and then you're into politics. And I know that isn't a priority of yours right now, nor likely to be one with your mostly average athletic prowess (don't look at me that way), and of course you've never wrestled, nor shown any interest in it at all, even when I offered to take you to a meet when you were younger. I'm not complaining. You were always more of a basketball fan and I respected that. Heck, it wasn't like I was taking time away from the Cardinals' games to go to the meets, I'm just saying that in the four years you are going to be there, flags could fly. That's the kind of thing that isn't important to you yet but you never know what's going to matter to you come three years' time. None of us has a crystal ball.

"Let me get you a soda and finish my thoughts. State is two hours away, and I know that doesn't feel like a lot, especially compared to Boston, but it's enough to stop me and your mother from walking into your dorm room every time we see fit. I imagine both of us have had enough traveling to last us a lifetime. Guess I don't want to speak for your mother. Anyway, two hours is a nice buffer, but it's close enough that you can come home if you get yourself in trouble. Maybe run out of laundry or something. Need a home-cooked meal, although if you are counting on one of those it's probably best to call ahead and give your mother a few days warning, am I right? You remember when she tried lasagna that one time when you were kids? Jesus.

"Anyway, wrestling is one of those things that gets everyone on the campus pulling together and that's rare enough these days. Don't worry, I'm not off on one of those political rants you and Charlotte are always on me for. I know you've heard it all before. Listen, what I'm trying to explain is that sports—when you are in the stadium or the gym, with everyone cheering—everyone's together. Everyone wants the same thing and they get it or they don't, together. That's a rare occurrence, these days or any others. I'd hate for you to miss that experience.

"Now I know Charlotte didn't take to State, and I imagine she's been sneaking up into your room at night and filling your head with horror stories and it's not my place to say that she's wrong but maybe things will be a bit different with you. Things are different for boys is what I mean. Maybe you've figured that one out already?

"And I don't want you to be worried about your mom or anything like that. Charlotte will be trying college again real soon, just as soon as she gets regrouped, and your mother and I are excited to start a new path, a new adventure with our life. Maybe try some peace and quiet around here. She's got thicker roots around here now, so I imagine we'll be staying pretty close to home. Which means we'll always be around if you get yourself in trouble.

"You know what I wish? Sometimes I wish I took you out on the road with me more, gave you more of a sense of the country because I'm going to let you in on a secret. You went with me that one time so you can back me up on this: it's all just about the same, isn't it? You've been around long enough and it all blends together and all you want is to stay close to home and lay down those roots I was talking about with your mother. People always think there's something better right over the next hill, the next interchange, but there isn't. There's just you, wherever you are. That's partly why I got a new sales route, that's definitely a part of it. I'll tell you a secret: most of the best decisions I ever made were the decisions not to do something, and I'd wager that's true of most people. It's always easier not to do something than it is to try to undo it. When in doubt, do nothing, that's what I always say. Of course, your mother might tell you that there's a downside to that course of action. But I'm not sure that the other solution is any better. But I guess you know all of this as well as me.

"Look, go out to Boston or stay closer to home. We've raised you eighteen years to know the difference between right and wrong, to make decisions like this one the right way, so we trust you to decide for yourself what's best. I'm just saying that two hours seems like almost nothing but it can be a lot more than that when you need it to be. Nobody's holding you here, least of all me. I've never done that before and I certainly don't intend to start now."

Lord of Strife

Coming off the pick, you feel like your entire body is made of water. Fluid, although the coach has taken pains to remind you that this is a game of fire, intuition—characteristics you lack. It would be cosmic humor that you are chemically unfit for this game (the only one you harbor any real affection for), but still there are moments like this one, fifteen feet out at the top of the key and your left arm feeling like an extension, your whole body moving in concert, moments when things open for you as wide as the highway, the hoop spreading herself in welcome. You start back on your heels, your arms frozen in follow-through, and Jeff, also on the scrub team, smaller than you, garbage minutes last year as a junior, tangles his feet with yours in complement. The captain of the varsity, a four like yourself, isn't quite as gracious: "We follow our shots here," he reminds you, the sort of rah-rah hands-up-on-defense thing that all hustlers everywhere are saying, but his cliché carries to the coach's ear, so you nod and spread fingers wide on defense as the opposing center comes rolling through you.

When the scrimmage breaks for water, you assess your odds. If you were a guard you'd be in dutch, but (rare good fortune over the summer, a prayer well and truly answered) your body has shot upward and now you seem positioned to play power forward, or at least as power as comes in this middling-level high school. You move the water around your gumline, feel it dance to the back of your tongue, and then you spit it back into the fountain, right next to the captain, Gregson, who eyes you warily, your foil, even spotting you two inches and ten pounds. "Don't drink any of it," he warns. He is, statistically, the weakest link on a team that did well enough in its bracket, but his contributions, everyone is quick to acknowledge, transcend the numbers. His presence on the court is a reassurance, like having another coach on the floor. He has attitude, defense, spunk, and the gift of platitudes that wrap themselves around his mediocre body and siren-sing to those wishing to demonstrate themselves true connoisseurs of the game. To them he is the team's true MVP, valiant knight of its heart and soul. To add to this, he is popular with his teammates in the way of all middle infielders and tight-ends; come springtime he will morph into an Eddie Stanky second baseman who glares at each batter, concealing his limited range with chatter. In every sport he is considered indispensable, his batting average explained away by his hitting behind the runners, his lack of production on the football field a testament to his blocking. He is a con artist, a card sharp whose true talent seems to be in his ability to convince men of real ability that he is one of them.

But in this first tryout of the new year you've found Gregson quite manageable. Even without any help from the wretched refuse of your teammates, you've taken him inside and finished regularly. The coach has begun to call you by your name and now he motions you over and asks where you came from.

"The south part of town, near the diner," you reply.

"No, I mean where'd you play last year. You're a junior, right? You weren't on JV."

You tell him you've never played before, that this body is new to you.

"Lucky," he offers, and you agree.

After the break, you hit a shot from the key, following in a few feet even though you knew from the release that the ball was going in, and because of this, you are a few steps late in getting back to help when back the other way the starting center puts in his rebound. Gregson growls, as though it is his fondest wish in life that you do better, as though he is father and coach and mentor, as though you aren't trying to take his spot because such a thing is not possible. The next possession you are double-teamed and none of the other gray team seem willing to cut into the paint. Eventually you push the ball back outside where a young kid with no hope throws up an airball. You hurry back upcourt shadowing Gregson, who exerts himself unnecessarily (the ball not even checked back in and he's in a show-me sprint), and you are thinking about ways to exploit this eagerness when your head slams hard into the floor.

After Gregson has laid the ball into the net, you rise to your feet, your teammates waiting to push up court. "Call out those picks," you shout, but no one seems particularly eager. Again you pick up a double-team, and again with no movement you throw it back to the same hopeless case whose shot veers off the front of the rim, right to Gregson who feeds it in the transition and then lays it in after you are slow disengaging from a clump of players coming up court.

This time you are slower to your feet, and the coach asks if you're tired. You give him a look that you hope suggests determination, but in reality you are gassed. Your solitary practice in the backyard over the summer didn't prepare you for running and contact. You tilt subtly away from Jeff, who's manning the point, and he looks elsewhere, the entire offense stalled around you.

It is the third hard pick that puts you to the ground for a minute, dizzy. "Call out those picks," you'd plead if you had the breath for it. The coach blows the whistle but otherwise makes no move. Finally you go over to your center, the backup nicknamed by his teammates the Concession Speech, and explain how his man is picking you at the top of the key as yours breaks into the corner. "You've got to let me know," you say, and he gives you a pimply smile.

"Is that how it works?" he sneers, tossing the ball up in the air.

It is. Or rather it should be. Most of the other boys in the gym are relative strangers to you, a different circle, until now nodding acquaintances in the hallways. Now that your mother and sister have returned, whatever tepid notoriety your situation engendered has faded. They don't know you from Adam.

Your shoulder is throbbing so hard you doubt you would be able to shoot even if the ball made it to you. Gregson, with the same sort of instinct that has allowed sharks to fend off evolution for millions of years, dismisses his double-team with a sort of glee and then moves over to help his own center. When Jeff finally passes the ball to you again, it is too hard and unexpected, your rhythm broken, and the ball glances off your finger, hard enough to make you forget the pain in your shoulder.

On the next possession Gregson turns into your shoulder, the ball still with his guard on the perimeter, and maneuvers you in a bull rush away from the basket. You try to push against him (weak legs), but he turns a deft little pirouette you are surprised he has the quickness for, and you are on your ass. You hear a chuckle, and then more than one.

The rest of the practice continues much the same way: you keep your feet mostly by keeping to the perimeter. Your team, which got ahead early, falls so far behind that the coach has stopped keeping score. When the practice is over, he tells everyone to do wind sprints, and even these seem Herculean to you. You are paces behind when you feel the sudden rush of liquid moving through you. You look down feebly at the water all over your shirt and reach out to the wall for support, but you have misjudged the distance again and this time you hit your head against the cinderblock. Gregson reminds you that he told you not to drink too much water as he reaches down to help you to your feet.

Afterward you thank the coach for the opportunity but tell him you won't be coming back.

"You might try," he suggests. "It'll be easier once you get into shape."

You shake your head. Strangely, your body has recovered. You feel you could run wind sprints easily now, in the deserted gym.

"We could use another big man off the bench," he offers, all the while packing up his equipment into a pale blue bag.

"No, thanks. I'll be pretty busy this year and I've got to keep my grades up if I want to go to college," you explain. "I'd best leave basketball to someone else."

"If that's your decision," he shrugs, and says no more, already long past you.

You are here too early. Through some cosmic scheduling error you have been enrolled in an upper-level astronomy class although you are only a freshman, a tiny blip in the larger cosmos of the college. While your peers are streamed peaceably into composition and precalculus classes, modestly left to fulfill their foreign language requirements, their physical education components, the most pedestrian of intellectual footholds, it is your fortune instead to be ushered to the base of an enormous tower well past nightfall. Everybody here is older than you. Everybody further along the journey.

The professor, listed only as Racine in the course catalogue, has placed typewritten notes in each of your campus mailboxes requiring your presence at the astronomy building this Tuesday at eight o'clock, and then, handwritten, scribbled in the corner: "in the p.m., naturellement!"

So the evening finds you here, late August, Boston, your first week of classes. There are five other students standing around catching up with one another. Finally their attention pulls away from their summers, their applications to graduate school, to you. "Who are you?" they ask, and you tell them your name. "Why are you here?"

they ask, and this is a much harder question to answer. Taken at its most elemental, the answer is simply that you were commanded to come by the letter in your mailbox, that same letter that commanded them. Taken at its grandest, the answer contains trace elements of your father, your mother, the burden of your sister's college failure, and a hundred more of your own to pile on top, creating a tower of its very own. Between these poles are any number of nuanced markers, like cards in a deck waiting for you to pluck them from the pile, to parse their meanings, to employ their rationales. One of the students, a thin woman whose hair rises above her face, removes two cigarettes from a canvas knapsack and offers one to you. "There has been," you assure her, "some sort of mistake."

"I'll say," a bearded guy behind the woman says. "What are you, a sophomore?" When you tell him to shoot lower, he makes a face. "This class has prerequisites," he informs you.

Another man, directly behind him, thrusts his finger into his chest. "I've been on a waiting list for three semesters," he complains. "Professor Racine doesn't offer this class every term."

The woman leans forward to light your cigarette. "Think about all the wonderful things our new friend is going to do to the curve," she says, smiling at you. "You're not a physics genius or something, are you?"

"Me? No."

"See, so everyone's happy."

This groundwork laid, you are given a nickname (the Neophyte) and then promptly ignored by all parties for half an hour, waiting for the arrival of Professor Racine and the keys to the astronomy lab.

Professor Racine, when he finally comes, is so slight that you initially mistake him for a woman. He has the slender grace of a woman, juggling his briefcase and roll sheet as he removes his keys, gesturing you all toward the steep staircase up to the roof. He does a brief headcount with his finger, pausing at your unfamiliar face. He confirms your name and then speaks to the class as a whole: "This rather remarkable young man wrote an impassioned admissions essay about the importance of astronomy in today's world, its mysteries, and all it has to teach us. It was such good work that I allowed him to join our troupe." Your former ally glares at you, while behind her the bearded man smiles smugly.

Your admissions essay was about being vice-president of the high-school debate club, about your love of snow, and some filler about your affection for poetry. Much of it was penned by your mother. Not a word mentioned astronomy in even the most oblique of ways.

Professor Racine moves closer to you, maneuvering you to the first step. "I've got rather high hopes for you," he says.

You don't say anything, can't think of anything to say really, except this: that you know incontrovertibly that it is Professor Racine's destiny to be disillusioned, that there is abject disappointment to be found in his cards, that whatever else the future might hold, things are never going to turn out in the manner he hopes.

There must be a thousand stairs leading to the top floor of the Astronomy building, so that by the time you reach it, you can taste not only your recently smoked cigarette but the heavy fried food from dinner and the heavy fried food that had preceded it at lunchtime. You hope everything stays down. This term is only an hour old and you have learned many lessons, although few of them can be described as astronomical in scope.

"We're in luck," Professor Racine crows. "It's a clear sky and the Red Sox are in Detroit." He is hopping from foot to foot in his excitement. "What do you think that means?" he asks you.

"Probably a loss," you guess.

His eyes narrow for a moment before he chirps, "a joke!" Then he turns to the rest of the class. "Light pollution," he intones solemnly. "The bane of our existence."

The astronomy lab occupies the entire top floor of the building, the ceiling mountainous, fifty feet high at least. In the center of the room, an enormous telescope points upward through the slitted roof. The telescope is wrought metal with gears and wheels speckled red and green with oxidation. It is a breathtaking machine. It is so complicated that even if you were the person Professor Racine seems to think you are, you might still be hard-pressed to identify the complicated machinery at work within it. While you marvel at all of this, Professor Racine circles the telescope, lecturing about new advances in the field. He talks about the great work currently being pioneered with multiple mirrors, the behemoths they are creating on the West Coast. "Of course, who knows," he says, voice dreamy with longing, "what the Soviets are coming up with at their end. An endless supply of government funds and no light pollution to speak of…They must be witness to all of God's secrets." Behind you, the students take diligent notes on optical telescopes and all sorts of technical terms that you presume will find their way onto exams and essays. But you don't care about any of that. The telescope dwarfs you, and from your position at its base you can see up into its belly, into a thousand pieces that promise the answers of our universe. It reminds you of something you can't quite divine. Your fingers rub, of their own accord, the molting paint. Racine leads the others across the room to a giant drafting table where plots of the constellations with their complex mathematical mysteries lie. The group hunches over one such paper, Racine tracing a graceful curve with his finger, his students capturing every word in their notebooks. When he spots you, he comes over, the others trailing behind like a comet. He looks at your hand, still petting the metal, your mind still at work trying to place what the towering thing reminds you of.

"What do you think?" he asks you.

Everyone stands quietly, waiting for your response. And like your own gift from the heavens, the answer comes to you. It's the way the base rounds together, its casing like an iron skeleton. It's the way you stand underneath it, the arc of your neck inducing vertigo so that when you look straight up to its head you can't be sure whether you are falling or whether it is. It's the way it lumbers over you. "It's a dinosaur," you blurt.

"Well," Professor Racine says, his voice as hurt as a rejected suitor's. "It certainly isn't the Hale, but it isn't bad for our modest purposes." He stands next to you and looks up for a moment, the angle of his neck reflecting your own. "Let's try it out, shall we?"

Above you the cosmos radiates in its immensity and you understand how people might once have taken refuge in thinking it a gigantic tapestry. There would be something comforting in this, the notion of a weaver, but also the certainty of defined limits. As it is now, you are struck dumb by it, by the careful and deliberate patterns of the constellations on the inky blackness of their curtain, the heroic glimmer of starlight that, by the time it reaches your eyes, connotes only the death of its sender eons and eons ago, as though the star's only purpose in existing was to have died for this single moment. You were the last one to get to the eyepiece, so you are the last to get a look. Behind you, Professor Racine and the others have moved away again to the far end of the lab where he begins to diagram computations on the blackboard, to try to make sense of the incomprehensible mysteries of large numbers. The telescope is focused on a single point—a nebula, you have been told—and it is a rare treat to encourage your mind to go blank while all around you the world dances easily. You can feel something just beyond your grasp, the fringes of it tickling your chest. You stand there motionless through all of the professor's calculations, the wavering of the stars as graceful as hymns. You stand there while the others collect their books and pack for the descent to their dorms and apartments. You stand there as the professor puts his arm on your shoulder and whispers to you that it's time to go. And you will stand there until his voice turns from bemused through insistent to the cold edge of anger. You will stand there under the enormous responsibility of desolate stars throbbing their epitaphs to you and you alone, and you won't ever want to leave.

None of us directs the course of our lives. This is the truth held from you by your nattering professors. For two days you have ridden back on the bus, back from campus, back home, to this stretch of highway, the mangled cars and the human wreckage once your sister.

The drunk driver's car lies heavily above your sister's, the metals and glass and detritus so fused that you cannot imagine how either body was removed until you circle around to the passenger side and its manmade incision. You lean into her car, not sure what you are hoping for, but whatever it was, there's nothing left. Your father puts his hand on your shoulder from behind. "I went through it pretty good," he says, his voice breaking only the littlest bit. Together you face the highway, cleared after two days. You watch cars come and go, kicking tiny bits of safety glass onto the shoulder. Eventually the glass will be picked up or blown away, and this spot won't be any different than any other spot on any other highway in the country. For the first time you understand the roadside markers and flowers. Somehow you'd always missed the point.

While you are standing there, a state trooper pulls up. You think maybe there's going to be a problem, but he nods to your father. He introduces himself to you, "I'm Officer Harris, I'm handling the case."

"Why are the cars still here?" you ask him, and he explains that "when there's casualties the report's got to be a lot more thorough, and there were some delays with the photographer and otherwise." Then he reaches out a hand. "I've given condolences to everyone but you," he says. "I'm awfully sorry about your sister." You take his hand and shake it.

There doesn't seem like anything more to say but the trooper shifts from one foot to the other, binding and unbinding his wristwatch in a nervous gesture. Your father kneels and picks up pieces of glass, collecting them in the palm of his hand and staring at them for a good long while. Finally the trooper clears his throat and suggests maybe you'd both like to head home. His face reddens at the collar. Your father looks down at the glass in his hand, jiggles it a bit.

"We've pulled off to the side," you say. "Is there some sort of problem with our being here?"

The officer looks past you to your father and doesn't say anything. His hand moves to his watch and frees its tongue from the strap. "Head home to your wife, Garland. She needs you now."

Your father looks up from the glass and stares at the officer until the officer looks away. "If I don't move, is this wreck going to stay here forever?"

The officer shrugs. "One way or another we'll have to clear it off the shoulder," he explains. "It's a hazard to other drivers."

"It's dangerous," your father says. "Gotta keep people safe." Then he turns to you. "I wanted you to see this," he explains. "I've been doing my best to keep it here, thought it might be something you'd want to see."

You nod. The officer comes close again and says quietly, "He's seen it, Garland. Head on home, now." You feel bad for the man, who seems both patient and kind.

"That her?" your father asks, gesturing to the police car. You look over at the shade of a person in the back.

"She's there," the officer says. And for the first time, his voice takes on an edge. "After your threats, she needed me to come with her to see the site."

"Did she now?"

"Yes." The officer coughs. "Hell, Garland, I'd just as soon not be in the middle of this, but the woman's husband died too and I've got responsibilities. She'd like to see where it happened, maybe have a quiet moment or two with her thoughts without you screaming and throwing things at her." He gestures down to the granules clenched in your father's fist. "The woman's husband died too," he says again. "Now I know the circumstances, but you can't run her off again. And you can't run off the photographers again neither."

"You're pretty good at telling me what I can't do," your father says quietly. And then he turns to face the officer. He's three inches taller than the man, at least fifty pounds heavier. The officer doesn't look too happy, but he doesn't look scared either. "You are pretty fucking wonderful at telling me what I can't do and what I should do." He looks at you and grimaces, a poor attempt at a smile. "It's good you were around, Officer Harris. I was getting mighty short on people who know what's best for me. My luck that you came along when you did." He looks down at the glass in his hand, moves it around with his finger and then flings the handful toward the wreckage. "Fuckers," he spits. "Fuckers."

"The woman's husband died," Harris says. By now his posture isn't apologetic at all. His watch is on tight and his hand hovers near his belt. "She says you come after her again while she's trying to look at the crash scene and she's going to press charges."

"Is she now?" your father spits. For the first time you realize how drunk he is. He pushes the cop hard in the chest and then goes over to the backseat of the police car. He mashes his hand against the window and the silhouette inside jumps backward. Your father lets his hand stay pushed up white against the window, the tiny bits of safety glass still in his palm. "Are you now?" he asks the woman's darkened figure. After a long moment he lets his hand fall and walks back to his car and gets into the passenger seat.

The officer surprises you by apologizing again. "Get him home to his wife," he tells you. "Get him home to your mother."

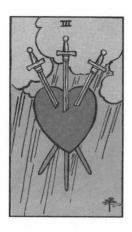

That Lord of Sorrow

Your mother hasn't come out of her room since the accident. Back from the crash site, you sit at the kitchen table with your father. He finds a bottle of whiskey and two glasses. He rinses the glasses in the sink and then flings them dry. A handful of ice from the freezer. You had forgotten how large his hands are, and you have a fleeting impulse, easily denied, to take his hand and measure your own against it. He pours a glass for himself, drains it, then pours another. Finally he fills your glass and pushes it over.

"We've got the funeral tomorrow," he reminds you. Then he looks down at his shirt and feels at the stubble of his beard. "I guess it doesn't really matter if I'm looking my best. All the same, we've got to figure out some way to get your mother out of there."

"Has she eaten?"

"I've been putting things by the door. I'm sleeping down here on the sofa," he explains. "I wake up the next morning; there's an empty plate. The door stays locked. I'm not used to seeing it from this side." He holds his glassy eyes up to yours. "I always felt like it was the two of us," he says. He swings his arm out. "You and me. Not just when they were gone. Even when they were here, it always felt like the two of us to me."

"To me, too."

He nods, a frown on his face. "I guess that's mostly my fault."

He doesn't seem to be fishing for absolution and anyway you're too tired, too stunned, not drunk enough to grant it. So you just sit there drinking.

"A lot of things are my fault," he says, after a pause long enough for you to hope he's moved past it. "But not everything. Sometimes I look around for someone else to blame."

"Sometimes I think it was all Lady's fault," you concede. He looks blank for a moment. "Charlotte's dog," you remind him. He shows no signs of recognition. "Cocker spaniel…"

He shrugs. "Sometimes I think I dreamt all of you while sleeping off a drunk," he says. "Sometimes I think I'm going to wake up twenty years old and none of this will have happened."

"Here's hoping," you say with a thin smile, raising a glass. He grunts and taps your glass with his, hard enough for you to feel it. "Lady?" you try again. "She pissed on your rug?"

Your father looks over at the den for a long time, then shakes his head. "Sometimes I think I wasn't even here. Right about now, that old disappearing act of yours would sure come in handy. Care to share your secret?" He opens his mouth to say something else when you hear heavy footsteps from the bedroom above you. A chair scrapes along the floor, then stops. After that, nothing.

"Maybe I'm wrong," your father whispers. "Maybe everything was my fault." He gets up and moves over to the window. "Starting to rain." He looks out. "Do you believe in omens?"

You tell him you don't know what to believe.

He's running his fingers along the moisture forming on the inside of the glass. He draws a heart and then runs his finger through it. Then, catching you watching, he wipes the entire design clean with the pad of his hand. Lightning strobes you both, and moments later the thunder rattles the panes. "Tell you one thing," he says. "Right about now that bitch is getting rained on."

It's a long time before you realize he's talking about the drunk driver's widow.

Your father sits down heavily. He pours himself another drink and tops yours off. "This making you feel any better?" he asks.

You move what's left of the ice cubes around in the glass. "Not really."

He sighs. "Maybe if your mother was down here." As if in response, you hear another heavy thud from above you. You both stare out the window. It's a real storm and the entire house is shaking. In the kitchen the dishes rattle and branches tap their own designs against the window panes. You watch it all. Only by timing the lightning can you guess whether the sounds you hear are your mother's footsteps or the thunder. Everything is coming from above.

Consequences

At Rest from Strife

At rest, Charlotte lies with her arms folded on her lap. She looks so peaceful that even though you are seventeen and not inclined to sensitivity about such things, you pause before waking her. Her bedroom looks emptier than before she went away to college last fall. Whatever possessions she abandoned in her dorm room still haven't found their way back home, her posters of bands with such improbable names: The Cracked Shells, I Ching. At Christmas, she told the family she wasn't going back, "not ever," and nobody knows why. Your mother has sent you upstairs to her room, ostensibly to tell Charlotte it is time for dinner but perhaps for a little reconnaissance work if the topic should happen to arise.

"Give her some space," your father grunted. More and more his answer to everything, and certainly his answer to Charlotte since her return. "The girl's entitled to some secrets."

"Ah, the authority has weighed in," your mother's voice floating from the kitchen. "How nice of you to join the conversation."

"Lu," your father said, adjusting himself in his seat, "she needs some space. If we don't give it to her here, she'll go searching for it elsewhere." He met your eyes briefly. "Trust me, I know what I'm talking about."

"Well there's a novelty," your mother's voice getting louder until her body emerged, holding a pot. "Jesus, Garland, I'm not recruiting him to the French Resistance or anything, I'm suggesting he take an interest in how she's doing." A wooden spoon handle rotated inside the pot, in orbit with your mother's shifting stance. "What I'm asking, speaking of novelty" she said, blowing hair away from her face as she focused on you, "is to try some compassion and see if that gets you anywhere." She gathered the pot in one hand and gestured with the spoon. "And stop taking advice from your father if you don't appreciate problems. That pearl I'll throw in for free."

On your way upstairs, you could hear the argument escalate and the sound of the spoon rattling its chime against the metallic rim of the pot, but once Charlotte's door closed everything became serene. You sit at her desk, careful not to disturb her, and find yourself matching your exhalations to hers.

It must be that you've gone into a trance because when she wakes to your bulk in her chair, her startled cry startles you to the floor, and so you find yourself collapsed in a heap while Charlotte straddles the opposite side of the bed. Her face (in repose nearly a mask) is now a distortion, her eyes wet, saliva welling in the hitch of her lower lip. "What the fuck do you want?" she snarls.

"Mom sent me upstairs," you explain. "Dinnertime."

You can actually see her body winding down. "God," she breathes. "You scared me. You're still doing that zoning thing?"

"I'm sorry."

She nods and pulls her hair away from her face. It is sad to say, but your sister is not a beautiful woman, nor will she grow to be. Your mother, hawkish, bony, angular, is not conventionally attractive but she redeems herself with an anger that infuses her actions with grace. The beauty of tyrants—as you will one day come to recognize it in newsreel footage of dictators and drug lords. Your sister has inherited many of her mother's mannerisms but brings to them the taint of your father's clumsiness so that what comes off as majestic in the mother seems merely apologetic in the daughter. Poor Charlotte, with her long hair and thin body. She has the outward trappings of the other girls—those you and your friends lust after, counting down the minutes until, as college men, you are finally granted access to the bounties of college women, never admitting, not even to yourself, that this sudden chrysalis is unlikely to provoke the changes necessary for a woman (college or otherwise) to offer you anything substantive. But still you dream, and so too must your sister. After all, what little you've grown to suspect about women suggests to you that, at least in this matter, you are very much the same. When she was asleep, your sister had a sort of grave dignity, but now, awake, you can see afresh how disappointing she must have been to college boys, the complete package somehow far less than the promise of its individual parts. Maybe this was why she left college.

Charlotte removes an apple from the dresser while you arrange yourself on the sheets. She fishes a small knife from the pocket of her jeans and starts paring the apple.

"You're going to ruin your dinner," you say, attempting a conspiratorial smile.

Charlotte huffs. "I was at college eighteen months. You're telling me she learned to cook in that time?"

"How was the food at school?"

"Hmmm?"

"How was the food at school?"

She adjusts herself at the foot of the bed. "It was fine, I suppose. The thing about college is that you don't wake up in time for breakfast, and then you get busy. By the time you eat, you're so hungry that anything tastes good. Everything is fried…The food isn't really such a big issue."

"What is?"

From your position on the bed you can see only the angle of her neck and the crown of her hairline. "Mom send you up here to spy on me?"

It is well that she cannot see you blushing. "No, of course not." You push yourself forward until your face is over her left shoulder, until your cheeks are inches from each other's. She is skinning the apple in a single coiled strip. "It's just that I'll be going next year."

"You thinking about following in my footsteps?" she asks.

"I'm leaning toward Boston, although Dad is giving me the full-court press about staying in state."

By now the apple skin is a looping snake down her arm. "That figures," she shakes her head. "Why does that not surprise me?"

"Sometimes I think it would be very nice to get away from here, even for a while," you say. "The way you and Mom did."

It's funny, but you and Charlotte never talked about where they had gone. They were missing nearly two years, but the few slender clues you have—a postcard from Chicago, one airy phone call (ostensibly from a diner in Montana)—give you almost nothing to work with. Sometimes, late at night, the phone would ring and your father would answer it. Those times, you suspected, it was your mother, but he never told you anything about it. At school the teachers were nicer to you, more lenient about missed assignments. It made you mad that even they seemed to know more about what was going on than you did. When they came back, Charlotte wouldn't talk. But sometimes, in the months before she left for college, there would be moments where she and your mother would exchange a look, just a look, and it was like a whole other lifetime, one that you weren't a part of and would never be invited to join. Sure, you hated her for it, who wouldn't?

"You'll get your chance soon enough," Charlotte says, distracted, her voice far away. This is your moment, when some combination of words will unlock the mystery inside of her, only you don't know what the right words are.

"When?" you try. "When?"

The apple has now been skinned. Charlotte lifts the skin to you. She forces it together gently with her hands, re-creating the hollowed apple, and then pulls it apart. She does this a few times. "Look," she laughs. "It's a Magritte. I'm a genius." Then, "We'd best be getting downstairs."

"We've got time."

"It's dinner," she says. "You know how they get when we're late for dinner."

"They'll wait," you say coldly.

Charlotte looks at you for a moment and then shrugs. "Your funeral."

"Dad is really pushing me hard to stay nearby."

"Can you blame him?" Charlotte asks. "Think of the history."

You are so angry that you have to wait a few moments, control your breathing, before you can talk again. "That really isn't fair," you say.

"No," she agrees. "It isn't."

"But I'll get my chance soon enough, right?" you say, in a cruel, mocking tone, that Charlotte accepts as owed.

She picks up the knife and then puts it down again. "The thing about Dad," she says, "is that he's always really just looking to keep things the same." She shifts her weight onto her elbow. "Sometimes I feel sorry for him because unfortunately the world just doesn't work that way."

"How about Mom?" you ask. "What's she looking for?"

"Oh, God." Charlotte's laugh, you realize, is exactly the same as your mother's, a sudden rush of air through the nose, a dismissal. "You know Mom."

"What on Earth," you finally ask in desperation, "would suggest to you that I know the first thing about Mom?"

This too Charlotte concedes. "I'm not back forever," she says. "It seems like I am but I'm not. One day I'll be long gone from here." Her finger traces the blade of the knife. "Can't you understand that Dad is worried about what's going to happen with Mom if you go across the country to school? If there's nothing keeping her tethered?"

"*I've* been keeping her tethered?" you ask, unable to keep what you need to out of your voice. "That was me?" Charlotte laughs again. "That was tethered?"

"But she came back." Charlotte shrugs at all the things you don't understand. The name Magritte barely scratches the surface of your ignorance. "Dad doesn't really know what to make of any of this."

"Is he worried that she's going to follow me to Boston?" you ask. "None of this makes any sense."

"He doesn't know why she left," Charlotte says. "And he doesn't know why she came back. So, because of all the things he doesn't know, he's afraid to change. All he knows is that as long as nobody moves, nobody gets hurt."

"It just seems stupid for me to go to State after what happened to you," you say. "I mean, would you recommend it?"

She picks up the knife and the apple. "Well, if we're not going to make it downstairs," she says, gesturing to the fruit and cutting off a slice. She puts the knife to her mouth and disengages the apple with her tongue. "I'm not one to read the cards, but I don't think you need to worry too much about me when you're making your decision."

"What happened to you?" you beg.

Charlotte smiles a bit, then flicks another piece of apple with her tongue, her tongue forked by the knife. "Not now. Soon," she promises.

"When?"

"Soon."

After a few moments of watching her eat, you say in a small voice, "Mom and Dad are going to start to worry."

Charlotte raises the knife to your face, a thin slice of apple on the blade. When you reach to take it, she flicks the blade with a sharp gesture of her wrist. You pull your fingers back in alarm. When you reach again, she flicks again. "Hey," you yelp, "that's sharp, you know?"

She stares at you over the blade. She flicks again. "Nobody move and nobody gets hurt."

In Celebration

Your father sticks his head through the doorway. "Dinner reservation is for seven," he reminds you. "Don't forget to put on a tie."

When you protest, he grins. "Better get used to it...college boy."

Now, the night before you head out by train, your romantic notions of hitchhiking quashed firmly, if good-naturedly by your mother, "If the school learns you did something that stupid, they're liable to pull their acceptance." Your bags are stacked neatly in your room. Your parents have made reservations at a fancy restaurant. When you protested, your mother stopped you cold. "Let's be honest. How often has this family had something to celebrate?" It was on the tip of your tongue to remind her that you hadn't done anything yet, not even boarded the train.

Charlotte, long moved out, living with a girl from high school, is slated to come to dinner. Her boyfriend, a scraggly young man with uncertain prospects (your mother's indictment), the kind of guy who looked like he'd leave a girl knocked up and stranded (your father's), has not been invited. This guy, whose name is forbidden inside the house, has somehow galvanized your parents and they're showing signs, hints really, of getting back to something. All this time it turns out what they really needed was a common enemy.

Even better, Charlotte let slip that she'd met the guy at State and this admission had somehow greased the wheels to your own leaving. "I can't pretend to be happy," your father allowed when you told him you were off to Boston. "But if that dirtball your sister's been bringing round is any indication of State's current product, then maybe things are changing. Maybe you're better off. We'll hold down the fort here," he promised. "Just make sure to get yourself a part-time job, see if you can save up for a car, all right?" As easy as that, after months of worry.

Dinner at seven and then off to a party at a schoolmate's house. Last week, after your months and years of passive yearning, Jenny Hempel had given you an opening. Bumping into her at a parking meter, you'd found yourself suddenly empowered (your short time surely a factor in your bravado) to ask her to a movie. Since that first date, you've gone out nearly every night (the two of you making a running joke of your ill-fated timing). Neither of you talked at all about the future. On your end, you had no desire to spoil things or clutter them up. It was complicated, true, but maybe it was better to pretend instead that things were simple, that things were all part of a larger plan. Last night, in the backseat of your father's car, you'd been bolder and she'd been receptive. The way she reapplied her lipstick afterward in the car's vanity, then shot you a sidelong look and confirmed that you'd be at tonight's party? Well, it was more than all right.

But now seven o'clock is a memory and still no sign of Charlotte. Your father has called twice to delay the reservation, and your only consolation is your parents' agreement that she is damned inconsiderate. "The hell with her," your father decided five minutes ago. "Let's go without her."

If he expected a fight from your mother, he didn't get it. She only laughed and finished her drink and hooked her arm around his. "One thing we can say about this family, at least we're consistent."

Your mother is upstairs collecting her things, your father in the bathroom when headlights appear through the living room window. At the front door, Charlotte kisses her boyfriend and then saunters past you into the house.

"Mom and Dad are pissed," you warn her. Her boyfriend, meanwhile, is leaning against the hood of his car, glaring at you. "He knows he's not invited, right?" She doesn't seem to have heard. Instead, she reaches up to wind a lock of your hair around her finger, tight, before pulling it loose. Then tighter again.

"What are you doing?" you ask.

She puts her hand to your mouth and moves your lips around, posing them in various shapes. "Mr. Potato Head," she giggles.

When you swat her hand away, she pouts. She's wearing what all the girls are wearing, some sort of cotton sack with far too many colors. She shifts her weight. "You'd better go change," you scold, and she finds something delightful in your tone, something that makes her reach again to your mouth to re-create it.

"Hurry up," you say. "Focus."

"What's the matter," she retorts. "Jealous that someone else is stealing your act, my little spaceman?"

You're about to respond when you hear the bathroom door open.

Quickly, you grab Charlotte's hand and race up the stairs, locking yourselves in Charlotte's old room just as your mother's door opens. The two of you collapse, laughing, on the bed, although exactly what's funny isn't apparent to you.

While Charlotte lies on her bed, humming, constructing shadow animals on her ceiling, you move to the closet. "You've still got some old clothes in here, right?"

"Nearly everything," she answers after a long pause. Then, in a newscaster's voice she incants, "Always travel light."

"Perfect," you mumble. You pick out a dress, one of her longest, just past the knees, and hold it up to your chest to match shoes. When you present this pairing to Charlotte, she pouts again. "Squaresville," she decides.

"It'll be fine," you cajole her. "I promise you that no one you care about will be there. And considering what you've got on right now?" You shake your head. "No one will even recognize you."

"It's a five-minute drive," your dad calls from downstairs. "Assuming there aren't any other cars on the road."

"Change clothes," you command.

"And if I refuse?" Charlotte taunts. You give her a flat look and she tries to wiggle her eyebrows. Then, sighing, she pulls off her dress even before you can turn away.

"Jeez, a little warning," you protest, burying your head in the crook of your arm. "You've been living with girls too long."

"What girls?" Charlotte snorts. "Prissy? She's my beard. I've been living with Del since February."

There's something comforting about the way she trusts you. You're flattered, even considering her present condition. "Our little secret," you promise, and she laughs.

"Oh, I doubt it's much of a secret," she admits. "It doesn't seem like the kind of story that would dupe Mom, anyway."

"So why?" you ask.

She shrugs. "I can't really explain it," she says. "Sometimes it's better to hide the truth, no matter how obvious. Sometimes it's just best to let people get on with their lives." She has finished putting on the dress and even unearthed a gold heart necklace from somewhere in her drawer. She shrugs again. "Maybe Dad doesn't know. Nobody ever accused that man of intuition." She looks down at the necklace. "God, if Del ever caught me wearing this, he'd dump me in a heartbeat."

"He's okay, right?" you ask. "Tell me he didn't have anything to do with you leaving college in the first place."

Charlotte's brow narrows at this oblique mention of her past. "Why would Del have had anything to do with that?"

"Because you guys met there and all."

Charlotte looks blank for a moment before she starts laughing. "Here," she says, pulling the rope of her hair away from her neck and raising the necklace. "Give me a hand with this thing."

As you fumble with the clasp, Charlotte chuckles. "Del didn't have anything to do with anything," she assures you. "He didn't go to State. Del's not the college type." Her upper lip does something funny as she says this.

"Then why'd you tell Dad he did?"

"Why do you think?" she asks.

"If you were hoping he'd like Del more, that plan didn't really work."

"The plan worked fine," she grins. "You're off to Boston, aren't you?" Finished, you let the clasp go, the necklace catching neatly around her neck. She watches you in the mirror for a second. "My little going-away present."

Your parents are so relieved to see Charlotte in a decent dress that they forget (or pretend to) how late she is. She curtseys a little, and however she means it, they accept it in good spirits and you're nearly out the door when the phone rings. "Oh, for Heaven's sake," your mother sighs. You go into the kitchen to take the call while your father points to his watch and mouths "one minute."

It's Jeff.

"Brother," he says, "if you know what's good for you, you'll find your way here pronto." You can barely hear him over the music and the noise of people.

"I can't," you explain. "Dinner with my family."

"Isn't that over yet?" Jeff says. You look at your watch. It's nearly eight.

You swear.

"What's that?" Jeff asks. "I'm having trouble hearing you."

"It's nothing. I'll be there in a couple of hours."

"Jenny Hempel's been asking for you," Jeff sings. "All night."

"Well," you say gamely, "she'll just have to wait."

"I'm not sure she will," Jeff replies. "She's been drinking pretty heavily. I'm not sure that filly's got the stamina to go twelve furlongs."

"I'll be there as soon as I can," you promise.

"Hurry," Jeff exhorts, and hangs up.

You can't explain everything to your parents, so begging off dinner doesn't go well.

"For a party?" your dad shouts. He looks over at Charlotte, sitting on the sofa. "Did you put him up to this?"

Charlotte raises her arm above her head, riding her dress up. "Guilty," she says.

Your mother checks her watch. "We can have you there in an hour and a half. You'll get a ride home from a friend?"

It's a good offer. You almost take it. But an hour and a half seems somehow a lifetime. You shake your head and lean over to kiss her cheek. "I'll be back late. Don't wait up."

You go upstairs to change clothes, and when you come down, your parents are haggling, your mother having wrestled the car keys away from your father. She tosses them to you over your father's protests.

"We're not worth one hour?" your father demands.

"I've given you nearly two," you point out. "You knew I had other plans." It feels wrong to blame Charlotte but she doesn't seem to mind, sitting on the sofa, inspecting a shoe she is holding up to the light.

"Break them," your father commands.

"No way," you reply. "The time for people to tell me what to do ended yesterday."

"Way to go, College Boy," cheers Charlotte from the sofa, dancing the shoe in a jig.

"Keep out of this," your father says, and looks over at your mother. But the fight's gone out of her, so he deflates and lets you walk past him into the carport. By the time you've adjusted the seats and mirrors, your entire family has moved onto the driveway. Your father watches the car clear the carport and then taps the trunk twice and shuffles back into the house. Your mother leans through your window. "Be safe," she says and brushes your assurance away.

"Afterward, leave the car and call a cab," she advises. "We'll pick it up tomorrow morning. Just get home safe. Hitchhike if you have to." She tucks your hair behind your ear fondly, adjusts your collar, and then goes back into the house.

By now Charlotte is playing hopscotch along the tiled walkway. You honk and she skips over. "Be safe," she says, winking, mocking.

"You too," you grin. "Still going to dinner?"

Charlotte points out that you've got the car. You apologize.

"I don't think that was in the cards anyway," she admits. "Now I've got to sneak back upstairs to get my stuff." She rubs a fold of her dress between her fingers. "God," she shudders.

"Spend the night," you suggest. "We'll have breakfast tomorrow. seven a.m. departure."

She raises her eyebrows. "Tempting," she quips. "Very tempting."

"I'm sorry about all this," you say, finally.

Then, like your mother before her, she pushes the lock of hair behind your ear. She raises her arms to the fates. "One thing this family's never done well is goodbyes."

She holds that pose as you pull down the driveway. You angle the side mirror to frame her just so, and she curtseys again, low and deep. You drive away like this, watching her as she disappears into the mirror, stoned, wearing a dress (you now realize) from junior high, with the patent leather shoes you'd selected, rising from her curtsey into a military salute, a jumping jack, a twirl, a wave as you turn the corner. And of course she's gone long before you wake up.

All Kindness

The morning of Charlotte's funeral, your mother addresses you both from the base of the stairs. She is dressed, seems sober, holds a coffee mug. "Get up," she orders. Then she heads back up the stairs.

The manner in which you were woken, the fact that you were sleeping on a living room easy chair, and your spectacular hangover all contribute their share to your disorientation. For at least thirty seconds you aren't sure whether you are at home or back at school, aren't sure why you need to wake up, aren't really sure who your mother is, dressed as she is in severe black, her hair pulled back into a bun. Considering the events that will follow, these first thirty seconds of disorientation mark the best half minute of your day.

Your spine seems to have conformed itself overnight to the shape of the chair and you can't stand upright. Your father rolls himself off the sofa and massages his temples. The booze seeps from your pores, the both of you, and the smell itself would be enough to induce vomit even without the circumstances, the empty stomach, and the unnatural angle of your neck. You steady yourself against the banister, mutter something to your father about a shower, and stagger up the stairs.

Your mother's door is closed. You're thinking about knocking when you hear an animal sound from inside, something difficult to articulate, but more than enough to make your hand recede and your legs shuffle toward your bathroom.

You had hoped that the hot water of the shower would loosen whatever it was that locked your spine, but no luck. The hot water runs down between your legs and jogs your circulation, making you realize that you are still a bit drunk.

Downstairs, your father is finishing his coffee. He has poured you a cup, and once you sit down to drink it, he brushes past you to the stairs and the waiting shower. The acid in the coffee churns in your stomach, a dancing, jolting train, and you barely make the sink before vomiting, the liquid flowing upward like the shower in reverse, like the rain from last night, small bits of your stomach mixed in with the coffee and whiskey. You run the water and the mess flows down the drain in centripetal motion. When you cup your hand to the faucet and fill your mouth with the cool, metallic water, you can feel it against your gums, feel it swing from one side of your mouth to the other until it gets warm, and then you spit it back into the sink and go upstairs to brush your teeth.

Your bag remains where you had thrown it before heading out to the crash site with your father. You gather your toothbrush and, since your father is using your bathroom to shower, you brush over a cup on your bed, swallowing the froth. You are unaccustomed to seeing your room so empty of clothes and possessions. At some point this morning, your mother has laid out a white shirt on the bed. But even as you reach for the closet door, you can picture your suit back in your dorm room, hanging there, waiting for its Spring Formal.

The gutted closet holds no surprises, nothing of use. You put on the white shirt and a pair of dark socks and wipe your mouth carefully with the edge of the bedskirt. All of your father's suits are in his bedroom, or what had been his bedroom prior to the accident. You knock on the door, but if she hears, she doesn't answer. You've got half an hour until you need to leave for the funeral home. You knock again and then walk in. Your mother is nowhere to be found.

The room smells terrible, like sweat, like sleep, all the trapped human odors. When you open the bedroom window, you can feel the cold January air against your naked legs.

Your father's old suits hang in the closet, and you guess at one he won't be needing. He remains so much bigger than you that the shoulders run halfway down your bicep. The pant legs eclipse your feet as you select an appropriately subdued tie and move over to the bathroom mirror to tie it. Maybe because you are still drunk, your hands are shaking and you have to undo and redo the knot a number of times. You are about to move when you feel a sharp tug on your pant leg. You look down at your father nodding up, wearing only his towel, pins in his mouth. He tucks each cuff until it looks presentable, first one leg, then the other. He's still wet from the shower, his hair moving away from his bald patch in perfect circular orbit, and there is a pool of water around his feet where he has dripped. But his hands are steadier than yours as he runs the pins through each cuff, giving each one a surveying tug. He trails a finger up the seam of your left leg to the calf. "That should hold," he tells you, his hand still on your leg. "That should get you through today."

No one in your family has been inside a church for years. Your mother, it seems now, practiced once but since the marriage to your father has long lapsed. When you asked her about it, she'd sighed, "Something else to fight about when God knows we didn't need another." But at a time like this, the Church is open-hearted and your sister is accorded all respect. The priest is a young man, nearly as young as you, and you can see something of yourself in him, or at least something of the man you are becoming while away from here. The priest, thin, with a superhero's jawline, has the unsettled look of one who whispers apologies to inanimate objects. At the door he clasps your mother's arm firmly and directs you to the front pew.

Because of Charlotte's age and the manner of her death, the rows fill easily. Your father's eyes scan the faces, his lips counting the bodies, his fingers rubbing at the spine of the hymnal he holds in his lap.

After the readings, the priest clears his throat. "This is certainly the worst part of my job." He looks back at the coffin and then down at your family. "Nearly enough to make me regret my calling. It seems like the Bible should be full of answers. Certainly most of the men in my position seek and find them. Myself, I seek constantly but still do not find. But the act of seeking is itself my consolation, and sometimes that is enough for me." His eyes find yours. "I didn't know Charlotte, and in a room where everyone else did, it seems an aggressive form of hubris to speak of her, or for God, or to you. I am only a man, and these are hard times and hard questions. Forgive me. There is life in death, of course, which avails itself to me as a measure of grace. But if there is life in death, then the inverse, death ever-present in life, must also be true, and this knowledge robs me of any comfort. The two are not simply inversions of one another but parts of the same body, and while I know this spiritually, intellectually I find it"— his lips turn upward—"repugnant."

He looks out with a shy smile. "I'm sorry," he says, shaking his head. "I honestly don't know what to make of a God who permits me the knowledge that the answers are hanging up in the stars yet denies me the wisdom to interpret them and the language to share them with my congregants. Why give us fingers with arms so short?

"Charlotte's death is a reminder of something we must learn and forget perpetually throughout our time in this world, as the serpent eats its own tail. There is no reason to Charlotte's death, no plan to it that I can fathom, and any lesson you learn from it is, I pray, short-lived. That, then, is my only prayer for you. Go from here and forget enough to live your lives. Amen."

Amen.

Nurturing

Your mother, at work on her fourth gin and tonic since the sun went down, professes a fear for your mortal soul. She swirls the drink in her hand, leans forward, implores you again to go see a priest. It has been seven months since Charlotte's death and you're all finding your own ways to cope. Your father, always a fan, has been lost to an elaborate baseball board game in his study. His lips move in murmur as he shuffles cards placed in intricate lineups on the fringe of the desk. He rotates in his seat while rolling the dice, the dots representing numbers, the numbers representing actions on cards representing players. You can hear him late at night, rolling dice in a plastic cup, their sound identical to the rotation of ice in your mother's glass. His cheers as three black dots denote another strikeout, another perfect inning, another shutout. He keeps a ledger in a notebook, meticulous in a way his bookkeeping never was.

Your mother drinks.

During the days, while your father is at work and you are home, in these strange and transient weeks before returning to college for your sophomore year, your mother dresses up in clothes you do not recognize. She wears her hair like a younger woman. When she passes you on the way to her car, on the way to the church, her perfume showers over you. Each night, another drink in her hand, your father midway through a doubleheader, she invites you to come with her to the church and meet the priest. "Please," she begs. It would be an easy concession, a gracious one since you have not done anything of note this summer and neither she nor your father have mentioned it. Since you spend your own nights drinking beer along the riverbank, letting your thoughts dissipate into the atmosphere. Since it is something your mother clearly wants, and it has been years since she has asked you for anything.

And yet you do not go.

He is the same priest who buried your sister. But this alone doesn't account for your reluctance. After all, he had done admirably in that difficult circumstance. Later, after the burial, your mother's friends had held conclave, to gossip about the priest and his strange and reluctant homily. "For God's sake," one of them hissed, chasing a piece of salmon with her fork, "we go to church for answers, for comfort. That man seemed like every garage mechanic telling me he didn't know what was wrong with my car. If I wanted helpless confusion, I'd see my gynecologist." The other women, sturdy, with hearty appetites and thin lips, nodded. The priest, they all agreed, was not long for this parish.

Your mother finally put a stop to it, mentioning how she had found the priest honest, and how if his tactic had been unorthodox, "it had, at least, been a comfort, which is more than I could say about the police." The police, the authorities, your mother's new punching bag, unable to do even the slightest thing right during this entire ordeal. For your own part, it wasn't clear what was left to be done. The offender was already killed, and if there was any further justice to be meted out, it seemed outside the jurisdiction of man. When you ask your mother, on nights like this one what the police could have done differently, you are met with a varnished stare. "All those years, you pay taxes with the expectation of something in return. It's like a promise, like a contract. All those years and all that money and at the end of the day you get nothing but a big fat goose egg. What a cheat." So now she goes to church during the day, and begs you to come with her, and marvels at your ingratitude, and pleads and promises and wheedles like a drunk.

But still you withhold this from her. If it isn't the priest or the church that holds you back, then it must be your mother. What else is left? And the very notion tires you. She is sitting across from you, tilting the gin bottle carefully above her glass. The bottle has an elaborate design of a bird on it, all reds and silvers. The bottle, the glass, your mother's breath all have the astringent smell of paint thinner upon them, and as she begs, you can feel the ghosts of her saliva flit onto your eyelids and your lips. You close your eyes, your mouth, barricade every voluntary part of yourself. Her left hand snakes out and swallows yours, her right one still holding the glass as if in toast. She tells you how tired you look. Rather than focusing your thoughts on anything taxing, it is easy enough to divert them to the face in front of you, the peacock purples and pinks, the remnants of the morning's eye makeup, the bruising of another day, the cradle of her voice as she rises to run you a bath and you rise to accept it.

Surfeit

It will be years before you can get this fish story right. Home from college for the summer, this first summer since Charlotte's death, and drunk again. A regular occurrence in the summer months, nothing else whatever to do in this claustrophobic Midwestern town. Every night, Jeff, your only remaining high school buddy, picks you up in his father's dented, rusted-out Ford pickup. Every night he nods his hellos and reminds you that if he happens to get lucky, you're on your own getting home. It has not yet been a problem.

Generally, you start with a six-pack, driving the pickup to the riverbank that runs parallel to the highway. It's the same highway Charlotte was on, of course, but in a town this size there's no real way to avoid the markers. Most everything runs from, or flows to, the highway. Even at its core, everything in this town leads away from itself. Jeff stays quiet when you pass the accident site, long cleaned despite your father's best efforts. Sometimes you look out the window, sometimes you don't. Sometimes you're two exits past, turning off onto the gravel of your favorite drinking spot before you even remember to look. Nights like this, you admonish yourself to remember, and the next night you generally do.

Between you, you'll finish the six-pack, talking about your

separate but equal college experiences—the girls you almost got. By mid-July you've heard each other's fish stories so often they've merged together, and sipping on warming beer in the truck bed, looking out across to the far shore, to the lazy waves, the fallen branches and rusted mufflers, you'll pick a story out at random and gut it again, yours or his, the point of origin forgotten, the whole exercise there to ward off the silence. Your hand under her blouse, your fingers on the clasp, your lips on the cheek as it turns away. There is something comforting about the stories in repetition, and their doubling does nothing to taint this. Stories, you will find, often happen twice, and sometimes twice again. There's no reason for them not to, really. Things happen, or else they don't. Like the fish in the current below you. There's nothing different about any of them. One is no better than the others, no bigger, stronger, faster, braver. She wasn't any of those things, or maybe she was all of them, nearest to the hand reaching in. Made distinctive only in the choice.

Tonight each of you brought a six-pack (confusion over the schedule), and so you each tackled your own. It was a temperate night, summer taking a respite, and because of this, and because of the extra beer, you began talking about your high school experiences. You'd been reluctant to do so, and to his credit, so had Jeff. You sensed that talking about these things, the bold caricature of it all, would cut off something salient between you and effectively cauterize the friendship. A six-pack of beer each, but when Jeff dropped you off half an hour ago you made no plans for tomorrow night.

The story of Jeff, then, is the story of a week ago, on another night, hotter than this one. A night so hot the truck bed seemed to nurse it, until the two of you were back in the cab with the air-conditioning on, the headlights thin and plaintive against the surface of the river. The single shared six-pack, the recollection of a girl's perfume, the patch of razor burn on her high ankle, the almost inaudible acquiescence of breath. Jeff's story and your own. Jeff telling this story this night, shifting in his seat at the climax, his knee releasing the parking brake, the truck accelerating gradually, inexorably into the soft welcoming swamp of the shallow river. And afterward, scraping out the wheel wells with your cupped hands, the cold muck a miracle against your sweating forearms, the heaving of your chest, the pressure on the small of your back, the fluid curve of your bended knee as you and Jeff delivered his father's truck back onto firmer terrain. A sudden sucking sound and then it pulled free. Your broad smile, Jeff's throaty grunt. The marvel of it all. How easy this mistake (this mistake, this once) was to undo.

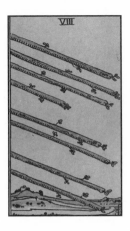

The Lord of Swiftness

This is something you've kept secret for a very long time.

Freshman year, just after Christmas break, back at school only a few weeks, barely in the swing of winter courses, your eye on a blonde in your American Lit survey (the one who seems to have the answer to everything), you come back to your room one night from a pickup basketball game to your roommate Mark's ashen greeting. "You need to call your parents," he says. "Something's happened."

You pack in a blur, get to the airport and board by muscle memory alone. Your plane transfers in Denver, overshooting your final destination by a thousand miles, but who can divine airline strategies? Denver, the sort of innocuous detail that can have unforeseen consequences, like the fabled butterfly's wings, like a girl developing a powerful jones for a milkshake at ten p.m. and choosing to indulge herself rather than shine it on until morning. A connection in Denver rather than Dallas, rather than Chicago, a decision of absolutely no consequence until a massive snowstorm locks the Denver airport down tight, the customer service employee sympathetic, offering a hotel voucher but little else other than the ominous prognostication that no planes will take off tomorrow either, and after that, well, who knows?

At times like these you love the capitalist system, under fire though it may be, a system that dictates that the needs of those who are willing to pay will be met regardless of obstacles, a system whereby a snowstorm that closes the airport will prompt a national bus line to divert as many extra motor carriages—converted school buses, some of them—as it can spare to supplement its regional routes. Since it is a capitalist system, the competition for seats on buses traveling eastbound is particularly fierce. But you have your ace in the hole, your hardship story, and this, along with the bartered hotel voucher, is enough to ensure you safe passage home, barring even more inclement weather or a traffic accident.

So this evening you are in the back row of a school bus somewhere outside of Goodland, Kansas. It is dusk and there's more than a foot of snow on the ground, although as the driver joked earlier, that's less of an issue in west Kansas than in most places since there is nothing to hit anyway. The passengers, the delays on the airport's flipboard still vivid in their minds, applauded this bravado heartily. Compared to the airplane, this rumbling bus seems stolid, like a pronouncement, impervious to natural forces. It is very nearly full, and not adherent to standard routes due to its circumstance, but a few passengers have disembarked at major exchanges for arteries north to Omaha and south to Dallas. The rest of you have become a surrogate family, your spirits buoyed by rapid motion after the hours of waiting. Enough passengers have now bled off that a few lucky souls have benches to themselves, yourself included, which is not entirely good luck since your seat is directly above the rear wheelwell and is therefore most susceptible to bumps (this too admittedly less of an issue since you passed over the border into flat Kansas) and its window side nearly useless to anyone still in possession of their legs. Since it is an irregular route, it is something of a surprise when the bus pulls over in Goodland, the driver having been radioed of a customer in need, and since there are other rows with only a single rider, it is a surprise when said patron, a wisp-thin blonde girl (whose colorful clothing and strongly herbal smell test the goodwill of those passengers who have already endorsed Barry Goldwater as their candidate, two months in advance of the Republican primary), elects to become your seatmate. The girl, no more than a girl, no younger than you, wins some measure of popular support when her knapsack reveals a Jayhawks logo, and then gives it back when she manages only a timid and befuddled smile in reply to a Rock Chalk Jayhawk greeting from the beefy insurance adjuster seated directly behind you (headed to a conference in Cleveland, he has informed the wider vicinity). You rose to help her with her bag so now, as the bus rumbles back to life, pulling back onto the highway, the two of you stare together at the bench and the massive hump at its far end. The girl offers to slide in since your legs are longer. "Nah," you reply (oh, how a mother might swell with pride in your chivalry), "I've had the aisle long enough." She thanks you and assures you she won't inconvenience you for too long, "only a few hundred miles to Lawrence," looking out to the snowflakes and the darkness in the window, "if we get there at all."

As it turns out, the seat is every bit as bad as one would imagine. Untenable, in fact. You think about going through your pockets for something to bribe the girl (who tells you her name is Azalea, and although she admits there is something else on her birth certificate, she will not reveal it under pressure) but you've already bartered your coupon, and anyway it is unlikely she would be swayed by a now-expired voucher for a mediocre airport hotel two hundred miles west of her eastbound body. Something about her smell, her clothing, her ridiculous name indicates that even the modest sums left in your wallet won't do the trick either. By the time the bus has merged back onto the 70 and traveled a few miles, you have already lost feeling in your legs and you're becoming increasingly desperate. So you engage her in small talk, ask why she's heading to Lawrence, what brought her to Goodland ("a beautiful group of people trying their hand at working God's earth"—"In the dead of winter?" you retorted, to your own detriment) and then, after a few minutes of pins jangling the nerves of your leg, you let slip the purpose of your journey. "Oh," she gasps, putting her hand on your knee. Nothing but a human gesture, there can be no other way to interpret it, but what had been merely a pity grab for the legroom has become something else entirely.

Within minutes you have maneuvered your bodies so that you have swapped seats, the rocking motion enough to prompt a jovial "hey, what are you kids doing up there?" from the Cleveland-bound Jayhawk fan, the feel of her body as it passed over you to the window seat, the rushed melody of her apology as her leg transferred its weight onto yours enough to silence any remaining qualms. To recompense her for the loss of legroom, you suggest that she stretch her legs on your lap, assuring her with open palms of your innocent intentions. She worries about what the other people on the bus might think, worries they might get the wrong idea (unswayed by your argument that "since when do people named Azalea worry about what anyone else thinks?"), but these reservations are overcome by a blanket stolen presciently from the Denver airport lounge.

By WaKeeney, your hands have drifted casually onto her leg. You ask her about her eventual major ("Oh, nothing too practical," she laughs, and then blushes at the sound, apologizing again until you squeeze her calf gently to assure her that it's all right) and about her parents. You tell her about your astronomy class (you don't mention that you'd lasted only two weeks, pushing the eject button moments after your first quiz results were returned to you) and you tell her about your roommate and pickup basketball in the gym. It is actually a very nice time, and the hours, which had seemed so daunting as you'd waited in the cold of the airport, now gather a momentum of their own. Everything you say provokes a laugh, and every laugh prompts a tiny shudder of recollection, her hand covering her mouth. Every apology demands an assurance from you, the gentle squeeze of your hand on her leg letting her know it's all right to laugh, to be brave, to live.

At some point you look up to the ceiling of the bus, to its marbled pattern and the slats that run like arrows up to the front. You can't imagine what they do, but of course they, like everything else in the machine, must have their purpose. The slats are attached by screws, which you count, each one in your section individually and then a total estimate based on the remaining length. You admire the way the light from the headlights and the snow reflects back into the windshield, onto the driver's face and then back out again to the reflection you can see on the windshield, like a half-life, like a ghost, the driver's eyes steady ahead, rarely blinking. When you look down, you realize that your finger has been pressing rhythmically onto Azalea's leg (a bit higher now), tapping along with your counting of the screws and then in time to the windshield wiper as it passed over the glass. If Azalea had been talking, she isn't now. She is looking at the dune of your hand underneath the blanket, as if it too is covered in snow, rising and falling like a metronome, a quizzical half-smile on her face, and now it is your turn to apologize to her and her turn to assure you that there isn't any problem at all. It is nearly two in the morning, the bus moving steadily through the prairie snow, and everyone else is asleep or quiet. Behind you the Jayhawk booster is snoring (you have already shared a laugh at his expense). Your hand still on her thigh, the blanket covering your lower torsos, you lean over and kiss Azalea firmly on the mouth. It is a nice kiss, your lips pressed as tightly as your bodies, your tongue dancing between her teeth. Curse, then, whatever impulse makes you open your eyes in midkiss, to the jolt at seeing Azalea's eyes open too, mere inches away, so that they look enormous, liquid, so that you can see deep, deep into them. There is no passion there, nor hate, nothing but bereavement, and a chastisement so gentle it will be years before it reaches you, no matter how short the distance it has to travel.

Teacher and Helper

Beauty

So you're at this party where you know no one. A college party, actually, which is bad form for you since you're four years out of college yourself, three thousand miles from your alma mater, and frankly the idea of asking someone her major is enough to make you puke even if the bad wine and worse pot and ridiculous squeaky sitar music weren't. You are here with Mark, naturally, knowing no one else in Seattle. Your old roommate, Mark, whose girlfriend has transferred back home for the in-state tuition and is graduating in the springtime, only a year later than she'd anticipated, which makes it about a century earlier than you'd anticipated since you've had to converse with the woman over breakfast. She's been sleeping a wall's width from you for six months, off and on, since you moved onto Mark's couch, but this is the first time you've ever been inside her apartment. It's nice enough. A few blocks from the campus. She's got roommates and a cat that spends most of the party hiding under furniture, except in those fleeting moments when instinct compels it to dart across the room to safer haven. An impulse with which you are completely sympathetic.

Everyone here is young. Everyone here is slender, good-looking. Already college has evaporated from your mind. Not just the calculus, geology, the agonizing literature prerequisites, but also something more elemental. In college, for a time, you had been happy and cocksure. Now, seeing shards of yourself in these newer models makes you wonder how much of it was artifice. Mark is long gone into a bedroom, leaving you with the roommates and their friends, their self-assured (half-baked) discourse of war and politics and philosophy and music. If Heaven is a place where no one talks about the Grateful Dead or Fellini films, then Heaven is a place far, far away from here.

Everyone is fitting into their slots so beautifully, and you are aware that you are too. The grumpy, off-putting older guy who came with somebody and stands apart, examines titles on the bookshelves, checking his watch like a Tourette's tic. Even knowing you're doing it can't make you stop. Mark had promised that the two of you would just duck your heads in. Yet here you are, staring blankly into a stranger's refrigerator, lost somewhere in the colors of the packaged goods within. *We'll just make an appearance*, his exact words.

"The hummus didn't appeal to you?"

You close the fridge quickly. It's an older woman, or rather, older than the children in the living room and maybe, yes, older than you, too. She smiles through your apology. "I don't even know what I was looking for," you admit. "I was just looking…"

"Um hmm?" Her tongue flirts with her lips.

"I'm sorry," you say again. "Have you always been here? I didn't see you earlier."

"I'm Hannah's older sister," the woman says. She gestures back out to the living room. With the pot fumes, your half-finished beer, it is taking your mind a long time to return to your body. She follows your confused stare out of the room. "Hannah?" she repeats. "She lives here." Then she whispers: "Are you robbing the place? It's all right, you can confide in me." She moves around you to lower her head into the refrigerator. "They've got olives," she says. "Some sort of salad dressing. Something unidentified in a cup." She waits for you to reply. "Not interested? That's about all, I'm afraid, unless you want the lightbulb."

"No," you say, smiling, not that it matters, her head in the fridge.

"Nothing, then." Her voice floats out. "Is it okay if I come out now? I'm feeling like Plath in here." When she emerges, her eyes narrow with suspicion. "You didn't even bring a bag," she says reproachfully. "For a food thief, your technique is awfully sloppy."

"I'm sorry," you say.

She's got small wrinkles around her eyes. A tiny bit heavy in the chest and hips. She has an absolute mess of curly red hair. You can tell right off it's the sort of hair other women would kill for, the kind that elicits adjectives before the color. She waits patiently through your staring, brushes loose locks away with her wrist. "Do I have something crawling on me?" she asks, still not breaking eye contact. "Hannah's letters are always mentioning roaches."

"I'm sorry," you say again.

"Congenitally," she agrees.

"Where were we?" you ask.

"You," she says, moving a step closer, "were asking if I was always here. I'm Meg." She extends a hand.

You didn't even know what you were looking for. You were just looking.

A Feast Day

Meg sings, "Who loves blueberry pancakes?"

Her head ducks into the bedroom. She keeps eye contact, making sure you're awake. Then she squats and rises, the doorframe blocking everything from her neck down in the sort of illusion that befuddles small children. "Who loves blueberry pancakes?" she asks again. "I'll tell you who, this ghost does." Her head floats up and down, giggling.

When you wake up again, you get out of bed and walk into the kitchen. It's a cold morning, the floorboards cold. For whatever reasons (humidity? the loamy air?), you can't see your breath, but it's that kind of morning nonetheless. Meg is leaning over the stove. She's wearing your shirt and nothing else. You move your hand to the small of her back under the shirt, and she rubs up against you. "You fell asleep," she pouts.

"That I did."

Still looking at the stove, she gestures behind you both to the kitchen table and a stack of blueberry pancakes rising nearly a foot.

"My God," you say, rubbing at your jaw. "What on earth are we going to do with all of these pancakes?"

"I wanted you to have hot ones," she explained. "So I just kept making them."

"That's unbelievably thoughtful," you say, although there are other words that spring to mind. "How much pancake mix did they have in the cupboards anyway?"

"A lot," she admits. She holds up a glass tin, still not empty despite her best efforts. "We'll have to buy them more before we leave."

You remember passing a grocery store coming in off the highway. This is Meg's best friend's summer cottage and she has offered it to you for the Labor Day weekend. "It's a beautiful place," Meg's friend had promised. "You'll love it." Then, throwing you a weighted look, "It's a perfect site for grand gestures." It seemed premature. After all, you've only been together six months and this is your first getaway. Two hours in the car up into the mountains to laugh at the friend's brazenness. But then: a beautiful spot, a lovely cabin that makes you forgive her instantly. Like those perfect summer ballads that make you forgive pop music its faults.

Meg moves past you with the skillet and adds three pancakes to the stack. Then she picks up the tottering plate and leads you outside to the back porch. You are wearing underwear and the bedsheet wrapped around your body. Meg excuses herself and returns with coffee. You open your arm. The outstretched wing of the bedsheet folds neatly around her. You sit together for hours, nibbling, never reaching the bottom of the stack. Periodically, Meg disappears to the kitchen for more coffee. Every time, the sight of her returning makes you goofy. For once there is nothing else in your mind. For once everything is quiet. You sit, eating pancakes from each other's fingers, drinking coffee, the sun overhead. The porch rests a half-story above the ground, and at noon a snake moves through the brush. Meg grabs your forearm and whispers: "Look." Some fifty feet away, at the edge of the clearing, a feral cat stares at you, one gene shy of a lynx, drawn out by the snake's movement. You don't dare breathe for fear of disturbing any of this. A bird sings out, shifting the cat's attention. There is one pancake left on the plate and you throw it down near the cat's feet. She runs off and at first you think you've ruined everything, again, but then she reemerges, tentatively. She sniffs at the pancake and then inhales it. Still staring at you, she moves a giant tongue over her muzzle. She stays there for a long time, perhaps waiting for more food, as you and Meg sit motionless above her. None of you is in any rush to leave. Under the bedsheet, you and Meg are perfectly comfortable. You let your entire body relax. "God," you whisper. "This is really something." Love, after all. Love. Just like they'd promised.

Stalemate

The road breaks slightly to the left, and you adjust the angle of your arm. On the radio, a woman picks at intricate chords with a harp. Meg's hand hangs loosely out the window. She makes waves with her fingers, feels the wind above and below, looks at you, smiles.

"Laminar flow. Like the dolphins."

This morning a giant bird passed across your window. Now you're driving south, sixty-five miles per hour, a straight shot. You tell Meg about the bird and she laughs. She's always seeing things like that. You are only twenty-seven years old, but in the six months you've been together, the voices in your head have started sounding different to you too. Up ahead, the mountains come at you faster.

Meg's fingers play at your inseam. At night, in bed, she keeps an arm locked around you like she's worried that you'll disappear. Times like those, you want to hug her so hard she could fold up inside of you. You would protect her if only you knew how.

And so you head south, the two of you, with a picnic basket in the backseat, olives and hard bread, a bottle of wine. Emerald Ridge, because everyone tells you it's lovely this time of year. It has finally stopped raining. The farther you get, the further away your job seems, your father and his nagging ailments, all of it. Life's leaden problems can't keep up with your Chevy. If you never stop, they'll never catch up. Who knows, wait long enough and they'll give up trying. You're yearning for something more, and in the thinning air of the mountain's incline, such a wish seems possible. You turn and try to explain to Meg, making a mess of the whole thing, but she smiles her understanding and tells you there's an equation that got lost to us somewhere along the way. When you push down hard on the accelerator, the smell of gasoline follows you for a few minutes.

At noon you stop for drinks inside a postcard. Your beer is ice cold, Meg's martini so clear it's like a jewel. Over the hedge you can see cars speed past, blurs of color. Things rush toward you. Things rush away. This is life at high speeds. The ring in your pocket is the rocket fuel pushing you forward.

When your drinks are finished, you pay and move back onto the road. The car starts easily in the warm air. By now the highway is filling up with traffic, and you stumble across an outlet road that seems to be heading the right way. "Take it," Meg urges.

But you don't. You continue onward to the gridlock of the main highway, hours and hours, and by the time you get to the mountain, it's too late to do much of anything, so you don't climb to the top and the ring stays in your pocket for another day. Story of your life.

The Cusp of Aries

Past the big top, past the trapeze artists and human cannonballs, there is another part of the carnival few people see. In this section the grass is untrampled. In this section the tents hang uneven, jury-rigged, the backside post replaced with a partition of rusty mattress. In this section the walkways are narrower, the carnival workers less careful not to let you glimpse them standing around smoking. There aren't many children in this section, no food stands, no games of chance. Meg and Hannah walk ahead of you and Tim, talking. You are far enough behind them that you can see the carnival workers stare appraisingly at your women, never breaking their own sullen conversations, flicking cigarettes off their fingertips. "C'mon," Hannah shouts over her shoulder. "She's just up ahead."

Hannah has led you to this refugee quadrant of the circus to meet the fortune teller. She and Tim, newly dating, Mark now seemingly out of the picture forever, came last night with some of their friends and paid their money to have their palms traced, or their cards read, or whatever witchcraft this one uses. "Don't give me that look," Hannah scolded you, mostly in good humor. "I don't need tarot cards to read your opinion of fortune tellers." Tim was watching the opening kickoff of the football game and Meg was clearing the coffee from breakfast. Hannah leaned in closer. "She told me things that she couldn't know, things that you wouldn't understand." Meg put her hand on Hannah's shoulder and promised that you'd all go this afternoon.

And now you're here. Sidestepping Jurassic-sized animal droppings, the soda cans and popcorn tubs and refuse blown to this dead end of the carnival's rat's maze of tents and stands and outhouses. Indian summer, the weather as warm as a kiss. Hannah hikes up her long skirt. "We're almost there," she says. "Just past the Hall of Oddities."

"None of this," Tim gives you his opinion quietly, "looks particularly familiar."

As you watch, a carnival hand with no body fat and Neal Cassady hips maneuvers past you carrying an amber-colored glass jar. "S'cuse me," he coughs. You watch him shift the jar on his hip, something barely identifiable inside of it floating to a stop along the side of the glass. You look at Tim for a hard minute and then hurry to catch up to the women.

Finally, you come to the Fortune Teller's tent, roped closed. Tim goes to ask when it opens, and you three remain, sitting in the tall grass at the tent's entrance. You can hear all the sounds of the carnival from behind the hill you've climbed. "It looks different at night," Hannah apologizes. She gestures to the dirty fabric, the faded paint of the sign. "Last night was a full moon, so you stood at the threshold deciding until a voice beckoned you in. The fortune teller sits in a high-backed chair with a book open on her lap." She looks around for a moment then back at Meg. "I guess because of the moonlight, and the halogens of the circus, everything seemed brighter...I'm not doing a very good job, I'm sorry." She gets a faraway look as she calls up the scene in her mind. "There's crystals hung up everywhere on the inside of the tent, and painted glass and the shadows from the branches of the trees. Meg, you remember when we were kids and we had those kaleidoscopes you'd look through, and the faster you turned the tube the faster the patterns evolved? This tent, last night, it was like being inside the kaleidoscope." Meg nods, but Hannah isn't really looking at her, her eyes back up at the seams of the tent, its hanging flesh. "It's just beautiful. And you're expecting some old woman with a third eye, some Gypsy with a head rag and a gold tooth. But this woman inside, she's dressed in these white and blue robes. She looked like the Pope, like Florence Nightingale. She knows just what to say. She's so clean. And the tent smells like something out of the Bible, like hay burning, and you should see how white her wrist was in the folds of her robe…" She breaks off as Tim cuts back onto the grass.

"Sorry, kids, no show for us. She only works at nights." Poor Tim has missed everything, so the pitch of his voice is jovial and wrong. You walk back to the car, through the fairgrounds, the smells of hay and animal shit and sickening sweet caramel apples. Meg keeps her arm around her sister, pushing her forward, holding her up, promising that all of this will be back next year, back before you even know it.

For today is the last day of the circus, at least until the weather turns and then starts to turn back. Within hours, the workers will load everything into crates, perfectly labeled, for transport on the wagons. You never see the Fortune Teller, of course, so for you the real magic is in how these people, these wizards, can squat an empty field for two weeks of Indian summer, unpack their tents and cages and stone jars and garbage, and make it look like they've been there all along, like the entire modern world has sprung up around them. That's the illusion. That's the con.

Communion

Eastertime and you're a step slow. Meg is wearing taffeta, the curse of bridesmaids the world over. You'd have guessed her sister to be kinder. You're slumped down in a chair, at least halfway drunk, the buttons on your vest pushing up into your sternum making it harder to breathe. Meg's father catches you loosening them and punches at your arm. "How about those shrimp?" he says again.

The shrimp were excellent. The entire wedding, in fact, was beautiful. Meg's parents have money, apparently, and decorum if not actual taste. The ceremony took place on a lawn. There were chairs set up and a giant ice fountain with flowing champagne. For a horrible moment, you worried they might release doves into the air. The minister, a family friend, spoke somberly. Meg stood beside her sister. Perfectly rehearsed, everyone moved in lockstep, and so throughout the reception you have all been rewarded with sloppy kisses from the increasingly drunk bride, who thanks each of you for making this the most beautiful and important day of her life. She speaks formally. Because her lipstick is smudged around her lips, and because she is deliberate in feeling out each word, and regrettably because she has inherited her mother's long face, Hannah looks quite a bit like Mr. Ed. But she's a bride, and even though you're drunk, you don't make a single joke about grooms and grooms. She'll never know it, but that's your real wedding gift to her.

It was a nice wedding, a nice afternoon. But there was a moment at the beginning where you'd thought it could have gone either way. "My maid of honor," Hannah screamed as you and Meg pulled up in the car. The two of them rushed off to hair and makeup, the movie-star moment in Hannah's movie-star day, leaving you alone with Meg's parents. It was a nice day for a wedding, you all agreed. Nice weather, not too hot. A thick blue northwestern sky. Late April in Bellingham, Washington, one of those days the tourism bureau lives for. You tempted the fates by concurring that rain was unlikely. Then Meg's mother went off to handle floral arrangements, leaving you with Meg's father. You'd met before, of course. Carl is a quiet man who, in the contradictory way of some quiet men, affects a jokester persona in social situations. The punches on the arm, the punchlines of jokes whispered in a rush in the ear. Every time you see him, you want to take him into a back room and sit quietly with him, beg him to stop trying so hard. But it isn't your place, and anyway, as Meg sometimes pouts, maybe it's you who isn't trying hard enough. Carl leaned in and began a joke about a Glaswegian and a librarian while above his head you could see his wife arguing with the florist, moving an orchid to the front of an arrangement. When Carl was done with the joke, the air hot on your neck, you'd smiled and patted his arm. "We'd sort of been thinking Meg might be first," Carl said, tentatively. So had you. Since the fall, since your second trip up to the mountains, since you didn't propose. Now you feel out of step with everything, things with Meg cooling. Whenever you look at her you feel it, heavy inside of you, congealing your blood. The ring has migrated from bedside table to closet to attic. Any higher and it will be no more tangible than the stars above. The palest star in the firmament. "Matron of honor was, I guess, what we'd had in mind," Carl finished. He was uncomfortable with you, and with his suit. He owns a pharmacy and works long hours. Finally he let out a sigh. "It's a hell of a thing," he said. "I can't say where it comes from but you wouldn't believe the pressure to marry off your daughters." Then he laughed a bit, grabbed your shoulder and remembered that he'd "just heard another good one about two blondes and a shark tank." Meg's mother returned before this joke had run its course, bridegroom in tow. When finally Meg reemerged, wearing the taffeta gown, you entertained thoughts of saving her, but then she looked over at Hannah and smiled, and you realized that she wasn't embarrassed or distraught or jealous. She was happy for her younger sister and happy to be a part of all of this. This fact, which should have made you happy, made you unbearably sad, and the ribbon of pity made you feel even worse.

Now, half a day later, the six of you are all that's left of the party. Most of the guests left with the sun, at least an hour ago. You watched the band depart, the caterers shortly after. As they were packing up, Meg's mother rushed off and demanded that they keep the ice sculpture in the middle of the lawn and now it was melting, the champagne fountains running water into the grass. The bar has also gone dry, but Meg's mother again (and times like these everyone loves her for it) somehow convinced the barman to leave some of the half-empty bottles behind. Now the groom is singing his wedding song into his glass and, astonishingly, he is rather good. As if reading your mind, Hannah jackknifes herself over your shoulders. "Tim used to be a singer," she whinnies, "before he gave all that up to go into business with his father." She's telling you how they met and the story is getting graphic (it was a successful gig, Tim deadpans) when suddenly she notices grass stains on the bottom of her wedding gown and runs away in hysterics. Her new husband, watching you across the table, raises an eyebrow and continues singing: "Though kismet once was missing you, Now the fates are wishing you all the happiness you deserve…" Meg plants herself on his lap and croons the rest of the verse and the two of them collapse laughing. You exchange a glance with Meg's father and he shrugs. "Would have guessed Hannah and Tim could have thought up something better to do on their wedding night, myself." It turns out Carl is a pretty funny guy when you've both got enough booze in you. Hannah returns, calmed, and Tim repeats what Carl has said. Hannah snorts and stares down at him, Meg still on his lap. "Seems like you're doing all right for yourself as it is." She staggers a bit, holding steady to the table. "I'm going to have to watch you two." She points to each of them in turn.

"Not if you keep Meg dressed in taffeta," you suggest, helpfully. There is a moment of silence as everyone turns first to you and then to Meg's monstrous gown, as crumpled as a bar napkin. Then everyone laughs. Meg raises her arms and her sister pulls her from Tim's lap. "Help me get these grass stains out before they set," Hannah says, and Meg's mom rises with them. Meg turns to you, smoothes out the wrinkles in her dress and mock pouts. "I may, or I may not, be back," she says archly.

"Glenda the Good Witch," you reply, "go get us another drink."

Laughing, the three women move away from the table. Midway to the bathroom gazebo, they come to the ice sculpture, or its wreckage, and as if in a trance they start dancing, all of them barefoot, all of them suddenly full of grace. Tim finds their rhythm and sings along while Carl hums quietly. Laughing, Hannah scoops some flowers from the arrangement and showers them over Meg's head. You move toward the women, still holding a bottle, and when you are a few feet away, Hannah breaks off and rushes toward you, "Meg just caught the bouquet. Now you've got to marry her." And in that moment, with the fountain and the moon, you can't think of anything else you'd rather do and you tell her so. It's Easter after all, the season for second chances.

Toil

Your father ordered his eggs over messy. "Crack them," he told the waitress, "you know how I like them," although he had never seen this waitress in his life, never having eaten at this diner, a function of his never before having set foot in the state of Washington. The waitress, midfifties, her hair a synthetic burgundy, wrote down the order and sashayed down the aisle into the kitchen. Your father, also midfifties, watched her go. Meg admired all of this like a play put on for her benefit and squeezed your hand under the table.

"How's Mom?" you quizzed your father's turned back, his eyes still watching the waitress disappear behind the swinging doors. He didn't answer. Instead, he removed a pack of cigarettes from his breast pocket and whacked it hard on the base, then rotated his hand deftly so that a single cigarette leapt halfway through its opening. He offered it to Meg, who declined, before inserting it into his own mouth. A fleck of tobacco migrated from his lip to his tongue, and it was only after he had spit this onto the Formica that he directed his attention at you. "What's that?"

"Mom," you reminded him.

"You know your mother," he answered. "She's always got a bee in her bonnet about something. Wouldn't be happy otherwise. This too shall pass, as the Big Man says. After all, you know women," he remarked to Meg and, on her best behavior, she assured him that she did.

Your father, still looking at Meg, returned to you. "She's a looker, this one." Then he reached out and took a lock of her hair in his hand and lifted it to the light. "Zazoom," he whispered.

You pushed his hand away. "Jesus, Dad, you just met her. You might want to wait until your second date before you reveal this side of yourself."

"Just trying to get to know the lady," he muttered, rubbing at his paw.

"In what capacity, exactly?" you asked. Meg, still playing her role, giggled.

"Besides, what good ever came from waiting?" your father said, still looking at Meg. "This one here, I'm guessing you didn't do much waiting yourself, am I right?" He raised his coffee cup nearly to his eye level.

"Absolutely right, Garland," Meg replied, raising her own mug to toast.

Your father exhaled a long breath that skimmed the top of his cup and emitted a clear note that held itself in the air. Then he put his cup down and reached for the cigarette again, his hand unsteady as it felt for the filter. "Got me a plan," he grinned. "Going to wait until my boy goes off on one of his mental vacations and steal you all to myself."

"My bags are packed," Meg said. She leaned in and stage-whispered, "Let's stiff him with the bill."

"That'll be the day," your father crowed.

Some part of you is curious about him. It has been nine years since you graduated from college and followed Mark out here to Seattle for the cheap rents. Nearly five since you met Meg, longer still since you've been home to visit your parents. "Not a lot of reason to," you'd answered Meg's questions with a shrug, and meant it too. Not a Hollywood epic or anything, just no reason compelling enough to get on a plane, fuel costs suddenly what they are, your own monthly salary barely enough to put gas in your car. The country is evenly split as to whether the fault lies with Carter, Iran, or some combination of the two. So few years, but your father seems to have aged two decades. You'd already asked about his job and he'd brushed the question away. "You've seen the price of gas, same as me," he shrugged. "No one can make it on the road these days. They've got me riding out short time in the back office. They'll offer me a package and I expect I'll take it." When Meg offered some words of condolence, his face broke into a smile. "I sold pipe fittings," he said, "so my family could eat. Let's not turn this into a tragedy or anything, all right?"

"All right, Garland," Meg replied sharply, and deep in her voice was something of your mother, and the sudden way in which your father adjusted in his seat, brushing his hair back off his face, looking guiltily into the cigarette in his hands, told you he recognized it too. It made you wonder how much of what you've known of your father was a product of your mother, an unanswerable question of course, and anyway not one likely to explain the mystery of the man in front of you, in his third incarnation at least—this one the faded huckster, watery eyes and slight tremor, an unconscious groan as he'd risen from the booth to the bathroom. No longer the fool, that time long gone. But too, no sign of the anger that dictated your childhood, submerged now, or else eroded by events or simply by time, again nothing remarkable, the sort of thing that happens to everyone eventually, the sort of thing that happens every day.

"What is your calling again?" he said, turning to you and then, seeing your look, turning back to Meg, laughing. "Forget it, he's off and running." After a rough couple of years, you'd finally settled at a job with a local marketing agency. You had a desk and a title, Assistant Marketing Manager, that effectively masked your role as phone bank operator. Now, when you reminded your father of this (not for the first time this meal), he'd given you a fish-eyed stare borrowed from your mother's catalogue and deemed the title "flashy" before returning his attention to Meg. "Yeah, not too long until I get handed the copper parachute," he'd said. "Not quite sure what Lu will do with me home all the time. The ideas she's floated so far don't sound too appealing."

"You'll make it work," Meg replied. "It happens to everyone."

"Nah," he'd smiled, and for a second you caught a glimpse into the valleys of newer, whiter skin beneath the sunburned strata of his face. "The lucky ones die in the saddle." Then he'd looked up at you again, and you could see his face reconfigure itself back into its new persona.

"You and Mom been doing any traveling?" you asked casually.

He raised his arms in response. "I'm here, ain't I?"

"I meant with Mom."

"This one here," your father said, turning his body toward Meg, "seems to have made it his life's mission to move as far away from home as possible."

You pointed out that since he lived in the geographical middle of the country, any place else would be identically far away, so long as it was on the coast, where places of consequence tended to be. Unimpressed, he'd ignored you. "First Boston, now Anchorage."

"Seattle," you'd corrected.

"Oh, I've heard your version," he quipped to Meg, who winked back. Then he turned to her. "How about your parents? They need to renew their passports just to break bread with you?"

"My parents live in Bellingham," Meg explained, and then mapped its relative location on her napkin, her pale fingers tracing gently over the ribbing of the paper.

"What's the matter?" your father asked with mock concern. "You didn't get the memo? Your whole generation has to flee from their parents, traverse the globe on their little hero quests."

"And here we go," you muttered.

"I'm just saying that when we got back from the war, we all had to move into our parents' basements. That's just the way it was."

"Sure," you'd replied. "Because they still hadn't discovered the lost continent west of the Rockies."

"Building supplies, you jackass." Then to Meg, "Look who I'm telling?" he groused to her. "Please tell me *you're* handy with a hammer."

Meg raised her arm into a muscle. "You know it," she laughed, her leg pushed up hard against you.

"I'm telling you, I read an article on the flight over here, something about genes. This boy finds the wrong woman to breed with and my grandkids are going to be born without any of the appendages we associate with humans. Then again, they'll have mouths six times the size of normal and a sense of entitlement that stretches all the way back to the old world, all the way back over those Rocky Mountains.

"I used to ask him to hold the ladder and, I'll tell you, darling," he shifted in his seat, "I am not by nature a religious man, but high up on that rooftop, the whole world stretched below you, and this guy," he gestured to you, his lips up in a smirk, "the thin veneer between life and death? Well, that's enough to make you start questioning all sorts of stuff."

"Gutsy," Meg joked.

"You're damned right."

"Yes," you'd said, aware of how flushed you were, your leg pushing back at Meg's just as hard, "it's a shame there was no one else around to help."

After this, a moment of quiet. The waitress came to refill the coffees, dropping the bill neatly in the center of the booth where it was casually ignored by all parties.

"You didn't need to find yourself?" your father asked Meg finally.

"I didn't know I was lost."

"That's a girl!" He slapped the table hard enough to rattle the cups, hard enough to startle the waitress and the few lingering customers near the door, hard enough to dislodge another cigarette from his pack, which he then raised in salute to those who had been brought to attention by the noise. "The whole damned world needs to run off and find itself now," he muttered. "New Age hocus-pocus." He squinted at Meg, suspicious. "That your kind of bag?"

Meg rose to cup his face in her hands, lowering her nose until it was kissing his. "Look into my eyes," she said melodramatically, "and I will reveal your future."

"Death is in my future," Garland replied, not moving his face a fraction. "Don't need magical powers for that." Then he shifted his eyeballs to you, his skull married to Meg's. "Yours too," he promised.

"After breakfast, we'll show you around," Meg offered.

"Saw my share on the hike from the airport," Garland returned. "Can't say as it impressed me too much. Just like the rest of the country, this place looks pretty well like it's been taking it in the shorts." He had kept his old timing, his evaluation voiced just as the waitress returned to refill the mugs. She leaned deep over him, with no recourse but to assume that this last comment was directed at her. Finally, she shrugged an acknowledgment. "Welcome to the Emerald City," she said. "It helps when you put on the special glasses."

"Where can I find me a pair of those?" he'd said to the body still draped above him, the cotton of her dress hanging down and obscuring everything in your line of sight, the seam opening on his side and therefore, from his vantage point, obscuring far less.

She hit her cue beautifully, removing the cigarette from his fingers as she straightened, taking a long drag that she volleyed back into his face. "Pawned them," she said, "for the gas money."

You'd explained about the Boeing Bust, the failed SST project. The massive layoffs. You'd explained how, in the wonderful world Garland and his generation had bequeathed, you and Meg felt privileged to even find gainful employment.

"SSTs, huh?" he'd nodded. "Wasn't that supposed to be the future or something? People scared that thing off with pitchforks."

There was no way for him to know that this was a sticky issue for Meg, who had protested long and hard against the 2707, afraid of the consequences to the ozone layer, unhinged by the sonic booms that would puncture the air. No way for him to know any of this when he raised his hands in mock consternation and said: "Who the fuck ever promised that the future would be silent?" Then he looked at your face and then at Meg's. "What?" he asked, in Seattle for the first time but on very familiar terrain. "What did I step in now?"

"It's nothing," Meg smiled, grabbing his arm.

He apologized again. "I'm always saying the wrong thing." Then he smiled. "I guess they'll need to rename the basketball team, huh?"

After a natural lull in the conversation, he'd asked again about your work and you'd told him, again. "Marketing," he'd confided to Meg. "He tells us on the phone but we still aren't quite sure what that is."

"Neither am I," Meg admitted.

"What it is, is one-ninety a week, pretax," you'd explained to them both, your hand reaching over the discarded plates for the bill. "In this case, it's Belgian waffles, blueberry pancakes, six cups of coffee and eggs over messy, cracked. Any other questions?"

Tonight, mummied in sheets on your living room floor with your father snoring prodigiously from the comfort of your bedroom, you lie awake until the wee hours and relive the day. "Yes," Meg reminds you at intervals, "I was there too."

" 'Go find yourself,' my ass. He's going to find himself in a Motel 6 if he tries this shit tomorrow, I can promise you that."

Meg sighs. "Oh hush. Stop getting worked up about all of this, he's an old man. And you're getting the covers all bunched up. It's only two more days."

Two more days. Forty-eight hours. A fifty-fifty proposition at this point with all sorts of colorful prop bets available. "He's already started hinting around about sticking around longer. You've heard him. I'm not even sure why he came, to tell you the truth."

"Maybe he wanted to meet me, Mr. Smartypants, did you ever consider that?"

You hadn't, of course, because you'd never mentioned Meg to your parents. Five years. And something in you softens at the recollection of how your father navigated that moment, never betraying your confidence, extending his hand out to meet Meg in front of the diner's cloudy plate glass window as if he had traveled two thousand miles for the simple pleasure of kissing her cheek, offering his blessing, and welcoming her into your family, such as it is.

It might have been enough if your synapses had not traveled the route, unbidden, to another epiphany, until you are sitting up, ignoring Meg's complaints about the covers, moving into the kitchen, far away from the bedroom, careful not to wake him as you pick up the phone and dial the familiar number, the number that had been your own for the majority of your years on this planet, and listen as the telephone rings through. You don't have to work hard to imagine the sound it makes, even two thousand miles away, even over the Rocky Mountains. The tinny heartbeat of a telephone in a deserted house. It is, after all, a sound you already know intimately.

The Golden Dawn

Inaction

"Just one of those things," you tell Mark. "One minute everything's fine and the next you're reaching for something heavy to throw."

He tells you again how sorry he is.

"She gave me the full-court press. An ultimatum." The word sounds sloppy in your mouth, the sequence of syllables.

Mark posits that maybe you had it coming, and even if it's true, even if you know it, you beg him to go easy on you.

He shrugs. "It's the nature of things to fall apart," he says and raises his beer.

"This is true."

He gestures up to the television in the corner of the bar. "Just ask Nixon."

"It's good to see him back in the news," you say. A joke. Three years since Watergate and nobody, not even his dog, misses him. Now, with the Frost interview, he's front-page news again. You look up at the screen, and for the first time it looks like even he wishes this would all go away. *I'm with you, Dick*, you think and then look up at Mark. "I've missed him." A joke, but something in the way you say it, your sadness over Meg, sells the line and there is a weighty moment until the two of you start laughing.

"Jesus," Mark says, looking down at the half-empty pitcher, "how many of these have you had?"

You nod.

"What are you always so afraid of?" she asked. "It won't hurt," she promised. "Not even a little bit."

The bartender is at the other end of the bar in heavy flirtation with a woman. They've been sequestered there all night, the two of them. Every once in a while, the woman will rise on her barstool and lean forward to whisper something in his ear, and he will lean forward to accept it. At these times, they look like an A-frame. She's pretty in a desperate sort of way, and you know you should be happy for them. "Nobody likes the Grinch," you say.

"That's not true," Mark replies, the voice coming from some other part of your brain. It takes an awfully long time to turn to him. "Our old neighborhood, we used to get together Christmas and put on skits. My father would put on long underwear and tiptoe around as the Grinch. Star of the show, every year. Everybody loves the Grinch."

"So I'm wrong," you say, raising a hand. "Again."

"Been wrong so long it's starting to feel like right," Mark says.

"There's our country and western song," you say, and warble it. But no tune presents itself, so you quit.

"It's been done," Mark replies.

"It's all been done," you say. "And yet we keep trying."

"Sometimes I think the Puritans had the right idea," Mark says. "Predestination. It's like a cosmic lottery."

"It's inevitable," you agree.

"Like Nixon," Mark says.

This stops you both. Mark traces the moisture ring on the bar, elongates the circle out to an infinity oval while you watch.

"Birds do it, bees do it," she sang, still crying. "Ask me," she pleaded. "C'mon. Just ask me."

Mark is watching Nixon on the TV. They are replaying footage from a decade ago: jowly Nixon wagging his finger at the nation.

"He always reminded me of a creepy uncle," Mark says.

"You and everyone else."

You stare again at Nixon, the television muted. Now it's debate footage against Kennedy. He looked so much younger. The pasty little hang dog.

"How the hell could we elect somebody president that you wouldn't trust alone with your kid sister?" Mark grunts. You raise your hands in surrender, a familiar gesture.

"What was the name of the dog again?" you ask.

"Max," Mark replies. He's emptying the rest of the pitcher into his glass.

That's not right. You can see the footage of Nixon in his living room. "No, man. The one from the speech. You know, 'we've got this dog and we're going to keep it.'"

Mark stares at you blankly.

"Checkers," you say finally. "Christ, that's going back. I was seven years old."

"Me too," says Mark, glumly.

"I can't wait for you forever," she said. The way she reached for her bag let you know you could stop her any time you wanted to.

"We need another pitcher," you say. You hold it up to the bartender, but he's long gone in that girl's eyes, and no one else is on shift on a Tuesday night. "Doesn't it seem like people stopped drinking?" you say. "Five years ago, this place would have been busier."

"It's a national crisis." Mark grins. "An epidemic."

"Smart ass." The pitcher is getting heavy in your arm and you put it down with a heavy thunk on the counter. The bartender doesn't budge. You and Mark shrug. "Max," you say. "Why the hell would Nixon name his dog Max?"

Mark guffaws loud enough for the lovebirds in the corner to look up. "Nixon? I thought you meant the Grinch."

This gets you both giggling. Mark reaches over, a loyal pal, and pours half of his beer into your glass. The head foams and then recedes. You raise your glasses. "To Nixon and the Grinch," Mark says. "Long may they roam."

You each down your shot of beer. "That was a nice toast," you tell Mark. "You've got a real way with those things."

"Handy at weddings," he says, then flinches. "Sorry."

You pull away from the bar. "A toast," you say, loudly. Everyone looks at you. You want to say something witty, or poetic. The whole moment's set up for it. But for once you can't think of anything to say.

"This is it," she said, her hand on the knob. She left her key dangling on its nail, swaying slow as an autumn waltz. "This is it."

You grab your coat and follow Mark out the door.

For Meg. Who was mine until she wasn't.

Victory

Downstairs at the U-Haul, Mark slaps the packing tape tight onto the last of your possessions and lifts the box to the top of the tower you've invested the morning in creating. "That should just about do it," he says, and you both race back up the apartment stairs cheering your prodigious feats of strength. You mock, but actually it feels like something.

"It certainly is," Mark huffs. "Forty-five boxes, which I presume deserves a beer." You produce one from the cooler you have iced for the occasion and hand it to him.

"I appreciate you spending your long weekend on this…" you begin, and he tells you to stow it. He looks over at the television in the corner, still plugged in. He turns it on and fiddles with the ears for a moment until the Seahawks game appears, at Oakland, down 10-7 at the half. "Do you mind?" he asks, "it's a rivalry game," and, after he has helped you pack and load forty-five boxes into the truck, helped tidy up the empty apartment just enough to assure the return of your deposit, and listened to you whine about Meg for over a year, you understand his question to be purely rhetorical. You've got a long drive ahead, but there can be no harm in postponing it another hour. There is, after all, nothing in particular waiting for you in New

York.

"I'm still not sure why you're so fixated on heading there," Mark says. "There's half a million people in Seattle. You think you and Meg can't share the city? Hell, I didn't take off for Oslo when Hannah married old Whatshisname with the dorky eyebrows."

"Meg isn't getting married," you remind him.

"Yet," he volleys back. When you glare at him, he shrugs. "I'm just saying that it's going to happen eventually. Look, it isn't my call. But you two were good together and Meg's a pretty special woman. I might try again," he shrugs again, "if it was me."

"Which it's not."

"Agreed."

"Hannah was pretty special too," you say, just as the game returns from commercial, so that Mark's attention immediately halves, so that you will spend much of the remainder of this conversation addressing the side of his head.

"Hannah and I tried to make it work," he explains. "We gave it the old college try and then some." Not that you needed the reminder, having turned up your stereo during any number of their breakups and then again during their inevitable reconciliations. Inevitable until the last. "Yes," Mark explains patiently, "and so I have devoted the Sunday of my Thanksgiving weekend and the ligaments of my lower back to your cause as a belated thank-you." Together you watch the Seahawks go three and out to start the third, a Zorn pass falling incomplete on third down. "Shit," Mark mutters.

"You know they're going to lose," you goad him. It isn't fair. Protected by your pedestrian interest in football, you can rib him all you want with no fear of retribution. "You think the Raiders consider this a rivalry? You think they circled this game on the schedule? It's pathetic, when you think about it, how one-sided it is. The Seahawks are losers, just like everyone else in this city. I can say that because I'm leaving."

"Going to pledge allegiance to the New York Giants?" he responds. "There's a powerhouse if I ever saw one."

"I'll just have to console myself with the Yankees," you remind him. "They finished ahead of the Mariners, right?"

"The Yankees had a few decades to iron out the bugs," he says, turned away from you to watch the punt, which sails out of bounds, causing him to interrupt his impassioned defense to swear under his breath. "Give the Mariners a few years and they'll get on track."

"They'll never be the Yankees," you taunt, "not if they eat their Wheaties every morning. Not even when they grow up. They'll always be the poor sister, never as good as the original."

Mark turns back to you just as the game breaks to commercial. "That's why me and Hannah finally broke up," he says. "Since you're leaving."

With little to add, you both watch through a scoreless third quarter and the beginning of the fourth. You wait until Zorn connects with Largent on an elegant crossing pattern over the middle for a touchdown, giving the 'Hawks the lead and then ask Mark whether he was serious about what he'd said earlier. About Hannah and Meg? On the small screen, Largent hands the ball to the referee with all the colorless tact of a future congressman, but Mark doesn't watch it. He peels the label carefully from the bottle. "Yeah," he admits. "There were a lot of reasons but...yeah."

"Wow."

"I'd try again," he says, replacing the label on the bottle. "If it was me."

"Seriously," he repeats. "Why New York?"

You can't answer him because there is no good answer. Because no decision you've made yet seems to have worked out particularly well: an undistinguished career at an undistinguished college, seven years in marketing only to be dinged during cutbacks, another year working temp jobs across the city for people older and dumber than you are. Meg. "Every time I've taken the initiative," you explain finally, "it seems to have worked out poorly. I'm thirty-three years old, I'm losing my hair, I've got no future and no prospects. Doing the unexpected seems to have produced disastrous results, so I'm going to do exactly what you're supposed to do in this situation. I'm going to move to New York and see if someone writes a zany television show about me."

"Welcome back," Mark croons, Zorn's pass putting him in a good mood, and before you know it, both of you are singing about your dreams being your ticket out, about being back where people need you. The song sounds hokey but who are you to judge? After all, you're heading to New York and have therefore forfeited any future objection to cliché.

You continue for two increasingly ad-libbed verses, and then Mark transitions into an upbeat number from *How to Succeed in Business Without Really Trying*, which ends abruptly in profanity unanticipated by the lyricist when Stabler scrambles out of the pocket to find Casper alone down the sideline to give the Raiders back the lead. "Hey, at least they missed the extra point," you offer.

"I don't know," Mark says miserably. In your empty apartment, the moving truck downstairs filled with the boxes of your sloughed cells, of little more value than a dumpster dive, it is easy enough to forget that the cards of Mark's life have also not been entirely favorable, that his own career has stalled out and that, since breaking irrevocably with Hannah, he has enjoyed little success with women. He holds his head between his palms. "Maybe you're right, maybe this is a place for losers."

Your apathy for football insulated you during your earlier razzing. There was no reason to feel guilty about this. As any guy will admit, it is perfectly acceptable decorum. In basketball, your adopted Supersonics have already won fifteen of their first twenty games, as good a team as you have ever been blessed with, a team that in half a year will finish as World Champions. Fandom is an emotional commitment. But it's more than early-onset nostalgia for Seattle that fuels the next five minutes, more even than the curve of Mark's spine as he hunches in your soon-to-be abandoned chair, straightening by increments as Zorn manages the clock like a ten-year veteran, the announcers explaining how a victory here would put an end to the team's expansion era. And it is joy, no matter what anyone says, when Efren Herrera converts a forty-six-yarder over the outstretched grid of Raider defenders, straight through the uprights, the clock expiring, to earn the Seahawks the win. And because fandom is an investment of a kind, we must count this as a victory.

The Material World

A friend of a friend of a friend; *two standard deviations* is the icebreaker you try over the phone. He asks you a few simple math questions, whether you think the market is going up or down.

"Up," you say, the break in your voice a testament to your optimism with the bold new economy.

"Think it through," he warns. "Don't tell me what you guess I want to hear. Tell me what you think and why."

You look at the newspapers spread in front of you, your ear pressed hard against the phone. "Down. Trade deficit, inflation, consumer confidence. None of the harbingers point upward."

"Everyone knows that," he says. "You think maybe the guys with power ties don't read the *Journal*?"

"I'm saying I don't think the market has finished correcting yet. I'm saying I don't think people are going to be buying for another quarter, minimum, and I don't think this administration has the political capital to turn it around." You bark this with a confidence you don't feel. The lifeline you grasp onto is the one everyone who has ever had a job interview in finance clings to: if this guy knew the answers for certain, he wouldn't be working for a living either. The financial district, that murkiest of crystal balls.

"Fine," he allows. "That's a valid outlook. You and the Hermit would get along famously."

You have no idea what he's talking about, but you're afraid to ask.

"I've got meetings," he says, his voice curt. "What do you look like? I'll pick you up at nine."

He picks you up in a sports car, drives back uptown. "We'll be here all night," he tells the valet, tossing him the keys. "Keep it under the roof. They're calling for rain."

"All night?" you ask.

"Right," Jensen replies and reaches into his pocket. He pulls out cab chits, signs one, and scribbles something on the back. Then he hands it to you. "Let's assume I'll be too drunk to remember later."

The club itself is palpitating. Between the driving bass and the crushing humanity, you have the strange notion that the entire structure is rising to meet you and then pulling itself back. Taunting you. Like the women inside of it, all of whom are far too good-looking to speak to you, their skin and clothing seal-slick.

A man with the pectorals and cheekbones to pull off pastels shakes Jensen's hand and escorts you to the back wall, to a brushed-suede bench curving elegantly around its table. Above you hangs a cherub, the beat making him writhe like a porn star.

"Nice table," you offer. "Are you a regular or something?"

Jensen examines the burnished wood and then reaches out his hand to show you a neat stack of fifties palmed like a magician's trick. "The shmear," he explains. "Expense account covers all." Then he looks out into the crowd. "There is an awful lot of talent here tonight."

When the waitress comes by, he orders shots, beer chasers. Two steaks. "This is a dance club," the waitress says. "We don't serve food."

"New York strip," Jensen says. "Rare. Fries or baked potato, whichever."

"New York strip," the waitress repeats.

"Yes."

"That's a cut of meat, correct?"

"Yes."

"And this is a dance club, correct?"

"Yes."

By now, she is squatting directly next to you, her impressive breasts pushed up near your face. The club is so hot that you can see beads of sweat on her chest. It passes across your mind that this entire ridiculous exchange is for you, either to impress you or else to arrange a good peek. The waitress rocks backward and steadies herself with a single fingernail against your thigh.

"You do notice the music, the ladies, the DJ?"

"Yes," says Jensen, a smile forming on his face.

"You do not, on the other hand, notice plates, or silverware, or napkins."

"No."

"Linens?"

"No."

"Salt, pepper, Heinz Tomato Ketchup maybe?"

By now Jensen is grinning broadly. Even the waitress seems to be getting into it, rocking more quickly. You can feel her but keep your eyes straight ahead, the thumping music gyrating your sightline from Jensen to the angel behind his head.

"Busboys? Candlesticks? Mood lighting. The guy with the big fucking white hat?"

"No."

"So we've established that your glitch is rooted in your processing functions rather than your perceptions."

"Yes."

"So we're focusing inward rather than outward."

"Yes, if I had to guess." Jensen grins.

The waitress rocks harder against your left leg. She steadies herself with her right hand against your knee, raises her left hand in a peace sign. "How many fingers, if you had to guess, would you guess I was holding up?"

Jensen leans in to the waitress, kisses her lightly on the forehead. He looks down at her chest and places a single fifty-dollar bill above her left breast, gluing it tight with sweat. "One," he blinks. Then places another fifty above her right breast. "And two. If I had to guess, I would guess two."

The waitress collects the money and rises to her feet. She implies something about his lineage and then turns.

When she has gone, Jensen looks back at you. "I suppose you think I did that for your benefit?"

You tell him the thought had crossed your mind.

"It's probably best if you understand this, and don't think I'm trying to be an asshole but your benefit doesn't interest me very much right now."

You agree.

"I did that to impart to you the importance of money in our society. And its"—he waves a hand through the air—"lubricating capacities." He moves along the bench, his knee close to yours. "You need to understand just how important money is to this job. I want you loving money. I want you worshipping money."

You tell him that you do, that you will.

"I don't mean the idea of money, those little lights on the computer screen. I don't mean theoretically, you understand that?"

You do.

"Leave that for the eggheads and the traders. I want you thinking of money in terms of goods and services. A good deal is ten Porsches. Your margin is an Armani suit." Then, for one second his face turns almost human. "These aren't idle examples either. I've found it best not to think of money in terms of mortgage payments or staple goods. I've found that that tends to tighten me up right here." Jensen cups his crotch. "Alimony payments?" It is a question.

You tell him you've never been married.

"Just as well," he says, his face reverting back. "Marriage tends to tighten me up down there too. These guys we're dealing with, they've got tons of money, right? They've got money that makes us look like…" his gaze, searching for something sufficiently squalid, lights on your shoes. His eyes narrow. "Pissants. Now, why do these guys need us flashing small bills if they've got equity wealth? Because their money sits down—pays for Harvard, pays for Westchester. It's big money, mind you, but it's doing a lot of fucking heavy lifting. Our money, on the other hand, it's like those fucking little dogs that never stop yapping, the little white ones. You know the ones I mean?"

You do.

He continues: "Had a maiden aunt with one of those dogs, Snowflake or something. Kind of a pain in the ass, little fucking dog a foot high always jumping up onto my sack. I'll tell you something, those little dogs can jump five times their height."

He waits until you stop smiling.

"That's our little money, you understand? Jumping five times its height."

He peels a slim stack of bills from the larger pile and measures it against the colored lights of the club. "They give us their big money so that we'll spend our little money on the things they can't buy for themselves. That's why the Dom Perignon, the Armani, the hookers, the Yankees tickets. That's how I want you thinking of money." And then he flips the stack into your lap.

"Buy some new fucking shoes. You look like a goddamned English teacher."

It is at this moment that the steaks come.

You've just unpacked your office when Jensen swings round the corner and tells you he's taking you to meet the Hermit.

He leads you down a hallway with better lighting. The doors are made of wood and there are blinds on the windows. "This must be the high rent district," you joke.

"Pretty much," Jensen says. "Two hundred a house." You look blank. "Like in Monopoly, the row with Boardwalk and Park Place? This is where we stash the wise old men. They're so toxic that we store them with the office supplies."

Near the end of the hallway, a woman in a white blouse holds a silver pot, her hand floating above the doorknob. When she sees you, her cheeks flush. She walks toward you. Jensen says hello, introduces you. Sylvia.

"Hello."

"Is there any chance you are going to see him this morning?" she asks. Her voice is breathless, the entire sentence escaping in a rush.

Jensen laughs. "Sure, we're going right now."

The woman, mid-twenties, dark hair pulled back in a bun, hands you the pot. "It's hot," she warns, too late, your fingers tingling from the silver. "Sorry," she breathes. "So sorry. Please forgive." She stares at you a moment, her eyes almost pink, whether from tears or pigment you can't be sure. Despite an almost ethereal beauty, she has the stature and dress of a woman who spends her lunch hour crying in bathroom stalls. "Would you mind horribly taking this in to him? I've been dreading it all morning."

"Sure, Sylvia," Jensen says in his easy way. The woman's shoulders relax and what's left of the air in her lungs pushes a loose strand of hair off her face. "Thank you," she murmurs, hands you a digestive biscuit in clear plastic and disappears, as neat as any magic trick.

You stare at Jensen, who stares back at you, amused. "The cookie's for the Hermit," he says. "Don't eat it." Then he raps sharply on the door and enters.

The Hermit is an Orthodox Jew. He wears a dark, heavy suit, a black hat that might have been popular in the time of Jack the Ripper, a long white beard that predates Noah. He looks at you for a long moment, at the teapot in your hand, the skin under his eyes nearly at desk level. "Sylvia," he announces gravely to you, "there was a time, I concede, when I found you attractive. But now I fear those days have gone. Perhaps I work you too hard?"

When you don't say anything, he motions you forward and directs you to put the teapot on the edge of a mahogany desk that dominates the middle of the room. While you wait, he takes a silver cup from his desk, cleans it with a handkerchief, and then pours himself a cup of tea. He looks at you from behind the veil of steam and then reveals, as sad as Eeyore, "that was, of course, a joke."

You nod. Jensen, not helping, has moved away to a love seat pushed up against the wall. The entire room is painted in heavy colors, the artwork oppressive, the overhead lighting off. The blinds are rubberized and drawn so tightly that the only light in the room comes from an old-fashioned desk lamp that lights the Hermit's face from below, to startling effect. He tugs at his beard for a moment. "I'm Crimble."

You introduce yourself, rush over to shake hands, but he is still holding his teacup. The result is an awkward sort of grasp, left hand on right, sideways and disjointed. He grabs at your wrist and then works your fingers apart, plucking his digestive cookie. "I wondered about this," he sniffs. "I shall have to watch out for you, I'm afraid." Then he winks, so slowly you can actually see the muscles of his eye socket deliberate on contraction.

"I'll leave you two to get to know each other," Jensen coughs. And then, like Sylvia, he disappears.

Crimble motions you to sit, and the two of you consider one another through the steam. His fingers go to work on the plastic of the biscuit. "Married?" he asks.

"No."

"Children?"

"No."

"Business school?"

"No."

"You are not..." he says, and then leans forward. "May I ask you something personal?"

"Yes."

"You are not another one of those goddamned shoe salesmen, are you?" There is almost no affect in his tone.

"I am not."

His head relaxes, lolls forward. "Thank God," he mutters. "For reasons that passeth my understanding, they are forever pushing a parade of shoe salesmen in front of me. I never understand what it is they want." He seems distressed by this memory, shakes his giant head as if to push it off. He sips slowly, moves his digestive biscuit around in the cup with a pinkie and then fishes it out with the claw of his middle fingers and eats it with gusto.

"They keep me here like a sibyl in a jar. You are not, I can assume, familiar with that story?"

"No," you say, shaking your head. "I'm sorry."

"Yes," he sighs. "No matter. They keep me here to dispense wisdom. Do they still call me the Magician?" he asks, leaning forward.

"I'm new here," you explain. "It's my first day. I honestly don't know what they call you."

He waves his hand. "No matter. Office secrets." He looks down at the teacup in his hand, sadly. Tips the dregs back into his mouth, stirs the cookie crumbs around the bottom of the cup.

"There's more, I think," you say, and pour another cup from the pot.

"Ah, so there is. Excellent." And he seems pleased for a second. But then his face drops. "Another biscuit?" he asks, as hopefully as a child.

You raise both arms, empty.

"No matter," he says again. And this time you catch the truth in the undercurrent, that to him such things are quite a big matter indeed.

"You don't, if you don't mind my saying so, seem quite like the other ones," he says. He looks at you again, his eyes mere squints, "not a shoe salesman?"

You laugh. "Honestly."

"Honestly," he mutters into his beard. "Well, they keep me here to dispense wisdom, so here you are. Ask away."

For a second, something about the lighting, and his beard, and yes, sure, his old-world religion, all of it makes you lean forward in anticipation. You have been waiting. It seems, despite everything, that this man might actually have all the answers. You can barely hold the words in your mouth. You can smell the tea, the bits of cookie lingering on his whiskers. "Tell me," you whisper finally, "what it is I need to know."

Carefully he puts the teacup down on his desk and then pulls out one of the drawers. It is so dark, the single lamp on the desk hooding his eyes, that it takes a moment for you to recognize the object he removes. It is a Magic Eight Ball.

"The source of all my wisdom," Crimble says, the saddest of smiles on his lips. He shakes the ball and then looks down expectantly. "Alas," he says. "Try again later."

You smile and thank him for his time. When you shake his hand again, now empty, he pulls his fingers through the crook of your thumb. "Still no cookie," he says. "You never know about cookies."

"That's true," you say, rescuing your hand and backing away slowly.

"Two years," he says in a louder voice. "Give it two years. If you're not out of here in two years, you'll never get out. Run for the hills."

You think about this for a moment, the two of you nodding to each other like owls. "They call you the Hermit," you tell him, watching his eyes. He considers for a moment and then starts laughing, clapping his hands together quickly. "Marvelous," he chuckles. "Simply marvelous." He is still laughing while you leave the room, still walking backward, bowing as you go.

Over sushi on a patio on a day that seems so bright it's overexposed, you mention to Jensen what Crimble had said. Jensen is rubbing his chopsticks together, chortling. "Fucking Mook," he shakes his head. "The Hermit is a waste of prime real estate." He tells you the story. "The Hermit used to be a big-shot trader," Jensen says. "He did V-O-L-U-M-E business. Turns fifty, he has a heart attack, a tiny fucking arrhythmia. I get one of those when I eat corned beef two days in a row. But Crimble goes off the reservation, gives his notice, signs on with us as a golden parachute. Like the glue factory, retirement, only with benefits like the tasty Sylvia. Fucker does volume business, world on a string, decides to take a knee and run out the clock. Do me a favor, you end up taking advice from that guy, let me know so I can wash my hands of you."

"He claims he's here to dispense wisdom," you say. "Are you going to put a price tag on that?"

"Dispense wisdom, is that what he told you?"

You nod.

"The Hermit's here because of his Rolodex. Anyone who says different sure isn't living in this world."

The Juggler

Jensen sits alone at the table while you dicker with the pimp over the price of whipped cream wrestling. Somewhere behind you, a trader and nineteen of his closest buddies are chatting up the four women, who do their jobs by looking impressed and bouncy. Four hookers, twenty guys, the rented bus to Atlantic City. You've got it budgeted just shy of twenty grand. Pretty standard bachelor party fare for a Big Swinging Dick. Over his suit, the bachelor wears a custom-made T-shirt that says "I'm Selling Short." It was meant, presumably, as a sardonic joke about marriage, but the hookers, in their vague and good-natured way, take it as an indictment of his endowments, to the delight of his friends. You and Jensen chuckle, apart from the party, here only to pick up the tab.

When the fun starts, you slide off into the back corner and then out of the hall altogether. The venue you've found is, improbably, an old VFW hall that rents to private groups and asks few questions. The veterans have moved—you are heartened to find out—to a newer building down the block, taking their photos, their swing records, their plaques and mementos. You stretch your legs on the concrete of the wheelchair ramp and look up at the sky. The air is so cold and thin that you can see individual patches and craters on the moon as you look up. The image distorts briefly as the warm air from your lungs floats upward and then comes back into focus until you breathe again. You do this for a few moments, breathing in and out and watching your world distort. It is a beautiful night, if a little cold, and being in New Jersey does not ruin it.

Debra does not like your job, of course. What woman would? Because she is an accountant as well as a woman, what bothers her most is the waste—*inefficiency* like a curse word through her pursed lips. Since you'd started dating a few months ago, it has become a familiar argument. Last week she'd started in again, "It doesn't make any sense. Cut out the graft, ratchet down your percentage a few points, go to bed at a reasonable hour. Who'd complain?"

"The traders," you explain. "Within six months the graft would be back and the bump would still be down. You can take my word for it. This is a rather balanced market."

"Don't give me that market bullshit. You're starting to sound like that ape, Jensen."

You know it but you're unable to stop.

"You can't think of brokers as logical," you explain again. "Think of us as a perk, like a company car or extra vacation days."

The arguments have extended for days, nights. Last Sunday morning over breakfast she'd looked up suddenly. "Have the brokerages cut their rates and direct the profits into bonuses for the traders. Hell, have a single in-house guy and dismantle the brokerages altogether."

"Both sides want us to do what we are doing. Everyone wants us to do what we are doing."

Debra reached an arm out and pinched at the loose skin around your chin, a fond, familiar gesture. "This cannot possibly be what you were put on this earth to do."

Jensen interrupts your musings with a cough. "They've got a contraption most closely resembling a pig greaser rigged up and it's spitting whipped cream," he says with a half smile. "It's not bad, as far as these things go." When he opened the door, the music leaked out and now you are aware of the bass even though the door has closed.

Part of your job is to be jaded. It's another way, Jensen explains, of separating yourself from the client. "Still," he shrugs, "sometimes things slip through." He sits down with a heavy sigh, pulls his leg out in front of him and rubs at his knee.

"Something wrong?" you ask.

"It's the cold," he explains. "And this fucking sea air. I ripped up my knee about ten years ago and it hasn't really worked right since."

"College injury?" you guess. And how Jensen stares at you reminds you that you don't know the first thing about him. In fact, from the blustery bus ride over here, you know more about the Big Swinging Dick, with his high school and college and b-school friends circling him like satellites.

"Remind me," Jensen asks. "What was it that killed the fucking cat?" He waits a second and then continues. "I fell off a boat," Jensen says. "And I swear to God, if you guess a yacht I'm going to fire you."

"No yachts," you nod.

"When I was nineteen, I quit college and went to work as a commercial fisherman. Stuck with it about seven years. One day I tripped and busted up my knee. Used workman's comp to finish college, got a job selling shoes. My old boss, my mentor, comes in one day for loafers and plays a hunch. Now I do this."

"You ever feel like it's getting to you?" you ask.

Jensen cocks his head toward you and doesn't say anything. For a long time, you think he might fire you anyway. Then you think maybe he's nodding his head in response until you notice that he's bobbing in time to the music. He slams a pack of cigarettes hard against the concrete, takes one, and then slides the pack over. From somewhere, over the dance music, you can hear the faint cries of the seagulls, the tinkle of a Ferris wheel. Jensen pulls a flask out of his pocket and you share it, finding your rhythm with each other. Across the highway you can see cars, their taillights like neon, pushing in and out of lanes. By now Jensen has stretched onto his back, and you would think he was asleep except for the pace of his hand pulling the flask from yours and then replacing it, the firefly bob-and-weave of his cigarette. You are back in your thoughts, and probably so is he, when you hear a sudden yelp from inside followed by the breaking of glass, raised voices, a crash.

And still neither of you move. Even when the voices get louder and the bass stops. Even when you can hear crying and then a short, sudden thump. The door opens and the pimp comes out, his fist around his police beatstick, the ashen faces of the fraternity boys peeking out from behind him. "We've got a problem," the pimp says, looking down to Jensen's immobile body, ignoring you completely. You wheel on your elbow and watch Jensen, worry for a moment you might have to do something, so relieved when Jensen's head shifts slightly. You can hear the weariness of his sigh. "Is this," he asks the pimp, his eyes still gazing upward at the inky sky, "the sort of problem that five thousand dollars will fix?"

Queen of Sorrows

Sylvia has the best posture you've ever seen. When you tell her this, she flushes. "I'm just saying," you tease, "that you have an erect carriage." She swivels her head, red, but maybe pleased in spite of herself. "Relax," you grin. "It's a quiet restaurant. No one can hear us."

It *is* a quiet restaurant, and quite a nice one. It isn't the sort of place you take clients to, of course. It has an air of femininity and restraint, like Sylvia, who is hiding herself behind her water glass, looking at you with magnified eyes.

"It's the chair," she explains. And it's true that the chairs are almost like thrones, straight up and down, plush and padded. But you tell her you've seen her in her cubicle and it's the same thing. "You're not fooling anyone," you chide, and she shrinks back.

You were concerned about asking Sylvia out. Partly because of the Hermit and partly because things with Debra have gotten a bit more serious. But nothing's been formalized with Debra, and the Hermit, archaic though he may be, does not have any claim to Sylvia. And so you sidled up to Sylvia in the hallway and asked her to dinner. She turned pink, of course, but agreed. For the remainder of the day, the two of you exchanged glances and it felt nice to have a secret.

It still feels nice. There is something about Sylvia, her birdlike frame, her librarian's demeanor, that makes you want to confide in her. For once on a date, it is you who does most of the talking and you find yourself opening up. "You're better than a priest," you say to Sylvia, and there is something of the confessional to all of this; the high-backed chairs, the darkness of the restaurant. Sylvia keeps her face hidden, talking to you through her water glass, veiled by her napkin, the tines of her fork. What should be disconcerting is instead very liberating. "There's something about you," you tell her, shaking your head, but you aren't sure what it is.

By the time the salads come, you realize that you've shared more with Sylvia than you have on all of your dates with Debra. You've told her about your parents and your history with Meg, and she's offered sympathies, the elegant wave of her hand an encouragement. She eats her meal in perfect tiny portions, and even though your eyes never leave her face, you cannot recollect her ever taking a bite. After the main course, she excuses herself to the bathroom, and you watch her float regally down the hallway. You sit back in your chair and take a large drink of wine, feeling superhuman, very unlike yourself. While she's gone, you order dessert for the both of you. The steward comes back, but you refuse a second bottle of wine. When Sylvia returns, you explain about the wine and she nods. The water glass magnifies her eyes and you can see the red of the rims, the hummingbird twitch of her blinking. You wonder if she's disappointed about the wine, but then you notice that she hasn't touched the wine glass in front of her.

She is almost unbearably beautiful, an ambushing beauty you did not see coming. She wears no jewelry, save a butterfly brooch on her blouse. The candles from the table catch the brooch at odd angles, and you want to ask her about it but you also want to cover it with your hand, and so you do neither. For a few seconds you watch her, without speaking, and in the silence her lips compact into a tiny smile. You lean in closer, your heart engorged, to tell her about Charlotte. "Do you mind if I tell you a secret?" you ask.

"People always do," Sylvia whispers shyly. And something in the way she says it makes you stop short. It's a long time before you figure out what made you pull back. There was something in her voice, a pain in her look that nearly overwhelmed you. Sylvia was resigned to dealing with life's disappointments, and in that moment you guessed that even your date must have been less than she'd hoped. You yourself must have been so. You did all the talking. You never asked her about the brooch. You never asked her about crying in the bathroom. You never even asked her how she liked her food. You pay the bill, drive her home, and promise to take her out again. But you never tell her about Charlotte and you never ask her out again and when you see her in the hallways, you smile as wide as Jensen and kid her about Crimble's tea set.

About three months after your father's death, a package arrives in the mail. You don't recognize the return address—Lawton, Oklahoma—so you leave it on the laminate kitchen table under the week's accumulated snowdrift of bills and flyers, New York never short of pizza coupons or bachelors to use them. It isn't until later, on your way to the sofa with a beer, that you remember to open the padded envelope. Because it spent the holiday weekend crammed into your catacomb of a mail slot, and because of your careless haste in extricating it, you've ripped off a sizeable chunk of an upper corner. Now the package is bent and the photo inside folded in on itself, a black-and-white of a man in fishing garb holding a young, naked child upside down by the ankle, the fold obscuring the man's face until you pull it back to reveal your father some time soon after the war, smiling at the size of his catch. Nothing can be done for the baby whose face, either through your clumsiness or the post office's various machinations, or perhaps only through the ravages of time, has been lost so that you can't tell how the child might have felt about being dangled by the ankle, smiling or frowning or screaming in fright, the grainy black-and-white photo with creases webbing in all directions, masking even those parts otherwise undamaged, making a mosaic of the naked child, a thread passing through the baby's midsection so that even the genitals are indiscernible, this young Achilles, this dangling sinner, inscrutable, as helical and sexless as any fish.

It isn't like seeing a ghost—after all, he's only been dead a few months and anyway there was a big photo of him at the funeral, a blowup of the one used at his retirement party, and afterward, in the basement of her apartment building, your mother escorted you past giant cardboard boxes, motioning with her hand—"take anything you'd like, before the rats get at it or the floods rise." When you mentioned that they certainly would—rats or mold or spiders— something at any rate bound to eat away at your accumulated family memories, she repeated her offer.

"Mom, I'm only back for a few days. Plus, my apartment in New York is the size of a bathmat. I haven't got room for this stuff."

"I can sympathize. I'm in the same boat myself. The condo board is very, very stringent. You've got to watch some of these old people. They nurture an impulse toward hoarding."

Your mother had, some years back, moved herself into a retirement community, although she'd just turned fifty-five. "Who's going to complain?" she'd retorted when you'd phoned to question her. "You think this is such a Shangri-la that people are fighting to get in? Besides, they like having a bit of youth around here." You could hear her mouth move away from the telephone receiver for a moment before closing in. "Such as it is."

"I don't think they're going to complain. But there's something unusual in a grown woman, a married woman, wanting to move into an old-age home before she needs to."

"Don't be ridiculous. This isn't a nursing home." She started explaining about graduated care systems before stopping short. "It isn't worth the long-distance rates," she finally sighed. "Anyway, we both know this has nothing to do with my apartment."

That had been five years ago, your mother jumping the gun on widowhood by nearly half a decade. The old vanishing act again, so that when the time came, five years later, your father would spend the last few months of his life in a VA hospital and then, ultimately, in a hospice.

A shadow of something unseen traced across the storage unit, and in response your mother rattled the metal of the cage. "I don't know what to tell you," she said. "So I sold the house. Some of Dad's stuff I took upstairs, but let's remember that I already had most of what I needed. What am I going to do with two toasters?"

"I'm not talking about toasters. I'm talking report cards, our first teeth, photo albums. Our stuff. Charlotte's and mine."

"Your dad went through a lot of that junk years ago, while you were living out there in Seattle. He told me he'd planned on shipping it to you, what was yours."

It came back, barely, his promise to send you a few boxes. You seemed to remember him grousing about the cost, you telling him not to bother with it, that you weren't sure how long you'd be in Seattle anyway, things falling apart on that end, that you'd pick them up when you made it back into town. At any rate, the boxes never materialized and now they were gone forever.

"Don't be so melodramatic," your mother cautioned. "I didn't run across them when I was going through his things. But then again, I had other things on my mind. Take a second look if you'd like." She moved behind you and dropped the key into your breast pocket. "Take as much time as you need," she said gently and headed back upstairs. "I've still got guests in town for the funeral. Mutual friends," she said, shaking her head as if in wonder that such a thing was even possible.

Three days after the funeral, you bicker on the train platform.

"I am at something of a loss as to why, exactly, you are yelling at me." She stubs a cigarette violently with her toe. A janitor on the far end of the platform, broom and dustbin in hand, raises an arm in protest. When she sees this she scolds, "Now look what you've done. You're causing a scene."

And, ridiculous as it is, you are. Your train is twenty minutes late and you're heading back to New York completely empty-handed. The picked-through remnants in your mother's storage locker have been eaten away by water and insects at some point over the past few years and are, for all intents and purposes, a complete loss. If your father had collected anything to send to you, those boxes were nowhere to be found, lost to time, adrift in the universe.

"And again with the melodrama," she says.

"You threw away all of the family pictures," you shout. "Every last one."

"I certainly did not," she huffs. "I haven't looked at a family photograph in fifteen years." You feel yourself turning purple as she twirls on her heel. "Here he goes, ready to lecture me again about being unsentimental."

"Yes."

"Heartless."

"Yes."

"Cold. Unfeeling. Calls me a statue."

"You are."

"A snake."

"And worse."

"A Dickens villain. A troll. An ogress."

"Are you honestly telling me that you can't understand why I might be upset that you seem to have systematically neglected or destroyed any evidence of my childhood?"

Another woman, near your mother's age, has moved closer on the platform in presumption of boarding. Your mother offers her a wry half-smile and informs her that you have just accused her of being Cruella de Vil. The woman looks her over closely and shrugs neutrally.

"I know you've structured your life around blaming me for everything," your mother mutters, rummaging through her purse for another cigarette. "It wasn't a role I was eager for, but it's what I got dealt. So, fine. But don't you think blaming me for a broken pipe in your father's basement, for furnace exhaust, for paper wasps, is a little bit much?"

"Don't you think admitting to your child that you haven't looked at a picture of him, of any member of his family, in more than a decade is a little bit inhuman?"

When your mother raises her palm, you think for certain she's going to slap you. And you can tell by her tremor as she flings the unlit cigarette from her mouth that she wasn't far off. But she composes herself quickly.

"I'm sorry you don't have any pictures," she offers sympathetically. "I can understand how that would bother you."

"Thank you," you reply. And had the train only come, everything might have been all right. But just then, a synthetic voice overhead informed you all that the train would be another hour en route, rubbish on the track, and thanked you for your understanding. So instead you squabbled over the food at the wake, and in the end she took off early, leaving you on the platform with the other woman still making her assessment and behind her a thin but growing cluster of people, fellow travelers on this Thursday afternoon, heading East.

You describe the photo to your mother. You've moved back to your couch, opened another beer. There is no date on the back, no clues, nothing to place the picture in time. Nothing to nail down the child's identity. Eventually you realize that what you had thought was a shadow at the lower left is actually a woman's leg, well-turned, the frame abbreviating everything above the knee. How can it be that with nearly its entire body you are unable to discern something as fundamental as the child's gender, and yet from only an inch of leg you know incontrovertibly that this fragment, this collateral image, belongs to your mother?

"Sure," she says. "Lake of the Ozarks. If there's a kid there, it's your sister. She was probably about a year old."

So that, at least, answers one question. In the time it takes you to process this, your mother continues.

"Sorry it wasn't you," she says. "But you were embryonic, at best."

You assure her that it doesn't matter.

"Lake of the Ozarks. That takes me back. We went fishing with one of your dad's work buddies. What was his name…"

"Hal Scott," you supply, courtesy of the brief note tucked into the envelope. *Thought you might appreciate this. Condolences on your pop.*

Your mother whistles through her teeth. "Hal Scott. Now that was a few lifetimes ago. Whatever happened to him?"

"He's in Oklahoma," you tell her.

"Goodness. What was his wife's name, the one with the Betty Grable ass?"

You inform her you know nothing more about it, a literal truth.

"Now that was a pretty fun weekend. Quite the stir on the beach when she arrived, I can assure you."

"Maybe I should look her up," you joke.

"How are things with your new trixie?" your mother responds.

"Debra," you remind her.

"Of course, dear. Debra. How is she?"

You tell your mother that she's fine. You don't tell her how the two of you have just returned from a long weekend in Chicago. Two states away, but still close enough to your mother's apartment not to mention it. Walking through Grant Park, Debra just ahead of you, the breeze off the lake pushing her hair from her face. Her fingers as she bent to help a child find her necklace in the grass. The gentle way she accepted your stare, leaning on one knee, hugging her cheek to her shoulder, smiling.

"Something you will find when you have children of your own," your mother explains, "is that they have too many suitors and beaus to possibly keep track of."

You remind her that she remembered Mrs. Scott's heart-shaped ass going back thirty-five years if it was a day.

"Thank you for that."

"I'm just pointing out, memory doesn't seem to be your problem."

"Those are my memories, just as you'll have your own. Small things that will stay with you forever. Like photographs. You'll see what I mean one day if you don't already."

Because you do know what she means, exactly, you repeat: "Debra. She might be the one."

"She might," your mother agrees. "But you said that about the last one, too. The redheaded one your dad was over the moon about. They're your beaus, your names to catalogue."

"Is this how you are with the widowers in your complex? You must have to fight them off with a cane." It was meant as a joke, but your mother gives back only silence.

"What's the matter? Did I hit too close to home?"

"Unlikely, dear," your mother says, not unkindly.

"Some pensioner pursuing you as fast as his artificial hip can carry him?"

"Skip it," your mother warns with a thin laugh. She sounds so different, some part of your memory surging forward to claim her, the woman she had been when you were a young child and before, the woman whose slender ankle in the photograph is the only evidence that she even existed.

"I promise to remember his name," you tease. "I've got a young mind with plenty of storage space available."

"No names," you mother replies after another long pause. "There was only ever your father for me. Always."

"Well, at least I've got this picture of Dad and Charlotte," you say and promise to make her a copy.

"Sure thing. Please do."

"Still none of me, though. Just your memories, I guess."

"More than enough," she assures you.

"I just don't understand where all of those photos could have gone," you wonder sadly. "Do you think if I wrote a letter to the post office they would conduct a search?"

Over the phone, your mother demurs.

"Maybe I could hire someone," you suggest. "Somebody who specializes in that sort of thing."

"You mean a private detective?" your mother says. "A sleuth. A gumshoe? A private dick?"

"Stop it," you plead. "I don't have any pictures at all, you can't imagine what that's like. Nothing of me or you guys or Charlotte. I'd do anything to find them."

There's silence on the other end of the line so long you think maybe you've gotten cut off. "You want my advice," your mother finally breaks in. "Forget it. Start over. They're just pictures."

"It's worth trying."

"It doesn't work that way," she explains, her voice hitting the alveoli hard.

"I'd do anything to get them back."

"Well, you can't. I burned them all. Fifteen years ago."

For a long time after you have hung up, you can't see clearly. You can feel the blood in your ears, your fingers white-knuckled against the photo. She destroyed everything. This photo then, this little snapshot, the entire family legacy. Your father younger than you can possibly remember, your sister inverted, her chubby legs crossed over one another in a figure four, your mother's leg slow to pull out of the frame, even then anxious to eradicate her presence, and higher up beyond the cross of that leg, all of those cells, your cells, growing exponentially, frantically, another fish story, restless to leave eternity and begin the short swim downstream and then the much longer swim upstream after that. Your father, your cherubic sister, that tiny portion of your mother she couldn't withhold and you, a cipher, purely theoretical.

Memorial Day. You'd spent the entire weekend with Debra, your first weekend away together and in the taxi from the airport you'd promised to call her in a day or two, maybe three, even sailors get shore leave, you'd joked, and she'd laughed. But now, nearly two a.m., it is her number your fingers dial, the phone ringing so many times you begin to worry, until her voice staggers onto the line.

"Hey, I'm sorry it's late. I didn't wake you, did I?"

"A bit," she admits. When you apologize, she laughs, Tinkerbell's fairy dust. "Noooo," she coos. "Talk to me. Tell me anything. It's just nice to hear your voice."

Later, you will remember very little of this. But here's how it all started.

Still driving, Jensen rolls down the driver's side window and motions for you to steady the wheel. Then he boosts himself halfway out of the car and swipes at the snow with his sleeve. Snow so wet, it lingers for a second before easing itself off the glass, caressing Jensen's stomach before coming to rest (much of it anyway) in the recently vacated driver's seat. You can hear Jensen swear over the sound of cars on the other side of the highway, although whether it's at the snow now melting through his pants or the wipers that bat at him aggressively, you can't be sure. You look to turn them off, but frankly it's disconcerting to be driving from the passenger side—with limited help from Jensen's knees. He's on his own. Eventually the condensation clears, allowing you a brief vision of the stretch of road ahead. "Good job," you tell Jensen, who doesn't say anything but directs you to keep the wheel while he scoops the snow out of his seat, cups it into a ball and tosses it far, far away from the car. You long to watch its arc but know it would be unwise under the circumstances. Somewhere during all of this, Jensen's shoulder has dislodged the rearview mirror so that now it points straight up. You tilt it with your hand, guessing it back into place.

While you pull off the highway and into the mansioned community, Jensen gives you a skeleton bio of Pan: trader, mid-forties, last name something unpronounceably Polish. "He's got one of those tight little beards. One look at it and you just know the guy's a prick."

"Is he?"

Jensen shrugs. "He's a trader. He's a money player." He readjusts the rearview mirror. The snowflakes are so wet you can actually hear the sound as they collide with the windscreen, over the traffic noise, over Jensen's voice, over the radio, over the horrible squeal of the vanquished windshield wiper, now bent and twitching half an inch above the glass. "He's a pretty weird guy."

"Remind me again what we're doing out here?"

"He wants to show us his house."

This is unusual. Most traders are happy to show you anything in the world except their house. Most of those guys, Ivy League from infancy, wouldn't have your state-college ilk in their foyer. Most of them wouldn't want you within three miles of their children, their wives, their live-in maids. It's only natural: no one bring the circus home with them.

You cock an eyebrow and then lower it when you realize that Jensen, fighting the weather from at least two different fronts, can't possibly pick up visual cues. "Why would he want us to see his house?"

"I don't know."

"Are we going to meet his wife?" You worry that you ought to be bringing flowers, or wine. Debra's influence, feeling wrong to arrive empty-handed. Meanwhile, the snow accumulates beneath the useless wiper blade.

Jensen swears loud enough to drown out everything else. "I don't know. I don't ask these questions, which is why my check clears every month. They tell me they've heard rumors of a topless Bolivian snake charmer, I make the call. They tell me one of their friends—and doesn't this just sound like a hoot?—found a guy who would let them fire Uzis at chickens somewhere across the river, I make the call." Jensen reaches out with his left arm and gives the windshield a violent swipe. The blade, halfway down its arc, clicks in disdain before retreating. "They tell me they had a dream about a Great Dane, a cantaloupe, Dag fucking Hammarsköld, I make the call. It's a simple fucking game, asshole, and yet three months in you're still peppering me with questions every fucking moment." By now, Jensen's head is back out the window but he's shouting louder to make sure you don't miss a syllable. "They want me to come over to their house to see their new fucking wine cellar or their sex swing or a Mickey Mantle rookie card, I tell them I'd love to." His upper half reemerges, his gloved hand tight around the windshield wiper, pried away from its mooring. He stares at you for a good long moment that feels longer with the car still driving straight ahead, impervious to the climate and the tilt of the Connecticut road. He raises the blade to your nose. "Riddle me this, Question Man: Why the fuck is the little devil on my shoulder warning me off beating you raw with this worthless thing and leaving you to die in a snowbank? What use can he see for you that I can't?" You look straight ahead until you hear Jensen's breathing calm. Then the wiper blade lands on your lap. "When we get out of the car, see if you can jury-rig that thing back on. Right now the damned thing is as useless as you are." Then he lifts his body out of the car again, this time the vehicle slowing nearly to a crawl in front of houses so large they boast servants' quarters. "Where the hell are we, anyway?"

Pan greets you at the door, ushering you inside with a sly squeeze of the bicep. He leads you off the foyer into a typical office: wood-paneled, with antique maps on the walls. He pours drinks, sits down close to you and then springs back up. "I'll be back in a second," he says, and vanishes.

You want to ask Jensen if the guy's always like this, but of course that's out of the question. You can't draw a bead on Pan, he's always moving. He reminds you of something you can't place and Jensen's earlier rant makes you wary of trying. You take a sip of your scotch, which tastes pretty much the way scotch always tastes, like peat moss.

"You like that?" Pan says, emerging from behind your right shoulder. He squeezes your shoulder, lightly. Even before he says it, you know he's about to tell you how much the spirit costs a bottle. He doesn't disappoint you, the figure coming in at least half again more than you'd figure. All for something you imagine could fertilize tomatoes.

You gush appreciatively. Jensen takes a big drink and you can tell from the flush of his cheeks, the sudden intake of breath, that it is the really good stuff. And you can also tell that Jensen's reaction is genuine and you understand a bit more why he does well at his job.

Pan claps his hands, twice, quickly. He rushes over to Jensen and starts telling him something about the way they cure the oak casks. He's like a hummingbird. And maybe it's the hazardous drive up, or the guy's perfectly manicured beard, or the shelves of books above his head, the whole Jay Gatsby set design, but suddenly you imagine bludgeoning him with the wiper blade, over and over, leaving him buried in the snowbank outside his front door. A strange and dangerous impulse.

"Hell of a drive out here," Jensen growls. "Especially in the snow."

Pan giggles. "It's the cost of having flowers and trees and wildlife."

"Wildlife?" you ask.

"Squirrels, maybe," Pan says. Then, his body at rest for a moment or two, he shrugs, "How on earth should I know? I'm out the door by five a.m. I work for a living. Ask my wife."

"He might do that," Jensen warns. "He's a curious little bugger."

"Don't do that," Pan chides. He waits to catch your eye, finally frozen. "Seriously. That kind of thing can get you killed in this business."

Jensen pleads with Pan not to waste his breath. "I've been training him to stop asking so many damned questions since I got him. I'm afraid the lessons aren't sinking in." He walks over and stands next to Pan. "Truth to tell, I'm thinking of sending him back to the pound."

"Don't give up on the lad so soon," Pan replies. He favors you with a smile. "I can remember when you were nothing more than a sapling, and look at you now."

In response, Jensen raises his glass. "Here's to me," he toasts.

Back in motion, Pan paces the periphery of the room, tracing his fingers along the spines of the books. He is whistling so softly that the tune vanishes the moment you think you've identified it. He has accessorized a very expensive suit with canvas Chuck Taylors whose tongues loll obscenely. As you take a sip of scotch, you brace your jawline to make sure you don't grimace. You can feel Jensen watching you. Last week he came to your desk and sat down while you negotiated a trade. When it was done, you hung up the phone and finished writing everything up. "Sixteen and three-quarters, the guy must have been fairly axed," you reported. "You think that's too low?" Jensen asked. "Yes," you said, ready to explain further but instead Jensen hopped off lightly. "What?" you asked him, as he started down the hallway. "You think that was the wrong answer? You think that stock's going up?" Jensen slowed down but you still couldn't hear what he was saying. When you caught up, you repeated yourself. Jensen grunted his response, "You ask me if the price was low or high? Who gives a shit? When I broker a trade you know what I'm thinking about? I'm calculating what my cut is, how much of that I need to pour back into each of these guys, how much might actually stop rolling long enough to find its way into my bank account. The fact that you are thinking about prices tells me something else entirely about you." He looked like he was going to say more but then moved away down the hall, and for once you didn't follow.

That was last week. When you were starting out, he told you that the best thing about this job was that, to the broker, there are no winners or losers, but it certainly doesn't feel that way now.

When you finally look up, Jensen is in the corner with Pan, hunched over a book. Pan is gesturing near the bottom of a page, his other arm wrapped around Jensen's shoulders. The two of them laugh. When you come up behind them, Pan shuts the book quickly and reshelves it. Then he looks at your mostly full glass and jokes, "How's that scotch treating you?"

Later, when he refills Jensen's glass, he will take yours lightly from between your fingers (ice melted, glass still half-full) and place it gingerly on the counter. He'll ask you what you'd like instead, pour you a Seven and Seven, put his arm around you and walk you out to the patio so you can scout the wildlife for yourself. Jensen will already be out there, smoking a cigar, and you'll infer from the geometry of his spine that you shouldn't disturb him. So instead you'll turn around, ready to head back into the study. Far, unfathomably far above you, the moon will send its reflection into the glass of the patio door and behind this reflection, back in the study you will see Pan, with something akin to pain in his eyes, raise your discarded scotch glass to his nose and inhale so deeply you can see his rib cage rise and fall, then flick his tongue into the liquid for a moment before tipping the remains down into the sink.

It takes a special kind of idiot to get drunker than his client and apparently you are exactly that idiot. Because after countless Seven and Sevens, you are buried deep in the soft leather of Pan's armchair, a throne so large it makes you feel like Alice, your legs dangling off the edge. You are sleepy, warm, numb. Somewhere just outside your line of sight, Pan and Jensen are talking, but in your condition you get only fragments that you can't pull into sense. At one point, Pan looks over at you. "I'm telling you," he says, voice rising, "he's perfect." When you smile at this and attempt a wave, Jensen looks away in disgust. "Maybe you're right," he allows. "God, just look at him." You try to struggle from the seat but succeed only in tipping your drink down into the folds of the armrest. The men stare at you for a moment. "Let's take a drive," Pan suggests, "and talk this over some more. Little pitchers have big ears, after all."

You get distracted watching dust particles. Pan comes over and rubs your hand gently until you tilt your head up toward him. "We're going away for a while now," he explains slowly. "Stay here and keep the fire warm, won't you?" He grins, all teeth, and then the two of them vanish and your eyes close.

"What're you supposed to be?"

It takes a very long time for your eyes to focus. When they do, it is on a belly button two feet from your nose. Inside the navel there's a golden pin with a tiny ruby.

"Jesus," a voice above the navel whistles. "They really did a number on you, huh?"

You follow the downy hair from the belly button up to a shiny tube top, filled out nicely, something straight from a music video, and then to a murine face with sharp eyes and enormous hair. Her earrings are as big as planets, circling her lobes in heavenly rotation as she leans forward to remove the near-empty glass from your hand and pluck one of its remaining shards of ice. This she drops into the loosened collar of your shirt. "There," she says. "That'll do you."

Everything feels like you're under water. The girl disappears and then returns with another glass. "Drink it," she commands, unclenching your fingers and then refolding them around the glass. "It's orange juice."

It might be. You'll have to take her word for it. But after a few minutes, you feel strong enough to sit up and take stock of the situation. Pan and Jensen are long gone, but with the snow and the moonlight you can't gauge what time it is. Everything is blurry. Nothing is where it should be.

The girl's name is Tina and she is twenty-three. She isn't particularly attractive but then at twenty-three, with that body, she doesn't really need to be. She is wearing a slip of a skirt, that lamé top. "Do you live here?" you ask her. "Are you the maid or the babysitter or something?"

She ignores your questions. She has a dishtowel and a glass of cloudy water and steps toward you before something in the pattern of the dishtowel diverts her. While you try to speak, she dabs your forehead with the towel, interrupting your verbal thrashing only to tell you what an idiot you are for trying to keep up with Peter.

"Who's Peter?" you ask, which makes her toss the towel onto your face.

"Still clinging to that juvenile nickname, his ridiculous games. Still pulling crap on poor guys like you." You're not sure you like the pitying tone, but it's clear that you deserve it. It's market price for her ministrations.

When you ask about Pan, she tells you, "It isn't what you think." But she doesn't say what it isn't and she doesn't say what it is either. She pushes you up to sitting and commands you, like a dog, to stay. "You'll be fine," she says, "or else you won't."

A few minutes (or perhaps longer) later, she comes back into the room and lifts one of your eyelids with her thumbnail. She stares into your eyes for a moment and then, in a single gesture, lowers your eyelid and slaps you across the face.

"Ouch." You recoil. Pure reflex. You hadn't felt a thing.

"Oh, good." She smiles. "You're alive."

"Barely," you reply. But the truth is that you're feeling a bit better. "That orange juice is a life saver. That and the dishcloth," you add shyly.

"Don't mention it," she says. Then she repeats this, more slowly, her tone almost plaintive: "Don't mention it. Okay?"

After securing your promise, she encourages you to get out of the chair, an act mustered with only moderate trouble.

"Let's take a walk," Tina suggests. When you suggest that might be a bit ambitious, she grins. "Dream big," she says. "I've got something I want to show you."

"Now?"

She's wearing a man's coat, far too large for her, too large even for the diminutive Pan.

"C'mon," she urges. "It's a full moon."

Fueled by alcohol, the moon, the sway of Tina's body draped in that giant coat, you follow her mincing steps across the snow to a thatch of trees a few hundred feet down the sloping yard.

"Where are we going?" you ask, although in this state you'd follow her forever.

"Right here," she says. "I come here sometimes to get away."

When you ask her again (sensing perhaps the time is right) about her relationship with Pan, she unfurls a leg from the bat wings of her coat and imprints an X into the snow. "This is the spot. Look up," she says.

The moon is full, just as she'd promised. And so heavy, so white in the night sky, it seems almost milk laden, the fairy tales you'd heard as a child somehow come true.

And then, as if in response (although you're never sure whether you'd spoken or not), Tina starts telling you about how when she was a little girl she used to wait for the winter, Northern Michigan, those nighttime storms, the way the snowflakes would look like they were coming straight from the moon, as if it was overflowing with them, as if it couldn't contain itself, as if it couldn't bear to keep itself from her for a moment longer.

The two of you stare upward together for a long time. Then Tina stamps her feet and pats at the pockets of her coat. "No cigarettes," she concludes sadly. "I guess your friend Jensen's a real Boy Scout, huh?"

You smile a bit. "I didn't recognize the coat. Looks different on you."

She affects a model's pose before laughing it off and pulling the coat tight around her. "Well, that's enough of my Little Girl Lost stories," she says. "If I don't watch it, I'll freeze to death, dreaming the world a way it'll never be."

You ask her how she got so smart, young as she is.

"I'm twenty-three, remember?" she corrects you. "And I'm getting cold. Coming?"

You'd like to, the promise of her retreating shape a powerful spell, but you decide to stay outside for a while. "I'm not done daydreaming yet," you call after her diminishing form. You watch her disappear back into the house, slightly above you on its incline, so that with the snow swirling like a cloud beneath it, it appears to you, in this drunken musing, this daydream, this strange and wonderful fantasy, like a castle in the air.

It's so beautiful, so disorienting that your chest tightens with loss of breath. You steady yourself against a tree, and the snow from its branches falls all around you, falling obliquely against the light from the house, amassing on your shoulders. You gather it into a ball and start to pitch it against the trunk of the tree, already into your windup when you stop short and then, looking both ways to be sure you are alone, lean forward shyly to offer the blue-white mass of snow a kiss, just to taste it, just to feel it melt on your tongue.

The front door opens in a rush, and Pan and Jensen are back, stamping snow from their boots and pulling off scarves and hats. Jensen leans in and brushes snow from the nape of Pan's neck and Pan shivers, his cheeks flushed. "It's a blizzard," he tells you. "A cataclysm."

You and Tina have been talking, it seems, most of the night. Between you, you have killed most of a bottle of orange juice. Tina is curled along the el of the modular sofa, watching all of this unfold, a single painted fingernail tracing the seam of the calfskin. When Pan steps toward her, she smirks. "Come any closer to this sofa, dripping like that, and your wife is going to have it reupholstered with your skin."

Pan considers this. "Nah. The way it's snowing, I'm afraid she and the kids will be stuck at her mother's house indefinitely." He hoots and his heels actually rise off the ground. "In—def—i—nitely," he elongates. Then he sits himself on her hipbone. Tina tolerates this until slush from his clothing beads down onto her exposed thigh and then she flicks him off. "Fly away, little bird. Fly far, far away."

Meanwhile, Jensen comes up behind you and takes the orange juice from your hand. "What is this?" he asks, taking a healthy swallow. When you tell him it's orange juice, he stares at you, inscrutable, and then hands back the glass. "Well," he says, glancing over to where Tina and Pan are reconfiguring themselves on the couch. "I don't mind telling you that you missed something unbefuckinglievable out there. Isn't that right, Pan?"

"It is."

"Something monumental."

"That would not be an overstatement," Pan giggles.

"Something unlikely to reoccur in our lifetimes."

"Not in your lifetime," Pan agrees.

"Nice skit," you mutter. "You work out this banter in the car?"

"Ah, the car," Pan says, his face dropping for a moment. "Remind me to tell you later about the car."

"Since you're feeling better," Jensen asks you, "would you be a doll and fix us a couple of drinks?"

He meant you but Tina's a saint. She gets up instead and pushes against Jensen for a second on her way to the office and the bar. "Jerk," she says.

"Hold the orange juice," Jensen calls after her.

When she comes back, it is with a glass of scotch for Pan, who thanks her with a nod, and a tall plastic cup of something indeterminate for herself. Jensen watches her strut across the room, an impenetrable smile on his face, and they keep eye contact throughout until she positions herself next to him on the sofa.

"You owe Pan here a thank-you," Jensen tells you. "He's taken quite the shine to you, convinced me to work with you a little longer."

"Nonsense." Pan smiles. "All I did was remind him that we all have our strengths. It's the good manager who recognizes and makes best use of them."

"He reminded me to whack you across the muzzle with a

newspaper," Jensen says. "Often."

You thank Pan. "I owe you one."

He gives you a crooked look in return. "If you insist."

"Pan here reminded me of a few principles I might have forgotten," Jensen continues. "The trick to business: find your horse and then ride him until he drops."

"Lovely," Tina says, giving him a cool look, unflattering in its appraisal.

"You're my horse," Jensen reiterates, "in case you missed that in your current state. Still a promotion from dog, I guess. You're like your own Chinese New Year."

That's what Pan reminds you of, the recognition coming to you in a rush. A jockey. It had been bothering you all night and into this morning.

"So we're agreed, then?" Pan asks Jensen and sits next to him on the sofa, crowding Tina closer.

"Why not? 'Give everything,' that's our company motto," Jensen replies.

"That's funny, it's sort of our house rule too. Wouldn't you say, my dear?" Pan asks Tina. When she doesn't respond, Jensen puts his hand on her thigh.

"There are times," he admits, "when I love my job." Then he looks at you. Hard.

You can see something pass over Tina's face, something like resignation, and you take a few steps toward the couch before Pan rises to block you.

"We're full up over here," Pan says apologetically. "And I'm afraid, after your earlier mess, I can no longer trust you with my armchair." Instead, his finger directs you to the floor. When you hesitate, he pushes his finger down harder. From this new angle the three figures on the sofa look huge, backlit majestically.

"What about you?" Jensen asks you, his fingers climbing Tina's thigh. "Don't you love your job?" With such a sour stomach, it takes a lot to reply. The house feels like it's shifting underneath you. "It has its moments," you say, finally.

Jensen's fingers start to climb up Tina's thighs. "And the fringe benefits *are* often excellent."

Tina swats his hand, hard, the sound like timber cracking, and you look down to see a red hand imprinted on her impossibly white thigh, like a Rorschach, like a face, with the silhouette of Jensen's two fingers like devil's horns peeking out from the top. "Asshole," she hisses.

Jensen rubs his fingers for a moment, then sticks them in his mouth. When they reemerge, he looks at them for a long second and then replaces them on Tina's thigh, tracing gentle, ever tightening, spirals over the red mark. He raises an eyebrow like Groucho, a trick you never knew he had, and quips, "I did say excellent."

Tina feints another swat, but Jensen doesn't move. They lock eyes. "Now that's two you owe me," Jensen says.

Tina pulls her leg away, underneath her. The early hours have stripped away any allure she may have had, and you can see the tiny hairs of her nose and the blood moving through the veins of her temples. When she looks down, it is with your own thousand-yard stare echoing in her pupils. There is somebody waiting for you at home and this tiny little comfort binds you together while you fall asleep.

The phone rings. Pan answers and all of a sudden everyone is moving. It is very difficult for your abused brain to process, so you sit quietly while hurried legs pass through your line of vision.

"It's one o'clock and his wife and kids are on their way home," Jensen shouts down at you.

"What day?"

"Sunday." Jensen pushes his socked toe deep into your ribs. "You missed church. Now help us clean up."

In the bathroom you splash water on your face, pulling down at your cheeks, exposing the very thin layer of white beneath the flared capillaries of your eyes. You stretch and coil your hands; red and splotchy, they function about on par with the rest of your body, which is to say petulantly, and only after debate.

As expected, the sun has melted most of the snow, leaving dunes on the lawn but the streets navigable. Unfortunately Jensen or Pan, whoever had been driving on their late-night jaunt, missed the street by a wide enough margin that most of Jensen's car is tucked neatly underneath a blanket of snow with only the rear bumper and tires peeking out. The four of you come at it from different angles, surveying, looking for some way to reason through the problem. Jensen opens the door and the snowbank calves down his leg. He looks up at you. "Well, that finishes the circle," and moves something around in his throat. Then he gets into the car. You can hear the hum of the engine and, if you reach your face close enough, you can see the tiny snow particles dancing up and down on the trunk. Unfortunately, the car itself is hopelessly entrenched, even when you all kick the snow off the tires, even when you drag the shovel from the garage and try to carve out a path. During the night, the car not only drove up over the concrete of the sidewalk but continued down the slope onto the lawn. It is a gentle slope, no more than a few feet, but enough to ensure that with all the snow the car cannot bully its way back in reverse. Jensen sticks his head out the open window. "Get to the front and push me out," he says to you.

"Why me?" you whine.

"Because you are the only person here that I can fire," Jensen replies and it is, you must admit, a very good answer.

You wade through snow no higher than your waist and dig to the hood of the car. Jensen hits the accelerator, hard. If his condition approximates your own, there is a chance that he has actually put the car in forward, yet when you shout this to him, he seems offended.

"It's in reverse," he snarls. "Trust me."

"Yes, absolutely," says Pan, safe and dry in the middle of the street, his energy faded but still present. "Why on earth would you not trust him? He, after all, who has proven himself so adept at the conducting of automobiles thus far. Whatever could have prompted you to doubt him now, young man?"

"Fuck you," Jensen replies.

"Watch the language," Pan cautions. "Think of the neighbors." And he is perfectly serious, and perfectly intimidating. Suddenly every inch the client.

Jensen motions to you with his left hand, "Push this thing out of here so we can get back to civilization."

But it is no use. There is nothing to brace against for leverage. Every time you push, you fall face forward into the hood, and every time Jensen barks at you to watch the paint. Twelve hours ago, six hours ago, this all might have been funny, but now nobody is laughing. By the time you give up, you are completely soaked and Jensen is furious. He threatens to fire you and you threaten to quit. He spits that you look like an idiot with your clothes dripping wet, and you remind him it is a two-hour drive back to the city and he has leather seats. "Don't worry," he assures you. "I'm strapping you to the roof like I would any other fucking bagged animal." Then both of you look around for Pan, but he has disappeared completely, leaving Tina, who leans against a tree smoking a cigarette.

Just when you think there is no solution, that you are going to have to wait until springtime, Pan emerges with two heavy iron chains. He tosses these casually onto the snow, the sound muffled, and slaps his hands together hard.

"What do you want us to do with those?" Jensen asks sullenly.

"I can think of all manner of things," Pan replies coldly. "I would try pulling the car as the pavement and curb will offer the traction that my lawn, or whatever is left of it under there, cannot. Alternatively, there is an oak just over the driveway. It might support this heavy chain were either or both of you to wish to martyr yourself over the loss of my business." He flicks something miniscule off his palm and then raises his hand. "Either way, I can assure you that if you are still present when my family gets here, I will make it my life's mission to ensure that both of you die paupers in some remote satellite office in the deepest South, glad-handing the Rotary circuit for leads. You've got approximately twenty minutes. Myself? I would hurry." Then he looks down the street and walks back into the house.

Miracle of miracles, once upon a time Jensen opted for the tow package, and now it is a simple manner to loop the chains through. You wait for Jensen, but he is still in the car staring forward into the snowbank. "You going to help me with this?" you ask.

"Give it a shot," he yells back. "I'll hit the gas."

With the chains and proper footing, you can feel the car rock on its haunches. It contemplates moving but the tiny hump of land, imperceptible in normal situations, the type of arbitrary landmass some fucking landscape architect put in a half century ago for texture (and you'd slit his throat but he's probably dead now anyway), is so close to the tire that the car can't work up enough momentum to get over it. You try again and again, the skin on your hands chafed and bleeding. After an effort so exhausting you can actually see stars in front of your eyes, you drop the chains and look in at Jensen, who is watching you from the sideview mirror.

"Let Tina hit the gas," you call. "I need someone strong to help me with this." And it is possible that he might actually have done it, gotten out of the car himself. When you think back later, his body language seems to prophesize an imminent departure from the vehicle. It is, by any account, the rational thing to do. And he might have done it had you not, in what must qualify as a substantial withdrawal from your near-infinite capital of stupidity, called out—to lighten the mood, to reestablish your rapport, "why do you think he had two giant chains anyway?"

The moment you say it, you know it is a mistake. You can see Jensen's back go rigid. It has been a very long twenty hours, and if you still don't know Jensen well, you know he can't have been happy with how things have played out. He says something, but your ears are clogged from the exertion. "Sorry?"

"I said fuck it," he says. "Do it your damned self."

"The guy's wife and kids are on their way," you point out.

"I don't care if the Apache fucking nation is coming down that street, I am not getting out of the car."

You find yourself talking like you might to a small child or a very large animal, "Pick up the other chain, put your back into it and let's go already. Tina can drive the car."

"Tina can pull the chain with you or Tina can disappear in a cloud of smoke. No kidding." He wheels around and frames his chin with both hands. "Look at my fucking face. This is it for me. I'm not moving."

The laws of the universe decree that shit flows downhill. You wrap the chains around your wrists and bark for Jensen to hit the gas. The pain is excruciating, but you can feel the car lifting. It is going to be one of those John Wayne moments, but your wrists and hands are slick from the water and the sweat and the blood, your tendons stretched and bulging, your muscles weakened by the weekend's labors, your veins still trafficking alcohol, and soon the car nestles gently back into the ditch.

It is enough to make you cry. The jerk of Jensen's head, the narrowing of his eyes in the rearview mirror. It doesn't matter if you cry anyway: with all the sweat, no one would notice, and you are pretty sure you'll never see any of these people, Jensen included, ever again. But then you feel Tina's hand on your shoulder as she stoops to gather her share of the chain. She weighs it in her palm and looks at your fingers. "We'd have better luck," she says, "if we had a better grip." She comes behind you and takes off your suit jacket and wraps it around your fingers. "At least it will hurt less," she says. You look over at her, at the thin slip of a girl with the thin slip of a dress. You fumble with the buttons of your shirt until she undoes them for you and then you pull the shirt from your shoulders and wrap it around her fingers. "Thank you," she says. Then you both pick up the chains and Jensen hits the gas and you can feel the car making its slow, inexorable climb up and over the hill.

When the car is safely to the street, Tina drops her chain. She looks down at the shirt on the ground by her feet and offers a small smile: "I think it's ruined."

"None of that matters," Jensen says. You can tell without looking up, something in his voice, that getting the car out has moved something within him too, that he is back, for better or worse, to the old Jensen. There is a sort of lightness in his voice as he speaks, "I'm never letting that shit on my seats. As the good man reminded me before, these things are fine Corinthian leather. Take off all your clothes, Buddy, even your socks and shoes. Wrap everything into a ball in the trunk. You can afford to sit naked for a car ride. Don't worry," he quips, talking to you but looking again at Tina, "I've got seat heaters."

You don't move.

"Drop the chains, ball up your clothes, and let's go," he says, getting back into the frontseat and revving the engine.

You want to. But you've been working the chain for so long that you cannot separate yourself from it. Your fingers, the metal loops, the frayed strands of your jacket are bound together as inseparably as a tree grows around a fence. When you try to pull them apart, the pain transcends your numbness and exhaustion. The harder you pull, the more acute the pain, until finally Tina calms you. "Stop," she tells you. "Relax." She makes gentle waves with her fingers in front of your eyes until your breathing stabilizes. "Just calm down," she says, and you can feel your body responding. It's strange but without the weight behind it, the chain goes slack and you can slide out quite easily.

On Wealth

Everything has been reversed.

Jensen, who takes lunch from twelve until half past every single day, has broken off a crown and fled to the dentist, leaving you at the desk at twelve thirty, when usually this time finds you hunched over a street vendor's cart selecting condiments. And so you are by yourself when Pan calls to arrange a trade.

"So nice to hear your voice," he sings. You haven't spoken since the blizzard. You don't know whether he's still working with Jensen or has taken his business up the street. He mentions a corporate bond. The company is expected to announce their earnings, one of those big moments that will either make or break them and no one quite knows which way it's going to fall. Pan offers you ninety-eight, a lowball number that casts his vote pretty firmly in the Chapter 11 camp. You ask him to repeat the price and he does so. Then he says "Fifteen million face amount." His voice sounds different somehow. "I've got a cold," he explains. "I'm working from home. Why? You want to bring me some soup?"

"I was just asking."

"Mother dearest, I wouldn't want you to worry. I have been drinking lots of fluids and at this very moment an electric blanket is licking its comforts onto my toes."

"That's fine," you say. "Ninety-eight?"

"Perhaps later, I may take a cup of soup and another dose of cough syrup. The stuff is most marvelous, really. An elixir. Highly recommended."

"I do remember your elixirs," you say cordially. The voice on the other end chuckles. Meanwhile, you check the number on the screen—it seems awfully low—four points off the market. He must really be expecting a blood bath. But then you remember Jensen's admonishments and, curious cat no more, you take the deal. "Feel better," you say before hanging up.

At ninety-eight, the offer gets snatched up in a hurry. "Seriously?" the trader asks. "Has he got an early look at their quarterlies?"

"Not that I know of."

"Tell the truth now: did he have a guy inside the room?"

"You'll confirm all fifteen million at that price?"

"I'll bid all you've got and more," Bill laughs. "Check under the sofa cushions. Nobody's talking ninety-eight. At those prices, I can lift like Atlas."

Bill is a likable guy. He's relatively new on his own desk, the rear guard of a horde you'd unleashed on Sammy's three months ago. He was the one who didn't say anything, the one the other traders delighted in making fun of, the one who got coerced into lassoing the heftiest of the dancers into submission. The one who'd passed out in the cab on the way home, the one whose new wife, as gaunt as a Modigliani, looked at you with something resembling hatred as you'd handed his body over the threshold of the walk-up. "He'll be fine," you'd assured her, and the disgust with which she'd waved you away from her stoop, the flick of her cigarette at your feet, the tenderness with which she'd cradled his head to protect it from the door frame, had a lot to do with your throwing him this gift.

"Done," you confirm.

"You know something," Bill says. "Three or four more like this one and I may start asking for you special. I may even put your number on my speed dial."

"Most kind," you say, and then you hang up and confirm with Pan.

"You're in," you tell him. It's true that some data has leaked, but it's all good news and the market has risen to 101, so for all the guy's scotch and square footage you can't make sense of this deal. "Ninety-eight."

"What the fuck are you talking about?" Pan's voice, in the few seconds since your last call, has dipped a register.

"Ninety-eight. Confirming the instructions for your trade."

"Ninety-eight, what the fuck kind of sick joke is that? I said 101, you fucking rookie."

It's funny, but Pan was the one trader who didn't swear, the one who sounded like he served in the House of Lords.

"You offered ninety-eight," you remind him. You are scrambling around for someone, Jensen, anyone, but the desk is like a ghost ship. "It seemed low to me, too."

"It did, did it? Now you're a fucking trader? Maybe that's what you should try next 'cause you won't be doing this much longer. Maybe lunch lady at the fucking school cafeteria. I said a hundred and one, mook. You aren't holding me to ninety-eight, that much I can promise you. Put Jensen on so I can get him to slap you for me."

"Jensen is off the desk this afternoon."

"That's right," Pan barks. "Tooth trouble, right? Well, time for me to start climbing the chain of command. Sit real still and hope no one notices you. Ninety-eight? I'm walking."

You race to the high rent area where Jensen's boss is on the phone. When he sees you, he motions with his hand and directs you to a seat. He doesn't say much on the phone, just grunts a few times and then says, "I understand. I'm sorry for the confusion and you have our word it won't happen again." Then he hangs up and turns up his lip. "Something you want to share with me?"

You start to tell him what happened, but he's already miles ahead of that and he cuts you off with annoyance: "he says you misunderstood, that he was saying a different coupon."

"Absolutely not. It was a consumer bond deal. Stupid, but simple."

"You didn't think to confirm the price with him?"

"I did confirm the price," you argue. "Twice."

"He's a valued client. You didn't think it might behoove you—behoove us—to point out it was *two full points* shy of the market?"

"I assumed there was information about to be leaked. And anyway, since when do we make sales decisions?" you ask.

"When you know the guy is wrong!" he hollers.

"Somebody's always wrong," you return, but it doesn't do any good.

"Some guy came in last month and told us he could wire the phones to record everything," the boss says. "Said that by 1984, three short years, everyone will have the technology. You know why I didn't do it?"

"Right now I have no fucking idea."

"Because you've got to disclose it to the clients, and I figured it would indicate a lack of trust, a lack of honor. I figured we didn't need it."

For a brief second you cling to the lifeboat that maybe Pan's company did take the guy up on his offer, that somewhere there is a recording, but then you remember that Pan was working from home, with a cold.

"I told the salesman," your boss continues, "that the Hasidic diamond merchants have been making billion-dollar deals for generations with only a handshake and that was the model to which we were aspiring. Now I'm thinking maybe of getting the recording guy on the phone."

"He said ninety-eight. Not a hundred and two, not a different bond. Maybe it was the cough syrup talking."

"I guess I should have done it," he mused, "but in our business, technology is the enemy. It's the technology that's gonna make us irrelevant," he says. "The robots are taking over." Then, "Call the other guy back and explain how you are a world-class fuckup. Beg him on your hands and knees."

You head out of the office as he calls after you, "Tell him your job is at stake."

"I'm sorry to hear that," Bill says. "I've already logged the trade."

"That doesn't mean anything."

"This was a big win for me," Bill says.

"I know it was a big win, I fucking handed it to you," you point out.

You can hear voices on his end, a curt discussion. After a few seconds Bill comes back on and says, "I'll take ninety-nine. That's the best I can do."

"I'm getting stuffed here," you say. The other guys at your desk are keeping a pretty good perimeter. "Usually people need to leave the city limits to get fucked this hard."

"I'm sorry," he says again, and you can hear that he probably is. You can also tell that there are other people on the line with him.

"I'll tell you," you try. "I can't even guess what something like this would cost in the backroom at Sammy's. Frankly, I'm not sure they've got a steer that big."

Silence.

"You remember Sammy's, don't you?"

"I'm sorry," he says coldly. "I'm obligating you to show me ninety-nine."

"I need this one," you say quietly.

"Join the club," he answers and clicks off.

By now Jensen has joined his boss. He has got a handkerchief pressed up against his jaw and his mouth is swollen. When he sees you he growls—literally growls.

You raise your hands. "He's holding me to it. I got him up to ninety-nine, but that's where he ends."

Jensen mumbles something you can't make out. He grabs a pen

and writes "quantity???" on the calendar ink blotter, so angry that the pen catches and tears into the months below. You tell him and he rolls his eyes skyward. His boss looks at him and the two start naming names, potential sellers, favors they can cash. You aren't even there. You don't exist. Finally they nod to each other and then look up at you. "Get out," the boss says. "Sit at your desk and we'll let you know the outcome."

"This isn't fair," you point out, and Jensen mimes a tear. When you tell him you're getting stuffed, he suggests both an alternate interpretation of the word and a locale.

"Pan is a valued client and a money player," his boss translates from behind him.

In the half hour it takes for all this to transpire, you catch a small break when the price dips back to a hundred and two. Jensen calls in a favor and gets another buyer to sell to him at 101.5, leaving you on the hook for the margin. All in, the tab comes to $375,000, roughly. There goes your bonus for this year and next. "Next year too?" you blurt. Jensen folds the handkerchief and then presses it to his cheek. "I don't think that's anything you need to worry about," he grunts.

Stagnation

All around you, people are working but your portion of the desk has gone as silent as a blighted field. Since the incident with Pan, you have become persona non grata among your colleagues (they would cringe to be thought your peers) and those traders who sent out tentative feelers in your first few months have crawled back into their holes. Your phone doesn't ring. Yesterday Jensen asked you to pick up lunch for everyone since you seemed to have some free time on your hands. You had. Each day, each hour, you can feel something slipping from you but you don't know how to staunch it.

Jensen, who had little enough time for you even in the first months, has almost none for you now. Twice you'd tried to talk to him about the Pan incident. "Nobody cares about that anymore," he groaned, looking over your head to the screen regurgitating numbers. "You are as good as your last trade. Take comfort in that."

You would, but it's been a week and that was your last trade. When you reminded Jensen of this, he shrugged. "Make something happen," he counseled.

"Like what?"

"Like a tuna salad on rye."

"Seriously," you said.

"Seriously. What's that old saying? From each according to his abilities…"

Debra seems to view all of this with a temperance you might not have anticipated. "It was a terrible job," she says. "It wasn't right for you."

When you remind her that you still *have* the job, present tense, the look she gives you makes you feel even worse. But at least she's trying, and you love her for it. You've been together almost a year, and this issue with Pan seems to have at least borne fruit in another facet of your life. It's like that expression your father used to scorn, "All things are in balance."

Debra, and Debra alone, will listen to you recount the trade. When you tell your mother about it, you can hear the jagged exhalation of her cigarette through the phone line. "What did I always tell you about finding a patsy?" she says. "Sometimes I think I talk for my own health." Then she tells you about problems with her homeowners association and a yapping Pomeranian next door. Then she warns you about too much sodium in your diet. Then she hangs up.

But Debra opens a bottle of wine and waits through the dissection. She sips slowly while you pull each word and phrase. "If only Jensen was at the desk," you moan. It is the type of misfortune that makes you want to decry the fates. Just simple bad luck.

"What bad luck?" Debra wants to know. "Nothing about this story makes me think of luck." She puts her glass down so quickly it threatens to topple. "An earthquake is bad luck. This is something else entirely." When you tell her you don't understand, she gives you an appraising look. "Just how good of friends would you say Jensen and this Pan asshole are, anyway?"

The second time you approach Jensen about the incident, he threatens to throw you through a window. "Look," he confides finally. "If I could fire you, I would, but I can't spare the time to train someone new right now. You put us in the red, get us out of it."

"How?" you ask.

He leans in close and whispers in your ear. "Make some trades."

"No one is calling me," you say, cognizant of the eyelash that separates your tone from a whine. "I feel stuck," you say.

"Then rob a bank. But do something."

Back at your apartment, Debra spending the night, you discuss the possibility of moving, a fresh start, while watching television on the couch.

"I thought you liked it here," Debra says. It is the middle of winter in Manhattan and your prewar pipes sound like they're the only ones who don't know that the war has ended. Every toilet three floors up sounds like heavy artillery on the beachfront. Through a missing slat in your closet, you can see the early morning go-getters rushing to and fro downstairs while you put on your clothes. All of this, ledgered with the lingering stench of sewage and the astronomical rents make a mockery of Debra's statement. You grin at her and she grins back, raising her arms in a flourish. She tells you about a cousin who runs a small brokerage in a small Midwestern town.

"No thanks," you say. She pulls closer to you on the sofa. "But I appreciate it. Hell, that's probably the first time someone has tried to help me since I've been here."

"It's a nice town," she says and you stare at her, incredulous, until you realize that she doesn't mean New York. "One of those bowling alley and fireman's parade jobbies."

You tell her about where you grew up, "probably the same blueprints," and she giggles. On your television a buxom man falls outlandishly into a fountain and emerges with his shirt soaking wet.

"There's something to be said for it," Debra says, then lists a few: "Lawnmowers. Potlucks. Lightning bugs. School plays."

"Nosy neighbors. Chain restaurants. All sorts of bugs. School plays," you retort. "Besides, I'm an institutional broker," you remind her, although in truth the switch to stockbroking would be as easy as passing a standardized test so simple it stands as a mere formality for anyone with functioning synapses.

"There's no failure in trying something and then rejecting it," Debra reminds you. "You don't always have to stick with a bad decision."

"You just want my apartment," you tease, although her place, down twenty blocks, is both nicer and cheaper than yours.

She rolls her eyes. "I'm being serious."

"Well, there's your mistake."

"Clearly."

"You are just trying to get rid of me," you tease.

Debra pulls back sharply. "No," she says, her hand finding yours. "That wasn't what I was doing at all."

"Cupcakes and picket fences? Thanks for the offer but I've seen that movie before," you say.

"Really, big shot? Then tell me how it ends." She swings her leg over yours.

Lord of Works

On the subway this morning, you sat across from a man dizzied by the world around him. He danced in harmony with the stops and starts of the subway car, seemingly unaware of the metal pole's assault on his body. At first you had assumed him drunk, but he was clean-shaven, in a heavy wool overcoat, dressed like everyone else on the train. Throughout, his hands rested peaceably in his lap. You found yourself staring at him. Not the usual half-glances of subway and elevator cars but the unapologetic gawking reserved for art galleries and strip clubs. When, following a sudden turn in the train's route, the man's body swayed toward you, your eyes met along a plane, and yet this produced no jolt of human contact. On his lips was fixed the rumor of a smile. He was lost in his own thoughts. Far gone. He was still sitting in exactly that manner when you got off and began the short walk to your office, and it was well into the morning rush before you stopped thinking about him.

Today marks the end of the second month of your ostracization following the Pan debacle, and in your most optimistic fantasies you wonder if perhaps this mightn't be some sort of hazing ritual. That would fit since Debra dubbed Jensen the overgrown frat boy and zerberts whenever you mention his name—like children do at a puppet show. Maybe this is simply a phase, an obstacle that Jensen, and his boss, and his boss's boss before him, a lineage all the way back to Crimble and beyond, had to overcome. The tiny sliver of this hope (embedded in your stomach) is enough to get you through the morning and you greet Jensen, when you pass him in the hallway, with a hail-fellow-well-met that earns a puzzled sneer, itself a vast improvement over his prior disgust. "Make something happen," he advises, brushing past you to pillage Sylvia and her digestive biscuits.

And so you do. Jensen's phone is ringing—easily distinguishable from your own since it's ringing—and when you pick it up a trader barks "Jensen?"

You correct him, tell him that Jensen is off the desk and you're handling things right now. Like an alchemist, you have stumbled on just the right combination of elements to push your bluff through. After the slightest hesitation the man, Davidson, whom you have heard Jensen mention in passing, puts in a bid at eighty-six. A very large quantity, a really big fish. Oh, what joy to start working the market, your fingers finding purpose at the keypad, your eyes scanning the blips of the monitor. It is a crowded market, and the guy's bid is too low to generate much interest. "It's ninety-two," one seller tells you, "and I don't see any reason for a tumble." As if he can't help himself, despite his audience, he asks: "Why? Do you know something?" With joy in your heart you inform him that you know nothing at all, that you are a mere conduit of the universe. "Like stardust," you tell him. "Let me know if the guy reaches into the nineties," the seller says and hangs up.

Other brokers are trolling the same market, but as you work the phones you can feel everything tightening toward you. You aren't thinking about Pan, or Debra, or the man from the subway. Instead you are thinking only about the commission this trade will bring, the staunching of the wound. You aren't thinking in allegory but you can see things just before they happen, a sort of Zen trance you hadn't known could apply to finance. When the buyer calls to raise to eighty-eight, you know what he will say before he does. "Eighty-eight might not get it done," you sing to him. "But I'll suss things out for you."

Meanwhile there's movement for the sellers too. Things are aligning for you. You find a willing seller at ninety and cover him without hesitation. "I've got you," you say and call Davidson back.

"It's ninety," you tell him.

"No soap," he counters.

"Alas," you say. "There's the rub."

"Speaking of rubs, I heard Pan gave you an unhappy ending," he says jovially.

"It's ancient history," you reply, and the easy way it passes your lips proves it's true. "Stuff of the dinosaurs."

His words tell you he's happy to hear it but something down in his gullet, something you wouldn't have been able to intuit this morning, tells you otherwise. He's a fucking shark. "It's the stuff of legend now," you say. "Things you outgrow at an age, like Santa or the tooth fairy."

"You mean there's no Santa Claus?" Davidson sniffs.

"No, Virginia," you reply. "A big fat man is not coming down your chimney and offering you eighty-eight. Take the ninety, big man."

"Ninety seems high to me."

"There's danger in complacency," you intone.

After a long pause: "Fuck it. Make the trade."

You do. Then you make another one. By the end of the day you've done your share and a bit more. "That wasn't bad," Jensen says, hearing your tale as you ride down the elevator. "Six more years of this and you might start paying off."

"The longest journey starts with a single footstep," you tell him, straight-faced.

"Yeah? Well, I'll see you tomorrow, Sensei."

A Man of the World

All of the planets are aligning in your favor. Last week you packed your belongings into a rental van and migrated the twenty blocks down to Debra's apartment and celebrated with Chinese food in bed. Now you sit up through the small hours recounting your victories, delighting even in the solace she offers your defeats. And these are easy to concede, dwarfed by recent victories. The long hours your work demands are a pleasure. You can still remember back eighteen months to the Pan debacle and now each ringing phone, each wheedled trade, each early morning feels like a gift for which you are eternally thankful. You've grown comfortable with the banter, the cajoling and needling that pushes buyers and sellers toward one another like teenage virgins. Evenings you apply the same tactics (you would blush to name them) at Sammy's and at other bars and nightclubs around town. Last weekend you took a group of traders on a riverboat cruise along the Hudson and then returned home to regale Debra with the stories of the women, the hijinks (no grander word would suit), the Coast Guard boarding party. She still does not approve—you can intuit this from her smiles—but she dispenses her indulgences all the same. Your cronies, as she is always quick to remind you, are nothing more than overgrown children.

It helps, of course, that the market is in unprecedented growth. Whereas once it grew in fits and starts, like a toddler, one glorious day this January it started scaling and that growth seems to be holding steady, up twenty percent from last year already. The rise is, you can't help but think, not only a cause of but a response to your own good fortune. "Look at it," you crow over the graph on the front page of the *Journal*. "It's a bright and glorious tower," you say to Jensen, to Sylvia, to anyone who will listen, and the constant ringing of your phone assures you that people are listening well. The planets, you explain to everyone, are aligning in your favor.

It is strange, but the intuition rooted in the desperation of that first lean year has grown into something formidable. Jensen warned you that the price on the trade doesn't matter and thinking about it is counterproductive, but over the past few months you realize this isn't true, or rather that this belief is Jensen's own deficiency, a limitation that, for all his enjoyment of scotch and indelicacy with women, will hold him from greatness. To know the market and its players is to understand how a trade will be consummated. It is true that you needn't know where the market will go in the days or hours after the trade is made, about *that* Jensen was undoubtedly right. But what Jensen doesn't understand, seems unable to grasp, is that knowing where the market will settle in the next two minutes is of incalculable value not only to traders but to brokers too. If you know the market and its players, you can anticipate the crosshairs and lead the participants to one another. Earlier this morning you secured a deal in a market as crowded as a Turkish bazaar by showing both buyer and seller a price midway between their margins. Each one had chewed on it and then agreed, as of course you'd known they would (as you'd pressed them to do), and the commission went to you rather than some passive sheep broker unwilling to make something happen. Make something happen. The tragedy of Jensen, you've come to understand, is that he underestimates the complexities of his own wisdom. It would be enough to make you pity him if the incidents of the previous winter did not still rankle deep.

"What's the good word?" Jensen asks, coming up behind you and swiveling your chair.

"Money," you suggest. "Money is always a good word."

"Yes it is," he grins back.

In a moment of benign curiosity you ask him, "you still trade with Pan?"

His face tightens for a second before loosening, "Every once in a while. He's gotten conservative on me. He's developed a hitch in his swing, can't pull the trigger."

"Poor Tina," you grin.

"Happens to the best of us," Jensen says. "Everybody gets old. Even Peter Pan."

"Not everybody," you say, and then grin. "The planets are aligned in my favor."

"Is that how it works?" he asks.

"Didn't anyone tell you that secret?"

"Nobody tells me anything," Jensen says. "Everything I know I've had to learn for myself."

"How sad for you," you say, not quite mocking.

"Yes," he says, not quite agreeing.

One day you will find yourself in Vegas and be astounded by the minutiae. In Vegas, everything is plotted. Floor plans maximize access to impulse slots. Mirrored ceilings imitate space. Rugs are chosen according to scientifically proven color-feeling relations. Vegas understands our neural impulses better than we do. Joyful jingling is amplified through brightly lit areas. You can't find a clock. Las Vegas makes you feel good about risking money. Las Vegas makes sin feel elegant.

All of these lessons, every one, are unheeded by Sammy's, your uptown haunt of choice, not quite Harlem but close. You take the traders there not for its perceived elegance but for its depravity—a condition it comes by honestly. The steak dinner at the best chophouse in town and then a trek way up into the three digits. The traders make faces at the peeling paint, the weathered posters on the doors. "You've still got your expense account, right?" they joke nervously. "If you think my wife is going to pay the ransom you obviously haven't met her…" You tell them the girls at Sammy's don't have the luxury of saying no. You wink. A slum like Sammy's a low-level trader can own for less than the Hennessy he'd been swilling an hour earlier. Once they get into the black light and the neon, they're yours. Sammy's: the sort of place where the girls gobble cigarettes, covered in towels, stretch marks, freaky circus hairy knees plainly visible. The sort of place where you could imagine things moving under the exhausted roast beef buffet. Sammy's, where the graffiti on the walls could school a marine, where a bad weekend's take gets the owner thinking of arson or donkey shows. Sammy's, one step up from a Jacob Riis photo spread.

You know the bouncer, of course, and the owner. The bartender waters your drinks while doubling your clients', pours sugar into the mixers to mask the bite. Each month you come in on a Monday midafternoon (seeing the place in sunlight is more than enough to cure any illusions), slip him a few bills, and look over the tabs.

Funny thing is that new traders want the bells and whistles but a guy who's been around five years has seen it all—sky's the limit— and the only thing left to show him is Sammy's—like a guided tour of Hell. First round of drinks comes with the hostess, who tells your patrons about the Champagne room, sequestered in the back. Champagne cocktails, you know from experience, are ginger ale and pink Chablis mixed with a baseball bat.

Tonight you've got four traders, mid-thirties guys, all from the same desk. They've got their Brooks Brothers suits, one of them failing to pull off red suspenders. Tomorrow morning they're going to take everything they're wearing (down to their silk boxers) to the cleaners, throw the shoes and socks in the dumpster. You've got the table right up front near the main stage. Any closer and you'd be at the stage with the dollar-bill crowd, slack-jawed, glassy-eyed, panting hard. Sniffing the dollar bills, adjusting their pants. Other than you that's Sammy's regular clientele: the fat guy who stares into gym club windows, sweating just from standing outside.

The dancer is an older, not-even-trying blonde. From your seat her skin looks unhealthy, but again it could be the light, which dyes everything the color of fly paper. In this light every thought you have makes you feel depraved. You feel rotted walking to the bathroom, like you'll leave skin on the sink top, and you wish that beer bottles came hermetically sealed even while you know that it wouldn't help. Sammy's is the hot zone. Trader to your left has a table dancer and from your angle you can see underneath her breast where she had a mole removed. Cancers must die for this sort of habitat.

The dancer's name is Lorraine and she's on again, off again with Jesse, the bouncer. You've spoken with her in the daylight when you've gone in to settle the tabs. As she gets up to leave, you exchange a smile and she slinks over to another group of regulars, a table filled with Japanese businessmen. They've been here every night for the past month, all of the nights you've been here plus (Jesse assures you) the rest as well. There's six of them and they play elaborate games involving shots of vodka, dice, and pornographic magazines. One of the men is younger than the others. Every night he looks embarrassed to be there, and the other men shift attention toward him, paying for his drinks and dances. They toast Yoshiro promptly every hour. The first night they came, you assumed it was his bachelor's party. Now you don't know what to think.

Gradually each of your charges disappears into the Champagne room with dancers, and Lorraine comes by to take a breath. Another girl, new, dances her hips up against you and is about to start the hard sell when Lorraine leans in and whispers a few words in her ear. The girl nods, and then sits. "I'm Sapphire," the girl says. She must have worked somewhere else before Sammy's—the dancers at Sammy's tend to have names like Esther, Georgina, Hallie. You look Sapphire up and down, wondering why she slid all the way down the pole to Sammy's. You can't see any scars.

When they're not working the tables, the two women take turns sitting with you and talking. Each of the conversations is different and, over the course of the night, rather involved, and the effect is disconcerting, like a chess expert playing ten boards blindfolded. With Lorraine you discuss the upcoming football season. An uncle of hers has tickets to the Jets and is forever promising to take her. "But you know promises," she shrugs, and this, for all of your hundreds of hours at Sammy's, is the first thing to shift something inside of you.

Sapphire, meanwhile, tells you about *Last Night's Makeup*, the memoir she is currently finishing. She discusses her publisher, problems with the cover art. "Agents and pimps," she says with a smirk, but she's fifteen years light on Lorraine and can't quite pull off the same world weariness. Still, the book does sound interesting. "I did a stint at Rutgers," she confides, leaning in so close you can smell the strawberry oiled into her skin. Then the boss taps her on the shoulder and points to his watch. "Off at eleven," he says. "Just like I promised."

She had been in the middle of a sentence, but with that tap her entire body went off shift. Even the way she pulls herself from her chair is different, although you can't quite figure out how. You offer a goodbye, but she's already long gone.

Later, home, with Debra curled up in your bed, you tiptoe into the bathroom. There was something you cannot quite articulate about Lorraine and staring at yourself in the mirror, the unflattering overhead lighting; you attempt to break it down. Her weight, her smell, her substance. But also the way she approached the traders with a certain amount of grace, the way she blotted the top of her beer bottle with a napkin between sips. Sapphire was younger, her skin and body tighter, her legs longer, her skeletal structure prouder. But that night, hunched over the toilet, perfectly quiet so as not to disturb Debra, it is Lorraine you find yourself imagining. After all, you know something about promises too.

The guy on the ferry takes your money and motions you down deep into the maw, into its endless procession of cars and vans. You choose a line, ease up to the back of a Pacer and kill the engine. Looking over, you ask Debra if she'd like to go up to the deck. She agrees and pulls down the vanity to freshen her makeup. By the time she's ready to go, there are cars stretching behind you. The exhaust fumes worm into the back of your skull and play at your gray matter.

Upstairs, on deck, you can see across to the distant shoreline. More bad air: gull shit and German tourists, but a welcome change after the parking level. You imagine the sea salt purging your brain. Debra has found a spot over the railing, looking backward as the ferry pulls away from the dock, the giant engines churning out oil-red water. On the bank, a worker unties the heavy jute line. The ferry rumbles through the strait like the parking lot it is. Debra waves to the man who has untied you. He reaches up and wipes sweat from his brow with the base of his leather glove. When Debra waves, he grins, and then, impishly, takes off his glove and raises it to her. Next to you, she giggles. When you cough she turns. "The people here are so nice." Her cheeks are flushed from the breeze and the briny air.

You both stand quietly for a few minutes, listening to people's chatter. There are kids running across the deck, parents in pursuit. Somewhere, someone is playing at a guitar, badly. It's already five p.m., the day's last ferry. You both overslept, emerging well past checkout time at the tiny lobby where the clerk greeted you sheepishly. "I couldn't bear to wake you," the old woman admitted. "Not on your honeymoon."

As it is, you are lucky to have made this ferry at all. You will reach the other side past nightfall, long after your dinner reservations have come and gone. The guidebooks were universal in their praise of the dill salmon (a perpetual favorite), so barring a kindhearted maître d', you will never get another table. On the car ride over, Debra ran her finger lightly over your jawline. "Don't worry about it," she said. "Go with the flow for once." She's wearing a sun hat you'd declared optimistic for early spring, but for most of the day the weather has sided with her. On the boat, the wind picks up and she stands with one hand draped over the rail, the other across the hat's brim, keeping it down. A strand of brown hair has escaped from her bun and dances around her ear. You move closer and put your arm over her bare shoulder and lean in to her. "Go with the flow for once," her tone meant to convey that she forgives you this alteration to the schedule.

You stand at the railing for two hours, feel the air lose its weight, heat, humidity, feel it turn cold against you. The land from which you are coming gets smaller, but that land to which you are going gets no larger. Seabirds play on the whitecaps generated by the wake, chirp greetings to one another, connect and then separate just as diffidently, while on the wooden slats a young woman passes with two cups in her hand. Without turning, Debra asks whether you want a drink, but the complimentary champagne from last night still sits in your stomach, rocking with the same uneasy gait as the ferry in mildly choppy waters. Slowly you find your sea legs, compensating with each step as you walk to the bathroom. There, you drink tepid water from your cupped hand, nausea suggesting itself and then retiring. You look into the water-spotted mirror above the sink and pull at the skin around your neck. The wedding ceremony made you feel old. If, as they say, this is entirely natural, it does nothing to dull the sting of it. You tell yourself you are only thirty-eight, barely kissing middle age. It means nothing, you tell yourself. You tell yourself not to worry. To go with the flow. When you return from the bathroom, Debra is standing alone, framed by the sea and the sky, her legs elongated like a crane's. When you come behind her and place your hand on the small of her back, she stiffens before undulating into you. A nearly inaudible sound escapes her lips as she reaches a slender hand out to the horizon and extends a finger. "Look," she whispers.

Across the water the sun is combusting. The pinks and reds and oranges are unreal, or hyperreal. If these are the colors of nature, then someone has been lying to everyone. It is as though the particles of the sky have burned themselves out, the fire that changes everything, the embers floating gently above the waves. Surely this sunset is a gift meant only for you. No one could bear to receive it twice. Debra's fingers feel for yours and find them, entwine and conjoin. Everything is new to you. Everything is a discovery.

The Familiar Lord of Failure

Winter in New York and you've got money in the bank. You've been with your company four years and your bonus, after the two years of forfeiture, comes laden as a Christmas goose. The bonus is very nice indeed, especially with a baby on the way, but your job's benefits extend beyond its income. Each trade is like dipping your hand into a stream to maneuver the current. You explain this to Sylvia one afternoon, tilting your hand just so, and she reaches up to trace the line cutting diagonally down your palm, her finger skimming lightly down onto your wrist. She looks up at you shyly and then disappears back into Crimble's office. Yes, things are looking up.

Before lunch, you bully two traders into a lucrative sale and reward yourself with a steak. You're not so old that you can't remember your early twenties and you smile at what you might have thought at twenty-four, fresh out of college, had you learned that one day in the not-too-distant future, red meat would constitute a reward and hard alcohol a medicine. Since you hit thirty, you've been diligent about your annual physical, and at this past one your doctor worried over your cholesterol, particularly after hearing about your father's congestive heart failure and early death.

"This kind of thing is bred in the bone," the doctor says while offering you a pamphlet advocating dietary changes. "Less red meat. They're doing good things with pork now you might want to explore."

"You haven't heard?" you ask, surprised. "I'm going to live forever."

He ignores you. "Maybe jog in the park in the mornings." He takes out a pen and circles your cholesterol on a graph, trending to the upper right quadrant, looking for all the world like the stock market. "The numbers don't lie," he warns.

You tell him not to worry. Numbers lie all the time.

Anyway, it's a lunch portion of steak, no bigger than a paperback novel, and you're sure to wash it down with plenty of water and a generous bourbon to thin the blood. Debra is fasting through most of her third trimester, so dinner has become a makeshift affair. Besides, every month they cure something new and you've got at least twenty years before your arteries start catching up with you. Plenty of time for science to pull another rabbit out of its hat. You enjoy the steak and that's the important part. The day you start thinking about what's going to kill you is the day you start swimming upstream.

After lunch you get a call from Davidson, who has become something of a regular pet. He puts in a bid at sixty, a large quantity but nothing extravagant. "Let's dip our poles," you respond. You quickly focus in on a seller willing to offer sixty-six. You know both of these guys so well, you've grown so familiar with their habits, that the entire procedure plays out in your mind long before it concludes in reality. It isn't boring (the stakes are too high for that, and the commissions too rich), but it has become predictable. They'll meet at sixty-four after some teeth-gnashing on the seller's end, and next weekend you'll reward Davidson for his loyalty with something special, although special is getting more and more scarce in the arms race of depravity that constitutes your nightly obligation. Debauchery is starting to wear a bit thin. But what are the options? Nobody moves over to trading, and anyway your company isn't equipped for it.

Davidson and the seller (a guy named Franks, who sweats so heavily there's jostling to avoid sitting next to him at clubs) do their dance for a while, circling like bears. By now it's the middle of the afternoon and you're ready for a nap. You always feel it at about this time. Naps are a funny thing, one of those habits you resisted so desperately as a child and yet the most precious of commodities now that you're older. A strange phenomenon, you can't think of much else like it. Eggs maybe (your cholesterol hovering over you again). Davidson rises to sixty-three as predictably as any rube and Franks coughs out sixty-five on his end. These few minutes are always a grind, listening to both of them complain like old women with creaking joints, *I'm not sure I want that price.* Sometimes it feels like you're pushing product at Sears. But when it works, it feels like three-card monte. Some part of you wants to get them on the line together and lay it out for them—explain to Davidson that he is fairly axed and therefore pushed to rise to sixty-four while reminding Franks how he read something last week about this market and how it's in for a bit of a drop and anyway he's given less ground than the other guy and has some sense of obligation not to leave everyone with blue balls. In ten seconds you could make everything happen, but instead you need to wade through these soporific minutes—not many, but enough, with their attendant snivels. "If you don't like the game," Debra counsels at night, her patience not infinite, "get out of it."

Davidson rebuffs the sixty-five as you'd known he would. "I can't do sixty-five," he says. "My wife would have to start looking for a job again if I did sixty-five." He pauses and you can hear the sound of keystrokes over the phone. "I'm off at sixty-five, sorry," he says.

You look at your watch. It's been nearly five minutes completely wasted. Jensen is sitting idly in his chair, looking out the window. In the last months, seemingly overnight, his facial muscles have started to sag. Alert, he tightens his jaw, which preserves the illusion, but if you catch him at rest, the weight of his years betrays him. From the reflection off the glass you can see into his eyes but nothing much is happening there—a daydream rather than a scheme, you conclude. He was out late last night with clients and confided in you half an hour ago that he was dragging. Probably he too would appreciate a nap. He seems at peace, his feet elevated on the radiator. You cup your hand over the mouthpiece and bark at him, mostly in jest, "make something happen!" His legs shoot up and he falls back on his tilted chair before steadying himself with an arm. He gives you a ha-ha look and directs his attention to the computer monitor beside him. The sudden exertion of steadying himself must have tweaked his back and he rolls it with his palm while he reads, his jawline ratchet tight.

You call Franks to try to resuscitate the deal and inform him that Davidson isn't biting at sixty-five. "Oh well," Franks mutters. "It looks like it's not in the cards for today. I appreciate your help and I'll speak to you when I speak to you."

"He'd take sixty-four," you prompt. This is, strictly speaking, not your purview, but every broker makes his own rules and your volume in the past six months gives you leeway a rookie might not enjoy.

"I'm sure he would," Franks says. "But that's theoretical since I ain't offering it."

"Give him sixty-four, send him home happy," you suggest. This is the delicate part, knowing how hard to push and where. When you explain to someone at a party what you do for a living, they look at you sadly, like you're a middleman. They look at you like you do nothing at all. They have no fucking idea how hard it is to pull the strings, what it takes to make someone dance for you.

"Not today, my good man." But there is something down deep in him, something he isn't going to be aware of for another thirty seconds, some portion of self-doubt getting itself mobilized. Thirty seconds and he's going to be grasping at sixty-four like a life raft. No one likes to push themselves away from the table. Thirty seconds. After a few moments he asks you, "He'd take sixty-four?" and you have to restrain your own voice to tell him you'd bet on it. He coughs again and says, "nah, sixty-five firm. Live to fight another day, right?"

You make a lot of trades a day, many of them bigger than this one, but for whatever reason you're getting annoyed. Right now Franks is running the numbers on his calculator, wondering about global holdings, thinking about that article he read. Right now he's reconsidering, wiping his brow with whatever beach towel he must keep wedged under his desk. Right now he's reaching for the phone...

And it rings. Sometimes you make yourself feel awfully good.

But it isn't Franks, yet. First it's Davidson, who has been having the same thoughts on his own end. "Where's he at?" he asks you.

"Sixty-four," you tell him, and yeah, sure, it's a bit of a slip but it's more or less true.

"I'll do sixty-four," he agrees, letting the air out of his chest. "I'm locked in at sixty-four."

You wish him the best, tell him you've got something really special planned for the weekend. "Oh yeah?" he says. "Bring a raincoat," you reply. "Ooohh." He laughs and hangs up.

Now all that's left to do is to wait for Franks to call back. Of course, if he doesn't, you're in dutch, but that isn't any kind of option. You figure it at ten seconds. You count down slowly, almost like an incantation, but when you reach zero the phone doesn't ring. You smile, thinking it must take Franks a bit longer to do all sorts of stuff with those jelly-roll fingers slick from sweat, so you factor in ten more seconds.

Still no call.

You pick up the phone to reassure yourself with the dial tone and then hang up. Jensen cocks his head but you ignore it. You count to five one more time, slowly, and then dial Franks yourself. Fucking sheep couldn't find their way out of a pen with neon billboards. Cows won't cross a yellow line because they think it's some sort of insurmountable barrier. And then there's traders, who make them all look like Lewis and Clark.

Franks seems surprised to hear from you. "What's the good word?" he asks.

"Sixty-four is a very good word for everybody," you remind him. "Davidson will do it and so should you. Let's make this happen—

I've got a soiree planned for this weekend that makes Mardi Gras look like Lent."

"My wife and I are out of town this weekend, celebrating ten years of matrimonial bliss," Franks says.

"Next weekend, then," you say. "Hell, the entertainment will be slightly less barely legal but I don't suppose another week of growing ever hurt a girl that age."

"That sounds good," he says. "But I'm going to pass on this one."

"You've stopped liking women?" you ask, letting your tone get rich with merriment.

"The women I like, the sixty-four I don't," he says. "I'm walking away from the deal."

"You can't do that."

"Of course I can," Franks says. The idiot is confused why you care so much. "Are you hurting for commissions?" he asks you. "Grapevine says you're on a hot streak."

"It's not the commission," you tell him. "I just hate to see you make a mistake with this one."

"So I make a mistake," he says. "Who cares? I make fifty mistakes a day and get fifty-one calls right. What the fuck, this isn't life or death."

"Then make the deal," you push. "Make something happen."

And it might be that he will say yes. It might be that he is crumbling. It might be that everything will be okay but then the market shifts—this fucking deal taking longer to navigate than the Panama fucking Canal—and the price jumps two ticks and you are getting your info just as Franks is getting his (and somewhere Davidson too) and you can just barely hear his voice an ocean away as he chuckles, "Looks like I dodged something on that one, huh, buddy? See you next weekend—make sure you save something fresh for me." Your ears pop.

Then he hangs up.

You're on the hook for it. All of it. At sixty-four per.

Nagasaki.

Celtic Cross

All Light, All Sweetness

Debra sits cross-legged on the hospital bed, trying again to nurse. Cassie, the baby, your baby, newborn and pink and wretched, roots along the nipple, scouting with her tongue. There is a single light behind Debra's head, ten watts, but enough to make Cassie shut her eyes tight. The birth, after the classes and books, after the birthing plans and negotiations, was ultimately an emergency C-section—the first consequence of Cass's lifetime of impatience. Long hours of waiting, of labor intense then stalled. You'd been there to administer ice chips and meaningless directions. At first Debra had seemed tolerant, even loving, hopeful at the day's promise, but with the long hours her eyes turned hard. It had taken you an unnaturally long time to realize that your true purpose in this event, your only useful function, was to serve as focal point for her anger, a divining rod to draw it safely away from the vulnerable child (Debra running through her progressions: the sweet darling, the innocent babe, the beachball-headed creature so devoid of instinct that she'd rather wrench her neck toward the action than live, God forbid she should miss anything). And so your ridiculous commands to push, the hand grasped and swatted away, and grasped again until the swearing was retargeted at you: the ineffectual who, any second now, is going to get that flyaway look on his face and leave me to do everything alone, the only guy in this room with nothing to contribute, a man so impotent it seems almost a miracle, almost a curse, that he could even have sired this baby. The doctors and nurses, discreet behind their surgical masks, checking monitors, reading bips and beeps as divinations.

Finally they made the decision to operate, the orderlies appearing from nowhere to wheel the bed into a sterile room, the doctor's warm hand on your shoulder to explain hospital procedure, unnecessary risk of infection, the promise to come get you as soon as it was finished. Your whispered encouragement to your wife to be brave, be strong, and her gaze above your head to the nurse: *Would somebody get me away from this fucking guy?*

"It's the morphine," an orderly assured you half-heartedly. "Mind your toes."

Within seconds you were alone in the room. One of the sheets had been pulled to the floor by the cart's wheels, so you walked over to the corner and unbunched it. It was sweat soaked, sour smelling, stained with urine and tiny droplets of blood. You folded it carefully and put it on the chair. Then you began pacing.

You counted each tile along the floor, fourteen along the far wall, eleven on the bisection, worrying your fortunes like beads. You paced a deliberate course, stepping only on each third tile, gathering speed with practice. Periodically, doctors rushed by the open door, pausing to shake their heads at your calisthenics, and then disappeared to answer pages and alarms. One hour passed. Then another. And then the nurse with the indistinct Eastern European accent reappeared, asking whether you would like to meet your daughter.

The Lord of Defeat

"The first thing you need to understand is how lucky you are that I'm even agreeing to see you," David says. "My cousin Debra, she's good people. You, I'm not so sure about."

"Some days, neither am I."

This seems to placate him a little bit. David is about fifty, five years older than you, and the years haven't completely swaddled the man he must have been in college, broad shouldered, another Midwestern All-American going to seed. He reminds you of Gregson, your old high-school nemesis, but in some ways the similarities are too easy. Here, in this small branch office of a second-rate stock brokerage with its hanging lights and cigarette-yellowed walls, he reminds you mostly of how far you've fallen in the six months since you'd cratered in New York. Since Nagasaki.

"You're good to work in this state?" he asks. You tell him that you are.

"Series seven, series sixty-three didn't molest you too much?"

"No." The series sixty-three is a ridiculous exam. At your old job, the standard joke proposed that passing the series sixty-three is as easy as completing the following sequence: sixty-one, sixty-two... You'd tell him this but who knows? Here in the hinterlands they might treat the series sixty-three, with its pedestrian computations and black-and-white ethics quizzes, seriously. You've been away from the Midwest for two decades but you still haven't forgotten people's affection for rules and the reverence they attach to following them. The land of good citizenry. Eisenhower folk, even a quarter century later.

Another man comes in, tan and slender, his age bridging yours and David's. "This is my partner, Bruce," David says.

"You're the guy from New York, right?" Bruce asks. He has unusually white teeth. He leans in confidentially. "Let me ask you something. How did you ever avoid going to jail after that stunt you pulled? How did you keep your licenses?"

Your lips pull up in a wry smile. "The fates must have been aligned for me that day."

David scowls.

"Seriously," Bruce presses.

"I must have a guardian angel," you say.

"Yeah, and her name is Debra and you'd be wise to remember it," David concludes. "I'm going to give you a desk, a phone, and a list of names. And every week I'm going to go over your records personally to confirm that you aren't doing anything cute. No churning. Nothing too New York."

You tell him you are from a town four hundred miles from here, but he isn't mollified. "New York certainly made quite an impression, then. Nothing too cute," he reminds you.

Bruce shakes your hand with a chamber-of-commerce grip. "Glad to have you aboard," he says.

You thank him and then extend your hand to David but he snarls at it. "Something you need to remember," he says. "I'm giving you this job for one reason and one reason only: to coerce Debra to move back here. Frankly, my seventy-one-year-old mother told me I wasn't welcome for Thanksgiving if I didn't give you this job. So you owe everything to my grandmother's fertile ovaries seven decades ago, and not to any fancy schemes you might be thinking of pulling.

Is that understood?"

"Come on," Bruce interrupts. "I'll show you around."

"They say the first day is always the roughest," you joke, when you get to Bruce's office.

Bruce smiles sympathetically. "The thing you need to understand is that David is a real straight arrow, a real moral absolutist."

"How about you?"

He extends his palm into the air and undulates his wrist. "I'm more fluid." He props his feet up on his desk and lights a cigarette. He offers you one and you take it.

"That's another thing different in New York," you mention, inhaling. "Getting harder to find a place to smoke."

"Really," Bruce asks. "I got the impression they were cuckoo for the cancer stick in the big city." He grins his boyish grin at you. "But I've only been there a couple of times to meet with corporate."

"Things change pretty quickly," you apologize.

"Then I guess I'd better start cutting back," he says. You can't figure out how a smoker can keep his teeth so white. Are they dentures? "What they're doing in New York ought to reach us in, what, ten years?"

You tell him that was your experience, growing up.

"Real rube in the big city when you got there, right?"

The funny thing is that you weren't. Of course, four years in Boston and then another ten in Seattle helped. But nobody in the city really had time for you, which was problematic when you needed the right cross-town bus, but it also meant no one held it against you that you didn't know the schedule for the right cross-town bus. Bruce nods at this. "That was my experience, too," he says. "Probably that hayseed notion went out when clothing got standardized. I mean, a pair of black shoes is a pair of black shoes, right?"

"It is," you say and smile away Jensen's voice in your ear. Your shoes at this very minute likely cost more than Bruce's entire outfit with his dandy department-store tie. One fucking trade goes south and you're cut loose to swallow fashion advice from the Duke of J.C. Penney Activewear.

Outside Bruce's window there's a public park and behind it the embryo of a downtown core. In the park a child tries to shepherd the pigeons while his mother laughs. Bruce's finger taps lightly on the filter of his cigarette. "You'll like this town, it's got all sorts of stuff to offer you." Then he gives you the name of a realtor. "She's high wattage," Bruce warns. "But she knows what's in your heart before you do."

"Debra is anxious to move back," you tell him. "She'll be excited to hear the good news."

"Knowing David's relationship with his mother," Bruce says, cocking an eyebrow, "I'm laying odds that the information has already reached her."

"I guess not everything takes ten years to get from New York, huh?" you smile.

"I guess not. Well," Bruce says, lifting and then dropping a stack of papers, "I should start shuffling some papers before people realize I don't do anything important around here."

You thank him for the tour and the realtor's name, and he tells you that if there's anything you need, "like the route of the cross-town bus," you should let him know. "Tell me when you and Debra get settled," he says, "and I'll set something up with my wife."

"That would be great."

"No kidding, regardless of how you came to us, I'm glad you're here. It will be nice to get some new ideas in the office."

"But nothing too New York," you promise him.

"No," he says. "Heaven forbid."

KING of SWORDS

Values

The division of labor is simple. Debra has secured the mortgage, scouted neighborhoods. You have hired Bruce's realtor. "I'm glad," he says when you tell him. He's distracted, jamming a magazine of staples into a stapler. "She'll walk you through everything."

New to the town, new to home buying, the entire thing feels like an adventure. Cassie, in the New Age papoose along your hip, loves the hotel room. She squeals in delight when the elevator greets you at your floor. "Of course she does," Debra says scornfully. "This crappy efficiency reminds her of New York." You are standing in the hotel lobby waiting for the agent to pick you up. She has promised a long day. "When I think," Debra shakes her head, "of all those months and years paying rent, the cockroaches, the bums…" her voice trails off. Debra is not unhappy to have left the city. But you are ambivalent. It is true there were things you could have done without: the old-fashioned steam heater that offered only intemperate extremes, the dolor of the lobbies, the commute in the early morning, the crescendo of traffic noise that, despite assurances from the natives, you never quite got used to. But there were more things, many more, a laundry list of things that you appreciated about living there, and in the valuation of checks and balances you would never have moved.

This new town, quiet, Midwestern, green and gridlike, reminds you a bit of a child's map of a town. Things are too linear, too discrete. But when you try to explain all this to Debra she scowls, "When I think that every month's rent could have been a mortgage payment, I want to stand in front of you and put a bullet through my own head." The realtor has promised a long day and you hope not to spend it fighting.

In the end you and Debra don't spend the whole day fighting, allied as you are against the common enemy of Pat Hart, realtor, whose card exhorts you to remember that she puts her Hart into her work. Pat Hart seems almost too easy—her helmet hair, southwestern jewelry, processional gold Cadillac. "Just move the golf clubs over," she screeches, her voice box jammed on a single unfortunate register. "I borrowed a car seat from my grandson." You and Cassie fold into the back, Cassie in a forward-facing seat too large for her, your body buried underneath the weight of Pat's clubs. You suggest maybe the trunk might be a better place for the clubs, "I'd hate for the baby to scratch them," but Pat says no, her husband used the car this morning to pick up supplies from the hobby shop and the trunk is full. There is a giant wooden club head inches from Cass's cheek, and when Pat sees you eyeing it she smiles from the rearview mirror, "Last year we were playing golf until November. Bet you can't say that in New York." You tell her you don't play, never learned, and she shakes her head sadly, "New York. I suppose they can have it." A pause and then brightly, "Did you know that the ice cream sundae was invented right here?"

Debra sits in the frontseat with a notepad in her lap. Whenever Pat turns to speak, Debra looks out the passenger window and makes notes about the coffee shop, the park bench, the lamppost just passed. From your vantage point in the backseat, the ruse looks incredibly obvious (it also looks like the two women are watching a particularly rousing tennis match), but perhaps Pat Hart and her commission are inclined not to notice. Cassie fusses, her head lolling, and you find a burp cloth in the bottom of the bag and wedge it around her neck.

"Well, isn't she just darling," Pat coos, in the exact same pitch you will discover she uses for smaller two-bedrooms. "My daughter used to be a tiny mite but now she teaches third grade." You smile and watch as, out of the corner of your eye, Debra's hand makes meticulous note of a bus stop. "We'll swing by the school later," Pat assures you. "We've had national commendations, you know."

You had thought, coming from New York, that your money would stretch astronomically in this smaller town, that a modest mortgage would secure a castle, that a dinner out here would undersell a cup of coffee in Times Square. You were under the impression that housing prices and cost of living were the modern milk and honey. By noon you are thoroughly discouraged. The houses are fine—no better. Antiseptically new and adequate, but small, with postage stamp yards. "We were hoping for something bigger," you had suggested. "Perhaps a larger yard for our daughter?"

"We can do that," Pat said, nodding vigorously, her helmet bobbing on her hairline. "but we're going to need to start looking at older homes. Is that a problem?" She looked hard at you for a moment. You told her no, before she patiently explained that an older home requires a certain proficiency with tools and plumbing. "Let me ask you," she said, her tone as gentle as her claxon would allow, "is your idea of a good weekend refitting a sump pump?"

So newer houses it is. At lunch you talk to Pat and try to feed Cassie while Debra uses a pay phone to try to secure a larger mortgage. She comes back with her jaw fixed and tells you, as a means of telling Pat, that there isn't a lot of wiggle room. "There's lots more we can do," Pat assures you. "If we can't get older or smaller, we can go farther away from the center of town."

"The center of town," Debra says in a dull voice. It is the first time she has spoken to Pat since early in the morning. "Have we seen that yet?"

The hurt look on Pat Hart's face suggests that you have.

By midafternoon, the houses all look identical. Like franchise pseudo-Mexican food, they all seem roughly the same component parts in slightly different order. There is absolutely nothing wrong with them, but still you both feel betrayed by your Horace Greeley dreams. In giving up theater for bowling alleys, you expect walk-in closets as compensation. Debra is sullen and Cass, picking up on your moods, fusses nonstop. You raise and lower her on your hips as you explore unfinished basements, admire recessed lighting. You emerge from a cellar to ask Pat the capacity of the water heater. Pat nods dutifully and promises to check. Debra is courteous enough to turn her face away so your daughter can't see her mother laughing at you.

You have not found a house and as you move further down Pat Hart's listings, it seems unlikely that you will. "Maybe after a year or two," you whisper to Debra, "when I've built up a better client base, we can start looking again." "Two more years of rent?" Debra whispers back. "How does that make sense? Besides, look around. Do you see any high-rises?"

"There are more doctors per capita in this town than anywhere else in the country," Pat drones. Earlier, she had suggested blithely that it was both a buyer's and a seller's market. You drive for miles in concentric circles, every listing fifteen minutes from your office. In the early morning, still chipper, Pat had extolled the virtues of the townsfolk. "People here are soooo friendly," she'd raved, "nothing at all like your New Yorkers." To prove this point, she had waved to each passing driver and now, in the fading afternoon light, she is honor-bound to continue the tradition, her defeated parade waves echoed by puzzled commuters returning home after a long day.

Finally, near dusk, Pat pulls into an older house in an established neighborhood. No for-sale sign and the grass is too long. But there's a warmth to the house that you hadn't felt earlier. You emerge from the backseat and look up to the second story (a rarity in this ranch-style town) and a light in the window. "I like this one," you confide to Debra, who lets her eyes fall up and down noncommittally. Then again to Pat, "I like this one."

"This is my home," Pat says. "My husband will be wanting his dinner. I suppose you'd better come in."

Pat finds her keys and enters the house. It isn't easy to turn off that portion of your brain, so you imagine yourself living here instead, evicting her, her furniture and throw pillows and clown figurines evaporating, leaving the hardwood floors, the elaborate backsplash in the kitchen, the stuccoed walls.

"We've got a high chair somewhere for when the grandson comes," Pat calls over her shoulder. "Gil, be a doll and drag that over, won't you?" Gil, Pat's husband, lurches forward. He has clearly suffered a stroke and the right side of his body droops. When he tries to smile a hello, the effect is reminiscent of the comic-book villains of your youth.

"Please let me do that," you sputter, but Pat pulls you back.

"I've got another job for you," she says and leads you back out to stacks of cardboard boxes piled high in the trunk of her car.

"My husband stains glass," she explains. "It trains him to do things with his left hand he used to do with his right."

"That's nice." The boxes are incredibly heavy and Pat waits for you to heft two and then leads you back toward the house. "Has he always been artistic?"

You have spoken to Pat throughout the day but mostly while looking at wainscoting or chair rails, or else through the perversion of the rear view mirror. So you don't even recognize her when she shakes her head at you. "My husband was a scratch golfer," she says. "I'd be obliged if you could stack those boxes in the garage." And then, as if she can't help herself, her voice goes higher, "It has been turned into a lovely home workshop."

With the boxes, some twenty in all, stacked neatly in the garage, you come back inside where Debra is helping Pat cut onions, talking about her new job, wiping away onion tears with a dish towel. Gil is sitting in his seat while Cass plays at his feet, pulling at his shoelaces. You start to apologize before you notice that Gil is asleep, breathing heavily. When Pat sees you, she explains that they often eat dinner earlier and that Gil tends to tire easily. She waves away your apology.

"Work comes first now; Gil knows the score."

When Gil wakes up, his left eye focuses on you. But confusion has become second nature to him and he recovers quickly. "It's good to have guests," he says and pushes himself to the head of the table. He leads you in grace, your heads bowed, thanking the Lord for this bountiful food, this loyal wife, this comfortable home...

The Lord of Ease

That first week, you head off to work early, anxious to make a good first impression. Bruce asks you how the housing search is going and frowns at your difficulties. You work your way through various periodicals and press releases, phoning to touch base with clients who, after your years of institutional brokering, seem almost ridiculously bucolic. They extend you an authority completely foreign to the Wall Street traders, who viewed you, as you once exhorted Debra, as a company car. These civilians defer to your judgment. Their financial plans, such as they are, trail off into vague mumbles. They ask only for the most conservative of returns. You have inherited the widows and orphans fund, it seems, the Volvo crowd, the people who came to investing halfheartedly after a turkey-day conversation with a go-getter nephew. You have inherited the rubes.

Still, there is something touching about their faith, their trembling voices. The feeling of familiarity colors your face. These people speak to you as they would their priest. Abashed, you want earnestly to succeed for them.

By lunch you have made a few trades, *moved some things around*, as Bruce would say. It is a quiet day, the market lurching forward almost predictably. Bruce returns, bearing good tidings. "I've looked into the finances and we're willing to swing you a company loan that might help with the mortgage."

The details are relatively unimportant. The company will float you a loan using your potential earnings and pension money as equity. This money extends your base incrementally. It is like play money or a pyramid scheme and all it costs is your future. "It seems almost too good to be true," you remark to Bruce and he laughs. "It's 1985, my man. There is money to be made and money to be shared."

Debra and Pat Hart are delighted. "Now I really get to show you some stuff," Pat says, her hand tearing off the tired listings of last weekend and producing a pristine sheet. "Wait until you see some of these beauties."

And, like a magical door opening, you are escorted to an entirely new selection of houses. These have upgrades, fenced yards, great rooms. This is what you've been waiting for. It is easy to see Cassie crawling around on each new carpet, easy to see Debra applying makeup at each stand-alone vanity. Pool tables in the cavernous basements. You are well pleased and Pat and Debra, now fast friends, move hummingbird-quick through each dining room, each guest bedroom.

It is a beautiful day and across from the home you know instantly will become yours, children ride their bikes in infinities along the street. Cassie looks up at the older children, raises her hand and squeaks, and even Pat Hart is dumbed by the gesture. "This house has everything you'd ever want," Pat says. "You will never outgrow it, no matter how hard you try." She winks at Debra, who nudges you with her elbow. "And the best part is that it is only slightly more than you can afford."

It isn't. It's quite a bit more. Even with the company loan, your depleted savings account, even with a lower equity mortgage. Your head is racing with the figures and Debra catches you, rubs the small of your back and purrs, "We'll find a way. I trust you. I have faith in you." Pat races ahead to open the front door and even before you've reached the top step you can see inside to the vaulted ceilings and the granite countertops. You and Debra stop at the doorway, turning to look across at the neighbor children, one of their mothers reading on her porch, her long, tan, suburban legs dangling off a wicker chair. Cassie is already inside, Pat hustling her up onto her hip to show her the nursery. And almost before you know it, you've swept Debra's legs out and lifted her into your arms. She giggles as you carry her over the threshold, laughing, whispering in your ear how much she loves you, how happy you all are and will continue to be.

All Good Things of This Earth

That Bruce and his wife Nancy are thirty minutes late throws Debra into apoplexy. She worries that the prime rib will overcook. On the living room table, the cheese dip persists in growing some sort of skin. When Debra yells, you transfer these frustrations to the dishes in the sink. Cassie alone remains calm and happy, bouncing in a spring-loaded seat hanging from the kitchen doorframe. That raised voices no longer worry her worries you.

"We should probably just take the roast off," you say, prodding it with a fork.

"And let it get cold?" Debra asks.

"It needs some time to breathe anyway," you shrug. "We'll just eat it a bit earlier."

"I've got the cheese dip and a salad course," Debra hisses. "When would you like me to serve those?"

"We could serve the salad afterward," you suggest.

Debra steadies herself against the sink and exhales a long breath that fogs the window and obscures the deserted street outside. "No, we can't."

"Why not?" It seemed like a good solution to you, a quick fix (understanding that Debra is forever accusing you of a quick fix and therefore these words, which seem in your mind to connote if not brilliance than at least convenient intelligence, have come to mean something lazy, squalid, and morally shady).

Debra doesn't pry her eyes away from the street. "You wouldn't understand," she says.

"They do it in France," you joke. "They might think we're classé."

"We're not in France." She walks into the living room to inspect the cheese dip and you follow her. "Ugh," she says, lifting the film with her fingernail before letting it fall with an audible splat.

"We're grilling vegetables, right? I vote we heat up the cheese dip and pour it over top."

"You *vote*?" Debra contorts the word. "Since when do you get a vote around here?"

It's true, of course, but it does her little credit to acknowledge it. "How bad can it be?" you ask. "They're the ones who are late."

"He's your boss," Debra explains slowly, in the tone of voice she generally reserves for Cassie's friends, although not, you've noticed, for Cassie herself.

"Serve the salad after the meal," you repeat.

"They won't think we're classy, idiot. You don't know people around here, you don't know anything. They'll think we have pretensions. They'll think we're ridiculous. This whole evening will become about the timing of the salad. Is that what you want?"

"I want to stop fighting," you say simply. You've gotten quite good at this role, although it certainly wasn't the one you'd wished for.

Debra trumps you on the punch line, producing a not-terrible Humphrey Bogart: "Yes, well, everyone in Casablanca has problems. Yours may work out." This problem, unlike so many others, resolves itself when the doorbell rings a few moments later.

You've been settled for a month but neither of you have met Bruce's wife. Debra herself rarely sees Bruce, aligned through blood with David, and it's certainly a symbol of something that her ambivalence toward him endears him to you. He carries a slender bottle in his arm. "It's ice wine," he explains, handing it to you. "It's imported."

"How exotic," you say. Then blurt, "We're having the salad after the main course."

He looks puzzled for a moment. "It's really more of a dessert wine."

Debra reaches around you and extracts the bottle from your fingers. She shares a commiserating laugh with Bruce. "I'll put this in the freezer to chill," she says. "Thank you so much. Please come in." She pulls you from the doorway.

"Thank you," says Bruce. "This is my wife, Nancy."

It isn't violins and angels, but it's as close as you'll ever come. It's the way she reaches gracefully for your hand, catching you by the wrist before releasing you. It's her autumn tan. The way she examines the living room and breathes contentedly before sitting down, the way one foot climbs gently over the other. The way she laughs without covering her mouth and demolishes a helping of meat that might give a Viking pause. "I hope you don't mind," she apologizes to Debra, "I was working in the garden all day, trying to resuscitate the last dregs of summer and I seem to have found an appetite."

"Goodness no," laughs Debra. "It's a pleasure."

"Remember to save room for salad," quips Bruce, and the three of them laugh for a beat before you join in.

After dinner Debra excuses herself to put Cass to bed, over the child's vocal objections. When she returns, wiping her hands on her skirt, you can still hear wailing through two closed doors and a flight of stairs. "I can turn up the music," she offers.

"Don't be silly," says Nancy. "Besides, we want to hear all about you." It's the way she leans forward in her seat, like she genuinely means it.

Even Debra is charmed. She gives them a brief synopsis of her history, how you met, the trials and tribulations of her life. "I assume you already know quite enough about the escapades in New York," she says, floating you a dark look.

"We've heard," says Bruce, amused. He's lounging back in the sofa, his arms stretched behind his head.

"Still," Nancy says, turning her body to you, her knee just touching yours. "It must have been exciting. Tell the truth," she breathes, "was it thrilling?"

It has only been eight months since the trade, since the investigation, since your dismissal, but so much has changed it seems a different lifetime. It seems, you tell Nancy, almost like another person entirely.

"It's been rough on all of us," Debra says. "Especially Cass."

"Really? She seemed happy enough," Bruce says. "Cute kid, anyway." He works at a piece of something in the back of his mouth with his tongue. Only when he reaches inside nearly past the knuckle does it occur to you just how enormous his mouth truly is.

"Thank you," you and Debra say in unison and Nancy claps her hands delightedly.

"Oh," she says. "Look at them, Bruce dear, so young. They finish…"

Bruce, still working at the food in the back of his mouth, looks up, startled. "Huh?" He pulls his hand away guiltily.

"…each other's sentences." Nancy's laugh sounds like thunder. "You missed your cue there, darling," she says fondly, and then winks conspiratorially at Debra. "Always a step late, aren't they, dear?"

"Tell me about it," Debra agrees. "Frankly, I'm lucky when this one catches up at all."

"Of course I've seen more of the world than Bruce has," Nancy says. "I'm older than him, too."

And it's true that she does look older than him. Whereas even in repose his body is still an assertion—the loudness of his tie, the angle of his elbows behind his head—Nancy's dress is muted greens and reds. She has a roundness to her, is what it amounts to.

"Look at these crow's feet." She angles her upper body back to

Debra, her knee still pinned to yours. "A whole murder of them by now," she laughs. "I know the sun makes you look older, everybody says so. But who'd want to hide indoors their whole life, like that poor Greek goddess, like one of the mole people? It seems rather a high price for such a small treasure. Give me my garden and hang consequence, I say. Although, if science wanted to hurry up and invent a cure for wrinkles, I certainly wouldn't turn it down." She throws her hands in the air like she's testing for rain. "I'm waiting, science!" she exclaims.

"I think you look beautiful," you say. It was meant to be one of those empty gestures, like the affirmation of a child's artwork, like condolences for a dead great-aunt, but it comes out all wrong.

"Watch it, buddy," Bruce jokes, putting up his fists like the Notre Dame leprechaun.

"Oh, Jesus," Debra rolls her eyes, "It's time to take the puppy out for his piddle."

Only Nancy knows what to say. "Why, thank you kind suh," she says in a faux Blanche Dubois—furthest thing from her heart. "You ahr truly a rheal gentleman." Then she looks up at Bruce, his fists in the air, his enormous maw in a twisted smirk. "Ahnd that, my love, is cahled hitting your cue."

"Yeah, well," says Bruce, laughing, releasing you, even Debra softening a bit. "Tell Rhett Butler over there that he forgot to serve the ice wine."

You rise quickly to get it, knocking Nancy's leg into the table in the process, her tiny squeal drowned out by Debra's derisive, "hitting his cue, now that would be a first."

Later, your arms mingled over the soapy dishes, Debra remarks how great Nancy seems. Once bitten, you decline the bait. She looks at you sidelong, her fingers feeling under the soap for a sunken dish. "In fact, she's so great she almost makes you reconsider Bruce, you know what I mean?" She raises a plate from the suds and starts scraping at the cheese crust with her fingernail. "You look at the

guy and think he's just a big lug, another stuffed shirt, just another
Jensen. But they've been together, what, eighteen years? I mean, to
have kept her for that long, obviously I've missed something, right?"
She tilts the plate into the light and examines it for a moment before
plunging it back into the water. "There must be something there,
anyway."

"I guess so."

"You guess so?"

A salad bowl tilts and floods the counter. "Shit." You turn around.
"Where are the dish towels?"

Debra tosses you one and you try to dam the flood pouring over
the precipice of the counter and streaming down your pants. "You
guess so?" she prompts.

"What the hell do I know?" you say. "Maybe they're soul mates
or something. Maybe they're cosmically aligned. Or maybe they're
getting older and figured it's better to do it together than apart.
Maybe it's the tax incentive. Maybe she hasn't found anything better
yet."

Debra reaches over and maneuvers the towel in a circular motion,
pooling the water away from the edge, safely into the fabric.

"You know what's sad about you? It isn't how transparent you
are, although that certainly is pathetic. It's that of all the carbon-
based life forms in the geographical vicinity, you're the only one who
can't ascertain just how out of your league that woman is. You don't
even exist to her. You're like an ant. You don't even show up on her
radar."

Perspective

Cassie hunches over the paper, the pencil clumsy in her fingers. She bites her lip in concentration and then draws a looping curve through the corner of the page. Her neck tilts up to you as she seeks affirmation.

"That's great," you tell her. "Really great."

Meanwhile, Debra has resumed her place on the love seat. Her fingers wreathe her face, tapping lightly, her eyebrows furrowed toward you. The fighting that has continued off and on all morning shows little sign of abating. Debra wants to go back to work while you would prefer that she hold off until Cass is a bit older.

"You keep saying that," Debra barks.

"When did I say that?" you ask.

"Every time we have this goddamned conversation."

She is wrong, because you've never had this conversation before. But she is right, too, in that every conversation for a while now has become interchangeable with this one. Everything is a fight, everything a struggle.

You sit glaring at each other until Cassie props herself up on your knee to pass you the colored pencil. "Broken," she complains.

Because she is drawing on the carpet, and because she is three years old and therefore often comes at things from unusual angles, the tips of her colored pencils break at a rate of approximately one per five pencil strokes. The result is that your fight with Debra has been interrupted at regular intervals in order for you to sharpen the pencil. By now, the one she favors exclusively is reduced nearly to a nub. You ask Cassie whether she'd like another color, but she remains partial to the metallic pink clutched between her fingers. "This one," she insists. So you sharpen again, leaving the edge blunt enough not to break off at the slightest instigation and also to prevent her from poking herself accidentally (there have been incidents). When you are finished, she stares at the little nub and observes its hacked top. She makes a face at you, the same face her mother has been modeling for the past hour, and then returns reluctantly to her drawing.

"We moved here so you wouldn't have to work," you point out. "This was always the plan," you point out. "All of this," you point out, arms spread, "is exactly what you wanted."

"Things change," Debra snaps.

Things between the two of you certainly have. You aren't sure exactly when it started, and it seems lazy and inaccurate to date everything to the move from New York. But there is no denying its share in it.

"But this is what you wanted," you repeat again, quieter. "We had a plan. Remember? We sat in our old living room, on that old crushed-velvet sofa, and talked about what you wanted and what was best for Cassie. You said you were afraid she was going to grow up afraid of grass."

Debra shrugs. "We had a plan? What the hell did we know, anyway? You say that word like it's some goddamned scroll of wisdom. Now I want a new plan, a better plan. Does that make you happier? Does the language reassure you?"

You tell Debra that you feel betrayed. "I did all of this for you," you blurt, and you can see the act of fortitude it takes for Debra to swallow back the violence in her head.

Finally she hisses, "don't hang all of this on me, Mister."

Cassie's hand on your knee alerts you that she has broken the tip again. "You're putting too much pressure on it," you counsel. "Ease up a bit."

One of the unanticipated things about this town is how far down Debra's roots spread. While her parents have long since moved away, long before Debra herself was born, they left a complex root structure of aunts and uncles and cousins and childhood friends. When it's just the three of you, masked by your last name, everything is fine. But when Debra's aunt or cousins are with you, everything changes. The town, big enough for hotels, freeway on-ramps, subdivisions, and multiplex theaters, suddenly shrinks in size until every butcher is Debra's aunt's former flame, every swollen contractor, backhanding shade into his eyes, leaning against a shovel for relief, is one of your father-in-law's Navy buddies, one of the ones who came home. And so, for you, friends have been hard to find. One Friday evening over beers you dipped a toe with Bruce, suggesting things with Debra were not entirely copacetic. He gave you a long, appraising look and advised you to make things work. "Did you ever stop to consider," he said coolly, "just how many of your clients went to high school with her mother?"

Somewhere over the long months of Cassie's first years, the moves, the job changes, you have lost touch with nearly everyone you used to know. Each year you get fewer and fewer birthday cards, fewer and fewer holiday cards. "What do you expect?" Debra snorted, when you mentioned this. "We haven't sent a holiday card in five years. Frankly, I'm surprised it took people this long to put us on their naughty lists."

But it hadn't been solely Debra's fault or Debra's choice. There had been something wonderful about it, about pushing the world away with four hands, insulating yourself and Debra and baby Cass in one another. It must have been the same impulse that leads people to build fences around their property. All part of a larger pattern, the way Debra treated Pat Hart, the way you mimicked a cashier's gentle lisp, the way you would both intuitively cross the street upon seeing someone's eyes widen in recognition, ducking into whatever store was available, Debra pulling herself into you, laughing, grousing into the crease of your neck about "distant cousins like ragweed." It was all connected, you realize. A sort of siege mentality.

Now you have regular Sunday dinners at Debra's aunt's house, Cass playing with children her own age, the extended family spending the hours gnawing at shared memories and shared correspondences, even David holding you at arm's length, unwilling to "talk shop out of hours."

One evening, with Debra and Cass away at some cousin's house for a barbecue, you had burned half an hour with directory assistance. Meg was long gone, of course, although whether this meant she had gotten married or moved, the operator was unable to tell you. Tim and Hannah had disappeared as well, no listing. Meg's parents still lived in Bellingham, at the same address, the stasis bred into their generation's conservativism, but you couldn't think of what to say if you'd called. Mark had his own problems—a failed marriage and a knock-down drag-out with pills leading him to rehab—and your conversations with him had long devolved into pleasantries and reminiscences. Neither Sylvia nor Jensen was an option, of course. So a failed excursion down memory lane, unprofitable for everyone save the phone company and Debra, who asked pointedly when the bill came whether you "were trying to track down Jimmy Hoffa or something."

A mound of pencil shavings lies at your feet. Debra mutters "it's certainly not like the extra money is going to hurt."

"I do all right," you tell her. "I'm growing a base of clients."

"Sweetheart," Debra coos. "Wilson High School's Class of '39 is dying faster than you could ever build up a new one. You think maybe you're the cold call wiz?"

"What are you trying to say?"

"I'm trying to say don't bullshit me," Debra says, and looks down to Cassie who is lost in her drawing. "Don't give me that C-R-A-P because I ain't buying it. I'm saying that I would feel a whole lot more secure if I had my own job with my own client base to build up."

"What about Cassie?" you ask.

"My cousin Adele, Regina's daughter-in-law? She needs extra cash and said she'd be glad to look after Cassie. Ronnie is nearly her same age."

You fold your hands into your lap. "We moved eleven hundred miles so that Cousin Adele could raise our daughter?"

You've played your ace and Debra plays hers, "Why don't you remind me again why we had to move. There's a story I'm always interested in hearing."

When Cassie's pencil breaks again, as it inevitably does, there is hardly enough left to sharpen. "Look," you explain to her, "when I shave this down there isn't even going to be enough space on the pencil for you to hold it." You reach down to the discarded box and try to entice her with a brilliant red or a shimmering blue. "Isn't this a beautiful color?" you ask her, trying to drum up interest in a pale violet.

"This one," she says again, holding onto the tiny stub. Then, "Please."

There is so little left that when you place the tip between the blades, you have to reach in with your fingertips to turn the pencil. What emerges finally is a nearly blunted tip that Cassie considers and then refuses. "Sharper," she decides.

"No can do, my little butterfly. This is the end of the line for Metallic Pink. It's time to move on to something new."

Cassie whimpers for a moment and then starts to bawl such hot, heavy tears that you think surely this couldn't have been spontaneous, surely this must have been stored up somewhere. You take her onto your lap to comfort her, but she isn't having it. You explain how the pencil is all done, no more, how it did such a great job but now there's nothing left and how pencils don't last forever and that's why they put so many colors in the box and how she's hurting all the other nice colors' feelings so wouldn't she please like to try another one, for Christ's sake?

She refuses your generous offer, her tears growing hotter and wetter.

Finally Debra, who has been holding her face in her hands, grumbles something inaudible and then bends to her knee to collect Cassie's drawing from the floor. "This is beautiful," she sings. "Tell me about it."

Cassie's demeanor changes instantly. The tears seem to flow backward into her eyes and within seconds she is pointing out intricate design choices in her scribbles. You bend down to look and Debra moves her body slightly to allow you space at the base of the sofa leg. "And here's butterfly," Cassie says, "and that's tree."

"Those are wonderful," you both say.

"And that's me in middle."

"Wow."

"And there, Daddy," Cassie shrieks, pointing to some jagged lines in the upper left-hand corner. "Do you know what's that?"

You wish you could tell her you do, but frankly your powers of divination are not that attuned. "I know that they're wonderful," you bluff and above Cassie's head you can see Debra smiling.

Cassie stands up and whispers into your ear, the moistness of her tears a kiss against your cheek. "Birds," she tells you.

"Of course! Beautiful birds. Way off in the distance, so far we can barely see them." You can't tell whether the birds are flying away or flying toward you. When you ask Cassie about this, her lips and teeth and mouth fight for a while over the word hibernating, the sound coming out "hinating." Then her mouth drops for a moment. "But I'm not done clouds yet." Her finger jabs roughly at a cluster of circles in the middle of the page, behind the stick figure meant to represent her, one arm far longer than the other and reaching up diagonally off the page, sticks of hair flying upward into the air. Then she closes your fingers over the nub. "Please," she says again.

In the kitchen you find a sharp knife. Then you carefully carve the edges away from the lead, so carefully that the pencil loses almost none of its height and you only slice away a thin portion of your finger skin. You return with the pencil and drop it lightly onto Cassie's lap and she sets about adding more vaguely circular shapes to the cluster.

"I still don't see why you couldn't have chosen another color," you grumble good-naturedly. "Who has ever heard of metallic pink clouds anyway?"

Debra reaches over to inspect your wound and winces sympathetically at the ribbon of blood. "Say what you want for the kid," Debra says, holding your skin together with her fingertips. "She's certainly loyal."

This moment you will always remember perfectly. The image will come to you at odd hours: In the last fleeting seconds of a dream that leaves you doused in acrid sweat. In the gestures and comforts and silences of all the women you will know and of all those about whom you have already gathered your memories. This picture will ripple your unconscious. It will imprint itself onto the microscopic eye specks that presage old age. The graceful calculus of her neck will accompany you into your final days, when your own bone mass has long abdicated its struggle, when the arch of your shoulder is nothing more than a girlish enticement to the executioner's blade. The Kinemacolor of the grass on her knees, the mingled smells carried aloft, the sound of her laughter. Henceforth the scent borne by every summer breeze will disperse its atoms before ever reaching your nostrils, its sweetness only a rumor, preserving nothing but its memory, as if from a just-vacated room. The weight and heft of her breast in your cupped palm will mock you every first cold autumn morning. For all the seconds and days and seasons of your life, every laugh will conceal a virulent echo like a Trojan horse. The taste of her will spoil the vintage of every wine. You will have only this reminder, this affliction, this burden, and of everything that remains (in the muddled and star-crossed devastation of your crumbled memory), this portrait alone will remain pristine: her arms outstretched at the fringe of the pool, her hair like a crown, the loops and curves of her body rounded to perfect infinity.

Talents

Bruce's hand drapes over yours like a lover's, his fingers entwined in your own. "Can you feel that?" he asks, his breath a caress.

Together, you run the sanding block over the wood, tracing its grain. "Can you feel it catch right there?" he asks you. You can. At certain points the board resists the sandpaper. He presses down on your hand and starts working the reluctant area. The sanding block slides up and down. Bruce's movements are fluid, precise in the control he exerts on everything underneath his fingers. He's pressing so hard that your body jerks as he forces you down—gently but deliberately. "Careful," he whispers. "That's an eye. A knot in the wood. You've got to be careful with those, they're tricky. Too much pressure and the knot will chip, which is going to cause problems later on. Occasionally the whole knot will fall out altogether."

"What do you do when that happens?"

"You start over," he says.

"Bummer."

His hand slows above yours. He pulls away and wipes his hand on his shirt. "I guess," he says. "But this is a hobby, right? So I prefer to think of knotholes as a gift, a chance to extend the project for a bit longer. Like overtime in a hockey game."

"That's a very nice way to look at it," you say.

"Sure. It's all basically an excuse to spend another hour out in the shed," he laughs.

You move out from underneath him toward a large dark stain along the board comprising the far wall. "What happened here?" you ask, thinking maybe he'd tried to paint at some point. But when you get closer, you can see that the stain isn't manmade at all but rather a discoloration in the wood, nearly a perfect circle.

"It's heartwood," Bruce explains.

You trace your fingers over the circle. It's been sanded so meticulously it feels like brushed velvet. "Heartwood," you murmur.

Bruce laughs. "It's a fancy name for something that died."

His woodworking shed is just that, a small hovel in the northeast corner of his property, along a diagonal axis from the house and Nancy's herb garden. Thursday he'd come into your office while you were on the phone with a client, an old friend of Debra's mother's, who was interested in learning what diversifying meant and how it might pertain to her meager annuity. You motioned for him to sit down. When you were done, he apologized for bothering you. "I can see you're busy," he said. "This is a social call. It can wait."

It had been more than a month since you'd had him and his wife over, but since then you'd heard nothing at all from Nancy and neither had your wife. "Obviously," you scolded him. "I was beginning to think we'd scared you off."

"I'm sorry about that," Bruce said. "We get pretty busy in the late fall. Which transitions to my attempt at amends. There's a football game on Saturday. You should come over to my house."

"You have football games?" you asked, confused. "What are you, a Kennedy?"

"The football game is in Ann Arbor," Bruce explained. "Jesus, you're in the Midwest now. Act like it." He smiled. "Kickoff at noon."

When you relayed the conversation to Debra, neither of you were sure whether she was invited. In the end, Cass went down early for her nap, which solved the problem neatly. When Nancy answered the door and looked over your shoulder, "Where's Debra and Cass?" you explained about the nap and she nodded. "We'll have to arrange something just for the girls," she smiled. Bruce galloped down the stairs, the whole house shaking under his weight. "A stag party," Nancy called to him as he jogged up to you. "Which I am going to take advantage of by heading downtown to run some errands. It looks like Bruce gets you all to himself." Nancy touched your arm lightly on her way out the door, the vibrations resonating through your chest. Then she let her voice drop into a mock baritone. "Be manly," she preached to both of you, "do as men do," and then she was gone.

Bruce led you into the living room and turned on the game. You'd sat in near silence listening to the announcer profess enthusiasm for most of the first quarter: every three-yard plunge a chance to go all the way, every dump-off in the flat offering the receiver an opportunity to beat eight defenders to daylight. You are a casual fan, and from the way Bruce was shifting himself on the sofa, his focus attuned to every bird's chirping outside the window, you suspected the same of him.

"Quite a game," you'd tried, eventually. He'd spent the last minute watching a squirrel pursue an unidentified target across the fence top.

His head jerked back toward you. "Sorry."

"Not much of a fan?"

"It's not that," he explained. "It's the thaw."

It was true. Overnight, Indian summer had descended and you'd awoken this morning to temperatures thirty degrees higher than at nightfall. The sky was crayon blue. "It's an awfully nice day to spend inside," you said.

"You mind if we skip halftime?" Bruce asked.

"Not particularly," you'd admitted.

"Music to my ears," he said, slapping his meaty hands against his knees. "Come on out, let me show you something."

And he'd led you down a short path to a small shed near the property marker. "My woodshed," he'd announced. It was so small that at first you'd assumed he meant an enclosure where he kept his firewood, immensely glad that you hadn't said so when he opened the reluctant door, "It sticks a little twelve months of the year," and led you inside. On a bench, Bruce had been prepping a board whose purpose remained a mystery. Before you knew it, you were hunched over, the sanding block in your hand, Bruce's body draped above yours, guiding your hand with his own, sanding down the board.

"Where did you learn how to do all this?" you ask.

"Gil taught me," Bruce explains, then notes your confusion. "Pat Hart's husband? I thought you met him?" You had, but had forgotten.

"How'd that come about?"

"Oh, we got talking after eighteen holes one day. This was before his stroke, back when we were a regular pairing." He shakes his head sadly. "Guy used to take money out of my pocket driving two hundred seventy yards with these ridiculous old woods." He looks up at you sharply. "Do you play golf?"

"That depends. How charitable is your definition of golf?"

"Pity. Anyway, we're in the clubhouse talking and he mentions he's got a woodshed in his backyard and invites me over to see it. Kind of like you, like now. If you know Gil at all, you can guess I'm expecting power tools, a real first-class operation. Instead he's got a shanty with a lightbulb hanging by a wire overhead. Obviously it was a letdown." He laughs.

You tell him you know what he means.

He nods. "He'd built the place himself, you know? I mean, cut every board, measured every edge. It's a hell of a thing." He looks around. "Anyway, he planted the germ of it and then I begged Nancy for a parcel of land here. She was happy enough. Gives us each something to do when the weather turns nice. Key to any successful marriage, right? Separate hobbies."

"So you built this all yourself?"

"Well, the plan was for Gil to walk me through the preliminary stages, show me the ropes. But he had his first stroke when we were only about halfway done with the frame. Since then I've been pretty much tinkering. Trial and error."

"That's amazing," you say earnestly.

"I don't know about that," Bruce says. But you can tell he's pleased. "The roof leaks any time there's rain and last winter there was so much shift that I had to reset the west wall. I'd still hate to put a straight edge to the corners."

"You built this yourself," you whistle, looking around again. "I can't even imagine that."

"I think maybe you've stumbled on the secret there," he grins. "If I'd have known what I was getting into, I'd have run the other way." He moves around you to the far wall. "Come take a look over here."

It is a shelf. A piece of board sticking out of the wall.

"It took me nearly a month," he says. "I know, I know, it's a shelf, right? Tree houses have them, for Christ's sake. I tell Nancy I'm putting in a shelf, she tells me she'll have sandwiches ready for lunch. This was early March, and it was opening day before I could use the thing."

"What happened?"

He puts his hand lightly on the shelf, holding some wood screws and a wrench. "Everything happened. What did I know, I went into it hell's bells. Put in four-inch dowels and split my outer wall down the spine. Once I solved that problem and got the board across, I ran into trouble with the level. There was always something." His face breaks into a wild grin. "About three weeks into the project, I call Nance in from the house, a real big deal, right? I've laid the board, dowels are rock solid, outer wall patched nearly good as new. She's carrying a cup of coffee—by now I'm waking up at daybreak to work on the damned project, coming into work smelling like Pinocchio so that David's riding me. A cup of coffee, right? I'm talking a mug, World's Greatest Wife, ten fluid ounces. So she comes inside, looks around. Now I've been real careful not to let her into the shed too often, I guess I'm hoping it will turn into something more. But she's fantastic about it, well, you know Nance, and she makes a show of admiring the roof and smelling everything." He looks around furtively. "Promised me we'd christen the thing properly, but it's too narrow to lie down and the floor splinters something awful... Anyway, we've got the whole thing like a ceremony and I'm feeling great about myself and so she takes this coffee mug, right, and puts it on the shelf."

"What happened?"

"Guess."

"The shelf fell down?"

"I wish. The whole wall tipped over. Counter-balancing was off."

"God."

"That's what I'm saying. Something like this—four walls and a ceiling, a shelf. Caveman stuff, real dark-ages work, took me nine months. Now I think about Gil's shed with that light overhead and it's like thinking about a cathedral or something."

"What the hell," he shrugs. "It's pretty much doing the same thing over and over again. Nance says it sounds mind-numbing to her and it's hard for me to disagree, but now I think maybe that's how you get good at something."

"Practice makes perfect," you say and his face twists.

He looks around. "I don't know about perfect," he says. "But I'll tell you something else: I learned more making that same shelf fifty times than I've learned doing any other fifty things once each." He rubs his hand across his face again. With two bodies in it, the shed holds its heat like a furnace. "I don't harbor any illusions about any of this. But the thing is—how many hobbies are there where your apprentice work is your place in the world? How many hobbies are there where you can touch your progress?"

"Touch it? That depends on how brave you are," you joke. You reach over to the shelf and push gently with your index finger. You have a pretty strong suspicion that if the shelf comes down, you'll be packing your stuff Monday morning, but a devilish impulse drives you to risk it anyway. Behind your ear Bruce laughs. "Go ahead, man," he says. "I've vetted it."

"Seems solid," you say.

"Should be. God knows how many hours went into it."

"I would have given up," you say, turning around. It's a very small shed and you turn suddenly, before Bruce can clear the space, so you are very close together. The afternoon light is streaming in from tiny fissures in the thin plyboard walls. He looks down at you, something inscrutable passing across his face. You are a tall man but in the tiny shed he is as tall as a giant.

"Probably," he agrees.

A Child of Success

Bruce taps once on the glass outside your office door and tells you that it's time to go.

You grab your files and head over to the conference room. It's Friday afternoon, late, and the place is deserted, the support staff gone for the day.

"Hope you don't mind the conference room," Bruce explains. "We thought we could use the extra space." He confides in you that he is hoping to generate an echo.

"Why do I feel like I'm being led to an execution?" you ask, slowing your gait, almost kidding.

Bruce waits for you to catch up. "I was hoping for more like a fraternity hazing ritual. Bring in the goats. An execution? That's the difference between you and me. You are an optimist." His teeth shine blue under the fluorescents.

"How about David?"

"He'll meet us. He's running late."

"I meant the other thing—what do you think? Optimist or pessimist?"

"David," says Bruce, finding the key to the conference room and moving over to usher you in, "is an asshole." He holds your eye for a moment. "But then I guess we both know that by now."

It is May of 1986 and time for your first-year review.

The conference table is a half-moon, ascending from the window. "Nice wood," you say, to say something, forgetting Bruce's predilection, and therefore earning yourself a lengthy, highly technical lecture about hard-versus-soft wood craftsmanship. Bruce is illustrating something on a base joint, the two of you hunched underneath the table, when David's legs and lower torso appear at the door.

"What the hell is this?" the legs ask.

Bruce looks at you. "Let's jump him," he urges. When you don't say anything, he looks disappointed for a moment, and then leaps out from his side. "Boo!" he shouts at David.

You emerge more slowly, just in time to register David's disgusted face.

"Bruce was teaching me about oak," you say, which does nothing to alter David's facial expression.

"He's worse than a Jesus freak," David sighs. "I hope his next flight of fancy involves sailing across the Atlantic." He glares at Bruce for a moment before punching: "Solo."

The banter would be funny except that it's every day now, you're always caught in the middle, and it's your first-year review so you'd just as soon everybody plays nice.

"Take a seat on that side," David says, directing you to the apex of the curve.

"Did you ever notice," Bruce rags, "that David won't sit with his back to the door? He's like a Mafia don that way."

"Let's get started," David says.

"Of course, only that way," Bruce continues. "I'm not casting aspersions about Debra's family, you understand." He flicks at imaginary whiskers under his chin. His Brando is abysmal.

"We're Dutch," David says, exasperated.

"Calabrian Dutch, maybe," Bruce quips.

"Sit down. Let's at least take a flying leap at professionalism, shall we?" David asks. Bruce mutters something inaudible under his breath. "Just to try it," David begs. "Let's drive it around the block a few times and see how it looks on us, okay?"

It's funny but last March, when you'd been hired, the park across the street had been nearly barren, more mud than grass, more dirt than mud. Now, fourteen months later, it is green and tidy. What's strange is that you can still remember the children and parents and dogs who'd played in it then, chasing one another like the Lost Boys and Hook's pirates and Indians, like a merry-go-round. Now the grass is as manicured as a fairway, as lush as an Eden, and nobody comes near it. It is funny, you finally conclude, but hardly an opportune time to consider such things. Across the table your bosses prepare their papers.

Bruce, of course, has brought almost nothing to the meeting. His copy of your yearly self-evaluation, given to him last week, is still virginal. Otherwise, he has scribbled a few notes on the back of a takeout menu. He makes an elaborate show of taking out his bifocals and cleaning them on his tie.

David, on the other hand, arrives with meticulous notes. He quizzes you on some of your decisions, on the specifics of the one or two clients who have left. He isn't hostile, exactly, but he's near enough to wade its shoreline. "I hope you don't mind, but I prefer to keep these reviews as professional as possible."

You tell him you understand completely.

"I'm sure you do," he says. "Although I wouldn't even hazard a guess how they handled things in New York."

"Pretty much the same, actually."

"Obviously not," he says coldly. "We feel as though we owe it to you to conduct a formal, thorough, rigorous first-year evaluation so there's no confusion, so we all know where we stand with one another." Next to him, Bruce gives you an über-serious nod. "I think it's important that we understand one another," David concludes and waits until you've affirmed.

And you do understand. *Nothing escapes the all-seeing eye* is the moral of this story. But you've had a good year—your guesses outpacing David's by a comfortable margin, your clients in gravy and, when it's all said and done, that story has its moral, too.

When David is finished with his questions, Bruce starts in. "I only have a few complaints," he says. "These won't take long. Two months ago," he begins, peering over his glasses at the takeout menu and then at you, "ah, here it is, you wore a tan belt and much darker, nearly black, shoes. Obviously that needs to be rectified in the future."

"If you weren't going to take this seriously, why didn't we just cancel the meeting?" David grumbles.

Bruce throws his hands in the air in exasperation. "You're preaching to the choir," he shrills. "Where you are right now? I've been here for weeks."

"You don't think we owe it to the company and our other employees to conduct a formal first-year review?" David asks. "Under the circumstances?"

Bruce doesn't say anything for a moment. Then he takes another look at his takeout menu. David, pacified, sits back down. Because of the angle of the chairs, there is a split second when Bruce's far eye winks at you before he starts talking. Enough time for you to gird yourself for the explosion sure to follow, but not enough time to beg him to abandon his quest. "I really must take you to task," he begins, "on your putting, which pales in its crapitude only in comparison to your drives and your abortion of a midrange game." David starts yelling but Bruce, prepared, talks over the sound. "Frankly," he continues, "when you get into the sand, it's like watching an archaeologist digging for bones and when you get into the rough, you'd be better off gluing your ball to the golf cart and pushing the damned thing onto the green."

"It's our name on the door," David barks. "I've spent a half century earning that name and nobody is going to fuck with it."

"Oh, for God's sake, David. His clients are the last people on earth who still balance their checkbooks by hand. Coupon clippers. These are the people who catch rounding errors at the bank. You think they're going to let a penny slide? That's why we gave them to him! You've interrogated every client who left him. Hell, I've done everything short of rummage through his trash. There hasn't been a comma out of place. It's time to let him off the leash."

The two of them are panting now, their ties flapping, and you sit, stunned, while they catch their breath. Bruce, not quite looking into your eye anymore, collects his tie back over his shirt and straightens his jacket. "He's good people, David. That's enough. This review is over."

"Says who?"

"Says all of us," Bruce replies.

The Lord of Happiness

Across from you the Hudson, oil-slicked, a jewel. You and Cassie stand on its banks, watching the sailboats play in the current. You keep your eyes tight on the shoreline, hoping for a seashell to gift to Cassie, worrying about the hypodermics you've read about in the newspapers. But thus far you've spotted only soda cans and driftwood. You help Cassie over a log. Her legs are losing that baby fat, their coltish inward angle correcting itself. She's seven years old and some days you can't remember a moment of it. You've come back to the city to visit friends and to show Cassie where she was born. It was a trip she'd been enthusiastic about. The plane ride, the plastic wings, the visit to the cockpit, the massive airport and taxi across the bridge have all been nothing more substantive than a fairy tale to her. Debra has stayed home, too busy for sentiment. The quarterly reports are due. So just you and Cassie and a small hotel on the Upper West Side. On this trip, away from Debra, you've conceded to spoiling Cassie and she, in her own way, has illustrated modesty in her demands. Having lobbied for room service, her order was parsimonious. She walked stoically by the stuffed lions at FAO Schwarz only to fill a loot bag at the Museum of Natural History gift shop later. There is something wonderful about the way she alternately pampers and denies herself, this miniature adult, and you find yourself urging her wants forward rather than reining them back. And so, instead of the scheduled walk through Central Park, you acceded to a stroll along the riverbank, far up from the crush of those avenues that house the heirs to the city. It is not a block, nor even an area, that you can ever remember visiting. Cassie had explained her desires to the only patient cab driver in the city and he had taken you up into Washington Heights, to Fort Tryon Park. When you'd asked where you might get a cab back, there had been a moment of pure serendipity. "My mother lives a few blocks from here," the cabbie had said. "She could always do with a visit. I'll swing back around in two hours and take you down." It is one of those days when everything seems effortless.

Cassie finds a park bench and lets you sit next to her. Early summer and her hair hasn't yet lightened, despite the lemon juice she squeezes in each morning. Every pleasure boat in the burroughs sails by while you explain to Cassie about boat ownership, the costs but also the freedoms, how on a day like today they seem purchased cheap at twice the price. You go on, it is only fair to say, for too long, her vision straying back to the brightly colored sails. When you trail off, embarrassed, Cassie pats your knee twice, neatly. "They're pretty," she assures you.

After a while she looks out to the horizon and asks what lies beyond. You explain New York's cumbersome geography using your outstretched hand as a guide. "We're here," you say, pointing to one of your fingertips. "We're here," Cassie repeats, covering your large hand with her smaller one.

While you sit, the sun moves slightly to catch a glint down on the shoreline. Still hoping for a shell, you approach quickly, before the waves pull whatever it is back into the water. Cassie is excited too, although she probably hasn't seen anything, roused by your sudden speed. It is, alas, only a discarded Coke bottle, its narrow waist clogged with sand. Cassie is delighted. There is no wrapper and she is free to imagine the bottle's far-off point of origin. "It could have come from China," she whispers. "Yes," you whisper back. She stoops, the hem of her skirt dipping into the water. "Oh," she gasps. "It's cold." Then she grins up at you. She immerses the bottle in the water, pushes it down to the bottom. She lets the tide fill it until there is no sand left, nothing but seawater. She stays like that for a very long time, watching the horizon point, imagining what lies beyond.

Eventually you have to remind her that the taxi will be coming back soon. "He's done us a favor and it won't do to not be there for him," you say. She nods, glumly. You can feel the magic pulling back as surely as the tides. But then, a little miracle: Cassie looks up brightly and asks you for the piece of paper and golf pencil she knows you keep in the spine of your wallet. You walk up a stretch from the water and, like the princess she has been this entire day, she commands you to kneel before her so that she can write on your back. "It's a message for the bottle," she explains. You can feel the pencil moving along your back, like the games you and Charlotte would play on car trips, *Guess what I'm writing*. But you couldn't then and you can't now, the loops and bows inscrutable. When she's done, Cassie tucks the paper into the bottle and stuffs a piece of seaweed into the mouth. She moves her arm back to throw it but then turns. "You do it," she says. "You can throw farther." You think about telling her that it doesn't matter, but something holds you back, and you take the bottle and throw it in a long parabolic arc into the water. The two of you stare at the splash site for a while, trace the white cap until the wave rolls back to the shore. "What did you write?" you ask, and Cass looks womanly, her pink tongue pushed up against her top lip, promising never to tell.

She offers you her hand and you escort her back up the sand to the grass island and the street. You have a dinner arranged with some friends who are anxious to see Cassie again and to tell you about their own children and their own accomplishments. They are good friends and it will be nice to see them, but for right now you cannot imagine anything better than Cassie's hand in your own, the grit of the sand, the promise of the bottle.

The Tree of Life

An Instrument of Force

The eleventh hole is a dogleg, so you'll want to ease up on your drive. You know this. You understand this. You caution yourself as you set your stance, you remind yourself as you raise the club head. It is the last thing you think before you start your downswing.

When you watch golf on television, the sound the ball makes off the tee is unlike anything you have ever created yourself. For a long time you'd assumed this sound was the product of the television coverage, some sort of audio trick, a distortion. But last year you had played eighteen with the club pro, his even par beating your score by a slender twenty strokes, and his drives had induced that same sound. From that day until this one you had secretly hoped that perhaps this was a sound one could only recognize at a distance and that your own meager drives still manufactured at least some fraction of it. But now, standing on the eleventh, your arms and legs in perfect cosmic alignment, your ear has no trouble discerning the glorious whoosh of a well-struck ball. Intellectually, you suppose this should make you unhappy, how this single well-hit ball has doomed a million of its incompetent predecessors, but nothing can mar this moment—not the sound nor even the sight of the ball, a pinprick on the Empyrium, in perfect parabola, long past the short fairway and beyond into a cover of trees.

"Wow," cheers Bruce, "watch that puppy go." He raises his hand to his eye like he's staring vast distances, before pivoting to finish the gesture as a salute. You salute back.

Even Nancy seems impressed. "For a second there you looked like you knew what you were doing."

Only David, naturally, has a different take on the issue. "You'll probably want to take the stroke penalty," he counsels, "and drop at the fringe of the fairway."

"Nah," you say. "I'll just hit another one."

"That's the spirit," Nancy says. "Nobody likes a mouse."

"That is ill-advised," David says. His ball is next to be teed and he juggles it in his hand while he talks.

"We're still keeping score, right?" Bruce says. He claps you on the shoulder. "At a dollar a stroke, you should feel free to take as many whacks as you see fit. The next foursome can wait their turn."

"That doesn't make any sense," David counters. "He'll have a lovely lie from his drop and an easy pitch for bogie."

"Bogie," you say, in mock horror. "Swallow a bogie as reward for that gargantuan blast? Your problem is that you don't have any faith in me."

"Well, that's true."

"Take your time," Bruce says. "If we can wait half the day for David to line up a seven-inch gimmee, we can certainly wait for you now." David's notorious deliberatation annoys Bruce, who, as habitual low score, must follow him. During the many fits and starts of a David swing, Bruce amuses himself by shooting imaginary skeet with the grip of his club. "Take your time, it's a beautiful day for golf."

"Take another swing," Nancy giggles. "Practice makes perfect."

"Take the penalty," David reaffirms gravely. "There can be no upside to this course of action."

"That's the problem with you, partner," Bruce says. He blows an imaginary airplane out of the sky and then releases the club head down with an easy gesture that strafes the grass. "It's all upside."

"One more," you decide, and wink at Nancy. Behind her, David practices his swing near the ball cleaner. You set your feet again, try to recapture the conditions, rock slowly on the balls of your feet and then raise your arms. You feel the club rise above your head and then start its inexorable arc down to greet the ball, everything a matter of faith.

Conquest

All week Debra has been checking the weather reports with a gambler's rabid fanaticism. Where once you might have woken to her soft breath on your earlobe or her hand on your thigh, now there is only the hissed intake carrying its cold data. "Thirty percent," she reports, already heading toward the shower, "up a bit since yesterday." If you followed the market with this diligence, you might have earned a bonus this year in spite of the general economic malaise. Instead, you have only David's vague gestures of belt-tightening.

Cassie's birthday party is scheduled for Saturday and by Thursday the possibility of rain has tipped over into probability and Debra is near hysterics. When you offer her the usual platitudes, she looks at you with such disdain that only self-immolation seems the proper penance. "I've waited all year for this," she spits. "I'm not surprised it's something you can't understand."

"Things will be fine," you say, putting out a hand that she rejects.

"And if they're not?"

"Things will be fine."

"You should get that printed up like a banner," she says and turns back to her newspaper. "You and your lazy aphorisms." She turns back to the newspaper and then says something else that you miss entirely. When you ask her to repeat it, she just shakes her head. "Off you go," she snorts. "All aboard. Your own little escape hatch from the world."

When you say you don't understand what she means, she apes a glassy-eyed look. "Even the possum had more than one trick."

You open your mouth in protest, but she snaps the fold of the newspaper. "You should see yourself sometimes, the way you really are. You act like if you sit real still, trouble won't find you." When you don't respond, she motions for you to pass the coffee. After she fills her cup you can feel her watching you over the brim. Then she turns her attention back to the weather page, looking like she's about to cry.

Then, moments later she lifts up her head hopefully and suggests rescheduling. "We move it to Sunday and that gives the storm a chance to move through," she says, her gesture as sweeping and definitive as a weatherman's. You point out that there are other factors to consider. Her parents, for example, who would have to extend their flight; your own mother, who would have to spend another night in your home. The rental tables and chairs. Your objections, with their tepid logic, are swept up by the cold front moving across Debra's mental map.

"It's their granddaughter's eighth birthday," Debra says. "You think they won't pay the upgrade? Anyone would understand. Even your mother would understand something like this."

"There are six children invited to this party," you say. "That's six mothers and fathers, brothers and sisters and weekend plans. It seems presumptuous to ask all of them to change because of a threat of rain."

"Fifty-five percent isn't a threat," Debra snarls. "It's damn near a certainty in this backwater town." She takes a pull of her coffee. She is dressed immaculately from the waist down, a pressed skirt and no-run hose. From the waist up she wears one of your college shirts with two decades' worth of coffee stains forming rivers and lakes and tributaries along her collarbone. She raises her cup and swirls the oil off the surface of the coffee. "Besides," she says, her mouth not quite a grin, "it's only five fathers. Ashley's mother just filed for divorce."

Later, when she has left the house and you are tidying up the remains of the kitchen, you pause and read the weather report yourself. It seems obvious from the almost nothing you know of weather patterns that the steady uptick in precipitation forecasted from now until Saturday suggests a rainier Sunday, but of course she's not here and anyway she wouldn't want to hear it even if she were.

The Buick pulls into the driveway, clipping the wheel of Cassie's bike. Your mother emerges to check her bumper, flicks a speck with her fingernail, and walks toward the house. Only after she has rung the bell a second time do you realize Debra has disappeared upstairs. At the door your mother looks you over. She pokes that same fingernail at your widow's peak and tsks slightly. "Something else to blame your father for," she smiles, and then leans in for a hug. Through the haze of her perfume you can see Cassie's bike wheel spinning with a wobble you will need to correct before tomorrow's party.

"Are Debra's parents here yet?" your mother asks, pushing her bag toward you with her leg. You shake your head no. "Good," she says. "We need to go to the store for coffee and I was worried we'd have to burn the whole afternoon waiting for them."

She buries her hand deep in her overcoat and emerges with a compact. "Just let me freshen up," she says. When you offer her the bathroom, she points to the bag. "You go put this in my room," she says. "I'll wait here. No sense getting everyone else riled up."

"Everyone else is gone," you lie. "Debra is at work. Her parents are spending the afternoon at Cassie's school." You can see your mother's reflection in the compact as she applies makeup. She catches your eye and speaks through the O of her lips.

"Must we wait for them?" she asks. You tell her they have their own key. You don't mention that they are on the approved visitors list at the elementary school whereas she called to inquire whether Cassie would like her very own subscription to *Seventeen* for her birthday. You don't mention that her drive across two slender states is fractional compared to their two-thousand-mile trek with its layovers and inevitable delays. You do tell her that you're pretty sure there's coffee in the house and she sniffs as she snaps the compact shut.

"Why don't I buy my brand," she says. "Just to be safe."

She is already in the car by the time you've moved her bag, and when you pause to carry Cassie's bike onto the grass, the horn of her Buick emits a sudden snort. Once you climb in, she apologizes. "My hand slipped," she says, pulling out of the driveway even before you've had time to close your door.

You stare at the sideview mirror, your right arm braced against the Buick's stirrup, and watch your street recede behind you. "Mom," you want to say, "you drive like someone's chasing you." But then again, she always has.

After dinner, your mother rises to help Debra clear the dishes.

"Thank you," Debra says, pleased. You use the dining room once a year, the night before Cass's birthday party. The rest of the year it's a repository for the things you can't yet resign yourself to throwing away.

Your mother stacks two plates, and her too-deliberate walk clues you to follow close behind. You motion to Debra to sit and clear the remainder of the plates yourself. Your mother is nearly to the kitchen when a fork slides off one of the plates she is carrying and sticks, tines down, between the slats of wood flooring. "Well, look at that," she marvels, and keeps walking. She drops the dishes unwashed into the sink and calls to Debra, "I guess I'll make a pot of coffee."

Debra's voice reminds her that there's still half a pot from breakfast.

"Wonderful," your mother calls back.

While she pours the remainder of the morning's coffee into

the sink, your mother asks you about work. You tell her about the slowdown and she furrows her brow.

"It was a lousy year for everyone, Mom. We're in a recession—maybe you heard about it?"

"Don't be smart with me, young man." She reaches into the grocery bag to remove her brand of coffee. "I've told you before that they're always looking for a patsy in that field. Looking for stocks to rise and people to blame when they don't. My father told me that." Her father was a dentist, but you're a bit busy finding the battery grinder and the filters and then running the water to rinse away the morning's grinds and the gristle from dinner and running the disposal to mask the sound of the grinder. Your mother empties the fresh beans into the coffee maker and hits the start button with a resounding jab. "You need an exit strategy," she says.

Your mother, after her brief churchly dalliance, now applies the logic and semantics of *The McLaughlin Group* to her everyday life. "You should listen to me," she warns. "My portfolio grew fifteen percent in the last year alone." You cannot quite eradicate the surprise from your face and perhaps in retaliation she gives you a cool look. "Your clients, I would imagine, should be so lucky." Then she tucks her head around the doorframe and says in a cheerful voice: "The coffee should be ready in a minute, it's just getting hot." Her head reemerges and she asks you more quietly, "I don't suppose she bought anything for dessert?"

That night, in bed, Debra enumerates the day's offenses—all the ones you have noticed and many, many more. It's been a long day, tomorrow promises to be more of the same and you'd just as soon nod off, but there's something in her voice that suggests that you would be wise to listen and for once you are wise. What started as whispers have gotten louder so that by the time the after-dinner drinks are being revisited, Debra is propped up on her elbow jabbing at the divide of the mattress with very near the same emphasis your mother applied to the coffee maker.

"She's absolutely intolerable," Debra says. Then does a credible impression of your mother's reaction to the veal. " 'Oh, goodness, such a color. Have they cured trichinosis then?' I can tell you that when Cassie gets a bit older, we're going to have a problem."

"Maybe things will get better," you say. And some part of you believes it, until Debra reminds you of your mother's return to the dining room with the coffee. She had apologized to Debra and your in-laws: "I'm afraid I couldn't find anything to serve it with. I believe I have some mints in my purse."

"Probably not, then, no," you say, lightly.

"At least Dad had a sense of humor about it," Debra recounts. "He suggested schnapps."

"I think she took care of that herself in the kitchen," you say. She did. You saw her.

Debra turns her body over in the bed, against you, and you can hear her struggling to regulate her breathing.

"I don't know what you expect me to do," you say finally.

"Honey," she says, not turning over. "Put that on your banner."

The next morning Debra is up before the sun, scanning the horizon for clues. She turns to you and arches an eyebrow. "No more sleep for you," she says. "Plenty to do around here."

There is a long list of chores to be done, work that seems superfluous to a child's two-hour party. You cannot think of why the air conditioning filters should need to be changed, for example, but Debra's scowl stems the flow of questions at its source. You tell her maybe you'll begin with sweeping the back porch. "No," she says. "Start by blowing the leaves from under the maple so that the kids have somewhere clean to play. I don't want leaves tracked back inside." She says it so logically that it isn't until half an hour later, when your mother's sleepy head emerges from the window directly above your throttling leaf blower, that everything becomes clear.

By noon, an hour before the party, you've moved the rental table underneath the second-floor patio and set up the folding chairs.

Debra has weighted each placemat with a plastic toy pony. Your mother emerges at intervals to refresh her drink from the pitcher of margaritas on the table. Around her, Debra and her parents sweep and tie and batten down the paper cups and streamers. You are hoisting the giant pink piñata, another pony, special-ordered for the occasion and pregnant with candy, and from your vantage point high on the ladder you watch your mother step gingerly above your father-in-law's prostrate body to the table where (with a look of befuddlement that makes you think all the way back to Charlotte's dog) she lifts the plastic pony from her paper plate and then, just as lightly, puts it back down to return into the house. Your father-in-law, at work stapling streamers to the deck's legs, bends his head slightly to avoid her return passage and Debra looks up at you for a moment. You are working through a fisherman's knot, and when you look back she's talking quietly with her mother.

Even so, everything might have been fine except for the rain. Debra, so tactical in the days leading up to the event, abandoned her reason entirely now, so the four of you (your mother gamely volunteering to wait inside and help Cass with her coloring) have spent a harried hour anchoring and weighting and stacking the paper plates and the plastic spoons, retrieving the napkins when the breeze picked up and dodging the cups when the shifting wind caught full-bellied in their rims. You did this long after it was clear that the party would have to be moved indoors and, because you loved your wife, you did this long after her parents had already moved themselves and the tattered birthday banner inside the house and you did this even when Debra herself sat down on the step and let swollen rain drops, big as broken promises, brush away her tears. You alone gathered and regathered napkins and plates, through the thunder and the lightning and the doorbell's ringing and the sympathetic smiles of the parents and their pastel girls in princess costumes, until the napkins were nothing more than paste and the plates collapsed inward at their centers. You might have stayed longer had you not spied the piñata, damp but intact, safe below the I-beams of the porch and climbed up the ladder to rescue it and bring it into the basement with a shout: "Hey, look what I salvaged!" For Debra, still crying, consoled by her parents who were looking at you with the same reproachful look they'd been sporting since your wedding day, never more than a rain cloud away, and Cass looking forlornly at the unadorned basement walls and her little friends clenched shy in a circle, and your own mother, a pink plastic drinking cup in her hand, gazing unperturbed out at the rain and then back to the naked table and the ravaged paper partyware, saying, "This is what I meant by the value of an exit strategy."

With the party indoors you need to work like dogs to amuse the eight-year-olds, and actually a dog might have helped to ease some of the pressure. The storm outside, while exciting to the kids, does not win you their sympathies, so you quickly organize relay races and simple crafts to kill the hour until that magical time of cake and presents and departures. During the greater and lesser drama of these activities, the piñata sits idly in the corner, its eyelashes as long and disdainful as any fashion model's. Finally, after a three-legged race that threatens to degenerate into a riot, you use the ladder, a bookshelf, and your curtain rod to jury-rig a beam from which to hang the piñata. The children cheer when you hoist it over but it's so unwieldy you can't tie its rope, so the piñata falls to the ground twice before your father-in-law ties an elegant slipknot that secures it perfectly. "I still remember a few things from the Navy," he says, graciously accepting his cup of punch from his wife.

Debra moves quickly to find the bat and recheck the tension of the curtain rod, and finally to inspect the pony's haunches for damage incurred during its falls. You have donated an old tie for a blindfold and Debra wraps it carefully around Cass's head while the other children look on. "Don't worry," Debra assures them. "You'll all get a chance."

When she slides back into place, you ask, "Won't they be mad if Cass bursts it before they've had their chance?" In retort, Debra guesses that "candy raining from the sky would be a pretty big distraction." Meanwhile the children are spinning Cass around. "Besides," Debra says. "It seemed to hold up when you kept dropping it, so if we're lucky it will last until it's time to serve the cake."

It only takes one swing from Cass to confirm that she won't break the piñata. She holds the bat so weakly that her first solid contact knocks it out of her hands. You move toward her, but her grandfather is there to level her swing and point her gently back toward the piñata. She takes a few more benign whacks before Debra asks whether she'd like to give one of her friends a try.

All of Cass's friends have their try. By the third child, no one is reapplying the blindfold. You'd held out hope for a taller girl with beefy arms, a girl who had beaten the others so easily in relay races that she'd seemed a decade older. This girl lets loose any number of direct hits onto the pony's chest, but while the ladder and the bookshelf creak and moan, the piñata remains impervious. Finally, after all the children have had their turns, Debra takes the bat. By now you have run over into cake-cutting time and some of the parents have filtered into the house hoping to see the presents being opened. Debra lets the cheers die down and mimes a baseball player cleaning his spikes, wiggling her hips in a way that reminds you why you married her all those years ago. She connects with the piñata and it sways. She swings for nearly a minute, the hollow thuds registering her successes. And maybe it is the rain that binds everything tightly together, or the hollow children's bat, but the piñata won't crack. After a minute or two Debra gives up and lifts the bat over her head to boos from the children and heckles from the parents. "Daddy," Debra asks, lifting the bat. You're about to step forward when you notice she is turning the other way, toward her own father, holding the bat out to him. He hesitates for a second, then shakes his head. "Tennis elbow, I'm afraid," he grimaces. "Sorry to disappoint you all."

You take the bat out of Debra's hands and peer closely at the piñata. Debra leans forward and whispers, "Let's see it, Hercules," and stands next to her parents, by the window and the strobe of the lightning outside. You touch the pink horse at its heart, tracing a finger down the paper. The rain has glued her tight like plaster on a cast, and the bat feels ridiculously light and hollow in your hand. You take a practice swing and the tiny bat, a baton really, constricts you. Then you peer in and swing as hard as you can, a tiny oomph of breath escaping your lips as you make contact.

The pony doesn't move.

From behind you, someone laughs, and while you know it's directed at the whole situation, right down to the mocking pony face, one eyelash having melted into a lascivious wink, you can feel your chest tighten up. You swing again, harder, and this time the pony sways away from you. By the fourth swing, it's rotating at its apex and you're timing the bat to meet it. By the fifth swing you can't hear the laughter anymore, can't hear the thunder, can't hear anything but the Doppler of the bat through the air and the thunk of the horse's belly. You can feel the ache in your forearm, the sweat lathering your swings, so close together that they're not like a batting stroke at all but something altogether different. There's a pinch in your neck but you notice, after so many strokes you've lost count, a tiny fissure opening in the piñata's belly and it can't be more than ten or fifteen strokes after that that the fissure gasps open and the candy explodes through the air like rain all around you. "Yes," you shout, your arms raised above your head, enough presence of mind to lift the bat so as not to hit any of the kids you expect to come forward to fill their hands with the candy. The candy inside the piñata has disintegrated under the shock of the afternoon's blows and now, freed from its shell, explodes in a cloud of sugar that blankets the basement floor, sticks in your hair and mouth, and blinds you. It is a few seconds before your eyes are clear enough to see through the sting and so everything comes gradually into focus, the children, their parents, Debra and Cass, everyone with faces as blank and open as monster masks in their mute shock and then your own, at what you've finally done.

An Ideal Pupil

"Put it into gear," Bruce urges. He drums his finger against a manila file. "It's intern day."

Ah, intern day. Every year the company hires a summer intern from a nearby university, always, but always, a woman. It is an opportunity to witness firsthand the exciting goings-on of a satellite franchise of a stock brokerage. In return, the intern is expected to help with filing and some light administrative duties, those time-intensive drudge projects that fell through the gaps during the prior ten months.

"Who've we got?"

Bruce looks down at the file. "Courtney something or other. Good grades, pretty high test scores." He turns the file over in his hand. "No picture, though," he complains. "These files never include anything important."

Ah, intern day.

As you and Bruce walk to the entrance, you see a thin kid wearing a suit still molded from its clearance rack hanger. He's got hair like the grunge rockers from the music videos, the ones you spend your evenings shielding preteen Cass from. "Please tell me this is her overprotective brother," Bruce mutters to you, still in stride, before coming into the boy's earshot, raising his hand and offering him a bright smile. "Courtney?"

"Yes, sir."

"We were expecting a woman," Bruce says. The boy looks up at you and you wobble your head in apology.

"I've heard the jokes," Courtney says warily. "Believe me."

Bruce hands you Courtney's file. "It was nice meeting you," he tells the boy. "If you have any problems..." After he trails off, the three of you stare into a circle for a while. Then Bruce says, "I've got a meeting." Then he stomps away.

"That went well," the kid shrugs.

"They say the first day's the toughest," you reply, and then feel a wave of déjà vu pass over you.

When you don't say anything else, Courtney looks up. "What did I miss?" he asks. "You've got this smile on your face..."

"Do I?" You can see your reflection in the plate glass of the outer door. You are smiling. An even fifty years old. The reflection hovers over the kid like a ghost. "Sorry," you explain finally. "What goes around comes around, I guess."

He doesn't understand but then he isn't meant to. Instead he gives the quintessential teenage look, the one you seem to relinquish at a certain age, the one that implies that anything he doesn't know already can't possibly be worth acquiring. "Whatever," he finishes.

"Come into my office," you say. "I'll give you the rundown."

Courtney, as it turns out, is a pretty good kid. Despite the hair, which makes him look like he's denying the existence of his forehead. Despite the glittering stud in his ear.

"What's wrong with the earring?" he asks.

"There's nothing wrong with it," you explain. Then you take a chance: "I'd have thought a boy named Courtney might want to keep his gender markers pretty well defined is all."

He considers this for a moment and then laughs. "You should try one," he says. "The missus would start looking at you differently."

"The missus would think I was having an affair."

"That's different, right?" he points out. "Or maybe not."

"There's two partners," you continue. "You've met Bruce, and David comes in later."

Courtney looks down at his watch then up at you. Now he takes his chance, "Real nine to fiver, huh?"

"Give the guy a break," you grin. "He's almost sixty. That's like a million to you, right?"

You laugh, but David has been coming in later and leaving earlier. Like nearly every man his age, he has been diagnosed with prostate cancer. Unlike nearly every other aging man you know, who rates this blow as roughly on par with a slipped disk or gout, David has, in his own special puffed-up way, declared himself a cancer patient, his voice lowering ridiculously at the words. Cancer patient. He will have to undergo a tourist's portion of chemotherapy, a few sessions. You and Bruce have been more or less good sports about this to David's face, but of course behind his back he has been wearing it very hard. "Do you think he'll lose his hair?" Bruce whispers of his nearly bald partner.

"Or his sense of smell," you reply.

"I don't know, I think his sense of smell is going the other way. You haven't noticed he's always holding a handkerchief to his face now?"

"I just assumed that's because we stink."

"We do stink," Bruce agrees.

"Look on the bright side," you return. "In two months we can stop hearing about David the cancer patient and start hearing about David, cancer survivor."

"Yes, that's true."

It's also true that you aren't particularly proud of this behavior but neither do you stop it. Your mother died of cancer, real cancer, metastasizing fucking armies of it, and you expect one day to succumb to it yourself. But not prostate cancer (the Cadillac of cancers, as your urologist calls it). Frankly you think prostate cancer is to cancer what a speeding ticket is to a rap sheet.

"But you're not a partner?" Courtney confirms.

"You see where it says 'Associates' on the door?" you point. "I'm the Associates."

"If it's just you, why don't they just go ahead and make you partner?"

"It's complicated," you say. It is complicated. Did siding with Bruce stall your career? Do you make fun of David because he won't let you buy into the partnership, or does your teasing spur his refusal? Scientists have postulated that there are a thousand different universes, and if so, then someone with access to them all could easily determine the answer. For you it must remain a mystery. Regardless, Bruce has promised that when David retires, new arrangements will be reached. "Let's face it," Bruce admits, showing off those gleaming teeth that never seem to fade in luster even as the rest of him slouches through middle age. "I don't want to be carrying this whole thing on my shoulders."

"Does that mean I don't have to get you coffee?" Courtney asks. Because you haven't been giving complete attention to the conversation, you aren't exactly sure how to read this line. You look at him for a moment, replaying how you've gotten here in your mind, and he returns the glance evenly. You consider your options. What goes around comes around, that seems to be where you'd left him. So: "Get me a fucking cup of coffee," you order. "Cream and sugar." And after you hold your jaw steady for a few seconds, he leaves. "Get yourself one too," you call after him. Sniveler.

It's nice having an intern around the office. You had them in the past, of course, but Courtney is different, or at least you treat him differently. It isn't that he's a guy. And it isn't just how the economy has continued to rise—a tower to the heavens, as you've resumed calling it. Debra assures you it isn't any of those things (although, she points out, anyone who's ever ridden in a car with you would conclude that you've got some serious issues with women). Instead, she thinks it has to do with your life stage, mostly. "Don't roll your eyes at me, Buster. You're the one who's always looking for answers in tea leaves, but life stages is suddenly too New Agey? I'm saying you're more open to generosity." She slides her arm under yours and smiles. "You haven't noticed things between us have been better for a while now?"

You'd noticed.

Courtney gets included in a way your other interns never did. He has become a regular lunch companion. He is a whiz with computers (kids his age seem hardwired in a way you cannot even fathom) and has streamlined the office system. He has even tutored you all (except David, who begged off any new tricks) on accessing the Internet. He types in a few key strokes and data floods the screen. "This is the future," he augurs and with the rest of you peering over his shoulders, it's easy enough to believe him.

Following your lead, even Bruce warms to the kid. He pulls Courtney off a tedious project, a waste of time and effort "unless inane number-crunching is your bag," and instead lets him sit in on meetings. "You were right about that one," he tells you fondly after Courtney well acquits himself researching a potential new fund. "You've got a knack for handling people. It's a useful management skill," Bruce declares. "That's good to know."

Late one Friday afternoon, Courtney drops by Bruce's office and joins a discussion on the delayed baseball season. You and Bruce have been drinking a couple of beers in anticipation of the weekend and there's an awkward pause while you consider offering one to Courtney. Finally he looks down at the can of soda in his hand. "That beer sure looks good," he says mock-mournfully. "And just think, only two more years until I can finally learn what it tastes like. Until then, I guess I'll stick with this fine carbonated corn syrup." The grace of this maneuver goes part of the way toward explaining the kid's appeal.

David, his briefcase packed for the weekend, sticks his head in the door and recoils. "Jesus," he sniffs, holding his handkerchief to his face. "Like a fucking coffee klatch in here. Like a bunch of women."

"Now you've done it," Bruce retorts. "Thanks to you, Courtney has grounds for a discrimination lawsuit."

"Don't sue us," you advise.

Courtney hides his smile behind his soda and regrets sadly that he can't make that promise before further consultation with his lawyers.

"This could be his big win," admonishes Bruce. "We're going to have to put his name on the door."

"We could do worse," David grumbles (you catch this neatly). "You guys are a barrel of monkeys. I'm glad you're amusing yourselves."

Bruce applauds. "Way to rally the troops. Brilliant leadership."

David throws his hands up. "I can't wait until my fucking IRA vests," he mutters. "I'll scrape my name off the door with an X-Acto knife. That is, if I can't think of something more enjoyable to do with the blade." He looks at each of you in turn and then departs. You can hear his footsteps down the hall, his key in the lock, his weekend in front of him.

You reach for another beer. It will be a few weeks before Debra mentions how violently he's been reacting to the chemotherapy, his stomach ejecting bile in ropes. You'll admit you had no idea and it will be a long time before she says anything else. "You know David," she'll finally sigh. "He's always been pretty good about keeping his office life and personal life separate."

You're in bed, nearly ready to turn off the lights. "Jesus," you whistle, your hand pulling away from the lamp.

Debra turns onto her side to face you and props herself onto an elbow. "Didn't you notice how he walks around with a handkerchief over his face?"

"Sure, but I didn't think…"

"He uses it to dab at open sores on his tongue. The acid's torn up his esophagus. He uses the handkerchief because it hurts too much to swallow. And because the fucking chemo has turned all his teeth black and he's self-conscious about the jokes you guys will come up with."

You can't think of anything to say to that and anyway it's getting late, so you just turn out the lights and vow to do better tomorrow. In the end, what more can anyone do?

If this is meant to fulfill a promise to your mother, it is thirty years too late. As it is you come to the church at an off-hour, avoiding the liturgical schedule, the bustle of Mass, the rigors of the altar service, in favor of the solitary late afternoon, that sliver between the noontime crowd and those who will arrive after their work is done for the day. You are careful to adjust your schedule accordingly and careful to share your reasons for doing so with nobody, although you can't pinpoint why this secrecy should feel so important to you. But you have learned some tricks in the past half-century, although to boast of them would be to risk another fight with Debra or a scowl from David, who continues to view your secrecy, even after a decade of faithful service, even on his death bed, as his mortal enemy.

The first time is nothing more than a whim, a passing fancy in late summer. Such a nice day that you decided to take an afternoon walk and ducked inside the church lest you should arrive back at the office sweaty and unkempt. Air-conditioning. It would be a lie to make any more of it than that. Nobody was around, the priest in chambers, the old women who seem to haunt all houses of worship still in their own homes tending to their own pensioners, their grandchildren with working mothers. You were shy of the sound of your footsteps on the marble, of the echoes off the impossibly high ceilings, afraid these might prompt somebody to offer his services. You didn't pray, of course, it had been too many years for that, so many years that the font at the entrance and the velvet kneelers in the pew were nothing more than furnishings to you, the stained glass stations on the wall nothing more than artwork to admire while you waited for your body to cool itself.

But still you came back. A week later, suspecting that this might turn into a ritual for you, the afternoon stroll as tentative assault on the paunch around your middle or, more likely, a justification for your morning donut. Again the church was deserted, no surprise since you arrived at the same time as before. Again the smell of it, the lemon cleaner for the floors, the wax from the candles, the pungent remains of the incense. And again you waited, your jacket lowered to your waist, your hands raised to expose your damp underarms to the air, so that you might return presentably to your afternoon clients.

By the third week, of course, you planned to come in advance. If there was a miracle, it was only that the weather for these three days remained so consistent, so that you had need of the church and the crosswind it offered. Three days nearly identical in temperature, so that the only change when you entered the church was the sun's shifting position through the stained glass. And yet this tiny alteration transformed everything inside. The world around you, once yellowed by Jesus's robe during the trials of the second station, now throbbed the red of the stained glass's overhead desert sun, as if when our own sun's path finally crossed into the third station it had created an entirely new church. Even the smell was richer, the pews saturated with polish. You began to spend longer and longer in your pew (first seat in the middle aisle, facing westward toward the sunlight, the first trimester of Jesus's passage). Even when the weather turned, even when you no longer welcomed the breeze but kept your suit jacket buttoned against its teeth, still you came. Once a week, never more. Into winter, you noticed how the heater produced yet another change, the incense now prevalent in the heavy air, the wood polish tangible only in the last week of the month, when the maintenance schedule dictated its use, the lemon scent of the marble wax nothing more than an autumn memory. You would look up at the stained glass, paying close attention to the panes just west of the sun, and wonder what would happen next. And you noticed one thing more: when first you started coming the hymnals were all stacked neatly into pillars along tables in the front of the church, but now a single copy rested on the stand in front of you.

You waited nearly a month for Mary's shawl to produce a winter blue, the light slanting diagonally across the church floor, skirting your toes in its path to the exit. She raised her head to Jesus, with a lead came separating the two. Some element of distortion worked at you in this light and you puzzled it for two weeks, focusing intently on the minute and the grand, the mystery eluding you until finally the midwinter sky pushed the sun farther west, tweaking the rays, and you saw how, through accident or design, the artist had misaligned the two pieces of the scene, lowering one or raising the other by the slightest fraction, so that Mary's eyes can never meet her son's, so that she must forever console herself with a fixed point along His forehead, the wavering shade of a glass wrinkle along His brow. So that He, in turn, looks not into His mother's eyes but instead over her head, as though He is already past her on His journey, as though He is already gone from her.

One day in early March, Bruce schedules a meeting that interferes with your ritual. "That's not a good time for me," you remind him and he apologizes. "I know, but now that David's gone we've all got to make sacrifices. You'll just have to tell your mistress to clear a different hour in her dance card." Office scuttlebutt about your weekly routine orbited around various low-grade scandals before settling onto a comical dominatrix named Mona who performs all manner of degraded activity (involving, in its salacious guises, a horse saddle, hot wax, a classroom desk, and even, ingeniously, zero-gravity boots), those passion plays satisfying Bruce's accounting of the missing thirty-nine minutes of your Thursday afternoons as well as your flushed cheeks and "general shit-eating grin." Since David's hospitalization, Bruce has settled on you as a foil, his ribbing more or less good-spirited and easily tempered by the rise in your compensation and bonus structure. "What are you going to do for a target when I finally make partner?" you ask him and he assures you he'll think of something. "This world has never suffered," he reminds you, "for a shortage of fools."

When finally the meeting releases you to the church, it is nearly an hour after your appointed time. Only forty-eight minutes but everything feels different. You have been moving inexorably toward the fifth station, Simon of Cyrene. For two weeks now, in the early mornings before Debra and Cass have come down to fill the kitchen with their activity—the bubbling of the coffee maker and the refrigerator's compressor unit clicking on and off every time the door opens, and the toaster oven heating the bread, all of the machines signaling the completion of their tasks with merry buzzers, Debra and Cass and their easy chatter and reminders of coordinated pick-up and drop-off schedules, the junior high cheerleading, the mother-daughter spa treatments, the girls' night movies—before all of this you have sat alone at the table imagining Simon's emerald green tunic and how it might look reflected in the marble flooring, brought back only by Cass's insistent nudging that "Dad's off visiting other planets again."

Forty-eight minutes push the sun directly into the center of the fifth station, a placement you hadn't anticipated for at least another week. You stand outside the church weighing the pros and cons in your hand, the temptation of the heavy wooden doors. Already you can feel the pressure on the back of your knees, your elbows finding their place. But you can also feel the slight fissure inside you as you consider the sunlight passing through the heart of Simon's tunic or, worse, a glancing blow through his shoulder. The iron handle at hand offers no clear indication of what you should do. Behind you a car slows, its wheels kicking up slush and road salt, its headlights reflected on the brass plaque listing the schedule of liturgical offerings. The sky above is cloudy. You enter the church.

Inside, a priest hunches over your pew, whistling to himself. When he sees you, he straightens before stepping backward into the aisle. He is very old, so desiccated you wonder how he could ever possibly whistle through such dry lips. He tugs at his cassock, looking embarrassed somehow, and you can feel the blood in your cheeks. "Father," you say finally, and he nods in return. He holds a hymnal, which you both look at for a long moment before he replaces it on the stand. "You're running late," he whispers and then moves back toward the altar.

Flushed, off-balance, you reach for the hymnal and cringe when it slams to the floor. The priest, nearly to the altar, jolts upright and you think it possible that this man, this octogenarian, might go into cardiac arrest. You pick up the hymnal, your hands shaking, and lay it on the seat next to you. "I'm sorry," you call. He raises a hand in acknowledgment but doesn't turn around.

Nothing is going right, save this: the sunlight at this time of late afternoon passes just shy of Simon's right shoulder, missing his tunic entirely, offering the same yellowed tinting you've already seen five or six times, the wood of Jesus's cross, no different in its new context. The green is tantalizingly close, protected by its lead came, dark and untouched. Your hand reaches for the hymnal, still trembling. After all this, a miracle of sorts: the light will last another week.

What Is Lost and What Is Gained

The new convertible handles beautifully on the blacktop. May first, May Day, and everything has bloomed seemingly overnight from browns and yellows into those deep, rich greens that seem somehow a confirmation. Every year you think you should remember to look for the signs (the buds, the birds changing course), but every year you forget, only to look up one morning to find an entirely new world laid out for you. Every year you forget, but maybe this is a blessing, like a surprise party. With the top down, you slow until you can hear the birds overhead and smell the ozone. You can barely remember the winter, such as it was, fading already into the shovels in the garage and boots in the hall closet. Debra will have even fewer reminders, able as she is to keep her tan throughout the winter months. The odometer on the car turns over, just at the second you look at it, to 00050, your very age, and in this light, with this leather upholstery, it is child's play to laugh at the coincidence. Who is afraid of big, bad middle age?

The car is a sweetheart lease from one of your clients. Metallic red, alternately winsome and toothy. She's the sort of car you might get away with naming if ever you had such an impulse. You move candidates around in your mouth but nothing feels quite right.

Apparently you aren't the sort of person who could ever name his car, or his home (Tara, Barrington…). So be it. Such things always seemed like a costume to you. There are puddles along the sides of the road (it must have rained while you were inside filling out the paperwork), and the sight of your car appearing and disappearing in the wet sheen of the blacktop elates you. You head down a steeper incline to watch the reflection of your wheels gather speed, the metallic paint like fire above them.

Another good day on the market, another good day in the world, and now home to Debra and Cass. You park the car on the street. You'd like the whole thing to be a surprise and don't want to risk alerting them. You let yourself in through the front door, so rarely used you fear its groaning hinges will give you away. You tiptoe upstairs to Cass's room, but it's empty. So is the living room and your bedroom, only Debra's perfume lingering. You stand in the middle of the kitchen, perplexed. There's no note on the table. Even more ominously, a pot of spaghetti sauce sits on the open eye of the stove. You walk into the garage, no longer concerned with surprise and don't know whether to be relieved or more frightened still to see Debra's minivan. The alarm system blinks lazily, unconcerned. Back in the kitchen, you're reaching for the phone when you spot, through the kitchen window, through the screened-in porch, Cass and her mother standing outside in the garden. Cass is laughing, her loosened pigtails bobbing up and down, while Debra stands on her tiptoes, her hand outstretched, beautiful. There is a white bird (you've never been able to identify them by species), hopping along Debra's tomato trellis while Debra holds a branch out toward it. Through the walls of the house, the windows, the screen, you can't hear anything and so, even as you walk through the back door and stand in the new grass, your keys dangling off of your finger, it isn't clear whether Debra is shooing the bird from her vegetables or making an offering.

"Daddy," cries Cass, grabbing at your hand. She has been outside all afternoon and smells like lilacs. Debra turns slowly, her face open as a saint, hand open, mouth opening to greet you. "You're home."

THE EMPEROR.

Simon of Cyrene, when at last he shines on you, is (you may say) worth the wait. All week you have counted down the hours, brooking no attitude from Bruce who, with something approximating a smile, attempted to schedule yet another conflicting meeting; offering Debra and Cass your body to ridicule ("Ground control to Major Dad?" "Major? That's stretching it." "Ewwwww, Mom!"), holding apart that part of you that imagined the light through the green prism of his tunic, how it would alter your perception of the heavy wood, the marbled veins of the floor, the age spots on your hand as it clutches the hymnal, no shaking now, an ordered path, no running away, committed.

You arrive on schedule to find your hymnal in place, the church deserted, your pew open and beckoning. You're careful to avert your eyes until you get into your seat (you can always count on the sun to be exactly where it should be) and then gaze up to the seawater-green washing over this entire section of the church. You have made certain to hold off examining this new station too closely; even during last week's debacle your relief was enough to blind you to its details, but now you let yourself go to it. The station shows Simon of Cyrene made to carry Jesus's cross for Him some appointed distance.

Whereas the earlier stations contained large pieces of glass, here the artist divided the portrait into much smaller segments, so that the faces are nearly mosaics, nearly modernist in their representation. Jesus, at the center of the portrait, reveals nothing. If He is relieved to be released from His burden, His body exhibits no signal. He stares ahead at the viewer, the red blood dripping from His crown the only color on an otherwise frozen visage. He offers Simon, hunched into an inverse parenthetical, dwarfed by the cross that overpowers his quadrant, nothing—not even a passing glance. Only the crown of thorns on Jesus's forehead distinguishes His visage from the centurion's in the upper right-hand corner. Otherwise, they are identical. Like Jesus, the centurion's face is a blank, inhuman, the face of a low-level bureaucrat, thinking only of that evening's respite, of the spiced wine curling his tongue, the salvation of his wife's soft flesh, the pillow of her breast under his head.

Simon of Cyrene alone improves with the segmented glass. His left eye, closest to Jesus, the right side of his mouth facing away, his visible ear, these parts are the lightest of browns and together suggest the traditional image of stoic generosity. In contrast, his right eye, his chin, and the left side of his mouth indicate hostility. These the artist has shaded darker so that your eye groups them together to follow the length of the cross to Simon's nearly hidden right hand, down near the bottom, his fingers mahogany like the wood, one finger pointing accusingly at the unburdened figure alongside him. To clarify his emotions you need only lift your finger at a diagonal. If you select a certain angle, you elicit a slavish devotion. But rotate your hand along its axis forty-five degrees and the look turns caustic. Remove your hand altogether and Simon's face atomizes and then reforms into its mosaic of ambivalence, his nose a bridge, his chin locked in determination, his mouth a grimace of surprise, his eyes betraying recognition of his plight: his fate is unraveling and he is powerless to stop it.

As you sit there, tilting your hand forward and back, you grow aware of the priest standing over you in the nave, watching your movements. He leans above you and tilts his body to see the window from your perspective. Together you look up.

 "I'm sorry about last week," you begin. He rests his arm on your shoulder to push his body back to standing. "Nothing to worry about," he assures you. He gives you a small wave, ushering you out of the pew into a small office behind the vestry. "I don't believe I recognize you from Sunday services," he coughs.

"Not yet," you admit.

His small desk is burdened with papers. His hand reaches into the pile and performs some elegant magic, emerging a second later with a pink sheet of paper. "Here are times for all the services, along with various other bits of information you may find helpful." Next he finds a clipboard with a pen secured via rubber band. "I'm always losing these," he remarks. "Why don't we start with some information?" He asks your name and it seems indecorous not to answer him. Your address. When he asks your phone number, you hesitate a moment before inverting the final two numbers. It seems kinder than explaining about Debra, how this needs to be something for you alone, something private, and how you still haven't learned the secret (if indeed there is one) of how to keep something private without keeping it hidden. You tell him about Cass; baptized across town, but not much since. Like some of the faces from the stained glass outside, his face offers you nothing. He fumbles around and eventually finds a brochure for youth activities. "The kids love it," he says with a crooked smile. "They eat ice cream and popcorn, have dances to their rock music, basically all the conventional ways of honoring our Savior." You fold this brochure neatly at the top of the growing stack in your lap. "I'm impressed you can find anything on this desk," you tell him. "The whole parish runs on forms," he replies. "We are, after all, a church rich in the traditions of bureaucracy. Sometimes I wonder whether this was the calling I answered."

"And?"

He waves his hand over the pile of papers, the motion stirring the edges into a current. "When they promised I was to be a bookkeeper, I had another book in mind." He chuckles at his own joke. "This is the mechanism. The body, not the spirit. That's why we keep it hidden here in the back. The real Church is out there."

At first you think he is gesturing to the world outside, a sort of grandiosity you have been programmed by television to expect from priests, but then with a blush and a jolt of self-recrimination you realize he means the chapel, nothing more. From your seat you can see through the half-open door to the pulpit and above it the familiar glass.

"I've grown very fond of the stained glass," you say.

"Ah, the stations," he says. "We've had them since the early twenties."

"Beautiful," you repeat.

He looks at you for a moment. "You know, I suppose they are. At my age, I tend to keep my eyes on the path in front of me at all times. And of course, too many eyes on the glass suggest to me that my homily has been going on too long. A sermon only reaches receptive ears. So I suppose I've conditioned myself to think of the church's artwork, for all of its beauty, as my enemy. Strange, wouldn't you say?"

You laugh and he pulls back a bit in surprise before laughing himself.

"Anyway," he continues, "if you like the glass, I would recommend getting your fill of it now. Rome seems intent on phasing it out." He roots around on the desk. "Somewhere in here," his voice emerges from deep within the pile, "there is a proposal for new stations of the cross more closely aligned with the gospels. The youth leader has suggested we allow our younger congregants to produce their own representations—as an arts and crafts project." Unsettled, one of the great mountains of paper lurches forward and you corral it back onto the desk. He thanks you. "I can't find it right now," he finishes.

"It would be a terrible shame to lose that glass."

"Yes, you seemed particularly attached to Simon of Cyrene," the priest says. He takes out a notepad and scribbles something before returning the pad to the summit of a pile. "You can see how my desk came to be in this state," he says. "Well, I've made a note of it. Should we decide to modernize our stations, we will undoubtedly be conducting an auction of the originals. So you might well have a chance to examine it from the comfort of your own home."

You tell him that would be an honor but it would still make you sad. "They belong in the church."

"Simon of Cyrene," he shrugs. "Never mentioned by John. Blame him."

"I will," you nod.

"Should anything happen, presumably I will make some sort of announcement during the service," the priest says. "I do not expect this to be imminent. One must always take into account the speed with which things happen in the church. In many ways, we are as far from Rome as we ever were."

As he walks you back down the nave, you stare up at Simon. If he did have to leave this place, wrong though it might be, he would find a proper home with you. You imagine how he might look in the early morning sun, imagine how guests would react on seeing him in your house, how awed they would be. Lost in your imagination, you realize you've slowed to a crawl, the priest waiting beside you. You look up one final time, the hour and your own station near the door having pushed the light outside of the portrait's frame.

The priest looks at you looking at the glass and places his hand on your shoulder. So deft you barely register its presence. "Still, keep your ears open for an announcement," the priest's voice says. "Be listening for it."

For the Many Pleasures of Childhood

"What if she doesn't remember us?" Your wife grabs for your hand and you squeeze her fingers, gently.

"It was summer camp, Debra, two months."

"Two months! For a child, that's like dog years."

"I'll be sure to tell her you said that."

Across the parking lot, other parents are having the very same conversation. Some of them have brought flowers, younger siblings hoisted onto forearms, beaming smiles and vacation tans of their very own. The woman next to you is holding a tattered stuffed bunny. "It was her favorite," she explains, "and she forgot it in the rush to pack."

Debra nods in understanding.

"She begged for it in every letter home for the first month. Said she couldn't sleep without it. I wanted to drive it up to her, the five hours, but my husband wouldn't have it." Her husband nods distractedly. "She didn't even mention it in her last few letters. Now we're worried that she's forgotten it."

You tell her you know how she feels. Your wife fingers her bob. Cut off six inches and she looks younger, everyone tells her so. "Do you think Cass will like it?" she asked this morning.

It is a hot day, so hot it seems silly that the kids are coming home already. Last Saturday in August and they'll be in school in a week. That's enough for them not to want to come home if the horseback riding and water skiing weren't. You don't reveal it but your own daughter's letters home have changed as well. At first long missives of detail and questions, they have shrunk to almost nothing. They had to write every Thursday, you know this, and yet the week before last, the envelope had nothing but a page torn from a book, carefully folded. Debra searched for clues but none appeared. Filler. This week you got nothing, and expect nothing. Too much for the kids to do in their final days with woodworking projects to finish and swimming tests to pass. There was a dance too. Debra seemed eager to imagine Cass at it, dressed in clothes you can't remember packing. "I snuck in a white blouse," she said, proudly. "I told her to keep it hung up, just in case." Her eyes were dewy when she said this, although why she got choked up imagining some boy's hands on Cass's hips, or waist, a four-minute slow dance for whatever a twelve-year-old can think to do, is beyond you. One look at her swimsuit and you wanted to lock her in her room as a preemptive strike. The two girls, your wife and daughter, laughing at you while you ranted. Summer camp. You must have been insane.

Every so often a loud rumble emerges over the gaggle of parents congregating in small groups. All heads instantly turn, conversation threads cut. The train tracks that run behind the shopping center fool everyone precisely every eleven minutes. The bus is running late. Behind you, in the rows and rows of station-wagon gridlock, a baby starts to cry. A parent hushes it (the tinkle of a music box), but it devolves to tantrum, from the heat and the waiting, or maybe jealousy at so many heads turned away from it. Debra's shoulders tense, everyone angry with the mother, who mumbles an apology and crouches back into her car. You should all be more patient, each of you knows. You are, after all, parents yourselves. But this is a ceremony: the plastic banner welcoming the campers into the parking lot, the cameras poised ready, the lipstick kisses. This is a homecoming. People have brought dogs.

You and your wife have brought nothing save some pictures from a long weekend in Boston. At home there is a T-shirt and a baseball cap, both Red Sox, and a new lunch box for the fall. You are, you imagine, much as she left you. You have shed a few pounds in the summer weather, but it seems unlikely that either of your women would notice it.

"Do you think we'll meet this Sally person?" Debra asks. Sally is your daughter's new best friend, appearing sporadically and then constantly in whatever letters reached you. By the sixth week they'd become a we, an unspoken coupling. You know little about her. Her father is an orthodontist and she has braces. Cass has already started hinting for them herself even though her teeth are straight enough without them. Sally is a better horseback rider, having had previous experience. Cass is better at tennis. They seem equal, roughly, or at least the distinction irrelevant, at basketball and soccer.

"I'll be happy if Sally isn't a boy," you say and Debra gives you a sideways look. "Who knows with kids these days?" you ask. "Could be Salvador."

Debra blinks and stares at her watch. "It's almost an hour late."

It isn't, you were all here early, but this doesn't seem worth the fight.

An expensive car pulls up behind yours and an expensive couple emerges. "Looks like we timed it right," the man says loudly. The woman with the pink bunny gives him a withering look. "Every year we used to come early, every year they'd get here late. Eventually you learn." This couple wants you to understand that they are expert at this. They are experienced. They are old pros. Their Johnny or Jenny has been going to this camp for years. Of such things are counselors made. You imagine dragging your daughter's duffel bag against the metallic finish of their car, scraping the zipper along its trim. You imagine that your daughter has just dumped their boy with a casual nonchalance that would be alien among girls her age. She has left him for his best friend. When he asks why she shrugs and bites her lower lip. "He's a better kisser than you." The wife is tweaking one of her impractically long nails with a file when she cocks her head. "I hear them," she says.

You smile, the train again, but damned if she isn't right. The bus comes up into the lot and a cheer stirs through the crowd. "Not yet," someone warns. "When the doors open."

Debra slides over to you. You can feel the seam of her shorts rub against your thigh. You wrap your arm around her waist.

When the doors yawn, the cheer breaks open again, and you wait for the kids to emerge, to come flying down. But instead nobody moves. The windows are tinted, the faces indistinct but focusing straight ahead.

"Is there something wrong?" Debra asks. You don't answer.

All of the parents are silent, wondering, and then you hear it waft out of the bus like smoke. It is a mournful song, an elegy if there truly is such a thing. Even the babies in the crowd are muted. The children sound like a choir but they aren't singing for you. The song finishes and the final few notes blend and then dissipate. The rich woman has pushed in front of you, her frosted hair blocking any view you might have had. She turns and smiles patiently. "The camp anthem," she reports. "It's a tradition."

Finally a camper walks down the stairs, and almost comically the crowd begins to cheer. It is a towheaded kid, Cass's age or no more, and he flinches at the sound. Then, almost without warning, his face explodes into a giant grin. "Do it," you whisper, and Debra's shoulders are pushing forward. The boy teeters for a moment against the cheering and then he drops his duffle bag. He nudges his Coke-bottle glasses forward onto his nose and you can see behind his head the arms and hands and elbows of the passengers waiting anxiously behind him. "Do it now," you urge, and then his arms rise above his head like a champion and he thrusts his face forward into the cheers. You smile and cheer with the rest as he picks up his duffel and disappears into the crowd, knowing like a migratory bird which station wagon, which couple, which family is his own.

Another child emerges, and another, the cheering growing fainter as trunks open and close. You would think the bus filled and emptied three times over, like clowns from a Volkswagen. Another and another, almost no claps at all now, and still no Cass. Debra asks you if you think there is something wrong and you don't know what to tell her. Surely the camp would have notified you had it been something serious, only you stopped for breakfast on the way and aren't compulsive about checking your messages. "She's coming," you intone with a confidence you don't feel. Maybe she got on the wrong bus. By now there is nothing but the mocking sounds of trunks and laughter. The bunny girl has come and gone, so too the expensive couple and their ordinary-looking son. Motorboats and two-ton horses, it's not like something couldn't have gone wrong. Maybe they were waiting to tell you face-to-face. You crane your neck, but the passengers getting out now are in their late teens, the counselors. They have their own parents and friends and rituals. Debra's neck starts twitching and you rub it with your palm. "She'll be here," you say. "She'll be here."

And here she is.

The Lord of Valor

Debra wants to know if this has something to do with getting old. When you promise it doesn't, she dismisses your opinion. "I don't know why I bothered asking you," she says, "since you'd be the last to know."

"It doesn't have anything to do with getting old," you insist. And you don't think that it does. This isn't some last-ditch effort at redemption or some fear of the great unknown. It isn't some weaseling desire to hedge your bets. After all, if there is a God, you are pretty sure He doesn't offer dispensations to those who sit in church pews on Thursday afternoons to admire the pictures, foregoing Mass altogether despite increasing pressure from the priest, who has now added a chastising "missed you last Sunday" to the weekly ritual of handing you the hymnal. A chastisement that prompted you to ask Debra whether she and Cass might want to try the church out tomorrow, a suggestion which prompted this fight, everything causal in relationship.

"Look, we got the kid baptized, didn't we?" Debra says. It's funny that she should bring it up since even then it had been a struggle, extending from Cass's birth in New York all the way to your move here, a minor but distinct vein of tension during those first few years, when everything with Cass had been uncertain. Then, paradoxically, it had been Debra pushing for baptism and you holding back. Ultimately the decision had been made that it couldn't hurt, that her parents would appreciate the gesture while your mother wouldn't care one way or the other, and that it might even be an opportunity to increase your visibility within the community, "for potential clients who are on the fence," Debra had argued. You can no longer remember specific details about the baptism, except that your mother had elected not to come. "If you'd given me enough warning," she'd explained, "I could have made flight arrangements, but you know what they do to you these days with short notice and besides, my dues are paid up in that pool, if you can remember." Nobody missed her, even the pomp of the ceremony blunted by your exhaustion. Like so many seemingly momentous decisions, the baptism turned out to be nothing more than a page in the photo album, reduced in scale by the upheaval of the move, a quiet note in the midst of a very loud song.

"I don't get it," Debra says. "Things are finally on track with our life, so now you want to start calling audibles? People turn to the Church when things go wrong. You're the only person I know who fights his way alone through all the bad times to find the Church when it can no longer do him any good."

"I wasn't alone," you say, since she has offered the joke on a platter. "I had you."

"Oh, God," she shudders. "Somebody tell me why I married Shecky Greene?" Then she corrects herself, "Shecky Greene had *good* timing. Look, if we started going to church while David was alive, it might have made sense. Although between you and me, it would have taken a lot more than that for you to turn that ship around. But Bruce isn't likely to make you a partner because of religion, and frankly you aren't going to pick up too many new clients with it anymore. I begged you when we got here to consider a church, and then you wait more than a decade until every possible shred of benefit has been extinguished and then you find a church in a part of town where nobody lives…Honestly," she sighs. "Maybe you *should* go to church and let God carry you around for a while. Lord knows, my back could use the break."

None of this would have happened had you not mentioned the windows, in passing, over drinks with Bruce and his wife last week. There had been a lot of wine (as always) and near the end of the night Bruce had started on his full-court press about where you disappeared to every Thursday afternoon. It killed him that you had a secret. This was news to Debra, who turned with amusement. "Found somebody younger?" she asked. "Maybe," you quipped, and were hurt by how cavalierly everyone dismissed the notion. Responding to your look, Nancy said, "I'll bet it's something mysterious," and Bruce replied, "I'll bet it's a haircut." You'd held them off through another round of drinks, the conversation eventually migrating to the Aberdeen scandal, but just when you'd thought yourself safe, Bruce smiled and asked whether your own little soldier was doing you proud and you were right back into the middle of it. Finally, sheepishly, you told them about the church and how you appreciated the stained glass windows and liked talking to the priest (this last a lie, the old man taken to mutterings about the most logistical of matters, his complaints about the youth leader as stale as his breath, although you wonder if articulating this might constitute a heresy or at the least a lower category of sin). Some part of you held back some part of the telling from embarrassment and fear that they might want to accompany you, for fear in your drunkenness (for you must have been drunk not to have denied everything from the start) that they might have packed up the last of the wine into the back of Bruce's SUV and embarked on a pilgrimage. So your telling did not do (could never have done, anyway) those portraits justice, your devotion to them weak, a diminishment. So that rather than any grander effect, all your description elicited from Bruce and Nancy was an embarrassed glance at the clock and then from Debra the opinion that, all things considered, she might have preferred the blow-job alternative.

With such a reaction, your offer to take Debra and Cass (or Cass alone, were Debra to prefer) to Sunday Mass could be described as courageous. You had waited until Cass was out, her regular Saturday trek to the mall, before broaching the subject. You predicted, of course, that Debra would not react favorably to the notion. "Then why did you ask me?" she said and then answered her own question: "Because this is yet another way for you to claim the moral high ground, to position yourself as Saint George and me as the dragon. Well I've got news for you, Mister, that isn't the act you've got going on, no matter how many times you try it. You aren't some Lord of Valor, you're a manipulator and a saboteur. What's wrong?" she asked, finally breaking down in tears. "Had we gone too long without a fight?"

It wasn't a fight that you were looking for, although your desires are not manifest even to yourself. The portraits were a private matter. To invite Cass and Debra with you into the church, to go on a Sunday morning with the pews full (what old woman, with elaborate hat and cloying perfume, might have squatted your place, thinking it her own after years of faithful worship?) would not have brought you joy, of this at least you are quite certain. It would have been a sacrifice for you. Ultimately Debra's refusal and Cass's lukewarm response (Did Mom say I had to?) were enough to prevent any of you from attending Mass and this, coupled with your rising aversion to the priest, enough to end your own Thursday visits, so that within a year they faded into nothing more than a memory. So it may be then that you did end up with exactly what you wanted (and what you deserved)—your long Lenten fast, your renunciation, the arrow fitting perfectly into the wound.

Dreams Rewarded and Denied

"Open the fucking door, you old codger. We come bearing gifts." Bruce's fist like thunder and behind him the breaking glass of laughter. Debra, nearer to the door, already halfway in her cups, peers through the peephole.

"Who is it?" she calls, innocently.

"Odin, God of Prophecy and War," bellows Bruce. "Open this door, I do command thee."

"Or what?" Debra asks. You've scurried behind the plate glass window to watch two carloads of your guests on the patio, enjoying this performance. You watch as Nancy leans forward to whisper something into Bruce's ear.

"Or I shall huff and puff and blow your hut down," Bruce declares.

Debra opens the door. "I'm pretty sure you've got your mythologies mixed up." She shakes her head. "Ask the birthday boy, that's his new hobbyhorse."

"Where is the dancing corpse?" Bruce asks, after giving Debra a wallop of a kiss that deepens her wine flush. When he spots you hiding behind the curtain, he raises his arms in greeting.

"That was some kiss," you say. "Droit du seigneur, no doubt?"

"Naturally. For I am Odin, God of Poetry and Magic."

"I thought it was Prophecy and War," Debra asks, a silly smile on her face.

"That too, and a hundred more besides. Asgard is a big kingdom."

Behind him Nancy collects his coat, which he has let slide to the floor. "He's been reading his old comic books. Wait until that one gets a few years older," she warns Debra. "Mine's a teenager now, so I figure that gives me, what, ten years until he's in diapers?"

"Nonsense," thunders Bruce, "for I…"

"Am Odin, God of pound cake and liverwurst, yeah, yeah, Hrothgar, we got the gist," Nancy hushes him.

Bruce comes up and grasps your shoulders, undeterred. "Birthday wishes," he pronounces. "A million congratulations on your safe passage through this world." Then he leans down and kisses you loudly on the mouth. When the crowd stops cheering, he wipes his lips on his shirt and exclaims, "And *that*, my child, is the droit du seigneur. Now where is that lovely daughter of yours?"

Debra giggles. "Oh no you don't. We've barred her door. Cerberus guards the entry." She looks at you for assistance.

"We've chained her to a rock."

"And also she's spending the night at a friend's house," Debra finishes weakly. "We had a suspicion this might get out of control."

"Nothing quite as rowdy as a group of Golden Agers sowing their oats, huh?" Bruce grins.

"Fifty-two," you correct, jabbing your finger into your chest. "Fifty-two."

"Ah, Thor, still so young," Bruce says fondly, tussling what's left of your hair.

"Thor?" Nancy asks Debra.

"That's pretty good," Debra returns, "considering I've been going with Bruce Junior all these years."

The rest of the crowd has dispersed into the kitchen to pour themselves drinks or into the bedroom to drape their coats on the bed. So there are only a few people left to see you bow to Nancy with a deep flourish. "My queen."

Debra blows a raspberry. "Junior Bruce," she smirks. "Is it possible that you relish playing the fool?"

It is a tremendous party. The guest list, some thirty people, was well-constructed: colleagues from work, Debra's office friends, of course, and a select group of clients. "Sure," cracks Debra. "The precious few you've managed to lasso who didn't go to high school with my mother. Now that's a diminishing pool."

"I don't know," you retort. "If they're anything like your mother, they'll be dancing on my grave." It's true that these past few years, which have seen the deaths of your own mother and many others, have offered no hint of Debra's parents' demise. "Where are they now, Greece?"

"Istanbul," she smiles. "Some sort of jazz festival."

"They're going to live forever," you reply. You mean it too, although maybe not in the way she takes it.

"You think he's going to announce it tonight?" you ask. Debra is busy fastening her bra in the mirror. She fiddles with a strap, her arm snaking behind her.

"Maybe," she says. "He does enjoy playing to the crowd."

For that reason, you've kept the guests work-related.

None of Debra's family is here tonight—there is a brunch planned for tomorrow. Another Sunday afternoon—"unless you had other plans, Pope Pius?" Debra asked, her hand blocking the holes on the receiver. You hope to be able to relay the good word then. No family tonight. A tremendous party, as you've said.

"Twelve years," you point out. "Twelve good years."

"More or less," Debra agrees (more or less).

"You know he could use the influx of capital."

"That's true," Debra nods. She holds two unmatched earrings up to her face for comparison. "Lorraine says he's been paying out David's pension in installments, borrowing the money from equity."

"We've got enough built up in the house to buy into the

partnership, right?" you ask her.

"What are you asking me for? Aren't you the financial planner?"

"Aren't you the accountant?" you retort.

"Division controller," she smiles. A recent promotion of her own.

"I stand corrected," you say, and move toward her.

Still comparing the earrings, she watches your reflection come closer. She doesn't move away. "We've got to get Cassie to her friend's house," she chides.

"We've got time," you say. You watch your hand and its reflection make their voyage to her shoulder, the tips of their fingers kissing one another in the glass.

At midnight Bruce proposes a toast. Everyone gathers around him in the living room. Debra catches your eye across the room and mouths—"this is it." You hold up two crossed fingers in reply.

"In three months," Bruce begins, "we will mourn the two-year anniversary of David's loss." This invites a generic rumble of sadness from the choir. "That he lost his battle with cancer is ironic since he certainly didn't lose too many battles with me." He looks down at you. "I never wanted to hire you in the first place," he admits, shaking his head. "Didn't like what little I knew. But you know David, never one to lose a fight. He beat me into submission." He pauses. "And I'm glad he did. You were a great hire and you've been a great friend. Hiring you was the best decision I ever got railroaded into." Everyone starts to cheer. "Except marrying Nancy," he sneaks in, the cheers turning to laughs. "Happy Birthday, Buddy."

You wait for more but don't get it. Someone starts singing and you have to stand there with a stupid look on your face until they all finish and you can mutter a few words in response and then, mercifully, escape to the kitchen.

For the remainder of the evening the revelry continues without you, but no one seems to notice. The more you drink, the faster everything seems to move. Debra, in discussion with your office manager about school uniforms, pulls away briefly to whisper in your ear, "we'll talk about this tomorrow," before returning to her conversation. "Great party," everyone assures you. It appears to be. Your stores of liquor are most heavily depleted.

Every time you try to catch Bruce alone, he is pontificating to a group. He has recently taken up windsurfing, or some other form of foolishness, and now boasts a crescent scar along the length of his shin. Throughout the night, with almost no provocation, he has been lifting himself onto whatever piece of your furniture he can find, hitching up his pant leg and offering peeks. By the earliest hours of the morning, your own personal bottle of wine running low, you stumble across him about to mount your coffee table, one of Debra's female colleagues tracing the raised skin up to the knee. "You should get one of those booths," you suggest. "Let them feed quarters into the slot." "Don't be ridiculous," Bruce laughs, looking down at the woman at his feet. "A beautiful woman like this, I would give it away free." He rotates his hips a bit (the divorcée makes a ridiculous wooing noise) and you slink away to search for more wine.

Legions of dead bottles gather on the kitchen table. Empty bottles of beer and wine and liquor, so many they form a necropolis. This confirms it: you are drunk and melancholy. You look up at the bottles from above and then squat to your knees, what's left of the dregs coloring the glass, distorting the kitchen light into a prism. It could be beautiful. Standing too quickly makes the blood rush to your head, forcing you to grasp the table to steady yourself, generating an earthquake in the city below.

Hands grab you underneath the arms. "Whoa there," Nancy whispers into your ear. "Hold steady."

You turn to face her. "Got up too fast," you explain. So drunk your tongue is like a thrashing serpent.

"Or the booze," she says.

"Or the birthday," you admit. "This old gray mare…"

"Tell me about it." When she laughs you can smell the wine on her breath and see the drunken remnants of a mushroom covering an incisor. "Wait until you hit sixty," she promises. Then she leans in so close, you can smell her perfume and see into the valley of her blouse. "I'll tell you a secret," she whispers. "It doesn't get any better."

"You're sixty?" you ask. It's funny, of course. You're aware of how old you seem to be getting but nobody else seems to age, like they know a secret you don't. When you tell her this, Nancy smiles.

"Now that is the nicest thing anyone's said to me in a long, long time."

"Yeah," you reply. Then: "Sixty?"

"Shhh," she says, her finger up to her lips, blowing her atoms all over your face. "Don't tell anyone, all right?"

You tell her that Debra turns forty-five in November and she clutches her hands to her breast. "You wound me. Want another secret?"

"Yes, please."

"She doesn't want a party."

When you laugh, she smiles. "There it is," she says, letting her finger graze your face. "That's been missing for most of the night."

"Since midnight, yeah." You can't help sounding petulant.

"Don't worry," she promises. "Good things are coming."

"When?"

"Have patience," she promises.

"Easy for you to say," you retort.

"No," she shakes her head sadly. Something flits across her face, but you're too melancholy, too drunk to read it, the light in the kitchen bad and your eyes weak. "It's never easy."

Her left hand is still under your shoulder, her face tilted up to yours. You're very drunk and so is she. In the living room you can hear war whoops and college fight songs, a bench tipping over and glass breaking. "Barkeep," someone shouts. Between you, you carry more than a century of years. "Before the Wright Brothers," you whisper, without context, so drunk. Below you the metropolis of bottles stretches out like a cityscape, the theater of your world, you and Nancy as high above it as the gods on Olympus. You smile. "What?" she asks. "I'm getting my mythologies mixed up too," you explain. Her lips open in response. She is beautiful. You kiss her.

At the sink, Debra inflicts her own special brand of justice on a sack of potatoes. Beside her, scrambling eggs for an omelet, you concentrate only on offering a smaller target. Twice you open your mouth and twice she mutes you. "Let's just get through this fucking brunch, shall we?" Sunday morning and Debra's relatives are coming to celebrate her promotion and, it was assumed, your own.

The party did not end well, of course.

Even before the kiss could end, before you were granted this tiny gift, Bruce pushed his way through the kitchen door, trailed by a group of his camp followers, all carrying bottles raised above their heads. His voice entered before he did, "Little Thor, I regret to inform you that your coffee table may have offered its last full measure…" The punchline was never completed. For the first fucking time all night, Bruce shut his mouth. He wheeled but there was nowhere to go, trapped by the logjam at the door, the room suddenly a clown car, suddenly a vaudeville skit, the mass of bodies behind him with bottles raised like pitchforks.

"Oh," Nancy cried. "You're hurt."

High up on the thigh his pant leg was soaking through with blood. He reached down to dab it, then raised his finger to show

Nancy. "An incident with the coffee table," he mumbled and she was across the room and ministering to him before you could even think to put your arms down, before you could even think of something to say.

Tomorrow at work you will learn all sorts of things. Paramount among these is this: you will keep your job. Bruce received eleven stitches, although he does not offer to show you the scar. "It's a bit high on the leg," he'll banter, unaccountably jocular, "and despite what you seem to think, our relationship doesn't warrant such shared intimacy." He'll hobble over to his desk and examine something on his blotter. "Because of my blood alcohol level they weren't able to administer anaesthetic." "Ouch," you wince. "Quite," he'll nod. "My blood was a wee bit thinner than usual. I thought I was going to bleed out in the cab." For the twentieth time in a two-day span you won't know what to say. He'll dismiss you from his office and only an oblique reminder that afternoon of Thursday's staff meeting will confirm for you that you're keeping your job.

But you won't know any of this on Sunday morning and this doesn't make things with Debra any easier. You'd woken early to fetch Cass from her friend's house, the smell seeping from your pores enough to engender a contact buzz. Her friend's father greeted you heartily at the door, a bagel in one hand and coffee in the other, before catching sight of your face. "Jesus," he recoiled. "You look like the living dead. Rough night?"

You told him he had no idea and he seemed to accept the truth of this statement. "Well," he said finally. "I can barely remember my college days." He pulled back into the doorway before reconsidering, "We can take Cassie to church with us. That would buy you another few hours. She can borrow a dress from Sally, they're probably about the same size." It was a hell of an offer, all things considered, more than you deserved, and you thanked him but explained about this brunch thing at noon. He put his bagel in his mouth and looked at his watch and then grimaced. "Good luck," he offered.

Thirteen, oblivious, Cass nattered through the car ride home about the late-night movie, the popcorn, a love letter they had crafted to some boy Sally thought was cute. Midway through a recitation of this letter, every precious syllable of it, she'd looked up at you. "Can we turn down the air conditioning?" she asked. "Sally put my hair up just right and I'd like it to last through the weekend."

"No."

"Well, can we at least roll up the windows? It's like a wind tunnel in here."

"No."

After a moment she moved to the third stanza, an epistle on his eyes like seawater. "Honestly," she confided, "I'm not even sure what she sees in him. Frankly, I think he's pretty much a loser."

"I'm sure he is," you admitted.

While Debra blinds potatoes, you lug a black garbage bag through the house and fill it with empties. Upstairs Cass auditions a borrowed cassette. The volume permeates the house, its tempo in pace with the throbbing in your head. You drop the bag with a thud and massage your temples. Through the open kitchen doorway you can see Debra's actions mirroring your own. You look across at her and smile. "It's like something died up here," you say. "There's a trumpet blowing taps." She says nothing in return. When you've finished emptying the ashtrays, gathering refuse from the mantelpiece and under the chairs and even a single paper plate wedged into the grate of the fireplace, you drag the bag out through the door and into the carport. "I'm going to keep both the front and back doors open to create a cross draft and air this place out."

You hear nothing in return except the low frequency of the bass upstairs, a counterpoint to the staccato of Debra's cutting. Back in the kitchen you watch the blade for a while, the way it levers, a simple machine really, the way it looks in the sunshine, cradled in Debra's hand. If she notices you, Debra offers no sign. Her eyes are focused down on the vegetables in front of her. She finishes with a potato, brushes it away with the back of her hand, and begins work on a yellow onion. Within seconds the acid begins to sting your eyes and, from the tears forming on Debra's lids, hers as well. The knife moves up and down, up and down, the onion parchment making the blade look like a ghost. It doesn't deviate at all while Debra raises her elbow to her face to wipe away the irritation from the onion. "What can I do to help?" you ask her. She sighs heavily. "Salad," she concludes. "How badly can you fuck up a salad?"

The lettuce tears easily under your fingers. In rinsing it, you notice that your hands are covered to the wrists in ash from the fireplace. You nudge Debra with your elbow and show her your hands. She stops cutting and looks at them for a second. Then she starts cutting again. "There was a plate in the fireplace," you explain. "Making a break for it."

The hash browns are cooking on the skillet, filling the room with their wonderful odor. For the first time all morning, your stomach feels stable enough to consider food. She pulls the remnants of an onion from the cutting board and shreds it into the sink, peeling apart each layer, watching the pieces fall. When it's finished, you present the salad to Debra for inspection. "Wonderful," she says.

And so it begins.

"It was a kiss."

"I heard."

When you don't say anything, she looks out the door to the stairwell. "I'm sorry," she hisses. "I wasn't there to see it."

"It was a kiss."

"Absolutely," she says. "No one is arguing that point. Absolutely no one on this whole fucking planet is arguing the point, okay?" She turns to you and speaks slowly. "Let's try to get through this fucking brunch."

"And then what?" You reach for her shoulder (admittedly a mistake) and she punches your hand down hard enough to bruise, although it will be an hour before you notice. In the meantime, there is this glorious fight.

"Then tomorrow. Then the next day and the next fucking day after that. They make these calendars that pretty much predict the future." She grins—an ugly grin. "Now I know what to get you for your next birthday."

"I mean..."

"I know what you mean, you moron. Do you honestly think I don't know...You're just..." She sputters. She takes a deep breath. "You're like the fucking horse that's so far behind the pack it thinks it's winning." This calms her down enough to look at the mess in front of her. "Help me with the dishes," she says. "We'll have enough to do once the company leaves."

There are more dirty dishes than you can ever remember seeing in your house. The empty cups and plates and bowls from last night and the cutting board and knives from this morning's prep. You start loading the dishwasher while Debra fills the sink with suds for the most fragile of the pieces.

"I'm saying it was just a kiss."

Debra carefully lowers the cup she'd been washing.

You try again. "It was a kiss. But I was at that party. I've been at all of these parties. It's been fifteen years I've been there." You place your fingers to your chest. "You know what I'm saying."

"Almost never," Debra spits. "But it's probably too late in the day to correct that problem."

"That wasn't a Boy Scout troop meeting, okay? Nobody there, not you and certainly not Bruce, was Saint Agnes, all right."

"That's the tack you want to take?" Debra whispers. She takes out a dishtowel and dries the glass. "Think very hard about your next step," she warns. When you open your mouth again, she cuts you off. "Very hard."

You sit down at the table and put your head in your hands. The adrenaline and the music drill at your temples hard enough to start your eye twitching.

"Do you think this is going to affect my chances at partnership?" You catch a glimpse of a smile before Debra looks over at you, her face adjusting quickly to disbelief.

"You really aren't kidding, are you?" she asks. "You truly are unique, I'll give you that."

"You don't know Bruce like I do," you argue. "This won't affect my client base. It won't affect my ability to buy in or the liquidity that offers him. You know the company philosophy: business is business."

"That was David's motto," Debra reminds you.

"You don't think Bruce believes it, too?"

"I think you've managed to convince yourself that all of these little parts of your life, your little compartments, are separate from one another. You must be the only adult I know who really can't see the way things run together."

"So that's it?"

At this Debra actually laughs. "I think he's going to bleed you so slowly you won't know you're dead until you read the obituary in the paper. I think he's going to string you along until he turns off the light behind him." She pauses for a moment. "At least that's what I'd do."

"I don't understand."

"There used to be something charming about that," she agrees. "I used to talk about that with my analyst, we used to suspect that was your fucking secret: your magical interface with the world. I used to marvel at how you could even get out of bed in the mornings, taxed with the burden of being you. And then it came to me: *you don't understand.* That's your gift. If I could just bottle it, just for a week, I could sell enough to keep this family afloat for the rest of our natural-born lives, long enough that I wouldn't have to pour my own self into my job just to keep the fucking wheels turning."

This time your "I don't understand" sounds hollow even to you.

"What I'm saying is that a million people fall into the bottom of a fucking bottle every single day searching for a fraction of the ignorance you seem to have been blessed with."

Upstairs you can hear a thud and realize that the music has been turned off. This quiets Debra until all you can hear is her heavy breathing. When this softens, the kitchen is perfectly still. She busies herself with the dishes and you rise from the table to help her. "Something's missing," she says. "Go into the china hutch in the dining room," she orders you. "Bottom drawer: you'll find wooden salad tongs." Then, seeing the look of confusion in your eye, she barks: "They're sticks. They were a gift from my grandmother. My family will get a kick out of seeing them today. Rinse them off, God knows what dust they've been accumulating in that drawer."

"So what should I do?" you say, and Debra looks at you. "About the other thing. Seriously. What should I do?"

"I think if you've got any good tricks left in the bottom of your bag, I'd use them because this feels like the end to me." She absently rubs her face with the dishcloth and yelps when a piece of onion grazes her eye.

"It's not too late."

She shakes her head. "You should see the view from where I'm standing."

"I can earn it back," you promise. "It's not too late. You've got to trust me on this. I can still get it back."

"How?" she asks, the towel pushed up hard against her face.

"Magic," you say, spreading your arms wide over the dishes.

She shakes her head again. It's a simple enough gesture, but because of the dishcloth still covering her face you aren't quite sure how to read it.

The Horseshoe

That Familiar Lord of Disappointment

Nowadays no one ever looks out the window of the plane. When you were a child, you and Charlotte could play for hours, designing houses in the sky, your father butchering scientific names for the cloud formations, ice crackling in his glass. Back then things were different, cityscapes distinct and varying. Even the planes were different, bone china and silverware, a roast beef cart. People ate meat, drank scotch, emerged hours later blinking into white light, hands covering eyes like visors, relieved and, yes, even a little astonished to emerge in another city, your mother pinching at your father's elbow, nudging him toward the picture windows and out to the sky from which you have just come, "Look at the color, Garland, the blue of it. My heavens, palm trees!" There was a time when a trip to California would have been a life's work.

Cass does not look out the window, not even once, blasé at age fifteen, and you wonder what's been lost. It couldn't have been her trip to Disneyland four years ago or your mother's funeral the following fall. She'd been too young then, nestled between you and Debra, with coloring books and crayons, packs of cards and plastic wings. This time she co-opts the window. Before takeoff, she lowered the shade and informed you sullenly that she wishes to sleep. "Should I order you a meal?" you inquire and are rewarded with a withering glare as she tells you that they won't be serving meals on the flight, probably no flights anymore and certainly not a two-hour jump to Atlanta. "My God," she exclaims, the words containing so much unhappiness and anger that you wonder how the plane could take off at all, the weight of it always on your chest, compressing the vertebrae in the small of your back, too much even for the monstrous engines. "God, where have you been?" she asks.

With you, this is always a valid question.

Before long Cass is asleep, as promised, and her head falls onto your shoulder. She has thin hair, your wife agrees, and skin so pale at the temples that you can watch the blood move through. It is, you suspect in your darkest moments, the only proof that anything at all goes through her head. She has acne, some, on her nose and forehead, what her dermatologist refers to as a t-zone, and is alternately anguished and pleased by this onset of puberty. She has developed slowly, or more slowly than her friends whose breasts you need now make a concerted effort to ignore. That your daughter wears a bra at all strikes you as unnecessary, pure assertion, her hands always hitching and pulling at the straps. You try to remember her at seven or eight, during the cute years, but somehow that face is replaced by the one you see next to you now, eye makeup caked in layers, lipstick for an autopsy. Her head lolls and you feel hot air tinged with peanuts and chocolate push past your nostrils. How long has she had bad breath?

Debra is up in first class, her company having paid for her ticket. By now she is expert at this route. What had begun as three weeks to cover for an emergency departure has now stretched to months. Long ago she came to you with numbers, her notebook folded under her fingers. "It's twenty-one days."

You wanted to find a reason for her to stay but came up with nothing but a plaintive shrug.

"It could be the opportunity we've been waiting for," she said, daring you to ruin this for her.

"Five hundred and four hours," she said. "I'll be home before Thanksgiving."

"It was our year to have it. You'll never be able to get the house ready in time."

"Adele will cover for me. She and her husband like doing stuff like that. They probably celebrate the day before, just so she can try out new cranberry recipes."

"That's not the point."

She raised her eyebrows. "The woman has soufflé bowls, for God's sake."

"Debra."

"It's 30,240 minutes." She smiled, her accountant's canines gleaming. "It's not like they don't have phones. I'll be back before you know it."

"I love you."

"Just 1,814,400 seconds," she laughed, her arm reaching to close the door.

Now the seconds grow and multiply, stretch as infinite as the horizon. There are fewer and fewer of her clothes in the closet, and neither of you mention it.

The man on the aisle has layers that fold over and under the armrest. He adjusts his weight constantly, burdens you with his yeasty odors and bony angles. His body is not an apology, even in this small space. It is an assertion, like the teenage girl who flanks you, and you imagine that they have much in common. He clicks at the top of a pen, alternately as slow as a grotesque heart and as fast as a turbine. He is, somewhere inside of himself, punishing you for him: for the lack of willpower, the genetic malfunctions, whatever it is that has shaped him in this manner. His meaty fingers play at the silver spring like an accusation. He needs you to understand how every goddamned greasy cheeseburger is your fault. Like your daughter, he wishes you were dead, if only for the extra leg room.

When he pitches forward, you panic, thinking you've killed him with your wishes, a power you didn't know you had. But he's only reaching forward into the seat pocket in front of him, the tray disappearing momentarily into his belly, and pulling out an inflatable pillow that he blows and sucks until he is winded, the pillow still flaccid, even his air apparently too bloated for our world.

Eventually, the pillow grows and he adjusts it around his neck. He looks like a mastodon wearing a lifejacket. Something out of Sandra Boynton that might once have made milk fly from your daughter's nose, and this makes you smile until his enormous girth slides into your area. At rest, his flesh melts down his face. His cow's shoulder incapacitates your left arm, your right already trapped by your daughter's pillowed sweatshirt, and so you sit quietly and try not to breathe any of the molecules that circle around you like buzzards, as you wait for the weight to bring you all down.

THE EMPRESS.

The lock gives itself up after only a few tries. You'd always assumed that picking a lock was one of those things, like kicking in a door, or leaping over the hood of a car, made to look easy in the movies. But two bobby pins jiggled for a few seconds and the door swings open. It has something to do with the number of pins, you remember a man in a bar once saying, all things in combination. In a way, you're disappointed. You have decided to break into your daughter's room very nearly on a whim, counting on hard minutes or even hours of stalled contemplation. It might even have been the idea of trying that appealed to you and somewhere in another universe of different cards you can imagine a feeling of relief as you slink away to replace your wife's hairpins in her jewelry box. But now there's nothing to stand in your way, certainly not your daughter who has replicated your wife in miniature, two small pieces of luggage with the promise of more on the next trip. "She's comfortable, Dad," Cassie says, her tapping foot the only concession to her betrayal. Sixteen years old and she looks at you maternally. "What's the big deal? I'm off to college after next year anyway." You ask her whether she has notified her high school to expect her back for senior year. If she isn't going, there are almost certainly forms to fill out, files to transfer. "We're playing it by ear," this girl, this echo, shrugs.

The room emits an odor you would not have known until this second was your daughter's, like earth or ripe fruit, and you move quickly to close the door behind you, to trap it in, conserve it. If they are anything like Debra's, Cass's possessions will move off almost of their own accord and take their smells and scents and fragrances—it is somewhat hard to tell with Cass what is perfume and what is Cass—with them. So many things go without warning or indication.

With the door shut firmly, you are free to take your time examining the surroundings of a room you haven't seen for years, Cass seemingly able to squeeze through the door without opening it. Once this was the sort of thing you and Debra might have laughed at together.

It is, you finally conclude, an absolutely typical teenager's room. Tonight seems very much to be playing like a Hollywood reel, with the lock and paint job and posters all coming directly from the prop house. Is there something reassuring in this? Or is it insidious that Hollywood knows you so well—because really, how often do those movies end happy?

Occasionally, yes, but first there are the trials and tribulations.

All of the bands (Orisha, The Gnostics) your daughter worships have bad hair, split ends. They are so pathetically of-the-moment that even their grimaces and glares seem apologetic, as if staring through the eye makeup you can see their older counterparts smiling gamely (we know, it was marketing, we are very sorry. It'll all be over soon). This fantasy puts you in such a good mood that you hum one of their songs; admitting to the room that you know it makes you redden, and you open your daughter's closet to the books she has kept since childhood, with her stuffed animals and her diaries.

Ah. A conundrum. Upon the cosmic scale that judges us all, breaking and entering is a relatively minor offense. She's been gone a long time and you can always alibi that her fire detector had gone off. You can claim mitigating circumstances. But the diaries are another thing entirely. To succumb to that raises ethical questions, or rather answers them quite neatly. You fan the diaries into a circle around the floor. There are twelve in all, spanning the teenage years and the four earlier. Cass, with an eye to detail you certainly would not have suspected from her grades, has labeled each one neatly on the cover. You finger the corners gently, inhale the gradually more sophisticated perfumes that emanate from the pages. You are about to open one, the nine o'clock position as it happens, when your hand stops short. In a sudden inspiration you examine the covers for carefully placed hairs, scotch tape, booby traps out of Nancy Drew and the Hardy Boys. Since there aren't any, you reward this trust by opening the diary to a random page.

It is unbelievably inane. Yes, of course she was only eleven, but still you would have thought her better than this. In one entry she declared her eternal love for a boy only to replace him with another Lothario three pages later. You wonder whether she ever went back to read these, these repositories of all knowledge (certainly she doesn't seem to have learned anything about boys, a new one at your house every night until the day she left, someone else's problem now). Classes, lunch room gossip. Ruminations on the happiness of a pet turtle long banished to the municipal sewer system. My God, for this you have sold your soul? It is true that you could maneuver from this diary to the one dancing in your peripheral vision, the one carefully dated through last year. But instead you prop yourself up onto the bed, the pillow folded to the small of your back, and read about your little girl when once she was happy. And she was happy. And you are greatly relieved. You would even tell Debra, if only you could figure out how.

Cass had stacked her journals in no specific order, or at least none you could discern, but you had painstakingly recorded their sequence onto a piece of paper so you could replicate it when you put them back There was a stuffed lion on top of the box, no doubt spillover from the larger zoo alongside, but you indulge yourself in thinking of him as a little velveteen guardian.

Beneath the journals, letters from boyfriends. These you read without pangs, your more subtle senses eradicated. The letters are from a congregation of boys, heartfelt in a suddenly pubescent way. "Coming into you is like coming into a new world." That sort of thing. You think back suddenly to the letters you yourself have written, and what comes back to you isn't their juvenile tone or spelling, elementary meter, overwrought emotion (for, after all, you still indulge in such things), or even (and this last is the tragedy) the girls themselves, the objects of your epistles, beauty and youth and experience wrapped up in the tight skin and downy hair of young women. For the girls seem to be lost to you, melted into a composite. Like those boys who have so earnestly written these letters to Cass, all of them stacked like cordwood. Instead you wonder whether someone somewhere is saving the letters you wrote decades ago. Is this, then, all the posterity you are to be offered?

Beneath the letters are Cass's toys, the sort purchased by catalogue. Brown bag stuff.

And finally the pharmaceuticals. There are, of course, the dime bags of pot, from their smell staler even than the months she has been gone, the small oily turds of hash you sniff and roll between your fingers before recoiling at the thought that they might indeed be, more innocently, the droppings of mice migrated down from the attic. But others have no plausible excuse, prescription medications hoarded from your ski accident three years ago, from Debra's broken ankle, even from your mother's long illness. Neonatal vitamins, suppositories, psoriasis medications. One bottle contains six tiny blue pills, star-shaped and pristine, that you remember Bruce carrying in his jacket pocket after a heart attack. Glycerine. There are so many bottles (so many drugs that cannot produce any desired effect for a young woman) as to suggest a minor compulsion.

Feeding a compulsion of your own, you reorder the bottles and pills and creams along the floor. On the left you place the drugs of the spirit, including after a moment's hesitation the mouse shit/hashish. To the right those designed to help failing bodies, under attack by injury, bad diet, age. The middle you reserve for the glowing pink orbs of her birth control dispensers. There are three of these, with careful markings denoting ovulation cycles and barren weeks. You spin the clear plastic, letting the pills pop out onto the carpet, like this is nothing more than candy, nothing more than a child's toy.

Which, in a way, it is.

Worry

It has been ordained that all bad things come in fives. For you the week has brought its misfortunes laid upon one another like plagues, the loss of portfolios large and small. Earlier in the day Bruce called to inform you, as if you mightn't have noticed, that "you've been hemorrhaging clients since Debra left town for good."

"A lot of people think it's a sign of loyalty on her behalf," you explain and he raises his arms in surrender. "Someone losing as many clients in a week as you have is obviously something people are going to want to take a look at. I answer to people too," he reminds you. It is, he leads you to understand, standard procedure. "Nothing to worry about," you suggest in finishing his sentence, but his mouth contorts. "Maybe," he allows. "What would you suggest?" you ask him, and he looks out through his window to the parking lot below. "Worry," he says, "is an underrated diet." Then allows you a thin smile. Do you deserve all of this? From inside yourself, searching for answers, it is not yet clear. Debra, the crackle of long distance, scoffs. "What does your conscience tell you?" she asks. You tell her you aren't the judge. Her long silence on the other end tells you that she is not buying. You ask her in a small voice to tell you a story, something of your shared past. "It seems so long," you prompt, "I can barely remember…"

Her fingers cover most but not all of the receiver's holes as she tells whomever she is with in the office to hold on a minute. Then a pause. "One minute," she says again. "Where were we?"

This last to you.

A few minutes later, another e-mail pings onto the screen directing you to close an account. Who makes their financial decisions after dinner? And this makes you question what Debra is doing so late in her office. When belatedly you realize that it's earlier in Santa Fe, this only makes you feel more isolated. You walk slowly through the hallways, slip into Cass's room and lie briefly on her bed, your ankles hanging over the sides. There is nothing left of her smell and again you curse yourself, your carelessness, your self-absorption at having left her door open the night you'd hurt your hand. In a few minutes you get into the car, and without even realizing it drive to the church where your daughter was baptized.

As you drive you examine the bandage on your hand. It emits a foul odor that embarrasses you in close quarters. You have taken to spraying it with your aftershave while dressing, but the alcohol doesn't seem to last and the gauze has hardened into plaster. You drive with your palms, your fingers the barest curve over the wheel, the ruts in the snow guiding you into the church parking lot.

Saturday evening services are letting out as you pull in and you have trouble pushing through the current of eager bodies. With their heavy winter coats, it is difficult to squeeze past these joyous congregants, unburdened though they might be. They have their weekends to begin, all services rendered. They are as free as lambs, their souls' accounts paid in full for another week. Finally, there are only two people left in the pews, you and a tall woman whose head is covered. You sit far enough away not to intrude on her sorrow. That she is in mourning is clear to you. The stained glass windows filter moonlight and from your seat you can see the moon swollen and heavy, the snowflakes. It is all quite beautiful but you have no earthly idea why you're here. And so you sit, listening to the woman's muffled anguish, feel the pew tip gently with her rocking. Eventually you hear the soft clicking of the lock, the doors barred to the outside. The cleaning crew must be on its way, getting ready for Sunday morning's service. But for right now there is time and you move forward to sit next to the woman, find her hand in God's deserted theater, squeeze through each others' bandages to tell each other that everything is going to be okay.

Disillusionment

Months later, the house under contract, most of your belongings boxed and categorized, you are amused to find the remnants of a family of animals taken up in what remains of your toolshed, their droppings scattered on the blue tarpaulin. The female must have littered there, leaving behind the hardened casement of the placentas, the blood streaks and mucous hinting at a hard birth. You wonder if that family returns here at nights and if you've ruined that now, the lingering smell of your body's oils enough to taint things irrevocably, like newborn kittens or freshwater trout. What type of animals are living or have lived in your toolshed, you cannot be sure. Someone else, someone who knows more about such things, would have no trouble identifying them, worrying the shit pellets between two fingers, sniffing indecorously at the frozen jelly of the afterbirth. Or else someone with even the most cursory knowledge of zoology—been in the town fifteen years and you've never bothered to learn the first thing about it. Raccoons, badgers? Every place has mice and rats, but these droppings look too big for that. Eventually your knees start to ache so you rise, bending parenthetically to stretch your back. Before long you conclude what you've been concluding for most of your adult life, that someone knows everything, but certainly not you.

The weak sunlight comes into the shed at a fractured angle and climbs your pant leg, dissecting your belly to trace your midsection. It's all about angles, just like Bruce said. It's enough to make you smile to yourself. The shed's lean grows more pronounced with every change in the season, every shift in the terrain. The structure probably won't last much longer but then again, probably neither will you, at least not here.

"I need you," Debra had begged, "to keep the house presentable." Back in town for a weekend to tie up a few loose ends. Cass visiting colleges along the coast. "Just a few months more. Just until we find someone willing to take it off our hands." She went room to room with a legal pad, jotting down chores. "Small stuff like making sure to run the water in the guest bathroom once a month. Do something with those weeds out back." Her pencil gestured beyond the window and your thoughts leapt to another time, long ago, a bird perched on her finger, the smell of lilac. Mistaking your expression, Debra groaned. "Fine. Pay someone," she said. "Get someone in here once a week if you need to. It'll be worth it if we don't have to unload the place at fire-sale prices."

You assured her you didn't need a maid. "I've got the time," you said. And you do. Without Cass, without Debra, your career dried up at your feet, the days expand around you. But even time can't be trusted anymore—the hours just sort of flit away. Now errands that used to take fifteen minutes take an entire morning. Daydreams. You can't quite figure it all out, even the calendar folding in on itself like an origami swan.

You straighten up the tools on the desk (surprising nobody, you quit long before you managed a shelf), shuffle the butcher paper and watch the wood shavings dance along the top. Before long they're rising into the air, floating and dancing, catching the light just so. When you breathe in they rush to meet you, when you exhale they tease just out of reach. They'll play this game as long as you want to, as long as you're willing to wait, as long as your hands are willing to dangle them suspended between the world above and the world below, as long as you don't abandon them.

Over the sink in the kitchen you wrestle apart the chunks of last night's sweet-and-sour takeout. The chicken skin, the sauce, all fat and artery cloggers, all ammunition for wifely nagging, all hallucinatory MSG, all congealed, lubricate your fingers and dye everything the shade of red #2 that wakes kindergarten teachers into a cold sweat. You feel the sinews give way under the force of your nails, flatten under the meat of your palms. When the chicken is stringy, you plate it, the tiny flecks of breading nestled in your finger hair. You walk out back to the shed and kick the door open with your foot. You leave the plate next to the tarpaulin for whatever is living in the shed. Four walls and a ceiling, kind of. You think about pushing the entire structure over. You can imagine the wood giving under your shoulder, the satisfaction you'd derive from it, but something holds you back. What the hell, this is their home now if it's anyone's.

The backyard stretches out in front of you, wood sorrel and spurge overtaking what's left of the vegetable patch. Behind some broad leaves you can identify the western marker of a sundial, a birthday gift offered to Debra five years ago. You reach over to switch on the patio lights, but somewhere along the line the circuit has been compromised so the string stays dark. Just another thing to add to the list.

Just another broken promise. You'd fix them all if you thought it would do any good.

The Lord in Ruin

Drunk, woozy, you climb into your daughter's bed to breathe deeply whatever remains. It has been a hard night. The full moon fills emergency rooms across the world. The problems at work have you cornered. Almost no clients left. No one has spoken to you about any of this. Bruce is suddenly a rumor, his office door closed. People look down in the hallways. You know the drill, having lived through it before.

Cass's bed smells wonderfully of her. You push your head deep into the pillows and your reality torques down from the lack of oxygen. You remember when Cass was a child, her impatience and her threats. She would hold her breath so long that she would pass out until Debra, worried, consulted a doctor. You can remember his wry smile as he assured you that Cass couldn't do any permanent damage by holding her breath. "Try to make sure there's nothing sharp around for her to hit her head on," he advised. "It's a phase. She'll pass through it. All kids try stunts like this."

"You're telling me that this is normal?" asked Debra, her arms crossed.

The doctor looked carefully at her before responding. "It is an extreme enactment of a very common impulse," he explained.

Debra was not mollified. "You're telling me that all that passing out isn't killing brain cells?" she asked. "You're telling me the headaches when she comes to aren't anything to worry about?"

The doctor smiled again. "I can't advise you what to worry about, but I can promise you that the human body won't let itself be shut down permanently, no matter how stubborn a child's will."

Debra had thanked the doctor curtly and left, but you lingered. The doctor sat down heavily at his desk, paying you no notice. It was as though you weren't there at all. He wheeled his desk chair over to the window and lit a cigarette. "Since C. Everett Koop blew the lid off, I've got to sneak these things like a teenager," he explained shyly. He kept his face turned three-quarters from you, still staring out the window. "If patients smell the smoke on me, there's questions. It's a trust issue."

"She really isn't burning too many brain cells with this fainting thing?" you asked, hesitant to return to the subject.

"Of course she is," the doctor exhaled, the smoke curling under the window frame. "So's this." He raised the cigarette over his head. "So's drinking, eating red meat, turning thirty, living." He was still looking out the window as Debra emerged on the street below, striding purposefully toward the car. Later you would get into a fight over how you'd lagged behind. "It's not my kid and I'd never mention this to your wife, but would I be worried about a kid determined enough to asphyxiate herself just to get her way? As a doctor, I'm saying no. As a parent?" He shrugged. "Good luck to you." At the window the two of you watched Debra pull a compact out of her purse and touch up her makeup. When she looked up at the window you flinched, but she showed no sign of having seen you. "What I can offer is not to worry about the brain cells," he said, inhaling deeply. "We've got millions of the fucking things. Millions more than we need, to be honest with you."

In the end, of course, Cass had stopped of her own accord, just like the doctor had promised. You were a little disappointed when that happened. There was something wonderful about her

Napoleonic will, and it worried you that breathing was just the first of a million concessions she would have to make in growing up. It wasn't the type of story you'd share with friends until years later, when Cass's intensities were far less frightening, more predictable and more predictably assuaged. It was the type of story designed to get a laugh, cutesy, but you always felt the sadness, just a little.

When you sit up, some of the liquid spills onto the comforter. You dab at it with your fingers but in the grips of melancholia you know in every part of yourself that it doesn't matter: that no one will ever use this comforter again. They're all gone, long gone, not coming back. "No matter what I do," you mutter. Outside you can hear a car drive down the street. "Not even if I hold my breath until I turn blue."

You put the bottle carefully on the nightstand and direct your head forward toward the pillows. You clasp your hands behind your back, the fingers holding onto one another so tight that your shoulders burn, until your hands come to feel unrelated to each other, as cold and distant as other people's. Then you let yourself fall forward into the cotton of the pillows and hold out for as long as you can. You can feel blackness coming on, the sharp lights dancing in the back of the skull, all those dead and dying brain cells in their throes. Finally your body betrays you with a spastic jolt, your arms flailing outward, the right one colliding first with the bottle and then with the wall. It takes a moment for the agony to register, for everything to come back on line and the pain sensors to navigate neural highways to your brain. But as you sit on the bed pulling tiny shards of glass from your hand and collecting them neatly on the ruined comforter, you think then that this must have been the sadness that Cass felt the very first time she woke up from a tantrum. The crushing disappointment of life. And for the first time in a long time, you feel closer to her, and understand why she left, and admire all over again the lengths to which she would go to escape. How terrible it is, how monstrous, that we are all subservient to these bodies, these incomprehensible cities that, even as they are born, begin to die, cell by cell, around us.

Practicality

The realtor is no one you know. It's only when you hear her key in the lock, her cheery litany of the house's many benefits—the oak fireplace, the garden, the bounty of natural light—that you are roused from your thoughts, only when you hear heavy footsteps marching through your kitchen that you are able to wrestle your belt through its buckle, calm your tremulous fingers enough, implore them to spend just a moment of today doing your bidding, for God's sake, just thirty seconds would suffice, only when you hear them walk into the dining room that you're able to run your hands through your hair and consider the task of brushing your teeth.

Your thoughts, still half in this world, half in another, stretched thin, tinting the bathroom fixtures into strangeness while your arm, of its own accord, in muscle memory, moves the toothbrush's bristles around your mouth.

You'd been dreaming, you realize with a start, about Pat Hart, probably a corpse herself this many years later, so obviously some ghost of you remembered that the house was showing this morning. But unfortunately not the part charged with cleaning, and you can hear the realtor's murmurs of apology as she walks two voices through your downstairs and orders them to look past the disorder to the house underneath. "Try," she implores the voices, who promise to do their best, "to overlook the smell in here."

"It's like death warmed over," a woman's voice offers.

"Nothing a good airing won't fix," a man counters. "Spring's coming on anyway."

This prompts the realtor to move the party out into the garden, leaving you to scavenge your laundry dunes for socks. The shape of the laundry is enough to suggest another memory, snowbanks this time, and it's only at the heavy thud at the foot of the stairs that you're pulled back, to your hunched form at the foot of the bed. Luckily the woman is pregnant and anxious to see the baby's room—it's a wrench to have people come into Cass's room like that, her possessions still spread across her floor, and while they talk about the house's relative merits you manage to get yourself into a (mostly) clean shirt and rub your fingers over your jawline to measure your stubble. It has been, you'd guess, three days since you've shaved, a bit longer since you've left the house. Your last day at work was ten days ago and nobody talked about throwing you a goodbye party. No one has called since.

The voices move into the guest bathroom—you can't imagine what they'll unearth in there. You wait but there are, at least, no screams. You plot escape but can't divine a route. The upstairs hallway is narrow and they'd see you. Worse, they'd have to step aside to let you pass. Your bedroom window overlooks the garden, a twenty-foot drop to the paving stones, and you're not quite at that state yet. Some imp within you, something you haven't felt for years, urges you to hide under the bed and it seems as good a plan as any, better than most, so you reorganize your weary bones, thankful that your bedframe has both feet to raise it and dust ruffle to hide you.

It has been many months, years probably, since anyone has vacuumed under the bed, and you find yourself among a repository of old coins, pens, scraps of paper (reminder of an orthodontist appointment made or missed a decade ago, a phone number with the last two digits smudged out). The light from the window penetrates the ruffles in odd patterns and you can see the dust resettling itself around your body. It's strange that in this house, your house, among so much detritus of your accumulated life, the tokens and icons and sloughed-off skin, you should remember back instead to your old apartment in New York, to its porcelain sink, the three chemical pots like ink wells, the applicator stretched across them like a bridge, like a blue-tipped pen, positive, and in the mirror Debra's inscrutable face and your own, both of them flushed, reaching to embrace each other in love, and panic, and to promise each other that nothing was ever going to change.

This memory, if that's what it is, is stolen away by the heavy footsteps inches from your face, the open-toed shoes in early springtime, the indistinct murmurs of the women and then the man's confident rejoinder—sensible and wise—that this house is a solid investment, nestled in a good neighborhood with close proximity to schools, mature landscaping, that the property is worth far more than its asking price, despite its disrepair, its stench of death, the years of neglect, that despite everything that was done to it, the fundamentals remain strong.

The Tower of the Tower & Terrace Apartments stands three stories high and houses six identical units per floor. "Yeah, all about the same. Roughly nine hundred square feet, counting closets. Carpeting every five years, paint every three or by law when the tenant changes. Water and electricity included but don't go crazy." The manager, Rodney, pauses to confirm (again) that you will not be running a business from your residence. "Nothing like that," you assure him. "I'm recently retired." Rodney looks down to your dark socks, your jogging shoes and then to your monogrammed luggage, a gift from Debra's parents several eons ago. "Yeah," he says. "We get a lot of that." He warns you that the owners monitor diligently for monthly spikes in the power usage to ensure compliance and that residents in violation of this stipulation will have their lease agreement terminated immediately, with no refunds, and that said eviction does not preclude additional legal action or even criminal prosecution. He recites all of this from a soiled card he has taped to the top of his manila file folder. After he finishes, he searches for the correct key from a ring attached to his belt loop by means of a nylon cord, a nifty device that makes a cheerful whooshing sound that you admire—"quick draw"—although when you say this, complete with cowboy mime, Rodney, busy cycling through thirty or so keys for the one that will open the door to your new home, gives you a crooked look. Then your door swings open and he stands aside. "After you," he says, ushering you in with a flourish, his rejoinder to your outlaw, his look turning to something akin to bemusement.

Whatever else you say, the new apartment is basically clean and freshly painted. Rodney walks you through the living room, pointing out the electrical outlets and cable jack, and then into the kitchenette. "The knobs tend to get loose," he explains, "but they're easy enough to fix." Together you look out the kitchen window to the parking lot below. "Notice the dumpster beneath your window," he says. It is hard to miss, both menacing and obsolete. "Garbage goes down to the dumpster manually," he says. Even before you can reply he continues, "in a couple of weeks, or a couple of months, maybe it's raining, maybe you're drunk, I don't know, you'll get the urge to open the window and let that garbage fly, bombs away. You're going to be thinking it's a straight shot, what's the worst that can happen?" He waits a good long while until you realize that it is not a rhetorical question. "The termination thing with all the subsequent legal action to follow?" you guess. "Damn right," he replies. "We got possums."

"As a deterrent?"

Rodney steadies his hands against the plastic sink top. "As a result of the residents throwing their trash out of their windows into the general vicinity of the dumpster," he says through gritted teeth. And the way he elongates general vicinity suggests to you that he might not always have been here either.

You cannot stop cracking jokes. The overwhelming smell of paint makes you giddy. When Rodney leads you into the bedroom, you are horrified to find yourself mentioning that you are relieved the space is big enough to hold your king-size bed. Undaunted, you continue about how much furniture you've got coming. Rodney walks over to the doorway and flips the switch on, generating a watery light above your heads. "Least she left you the stuff, huh?" he says, and you can tell he had responded in spite of himself, that he had never meant to open this particular can of worms. And now his look changes again to gratitude as you respond simply that she has moved out of state, the divorce not yet finalized. He reveals that "the lease can transition monthly if anything changes on your end," looking around like he is violating corporate trust. "There's an escape hatch if you search hard enough."

The bedroom has a patio door but it's barred shut. This is not a figure of speech; there is actually a rusted metal bar along the bottom quadrant of the patio door. "For safety," Rodney explains. "None of the windows in this place open—although when you get settled you can always invest in a screwdriver and change that if you feel so inclined." When you ask whether that might void your renter's agreement pursuant to legal action, he shares a smile you haven't seen before. "It will be fine," he promises. You shake his hand formally, just as the exhausted filament in the overhead bulb stumbles, plunging you both temporarily into the relative darkness of late afternoon. In a second, the bulb recovers. "Let me know when that thing finally quits," Rodney says. "I've got some spares stashed somewhere. I live down in the Terrace section." Then he gives you his number in case of problems. You thank him, still shaking his hand, which he finally extricates with some measure of diplomacy. "You never know," he says, something like a smile on his lips. "That lightbulb might have just needed that little break. Who knows? Now it might be good for another ten years."

The Arrow of Time

He rides in a pale beige compact car too small for his bony legs. He jogs up to the efficiency's thin door and pauses a minute before knocking. He sucks in air through his teeth and then leans over the railing to the concrete of the apartment below, suspending a grayish wad of mucous and phlegm and saliva in midair before gravity pulls it to earth with a wet splat. You know all this because you sit huddled in your bedroom watching him through the cloudy window, the screen segmenting your world into quarters. His arrival is not surprising since Debra has called in advance. "Be home this time," she warns you, in the tired tone once reserved for the babysitter, "I don't want to have to reschedule again."

And so you have kneeled here for most of the afternoon, enjoying the world from a new vantage point. From the bedroom window you can see the earth below you and the sky above. Earlier, a bird circled in long, lazy calculus, gradually closing in on itself, a dark bird against a milky sky. More and more you are finding the world quite beautiful. There are garter snakes in the shrubs dividing the parking area from the apartments. You'd never noticed them in all the months you've lived here and they don't seem harmful but the squirrels that occupy the trees and second-story landings give them wide enough berth to make you reconsider. It is an interesting perspective, on your knees between the plyboard and bed. Here you have an almost uninterrupted view of the sky and the meager landscape separating your apartment complex from the ones that surround it, only a thin metal bar marring the view straight ahead.

Finally, he knocks and you stare through the peephole for a moment, out of show and nothing more. He is tall and unusually thin, his head shaved tight to the sides. You wonder if maybe that is out of show too, but nothing about him seems particularly self-aware. He raises the folded paper in his hands as a greeting, or perhaps an explanation, and waits patiently for you to struggle through the deadbolt.

He confirms your identity. "You've been served," he says, without preamble. Then thrusts a clipboard in your face. "Sign here."

You wonder whether he is armed. He has no weapon visible, but surely he must come into contact with people at their very worst. People who have committed crimes, people just barely skirting the fringe. He's been in this complex before; something in the way he exited his car and walked surely to your unit suggests that he might even have been in your very doorway, speaking to another you a few years ago. Or maybe not: he seems too young to have been at this long. It can't be a job you hold forever with its incumbent danger and psychic toll. At any rate, you can't see a gun or a knife. He's a big man, which probably helps, but all the same when you serve someone his papers, he's not going to invite you in for coffee.

"You handle lawsuits or just divorce?" you ask.

"You've got someone you want sued?" He raises his eyebrows.

"No, just curious." You offer a smile, which he declines.

"Sign here, please."

You acknowledge receipt with a steady hand. "That's it?" you ask.

"That's it."

He hands you the papers and you glance at them briefly. "What God has joined together let no man tear asunder," you say, without inflection.

"Sure, buddy."

Generosity

At the head of the church, the Bishop anoints each Confirmand in turn, his hand passing swiftly over their faces. Meanwhile, sequestered near the back, you're trying to engage Debra in conversation. This is not as heretical as it sounds. The women next to you are gossiping about vacation plans, their husbands recalling a recent golf outing. Debra, looking younger than she did when she left five years ago, decades younger than when she first started boarding planes to escape, shifts herself in the pew.

It isn't your pew, nor what had been your church, all those many years ago. That church, miles away on the other side of town, waits empty for you now, its stained glass offering an absolution you refuse. Too near your old office. Too near too many old memories. You give that whole neighborhood a wide berth. Once, though, long ago, you had come here. More than once. This is, after all, Debra's family church. Cass was baptized here, how could you forget that?

Debra's fingers reach to still your mouth. "Hush," she admonishes. "How could you think I'd forgotten?" Then her eyes narrow in and focus on yours. "You're talking out loud now," she whispers. "Did you know that?"

You don't respond for fear that her fingers should retreat from your lips. She's intent on your eyes and when she smiles you can see the wrinkles and creases fall back onto her face. "All those years I wondered what you were thinking when you spaced out," she says, "when all I had to do was wait it out."

"You didn't." The words unbidden, impulse control shaved away by time spent in solitude and near-solitude, the forgiving company of drunks.

Debra, in good grace, ignores this comment. "Do you remember Cass's dress for her first Communion?" Her eyes are still watching yours, and she knows you so well there can be no disguising the fact that you don't. "Really?" An undercurrent of irritation.

You shake your head.

"White," she prompts. Then shrugs gently. "Of course, white. Satin trim?"

You tell her that you've been having trouble calling up memories. "At least on command," you explain. "Actually, it's memories pretty much full time for me these days, but I don't seem to have much say in which ones."

"Which ones?" she asks.

The hangman's bend of the neck. A certain faraway admonition. The smell of twine burning into fur.

"Regrets. It's the all-regrets channel for me."

"Oh, Scotty," Debra sighs. "Always thinking the whole solar system keeps revolving around you. Never ready to live in this world."

The Bishop is quizzing each of the students on their catechisms. Elizabeth, your erstwhile niece, stands half a foot taller than the other ones. She fields a question about the seven sacraments. More than a half foot taller than the other ones. Was she always so tall? Maybe a pituitary problem?

Debra snickers. "She's older than the rest," she says. "Ginnie was married to a Baptist for years. Henry Durnon?"

"Worked in a garage?" you guess.

"Lawyer."

"Oh, sure."

"Elizabeth went through some rough spots after the divorce and the priest thought it best to wait a bit on confirmation." Debra leans in close to whisper this. Some of the people around you surely know the family, or are a part of it, a wide and ranging root structure. And, in a flash, something comes to you.

"She probably gets it from her dad," you whisper back, grinning. "Remember that time he tried to slide down our banister and took out part of the wall?"

Debra snorts. "He was always threatening to run off to join the circus."

"Great quality in a lawyer."

This time Debra laughs, and has to wave her hand briefly in apology to those within earshot. "I should never have sat next to you," she giggles. "I don't know why I ever did."

"I don't know either," you say, although this isn't true. You'd come to the church early, invitation in hand (the invitation itself frankly something of a mystery since Debra's family had been quick enough to write you off. A matchmaking yen, perhaps, or an enactment of one of the seven sacraments? More likely a grab for more gifts, a low-risk bluff at a check in the mail). You'd set the alarm last night, a reenactment of a long-dormant ritual, gotten yourself dressed in an old suit, baggy now but presentable, you'd guessed, stopped early at a drugstore for cologne, even shined your shoes. There's a different light in the morning and you'd chided yourself for losing sight of it. The whole world. You'd forgotten how weightless you can feel, rising with the sun. Even when your hands shake so hard it takes a minute to wrestle the key into the ignition. You'd gotten to the church early and stood there, waiting. It didn't take long for whatever good feeling you'd generated to exhaust itself. Didn't take long to start overhearing whispers from surprised ex-relatives. Didn't take long for you to interpret their looks that maybe your suit wasn't as presentable as you'd hoped. The entire thing nearly enough to push you away from the church altogether and you were out the door and to the threshold when you'd heard your name and looked up to see Debra, glowing and young like the Santa Fe air was what Ponce de León was searching for all those centuries ago. Debra, and she smiled.

She's smiling now, waiting for your return. You smile back and she leans forward into your neck. "Better," she whispers. "At least you kept this one to yourself."

"That's good," you joke. "Keep talking to myself and they'll have me committed."

Her head is still buried in your neck so you can't see her face. But you can feel her muscles tighten around you.

"What is it?" you ask. Debra doesn't say anything in response. She takes your hand in hers and quiets your trembling.

"I'm glad you came back," you say. She blinks twice, still looking up at the Bishop, who is now offering his own prayers for the souls of the confirmed.

Memories more and more erratic, unbending to your will. Debra, in the threshold, backlit by sunlight. So beautiful your heart stopped. Wearing her years perfectly. The look on her face upon seeing you there, her involuntary step backward, her shudder as you reached for her in greeting.

"You came," you told her. And her face tangled in annoyance as she informed you, "of course I came. She's my cousin's kid. She's my cousin. Why on earth are you here?"

She was always happy to be the straight man and a decade ago, a year ago even, you might have relished the opportunity. "To see you," you would have said, letting the emotion hang for a moment before shaking your head in sadness. "Although I can't for the life of me remember why." You could see this all transpiring, down to the quick soft-shoe you'd use to maneuver around her, down the street, you'd mail the kid her damned check. But these days your brain isn't always yours to command, so the truth was out before you could even think to stop it.

"To see Cass," you'd explained. "She and Elizabeth were always so close growing up, I thought she'd be here."

"She couldn't come," Debra spit. When you stood there, palms out, she mocked you with a half shrug. "What?" she challenged. "What doctor on earth is going to let someone fly this late into their third trimester?" And for once you could see Debra's face square on. The anger morphing to confusion and then to sadness. "Oh," she said softly.

"Oh."

"Come on," she said finally, escorting you past the crowds of blood relatives congregating near the nave. "Let's go find us a pew."

Yes, you are glad she's back.

This one, apparently, you did murmur and Debra brushes your lips gently with her fingers, wet with salty water.

"Cass's communion gown was white with satin trim," you tell her and she nods. You both wait.

"I was furious because you'd let her get into crayons an hour before we left and she'd gotten smudges on the bottom," Debra says. "You can still see them in the photos."

"I'm sorry," you say. Then you say it again.

"They look like polka dots now," she smiles. "Like they were supposed to be there all along."

She reaches over and touches your face again. More salt water, and you think maybe it's you who's crying until she reaches into her purse and takes out a handkerchief. "I'm sorry," she says, wiping gently at your face with the cloth. "I've smeared mascara all over you."

"You, too," you point out.

"Me, too," she admits. "We look like a couple of sad clowns."

The both of you look around and it's true that people are staring as the confirmation winds down. "God," Debra moans. "Now I've gone and asked for it. I'm going to be fielding phone calls for a month when I get back to New Mexico. Every near relation in the family wanting to know if we're getting back together. Thirty minutes with you knee-to-knee in a pew and they'll be fooling themselves that I'm moving home."

In the parking lot, after the confirmation, after she has said her hellos and goodbyes to her relatives and they've all gone back to Ginnie's house for luncheon—"you're welcome to come too," Ginnie offers and then pats awkwardly at your arm, buried somewhere in the fabric of your suitcoat—you and Debra say goodbye. You ask a few more questions about Cass and she promises to keep you in the loop. "She's so busy she's spinning," Debra says. "I've been flying out to Baltimore nearly every weekend. Burning through frequent-flier miles so quick, they're going to confiscate my platinum card."

You nod at this, and smile. "I hope she has an easy time with the birth," you say.

"There's no such thing," Debra laughs. "At least not in my experience."

"I remember," you say.

"Yeah? I'm glad. You had me worried there for a while."

"Don't worry about me."

"There's things you can do for memory," Debra counsels. "You don't have to let it all slip away, none of us do. I read an article about it on a flight. Look through some old photo albums, that might help. The trick is to think of some way to make sense of everything, to put everything into an order. Find yourself a mnemonic. Make an effort. Find yourself something that works for you and stick with it."

THE MOON.

Dulled by alcohol, blinded by the shine of moonlight reflecting off the window, confused by the orientation of the apartment (the cramped quarters, the monstrous furnishings migrated from your old home—so enormous in this new space that you must navigate around them, so that even when you're not drunk it feels like they are the permanent residents in this arrangement and you the transient, simply passing through, bunkering here in this tiny efficiency with its stale smells of whatever the families downwind are cooking, its floors cringing whenever a car's heavy bass asserts itself on the interstate just behind the concrete partitions), out of sorts, you are nonetheless welcomed into your apartment by the comforting lilt of a female voice, and the feeling this engenders in your admittedly bloated heart, wine-soaked, melancholy, is almost too much to bear.

You maneuver to the sofa, unwilling to disturb whomever it is offering you this gift, terrified of scrambling the sound waves before they can begin reassembly into words.

It has been another hard night and, with the way you feel, you suspect nearly the last of them. With nothing now to fill your days, you wake later and later. This town, always claustrophobic, always suspicious, has taken in the daytime hours a malicious color, each car driven by a mother of one of Cass's former friends, each driver turning her head away upon recognition. Each grocery clerk, sliding your modest purchases over the scanner, reminds you that once your cart was filled, whereas now you frequent only the outer perimeter of frozen foods, cartons prepackaged for your convenience, portions predetermined, appropriate only for the very busy, the very successful or the very lonely. Mercifully, another town appears at nightfall, superimposed upon the shell of the one you've always known, a new town full of strangers, a town so discreet (drunk, chuckling, you add discrete as well) that you could have lived here not just twenty years but twenty times that again and never known it existed. The service industry of this new town, its bars and pool halls, its tattoo parlors and Waffle Houses and off-brand convenience stores, comes out with the moon and if anyone shares anything from your recent past, they don't admit it. So you stay out later and later, rise later and later, a born teenager. With your severance package—meager but, as Bruce was quick to remind you, far more than you deserved ("I guess Nancy doesn't know you like I do")—and your share of the house's proceeds, you have more than enough to keep you in your current condition until Doomsday or beyond. Indeed, the three years since your divorce and termination have barely cut into your worth, the figure on the statements seemingly impermeable.

You know the same can't be true of many of the town's other night inhabitants, those who pull their pockets inside out to look for change, those whose lips tremble when confronted by bartenders, conditioned by now to expect the back of the hand, so that even a humble drink request is fraught. These souls you feed with your own money, nodding your patronage to the barkeeps who have learned to look to you when the Emmett Kellys of their establishments run dry. These men (no woman could ever find herself so lonely) thank you with cups of trembling, their shy smiles, and most importantly their silence. That you are not where they are now is nothing more than chance, nothing more than the benevolence of fate, string theory, some cosmic accident—and if you've learned anything in your lifetime it is neither to question this nor to take it for granted, but instead to offer your tithes in a thousand inconsequential sums, each night a feast night to the Fates, every night a thanksgiving.

From where you have collapsed onto your sofa you can still hear the woman talking. You assume the voice to be coming from the alleyway beneath your kitchen window, marketplace to varying illicit forms of commerce. Knowing this, you are reluctant to make sense of the words for fear their meaning (almost certainly sordid) might pollute their music. And so it isn't until the voice is cut off by the sharp ping of your answering machine that you realize the voice was coming from your bedroom, and it isn't until you have finally felt your way (the full moon haloing everything in your apartment such that the hulking armoires and cabinets and bureaus seem to shift in their stance) into your bedroom, climbed onto the bed, and found with trembling fingers the tiny red button (why wouldn't they make it bigger, for Christ's sake? You'd need a doll's fingers to press it) that you realize that the voice was looking for you.

"Hi, Dad," the metallic reproduction of Cass's voice squawks, "I guess you're asleep, I'm sorry to call so late. Maybe you're not home yet. It's two a.m., where can you be? Don't answer that, all right? Anyway, I was just calling…I was just calling, I guess. I'll try again later some time, things are kind of crazy here now with Cal and the baby and the move to Baltimore, so my phone is going to be hit-and-miss for a while. So don't bother trying to call me back, okay? I'll try again. Where did you go? Anyway, I'll try to reach you later. Keep well, Dad, okay?"

Every New Day

Finally, The Lord of Indolence

It is, of course, a dead image. A bus station after midnight. There is nothing to be done with it, yet you are here, forced to sit on frozen plastic, listen to the stale air pushing out of the air vents. February in D.C. and even the snow seems exhausted. Coldest winter on record, or one of them: the weathermen giddy with the negative numbers, moving up in the news cycle. Hard to trust them, really. The depot is unlocked but deserted, with nobody behind the impossibly thick Plexiglas. You wait patiently for a while then stretch your fading body out along one of the benches. The lights glow phosphorescent and you shield your eyes with your jacket. Eventually you drift off, and when you wake up it seems as though days have passed. You reach inside your pocket and are surprised to find your wallet still there. According to the clock against the far wall, you were asleep less than an hour. If anyone else has been in the depot, they have come and gone. You walk over to switch off the lights and with the quiet and the darkness the entire place seems organic, like a giant body shutting down. When you sleep this time it is for much longer, a peaceful sleep unencumbered by the details of travel: the sleep of the dead, or at least of the displaced. And when you wake up again, you still have your wallet, and you are no longer alone.

Acknowledgments

To settle my debts first: thanks to Colleen, Patty, and Jennifer at Prospect Park Books. I can imagine no better home for this novel. And to Chris Kepner, my agent, for his patience and skill in handling a writer who is equal parts naïve and neurotic.

Thanks, too, to all of my colleagues in the English, Philosophy, and Sociology departments at Spring Hill, most notably Stephanie Callan, who fixed my commas, and Michael Kaffer, who (inadvertently) gave this book its title. And to everyone else at Spring Hill, thanks not so much for anything related to this book but because you haven't killed me yet.

I am grateful to everyone at Mizzou and Johns Hopkins whose own work illustrated just how much I had to learn about writing. And I am indebted to the readers on this novel—Michael Kardos, William Bradley, and Stephanie Carpenter. And to the late Timothy Findley, who was kind enough to encourage my writing when he had no particular reason for doing so, save kindness.

And finally to those I love: Barry Piafsky for teaching me about money and Don Piafsky for being generous enough with his that I could write a book. To Lory and Shirley for their support. And most of all to Julie, Ethan, and Sam, for making sure that my fortune turned out happily in the end.

ABOUT THE AUTHOR

Michael Piafsky is the director of creative writing at Spring Hill College in Mobile, Alabama. He earned a Master's in Creative Writing from Johns Hopkins University and a PhD from the University of Missouri. A former editor of *The Missouri Review*, Piafsky has published fiction and nonfiction in *Meridian*, *Epic*, *Bar Stories*, and many other journals. He was a finalist in the *Glimmer Train* Short Story Award for New Fiction, and he was a finalist in the 2012 Tuscany Prize for Fiction. A chapter from *All the Happiness You Deserve* was published by *Jabberwock Review* and nominated for a Pushcart Prize. Learn more at michaelpiafsky.com.